THE HEART OF A SHADOW

MERGED WORLDS
BOOK ONE

SAMANTHA MARSHALL

GLOSSARY OF TERMS

Want to know more about a specific character? You've come to the right place!

I keep a working Character Glossary for each of my worlds on my website.

Check it out here:

www.sliceofsammy.com/character-glossary/

For mum, who encouraged me to let these words out even though the timing was inconvenient. If not for you, and your love, Raiden and Liria would still be swirling around inside my head.
Thank you, and I love you!

HEARTH AND HOME

Liria Atlannon looked around at the cool marble pillars of Princess Ione's quarters and knew she wouldn't miss it for even a moment. There was something to be said for the elegance of gold-shot marble which glowed in the light of the noonday sun, and perhaps even something to be said for the open, breezy architecture and gauzy drapes in Atlantean aqua - but for her, the paradise island of Atlantis had only ever been a prison.

Moving quietly to the edge of the balcony, Liria set delicate hands on the railing and cast her gaze out over the cheery city which glittered in the sun, shimmering marble and deep gold sandstone broken up by swathes of cloth in all the shades of the ocean. Beyond that, the azure sea lapped lazily at a pristine shore of pale sand that sparkled with hints of silver silica. A pair of Atlantean Dreadnaughts bobbed offshore, one with her steel decks unfurled like a silvered ocean lily, and the other curled in tight upon itself in preparation for an underwater journey.

"Beautiful, and yet I don't see that I will miss it."

Liria lowered her head as the Princess Ione came up beside her, lest the other woman see the way her face set into an involuntary grimace. The motion shifted her focus to her fingers, gripping tight to the balcony rail. Her skin had begun to turn the mottled blue-grey of a storm-tossed sky, her emotions slipping their leash and causing the truth of her nature to creep through. Drawing deep of the salt-laden air, Liria forced her face into smooth lines and exerted just enough power to shift her skin back to the blemish-free cream her mistress preferred.

"You won't miss it?" she asked, her voice carefully modulated to be soft and submissive. "Surely Atlantis is in your bones, your highness."

Princess Ione tossed her head. She was beautiful - exquisite, even, with long black hair that hung in perfect curls midway down her back, softly tanned skin and deep, dark blue eyes - yet there was a glitter in her gaze, an edge to her cultured smile that spoke of bitter hunger.

"No," Ione said, her lip curling. "I am meant for greater things than to be the fifth child of the ruling family of Atlantis. I am meant to be a queen."

"And so you will be," Liria answered, bowing slightly from the waist. "Your marriage to the Pharaoh of Egypt will ensure such."

An arranged marriage sounded like the worst kind of torture to Liria, but Princess Ione had been the driving force behind the entire affair. In fact, Liria's eavesdropping around the palace had her safe in the certainty that the King and Queen of Atlantis had only acquiesced to keep Ione happy; no-one had actually expected Pharaoh Taos to accept.

"Yes. Soon, I will be Queen of Egypt," Ione breathed, spreading her arms wide and tipping her head back to stare at the sky. "Soon, I will witness the technological marvel of Egypt's great airships, and view their crystal-topped pyramids with my own eyes. I shall rule over the country which stands at the forefront of science and magic, sip wine with the most powerful of gods and be bathed in the adoring praise of my subjects – while Atlantis will become but a faded memory, a pale imitation to be laughed at and forgotten." The Princess clasped her hands at the base of her throat, gleaming midnight eyes locking on Liria's face. "Are you ready, my shadow, to follow me on this path to greatness?"

It wasn't like she had any other choice, but Liria knew better than to say such things aloud. Instead, she bowed deeply, locking her gaze on the embroidered hem of Ione's gown. "Of course, your highness."

Princess Ione ran her slender fingers across the shimmering surface of Liria's wings, the sensation akin to hot knives slashing her wide open. Her breath caught in her throat, the urge to protest becoming the very thing that ensured her silence as the magical chains which bound her to her mistress snapped into full effect.

"Such flawless mystery in you, Liria. The subtlety of twilight, of hidden, magical things. You are well suited to accompany a jewel such as I." Another caress of Ione's fingers, her movements flicking away the long layers of trailing gauze that served to shield Liria's wings from view. "I wonder if Pharaoh Taos' wings are as magnificent as yours?"

"He's of the blood of Horus, your highness, and thus carries the wings of the falcon - whereas I am but a lowly fairy. I'm sure my wings are as nothing in comparison to the strong, feathered pinions of the angels."

"Hmmm. I suppose we shall see, soon enough." Ione tapped Liria's spine, silent permission for her to straighten. "I've heard the angels can even carry passengers, should the need arise."

So had Liria, but she didn't say as such, lest the Princess ask where she'd come across the knowledge. Instead, she adjusted the many layers of gauze which hung from her shoulders so that they once more protected her wings from casual view and said, "Perhaps, once you are wed, you can convince the Pharaoh to take you flying."

"Oh, yes." Ione clasped her hands to her full breasts, dark

blue eyes shining. She blinked a few moments later, a crease forming between her brows. "And you will follow us, my shadow, will you not?"

Liria inclined her head again, glad of the way her hair swung forward to hide her face. "Such is my duty, your highness."

WHEN THE DAWN BREAKS

RAIDEN HORUSHOOD, YOUNGER BROTHER to the Pharaoh Taos and Prince of Merged Egypt, stood shoulder to shoulder with those in the Pharaoh's honour guard and tried not to look bored. He felt like he'd been standing on the docks in his formal armour for centuries, but the timepiece on his wrist suggested it was more like twenty minutes.

The elegant Atlantean ship that had pulled into the dock bare seconds earlier looked less like a battleship and more like a pleasure craft, but Raiden knew full well that to underestimate anything the seafaring people did was a fool's mistake - and apt to end with said fool decorating the bottom of the ocean. With that firmly in mind, he wasted no time analysing every sleek line and curve of the ship, comparing weapons and warriors to the soldiers he'd stationed both on the pier and more discreetly in the surrounding crowd.

"You've got that look in your eye," Taos murmured, face serene as he watched the Atlanteans arrange themselves into a formal procession on the upper deck.

Raiden flicked his older brother a glance. Neither particularly tall or muscular, the Pharaoh possessed a form trim from healthy eating and a sword he knew how to use but preferred not to, leaving that lifestyle to Raiden instead. Still, Taos' deep brown skin, golden-bronze hair and sparkling brown eyes made him popular among females of all species, an effect only emphasised by the striking chocolate and white feathered wings that arched above his head and stretched almost to the ground.

"What look?" Raiden asked, raising a single brow. "The look that says, 'I have no idea why you agreed to an arranged marriage with a woman you've never met,' or the look that says, 'as penance for making me put on my ceremonial armour and stand in the morning sun, if these crazy Atlanteans fire their laser cannons I'm going to push you in front so I don't boil like a lobster'?"

Taos let out a wild, most un-Pharaoh-like laugh. "Here I just thought it was your normal, questioning-your-brother's-sanity look," the Pharaoh mused, shoulders shaking with residual laughter. "I had no idea your facial expressions were so complex."

Raiden snorted, but felt none of the amusement which Taos basked in. "Are you certain this marriage is a good idea? Poseidon has never gotten along well with Isis and Osiris."

"One of the many reasons I accepted the proposal in the first place." The smile faded from Taos' face, his brown eyes flicking skyward. "Fostering goodwill between Osiris and Poseidon via a political alliance with the Atlantean people will ease some of the tension that's been brewing amongst the gods since that fracas at sea last year." A soft sigh slipped the Pharaoh's lips, his formally draped silks masking the stiff line of his shoulders. "If the people of Mu go to war, the merged cities will be drawn into it, and if *we* go to war, those who are still fully human will suffer - and I won't see any of my people, human, mixed blood, supernatural or otherwise, harmed when there are simple ways to help prevent such senseless violence."

Pride burned in Raiden's veins, and he couldn't have stopped his hand from clasping his older brother's shoulder if he'd tried. "And *that* is why you rule Egypt, my brother."

"Hah!" Taos spread his left wing, buffeting Raiden affectionately. "You'd hold this kingdom together well enough should anything happen to me."

"Unlikely, since as the Commander of your honour guard, the only way something would happen to you was if it had happened to me first," Raiden growled, using his own wing to shove his brother in a move that couldn't be mistaken as anything other than a sibling spat. "Now stop it, or your prospective bride will see you flapping like a chicken."

"Like a *chicken?*" Taos' brown eyes flashed in a way that usually precipitated a full body tackle - but at that moment, the Atlantean ship at the end of the pier lowered her gangplank amidst the blaring of ceremonial horns.

The Pharaoh flared his wings wide, baring the full expanse of his white and brown feathers and casting a glorious shadow on the smoothly polished wood in front of them. Raiden snapped to attention, the movement echoed by the royal escort until the dock was lined by fierce looking warriors in polished breastplates and leather trousers, their shoulders draped with fine silk scarves the same shade of green as a palm tree's fronds.

Atlantean warriors in shimmering silver chain mail and aqua tunics clomped down the gangplank, energy pistols holstered at their hips and ceremonial daggers strapped to their biceps. They spread out at the end of the pier, heads bowed as a beautiful woman with raven curls descended from the ship. Her generous curves were on full display beneath a close fitting formal gown the same dark blue as her eyes, the long skirts composed of layer upon layer of semi-transparent silks that fluttered as she walked and gave the impression of floating. A delicate silver and sapphire circlet glittered in the sunlight as she stepped with measured grace onto the pier.

"Her royal highness the Princess Ione, fifth daughter of Queen Coranna and King Theon, rulers of Atlantis and the High Seas of Poseidon," announced one of the Atlantean guardsmen.

When Taos would have stepped forward, Raiden stopped him with a low growl and strode out in his brother's place. "On behalf of the Pharaoh Taos, Avatar of the Gods and ruler of Merged Egypt, I bid the Princess Ione welcome to the great city of Selekhet, capital of our fair lands and birthplace of the Merge."

Raiden returned to his Pharaoh's side as the Atlantean procession approached. Taos' wings rustled against Raiden's as he leant close to murmur, "By all the gods, my brother, she's exquisite."

There could be no argument to that fact; Ione was a decadent conglomeration of pale skin, large eyes, dark hair and sultry curves - but there was something about her, as though she were a beautiful sculpture carved in ice that would freeze anyone foolish enough to get too close. Though that air soured any attraction Raiden may have felt, there was no denying the sparkle in Ione's eye as she appraised the Pharaoh, offering a slender hand bearing a shining silver ring set with an enormous sapphire so dark as to be almost black.

"It is a pleasure to be here," she said, her voice thrumming and soft, like the petals of some mysterious flower. "Long have I hungered to meet the man who will become my husband."

"I pray I live up to your expectations, Princess," Taos replied, bending to kiss her knuckles. "Welcome to Selekhet, fairest of the Merged cities, and your new home."

"Please, call me Ione," the Princess purred, pale fingers curling around the Pharaoh's darker ones.

"Of course." Taos drew her closer, wings partially unfurling and eyes bright. "But you must call me Taos in turn."

"Taos." Ione's voice was warm and intimate, as much a caress as if she'd brushed her hands over the Pharaoh instead. "A handsome name for a handsome angel."

Taos' smile held a sensual edge as he swept out one arm. "This is my brother, Prince Raiden, Commander of my honour guard and the angel most often by my side. Soon he will be your brother, too."

"I always wanted a brother." Ione smiled, drawing her hand from Taos' to offer it to Raiden. "Delighted."

"The delight is mine, Princess." Raiden accepted Ione's smooth hand in both of his and bowed atop it, keeping his wings tucked tight to his back and never once breaking eye contact. "It will be a welcome change not to be the youngest in the family."

Ione blinked, then laughed, the sound rich and chiming. "A curse I'm doomed to bear forever, it seems. Well then, brother-to-be and delectable almost-husband, allow me to introduce General Barin, one of my father's most treasured advisors."

General Barin bowed deep, the rich silver embroidery on his tunic shimmering in the sunlight. Raiden had crossed paths with the general at a variety of diplomatic functions in the past, and knew him to be gruff but honest. When the Princess shifted so they could greet Barin formally, he blinked to see a slender figure waiting calmly with the contingent of Atlantean guards.

With skin a pale cream and hair a strange shade somewhere between indigo and navy, she stood with delicate hands clasped and gaze downcast. On the shorter side of average, she wore a flowing gauze gown in Atlantean aqua that belted at the waist with a simple silver cord and did an excellent job of downplaying her feminine figure. A collection of light gauzes that weren't quite scarves and weren't quite a cape hung from her shoulders, trailing to the ground and further camouflaging the shape of her body. The elegant knot of her hair was held up by jewelled silver pins set with aquamarines, stray strands artfully arranged to highlight the way her ears swept up to a point. Though her bones appeared to be little more than match-sticks, she gave off an aura of strength that made Raiden look twice.

"What of your companion, your highness?" he asked when Ione stepped back. "You have yet to introduce us."

The Princess blinked and the delicate woman - fairy, Raiden corrected himself, for those ears did not lie - jerked her head up.

Her face was slim, bearing sharp cheekbones, a sweet bow of a mouth and a faintly pointed chin, but it was her eyes that were the true treasure. Almost abnormally large in her face, they were a bright violet framed with long, curled lashes the same shade as her hair and set with a black pupil that shimmered in indication of excellent night vision. Those eyes turned her face from other-worldly to ethereally beautiful, even if they were currently wide with shock and, if he was reading it correctly, more than an average amount of distress.

"My companion?" Ione looked around in confusion before following Raiden's gaze to the fairy. "Oh, she's nothing important."

"Will she be staying with you during your new life in Egypt?" Raiden asked, raising a brow.

"Of course," Ione answered, her perfect countenance frowning prettily. "She is my shadow."

Inclining his head to the Princess, he said, "As Commander of the Pharaoh's honour guard, I need to be familiar with your personal retinue in order to ensure the safety of both yourself and my brother, your highness. It would soothe my heart to know her name, at the very least."

The fairy woman looked like she wanted to run, but held firm as Ione chewed on her bottom lip. Finally, her generous bosom heaving in a dramatic sigh, the Princess said, "I suppose that makes sense. Come here, my shadow."

Raiden kept sharp watch as the fairy approached, but was able to glean little more information than that her dainty feet were bare and her gait oddly silent. The gauze scarves trailing from the back of her shoulders lifted in a light breeze, offering teasing shimmers of something delicate and glassy beneath.

"Your highness." The fairy dropped an elegant curtsy, her gaze once again on the ground.

"This is Liria Atlannon," Ione announced, flicking her fingers in the other woman's direction. "She is my handmaiden and my bodyguard."

A bodyguard who stared at the ground? How could she protect her Princess if she couldn't see anything? Even as Raiden wondered at the oddity, Taos greeted the female with formal warmth. When the Princess' handmaiden made to step back, Raiden snatched her fine-boned hand from his brother's grip and bowed atop it, staring up from beneath his lashes until he made an instant's searing eye contact.

"It is an honour to meet you, Lady Liria. I am Prince Raiden," he murmured.

Liria's lips thinned as Ione loosed another laugh. "Oh no, your highness, she is no lady - merely my shadow."

Raiden fought the urge to snap at the Princess and focussed instead on the object of his attention, making a mental note to research the term 'shadow' and how it related to this delicate looking creature who stared mostly at her feet and trembled in his grip.

"Lady of Shadows, then," he said, deliberately misinterpreting the Princess' clarification. Breaking his own rules, Raiden raised Liria's knuckles to his face and brushed the suggestion of a kiss across her skin. "Welcome to Selekhet."

STAINED GLASS AND SANDPAPER

THOUGH THE HEAT OF Egypt was significantly more than that of a standard Atlantean summer day, causing sweat to form on her brow and trickle between her shoulders, Liria had never felt so blessed. Brilliant blue skies stretched endlessly in every direction, unbroken save for the sweep of wings as angels and other skyfaring creatures flitted from one end of Selekhet to the other. Beyond the city's sprawling embrace, deep golden deserts spread out like a warm, rumpled blanket, the horizon shimmering in the heat haze and broken here and there by the glittering crystal peaks of the pyramids for which Egypt was renowned.

Selekhet itself was a chaos of laughter and light, buildings of all types and sizes connected by smoothly paved streets and bright fabric awnings in a rainbow of colours. Plants were encouraged wherever there was available space, and broad-fronded palms towered alongside fountains, pools and aqueducts, providing shade, water and decoration all at once. It was the most beautiful, gloriously alive place Liria had ever seen in her life, and she wanted to bask in its embrace forever.

"I'm covered in sweat," Ione grumbled, her smooth voice thick with disgust. "However am I supposed to live like this?"

Liria turned to glimpse her mistress fanning herself with her own skirts, her face twisted in dismay. "I imagine you will adjust to the climate in good time, your highness. In the meantime, perhaps we could explore different wardrobe options for you. I'm sure the Pharaoh can recommend a tailor who will help."

"Humph." Ione sniffed delicately, lifting her nose into the air. "If he had half a brain in his head, he'd have arranged such a wardrobe before my arrival."

"Perhaps he has, your highness. These are not your actual quarters, merely somewhere for you to refresh yourself before you join the Pharaoh for a late breakfast - if I may be so bold as to offer my opinion, I believe the Pharaoh wishes to make a grand gesture of presenting your suite to you, and likely hasn't realised you might find Selekhet's warmer climate uncomfortable." Liria crossed to the bathing pool in the centre of the room and bent to run her fingers through the water. "This is pleasantly cool, should you wish to take a dip."

Ione glared at the crystal water for a long moment, then sighed. "Very well, I shall bathe. Leave me."

"As you wish, your highness." Bowing low, Liria closed the window and drew a finger along the sill, whispering a warding spell under her breath. That done, she withdrew to the suite's outer chamber, closing the solid door behind her to ensure Ione's privacy.

Selekhet's palace was a grand affair far superior to that of Atlantis' in both size and design, every conceivable surface a stunning work of art. Sweeping her gaze across the intricately carved guest bed, elegant hand-woven rug and polished timber furnishings, Liria satisfied herself that all was as it should be before crossing to the tray of refreshments the Pharaoh's guard had left. She was just considering a selection of sweet, dried fruits when a sharp knock came at the outer door.

Smoothing her skirts and squaring her shoulders, Liria crossed to open the door, prepared to give whatever servant was on the other side the sharp edge of her tongue - and found that very tongue tied in knots at the sight of the angel on the threshold.

Prince Raiden had shucked his polished breastplate and stood shirtless in the corridor, his only concession to modesty being a rough linen shawl in Selekhet's palm fond green. It draped around his neck, across his shoulders and hung in long lengths past one hip, covering most of his chest but leaving his hard abdomen bare. Loose linen pants in a deep shade of cream were secured low on his hips by a gold and rust sash, from which twin swords hung. The colour offset the smooth, rich tones of skin somewhere between caramel and bronze, and the thick, dark brown hair that tumbled around his ears and brushed the back of his neck. He was a warrior in truth, his body tall, broad and fitted with sculpted muscles accented by the occasional scar that spoke of a life fully lived. Liria's initial impression from their meeting at the pier had been that Egypt's Prince was ruggedly handsome, but the opportunity to study the reality was almost more than she could absorb at once. Without trying to look as though she stared, she drank in his devastating smile, sharp bone structure and brilliant golden eyes, crinkled in the corners from a lifetime's worth of laughter.

"Lady of Shadows," Raiden said, his voice a rough, sandy caress. He bowed low, showing off the spectacular feathered wings that swept from his back in mottled shades of white, grey, and tawny rust - but never once did he take that intense golden gaze from her face. "I was hoping you might be here."

"The Princess Ione is bathing," Liria said, hoping her voice came out cool rather than breathless. Pharaoh Taos was lovely in a pretty kind of way but Prince Raiden devastated her senses, every inch of him custom designed to sucker punch Liria where it counted most. His scent curled around her, the rich, earthy aroma of hard baked sand tinted with the blistering heat of the sun – and surely it was some sort of joke that he smelt of everything she'd ever dreamt of, every rich image she'd ever conjured of what life would be like away from the waterlogged shores and dank caverns in which she'd spent most of her life.

Raiden raised a dark brow, his teeth a flash of white as he grinned. "I didn't come to see her highness. I came to see you."

"Hush!" Desperation had her hands on his chest, shoving him into the corridor with a frantic look over one shoulder. Dragging the heavy wooden door closed behind her, Liria shook her hands to be rid of the tactile heat of his body and glared daggers at the Prince. "You cannot say such things where my mistress can hear you."

"Why not?" Confusion stole his smile and drew his brow into a frown. "We're going to be working closely together from now on - I'd like to know you better."

Pressing her lips into a line, Liria held her breath lest she drown in his scent and tried to think. After a full minute, she exhaled in a gust and crossed the corridor to the empty suite opposite, shoving open the door and sweeping inside. She waited with arms crossed and foot tapping while Prince Raiden, his brows almost in his hairline, adjusted the twin khopesh swords that hung from his hips and followed her inside. He made as if to kick the door shut behind him, then caught her look, lowered his combat-booted foot to the floor and pushed the wood quietly closed.

"I am my mistress' shadow," Liria said once their privacy was assured. "I am forbidden from knowing you, much less working closely with you."

"That word again." Raiden's wings partially spread, filling the room with the rustle of feathers. "I asked the Palace scribe before I came, but we have no record of shadows in Egypt - certainly not in the way you or the Princess Ione seem to mean it."

"Shadows are rare."

He stared, and when she didn't divulge anything further, those rugged features beetled into a frown. "I still don't understand. Ione said you were her handmaiden and her bodyguard. Is that correct?"

"Yes."

"In that case, you should know that whilst I am a Prince by birth, I am not one by nature. Instead, I am my brother's right hand, his blade in all things. We are the same, you and I," Raiden said, waving a hand back and forth in the space between them. "Once the Pharaoh and the Princess are wed, it will be our joint duty to protect them."

Fatigue pressed down on Liria as she realised there was only one course forward - and for some reason, the idea of having to explain, to see the look in his eyes as his opinion of her altered irrevocably, hurt somewhere deep inside. Which was ludicrous, since she'd spent less than ten minutes total in his presence, ever.

"To be a shadow is exactly that; a pale imitation of a person." Liria lifted her chin. "My soul was extracted at birth and placed within a gemstone. That stone was then set into a ring, and whosoever wears that ring commands my soul and, therefore, me. My surname, Atlannon, means literally 'of Atlantis' and denotes my status as a shadow. I am not permitted to own things, to have opinions on things, to make any independent decisions beyond those allowed by whoever wears the soul ring." She saw the dawning horror on his face and moved her focus to the wall some inches to the left of Raiden's ear. "I served Queen Coranna as a child and was gifted to the Princess Ione upon her fifth birthday. I will serve Ione for as long as she lives, or until she willingly passes my soul ring to another - unless I die before she does, of course."

"But that's -"

Liria cut off the Prince's protest with a sharp gesture. She had neither the political or the personal right to do so, but it was imperative he comprehend her limitations now, before he did something foolish, like decide to trust her. "Anything you say to me, I would be forced to divulge should Ione ask. Whatever instruction she utters, I must follow like a marionette dangled from her master's strings, even should that involve taking my own life. My powers are activated or suppressed by her whim and my heart beats only by the grace of her good temper. So no, Prince Raiden of Merged Egypt, we are not and can never be on the same level."

"Blood of the gods," Raiden muttered, thrusting both hands into his hair. He began to pace the length of the empty chamber, his combat boots muffled by yet another exquisite, hand-woven rug. Liria clasped her hands and waited, counting the precious seconds while Egypt's Prince swam in the lake of his own thoughts. At last, Raiden stopped his back and forthing to pin her with those golden eyes. "I assume this means there are boundaries imposed upon you? Deep seated compulsions that cannot be denied?"

Surprise had Liria nodding her head. "I cannot attempt to harm the Princess in any way, nor can I touch or manipulate the soul ring in any way, unless it is given to me voluntarily. Neither can I speak foully of Ione, even should those words be truth, or undertake any form of action which may cause her harm. There are other, smaller things, but those are the ones most relevant to the safety of your Pharaoh."

"Hmm." Raiden's wings shifted restlessly, as though he longed to throw himself into the sky and flap his troubles away. "Can you be freed?"

Liria's jaw dropped. "What?"

"You heard me," Raiden returned, one fist propped on his hip. "Can you be freed?"

A knot formed in Liria's stomach and she closed her mouth, opened it, closed it again. Words bubbled in her throat and her body trembled violently, her hands clenching to bloodless fists as millions of tiny knives filleted her from the inside out. She swung away lest Raiden see the agony in her eyes but that just made her dizzy, taking her knees from beneath her and sending her tumbling. Liria spread her wings in an instinctive grab for balance but they wouldn't quite work and she knew that within moments, her face would smash against the floor.

Strong arms caught her, muscles bulging beneath deep brown skin, the scent of warm sand and burning sunlight filling her lungs as Raiden tucked her against his chest, going to his knees on the rug. His body was a living brand beneath hers, hot and vibrant, his feathers silky smooth upon her exposed skin as he curved his wings protectively around them both.

"Liria," he murmured, voice low and anxious. "Liria, look at me. Don't try and answer my questions if they hurt you." When she didn't move, he craned his head to try and see her face, rolling her limp body towards him. "Liria? *Liria.*"

As quickly as they had come, the knives dissipated and Liria drew a gasping breath. "It wasn't your question. Ione has realised I've left her quarters and is summoning me back."

"That's how she *summons* you?"

"Only when she's angry," Liria croaked, knowing she should scramble upright but equally aware she wasn't back in control of her body yet. She swallowed heavily, unable to stop her gaze locking with his. "Why did you catch me?"

Surprise flitted over Raiden's face, followed swiftly by temper. "You'd question my honour like that?"

"No, I..." she coughed, managed a minute shake of her head. "I'm only a shadow. You're a Prince."

Golden eyes narrowed. "That's not how it works in Egypt."

With no real defence to a statement like that, Liria struggled in his grip - but instead of releasing her, Raiden stood as though he'd carry her back to Ione's quarters.

"No," she gasped, jerking in his hold. "If Ione knows you helped me, things will be worse."

His jaw a brutal line, Raiden took a deep breath and eased her to her feet, his big hand a living flame upon her shoulder as he held her steady. "Is she really so cruel?"

"It's not like that - I'm her shadow," Liria said, shaking her head. She didn't know what else to say, how else to explain it within the boundaries of the compulsion. "I'm always there when she looks for me. That is my purpose."

"But -"

"If I don't go, she will call me again." Liria straightened her gown and fixed the loose tendrils of hair that had escaped her complex twist. "Thank you for catching me, your highness."

"Just Raiden." The Prince watched her resettle the gauze drapes over the top of her wings with a predator's intensity. "Your wings. Are they..."

Liria fought the insane urge to spread them wide, to display the gossamer and stained glass nature of her fairy wings for his inspection. Instead, she lifted one shoulder in an elegant shrug. "They keep me aloft when I need them to."

"As they should." Raiden looked as though he'd say more, but when she crossed to the door, he merely tugged it open. "I'll see you at breakfast, Lady of Shadows."

"Yes, I rather expect you will." Without bothering to look back, Liria crossed the hall and returned to her mistress.

PANCAKES OF CHAOS

The Pharaoh had spared no amount of effort on a breakfast
that usually only involved himself, Raiden and the open balcony
outside the Pharaoh's private suite.

Rather than kicking back to eat a simple meal and discuss the
day's proceedings with his older brother, Raiden had somehow
been cajoled into flying between the fluted columns of a
receiving room large enough to be a ballroom, using his warrior's
strength to bunch and drape a collection of enormous silk hangings with what he could only hope was artful precision.

"Has our Pharaoh gone mad?" Muttered his female compa-
triot, her white wings bright in the morning sunlight. She worked
hard to stay aloft in the relatively dead air of the hall, her body
draped with lengths of shimmering cord that would be used to
hold the hangings in place.

"Love is a kind of madness, is it not?" Raiden repositioned
his latest armful of bunched silk to make it easier for her to
secure. "I seem to recall a banner strung across the market
district only a month past, with the crudely painted words 'Be
mine, Yrini' stark upon the surface."

Yrini blushed deeply at the reminder of what her human

lover had done to shift their relationship into one of permanence. "If I weren't busy tying this perfectly fashionable knot, I might gut you, Commander."

Raiden laughed, the sound echoing off the walls until it boomed around them like a living thing. Yrini laughed with him, their friendship born of a lifetime training, fighting and protecting the Pharaoh. By the time their laughter faded, the final silks were hung and the breakfast table set. The doors of the receiving room were propped open, as were the windows, a soft morning breeze fluttering through the silks Raiden and Yrini had worked so hard to hang.

He was still swooping between columns when the Pharaoh entered, his Princess on one arm and the remaining three members of the honour guard trailing behind them. General Barin stalked on their heels, followed by the Princess Ione's shadow, hands clasped at her front and eyes downcast.

Liria Atlannon presented an interesting puzzle, one Raiden intended to decrypt with the same dogged determination that made him his Pharaoh's best protection. After all, once Taos and Ione were married, Liria would become part of the honour guard - and Raiden had no intention of allowing a stranger to be thrust into his inner circle. He *had* to be able to trust Liria, and she had to be able to trust him in return; and no matter how intriguing she was, if Raiden couldn't find that common ground, he'd be recommending her return to Atlantis as soon as possible.

The party entering the room looked up as his shadow fell across them, Liria's eyes going wide at the sight of Raiden's wings. He wished he'd managed more than a glimpse of hers, but the fairy seemed determined to keep them hidden beneath the trailing gauzes she wore wherever she went. Did she cover them in private, too? Or, when she was alone in her chambers at night, did she slide that gauze cape from her shoulders and set them free? Dark, primal greed sparked in Raiden's gut and as he landed before his Pharaoh in a flurry of snapping feathers, he vowed he'd coax Liria to spread her wings for him so he could inspect every glorious detail at his leisure.

"My Pharaoh," Raiden boomed, sweeping a generous bow whilst keeping his gaze firmly fixed on his brother's face. He flicked his wings to settle his feathers, then furled them tight to his back as he turned towards the Pharaoh's companion. "Princess Ione. Welcome to breakfast."

"Well met, brother," Taos chuckled, brown eyes dancing. "Well met, indeed."

"Do you always fly about inside the Palace?" Princess Ione murmured, one dainty hand spread across the base of her throat.

Taos led his fiancé towards the laden table, his smile charming. "Raiden and I fly whenever we can, my Princess. The sky is as much our home as the ground."

"Of course." Ione's dark eyes flicked to the open windows, her expression wistful. "The sky must be a truly wondrous place."

"Truly, my love, it is. Come, now, let me settle you for breakfast."

Ione lowered her lashes to half-mast. "Thank you."

Chairs scraped and fabric rustled as people found their places at the circular table. Raiden took up his customary position on his brother's left side, with Ione on the right and Liria beside her. The rest of the honour guard dropped into chairs without much thought, sandwiching a stone faced General Barin in their laughing midst.

Elevated bowls of fruit took pride of place in the centre of the table, their surfaces sticky with a honey glaze that dripped lazily onto the plates of pancakes arranged beneath. The kitchens had provided savoury options, too, but it was to the fruit and pancakes Raiden looked, remembering his manners just long enough to allow Taos to serve his Princess before everyone else tucked in.

Everyone except Liria.

"Does the Lady of Shadows dislike the Pharaoh's spread?"

Raiden asked, deliberately pitching his voice somewhere between curious and antagonistic.

Liria's jaw tightened ever so slightly, but she kept her gaze fixed firmly on her lap and her posture outwardly serene. In that instant, Raiden's decision to understand her for professional purposes transformed into a far more primitive urge - to smash that cool facade into glittering pieces, to push and poke and prod until he glimpsed the fierce woman who'd argued with him in the guest chambers earlier.

Unaware of the brutal demand of his instincts, Princess Ione looked up from her breakfast with a blink. "I beg your pardon?"

"Your lovely shadow," Taos murmured, his fingers brushing the back of the Princess' wrist. "She does not eat."

Ione's brow creased, and across the table, General Barin looked scandalised. "You would have my shadow eat with us?"

Raiden made an expansive gesture at the rest of the honour guard, who'd paused in their enthusiastic demolition of their own meals. "We eat with our Pharaoh all the time and now that you've come to join our family, your highness, your shadow is one of us. Does she have some sort of dietary requirement that prevents her eating from the Pharaoh's most generous table?"

"I..." Ione paused, and Raiden knew she'd at last caught the implied insult to Taos' honour. Chewing on her lower lip, she turned to Liria. "Eat."

The slightest flare of Liria's eyelashes was the only thing betraying her surprise. "Yes, your highness."

"From now on," Princess Ione continued, her fingers clenching hard around her fork, "if we are at a family gathering such as this, you may eat with everyone."

"Yes, your highness." Liria lowered her head, revealing the elegant twist of her navy-indigo hair and the two jewelled silver pins that held it in place. Ione reached out in a motion that smacked of ritual habit and trailed her fingers down the back of the shadow's neck, then returned to her meal. Only once her

Princess was eating again did Liria straighten, putting a single pancake and a smattering of glazed berries on her plate.

Raiden watched from beneath his lashes as she ate daintily, ignoring the polite chatter at the table until he was certain Liria was going to finish the pitifully small serving she'd allotted herself. He'd just begun to devise a scheme to get more in her belly when the enormous wooden doors to the hall blew open so hard they slammed into the walls either side, the silk hangings on the fluted columns streaming in a hot, dry wind that spoke of ancient secrets and carried a hint of smoke.

"To arms!" Raiden cried, gaining his feet by the simple expedient of flaring his wings and allowing the hot wind to sweep him upright. He had a khopesh in each hand before his feet touched the floor, the rest of the honour guard drawing their own weapons and forming a defensive barrier in front of the Pharaoh and his fiancé.

A single man sauntered through the door. Clad in the draped black silks of a desert nomad, his skin was a smooth, dark gold and his eyes the colour of old blood. Golden rings cluttered elegant fingers, matched by golden bangles on each wrist and a golden torc at his throat. Hair the colour of rubies hung softly tousled to his jaw and two long, black ears similar to a jackal's swept straight up in the air, their top edge squared rather than elegantly pointed. A long, almost feline tail hung down from the back of the black silks, covered in black fur that lightened to the same dark ruby of his hair where it split into two at the end, like a living tuning fork. When the man smiled and offered a mocking bow, his canines jutted like a wild dog's, turning his expression from silkily handsome to wild and deadly.

"Grand Pharaoh of Merged Egypt," he purred, his voice promising dark sex and twisted death. "I do hope I'm not interrupting."

"Set." Taos' eyes glittered with rage, but his words were calm. "It is bad manners to intrude on a private meal, even for a god."

Set merely widened his smile, sauntering towards the table

with a stride as liquid and dangerous as it was inherently lazy. "As the god of chaos, I believe an invitation would be entirely useless." He lifted a beringed hand, his dark gold fingers ending in black-tipped talons, and gave a languid wave. General Barin immediately flew out of his chair, sailing across the room to crash face-first into the wall and slide to the floor amidst a smear of blood. Raiden and his guard surged forward but Set waved his hand again and just like that, their bodies froze in place, muscles straining but unable to move.

"No, no," the god laughed, turning General Barin's chair around and straddling it. He crossed his arms across the carved back and clicked his tongue in reprimand. "Fighting at breakfast? How scandalous."

"Why are you here, Anarchist?" Taos demanded, his voice cold. Though he was as frozen and helpless as Raiden, the Pharaoh maintained an air of serenity, his muscles loose and relaxed. "Surely not to partake of a meal you could find as readily in your own home."

Set shrugged, reaching out a taloned hand to snag the half-eaten pancake from Barin's plate, roll it into a cylinder, and shove it in his mouth. Bloodred eyes laughed as he chewed, safe in the knowledge that the room was at his mercy. When he was finished, Set licked honeyed glaze from his fingers, then pointed accusingly in the Pharaoh's direction. "I heard you signed a marriage contract with Atlantis. I came to meet the woman so very special you'd risk swiping her from beneath Poseidon's nose."

"Princess Ione," Taos said quietly, "I formally introduce you to Prince Set the Anarchist, god of war and chaos, brother to Osiris, god of the earth, ruler of all Mu and King of Kings."

Ione looked royally unimpressed, her voice so cold when she spoke that Raiden was surprised it didn't crystallise the air around her face. "Are all the gods so very rude as this pathetic creature?"

Set laughed, throwing himself back off the chair to roll on the floor. His laugh was half hyena-mad and half sibilant hiss, an unnatural sound the likes of which Raiden knew he'd never hear from another throat even if he lived for all eternity. When at last Set composed himself, knuckling tears from the corners of his eyes, he rose and swept Ione a courtly bow.

"As the embodiment of anarchy, I'm afraid it's my nature to be rude from time to time." Eyes sparking with delight and something far more sexual, Set inclined his head in the Princess' direction. "I like you, little Atlantean. Perhaps we should play together and see what Poseidon has to say about it, hmm?"

The god took a lazy, arrogant step in the Princess' direction - and drew up short as Liria Atlannon appeared in the empty space before him.

"Stop," she said, voice quiet and chin high. Raiden's breathing turned choppy as the fairy who'd somehow escaped Set's magical bindings raised a cautionary finger and shook it beneath the god's nose. "You are not welcome here, god of war and chaos. Take your anarchy and leave this place."

"How did you do that?" Set asked instead, staring down at the woman he dwarfed by at least a foot. His nostrils dilated and he bent as if to sniff her throat, jerking back with a yelp when Liria palmed a sticky pancake from the table and squashed it against his face.

"I said," she repeated, her expression calm while the god in front of her choked and spluttered, "get out."

"Liria -" Raiden cut off at the blazing look she sent his way, her brilliant violet eyes flashing with rage. What on earth was she *thinking*? Not only defying a god, but taunting him? Rather than appeal to a sense of reason the fairy clearly didn't have, he strained to turn his eyes to his brother. Taos was already looking in his direction, lashes dropping in the subtlest of signals.

"You absolutely delightful creature," Set chuckled, spitting out a blueberry and wiping crumbled pancake from his cheeks. "What are you?"

When Liria didn't answer, Set's arm shot out to close around her throat and lift her high in the air. The fairy didn't struggle, wrapping one hand around the god's wrist in the most delicate of touches while the other remained by her side. Frowning at her silence, Set extended the index finger on his free hand and placed the tip of his talon against her forehead, digging in until a drop of dark, purplish blood began to blossom. Bringing the bloodied talon to his nose, he sniffed, then extended his tongue to lick.

"Interesting," Set murmured, his dark gaze never leaving Liria's face. Tightening his fingers perceptibly around her throat, he commanded, "Reveal."

Liria stiffened, the air in the room suddenly thick with magic. The skin beneath Set's hand began to mottle and at first Raiden thought Liria was choking, but the colour swept over her body in a swift wave, removing the pale cream skin in favour of flesh the bluish grey of a stormy sky. Sparks of purple light appeared in Liria's violet eyes, as though someone had thrown a handful of glitter and several of the flecks had gotten stuck. Her breathing came ragged and her lips peeled back, her canines and the two teeth either side of them curved like a viper's fangs. Set tilted his head in consideration and a vein pulsed at Liria's temple, the only outward sign that she fought to deny him as he revealed the truth of her blood.

Raiden's heart stuttered as the trailing gauzes at her back began to stir, her wings unfurling a slow inch at a time until they were spread wide. Shaped something like a butterfly's, they stretched high above her head and brushed against the floor and were composed of a shimmering gossamer he could see right through, patterned in a kaleidoscope of plums, purples and deep, midnight blues. A soft, oil-slick sheen played across the stained-glass surface as they fluttered in an imaginary breeze, the effect mesmerisingly beautiful. Though he'd longed to see her wings revealed, part of Raiden felt as sick as if Set had stripped Liria naked and violated her on the cold stone floor.

"Well, now," Set murmured, bending his elbow to draw her closer. The god brushed his knuckles across her cheek and Liria, moving as though caught in molasses, slowly turned her face into the caress. "A *dark* fairy. I haven't seen anything so exquisite in a long, long time."

Liria's lashes lowered over her sparkling eyes and Raiden watched her chest expand as she inhaled deeply, her nose against Set's wrist.

"You sense it, don't you?" Drawing her ever closer, Set's lips curled in dark, sensual promise. "The darkness within us which is kin."

Raiden's heart smashed against the cage of his chest, his body trembling with strain as he fought the god's invisible hold so he could go to Liria's side. By contrast, the dark fairy seemed serene as she lifted her lashes, fixing Set with the full impact of her violet eyes. "Yes," she whispered, lips moving against his skin. "I feel it."

Then she bit him.

Set shrieked and tried to let go, but the fingers Liria had wrapped around his wrist grew talons of deep indigo that dug into the Anarchist's flesh and prevented him from retreating. As blood welled, Liria reached into her hair, pulled out one of the silver pins and rammed it into Set's eye.

The god of war and chaos roared in agony, releasing Liria to stagger backwards and clutch at his ruined face. The aura of magic which had pervaded the room since his arrival abruptly dissipated, and Raiden thumped heavily against the dining table as Liria shimmered into existence directly in front of him.

"Do you mind?" she asked lightly. Before he got a chance to answer, she snatched a knife from his boot and threw it. The blade thunked hilt deep into Set's chest, eliciting another gurgling howl as the Anarchist fell on his backside.

"That's not going to stop him," Raiden said, shaking out quivering muscles and spreading his wings.

"I know."

He hesitated, then held out the blade in his left hand. "Khopesh?"

"Thank you." Liria accepted the weapon with the same

elegance one might accept jewels, twirling the sickle-bladed sword in her hand. "Protect your Pharaoh, Prince of Egypt."

Stained glass wings whirred into motion and Liria lifted gently off the ground, her flight controlled in a way Raiden's feathered pinions would never allow. Flitting across the room in a matter of moments, the sword held in a reverse grip down the length of her arm, Liria snatched up Set's tail and used it to toss him towards the receiving room's open doors. He hit the mosaic floor with a wet thud but instead of toppling, the god of war and chaos rolled to his feet.

"You," he growled, pulling the knife from his chest with one hand and the pin from his eye with the other. "I'm going to enjoy taking you to pieces, little fairy."

Liria slid her feet apart and sank into her knees, raising Raiden's khopesh so that the blade glinted in the light. "Come, Anarchist. Take my life if you can."

"Enough!"

Thunder rumbled through the room and Set paled as two figures shimmered into existence between the god and the breakfast table. The male was tall and regal, with dark hair and bright blue eyes. He wore white silk trousers and a wide collar of beaten gold inset with lapis, matching cuffs glinting at his wrist and ankles. A two-tiered circlet sat upon his head, the large golden ankh in the centre hanging so low as to be almost between his eyes. He held hands with a slender woman boasting generous curves and long, black hair bluntly cut across her forehead and midway down her spine. She wore a circlet that matched her husband's, her simple white silk gown cinched at the waist and throat with golden bands that sparkled with sapphires and emeralds. Her deep green eyes matched the vibrant green feathers that sprouted the length of her arms, overlapped with feathers of shimmering blue and brightest white. Like Set, their skin was a deep, burnished gold, their faces ethereally beautiful and their power a thrumming force within the room.

"Isis. Osiris." The Pharaoh swept a deep bow, tugging Ione

close to his side. "Thank you for responding to my call so swiftly."

"Not swiftly enough, it seems," Osiris rumbled, his voice shaking the very stones beneath their feet. "Brother, what have you been doing that my avatar felt it necessary to summon me with such urgency?"

Set bared his teeth, taloned fingers clenching on the weapons which still dripped with his own dark blood. "I merely came to welcome the Princess of Atlantis to our shores, my brother."

"A welcome as only you can provide, by the looks of it." Isis' voice was warm and throaty, one hand settling on her hip as she took in the scene before her. "For shame, brother."

"What can I say, other than that I am the Anarchist?" Set shrugged, seemingly unconcerned by his ruined eye and the vicious wound in his chest. "If it bothers you, dearest siblings, I shall take my leave." He paused. "But I want the fairy who drew my blood."

"No," Osiris and Isis spoke in unison, a tolling bell of implacable authority.

Set shrugged again. "It was worth a try."

"Wife," Osiris rumbled, his eyes never leaving Set's face, "won't you take our brother home and see to it that he gets medical attention?"

Isis' lips kicked up at the corners. "I shall attend him myself, husband mine."

"Unnecessary," Set gushed, dropping his purloined weaponry and holding up both hands in the universal gesture of peace. "I'm more than capable of looking after myself."

"And yet, your sister will do it for you," Isis purred. While Set sputtered and flushed a darker shade of brown, the goddess took Princess Ione's hand in hers and bowed atop it. "Welcome to Egypt, your highness. I apologise deeply for my brother's actions. I promise that I will return and make your acquaintance more fully."

Raiden's estimation of the Princess Ione went up a grudging

notch as his brother's fiancé squared her shoulders and awarded Isis a regal nod. "I look forward to it, my goddess."

Isis smiled and brushed her knuckles over Ione's cheek, then strode to Set's side and fisted a hand in his black silk clothing. "Come, brother."

"I really don't think -" Set began, and then the two were gone in a flash of light, the smear of blood on the floor the only evidence the god of war and chaos had ever been there in the first place.

Liria immediately relaxed her stance, her stormy skin returning to the pale cream shade with which Raiden was familiar. Stooping to pick up her jewelled hairpin, she wiped it on her dress and returned it to her hair, where its twin had done an admirable job of keeping her looking elegant the entire confrontation. Folding her wings down in a way that should have been physically impossible given their shape, the fairy rolled her shoulders to settle her gauze scarves back into place as Raiden arrived at her side in a flurry of feathers.

"Are you all right?" he asked, keeping his voice low.

Liria looked up at him for a fleeting moment, then pressed her borrowed khopesh and knife into his hands. "Of course."

Raiden should have said more, should have demanded she get herself checked or even checked her himself, but Liria Atlannon turned in a swirl of gauzes and walked away, the shadow with enough power to defy a god.

KING OF KINGS

LIRIA SWEPT ACROSS THE breakfast hall as fast as she could manage without looking undignified. Set's arrival had forcibly stripped away layers of well-cultivated armour, leaving her feeling naked in a room full of strangers - strangers who were likely judging even as they followed her to where General Barin lay in an awkward muddle of limbs and blood on the marble floor.

"Call for a healer!" Taos shouted, his tone every inch that of a confident, commanding ruler.

"There's no need," Ione returned, gathering her skirts to kneel at the General's side. "I can handle this myself."

The Pharaoh blinked, holding up a hand to stall the member of his honour guard who'd been about to rush out the door. "What are you going to do?"

"I have the blood of the naiads in my veins, my fiancé. Watch." Ione spread her hands across Barin's broad chest and closed her eyes. Her palms began to glow with a soft aqua light which sunk into the General's skin, spreading through his body until it, too, took on a faint aqua luminescence.

Osiris, Taos, Raiden and the honour guard gathered around

Ione in a loose circle, talking quietly amongst themselves as they watched her work. As a god, Osiris' energy was a blinding pillar of light to Liria's senses, and she was glad the boundaries of the compulsion forbade her from examining him too closely. The honour guard's single sand sprite was the next most magical, his energy warm and earthy. The two daywalking vampires were even more soothing, while Taos, Raiden and their female counterpart sparked with the peculiar effervescence unique to angelkind.

She'd fit in well here, if things were different. Even shackled by the compulsion that bound her to Ione, Liria's magic far outranked that of the sand sprite, and the characteristics native to a dark fairy meant she'd be able to keep up even with a vampire's legendary strength and speed should she need to. For a full minute, Liria allowed herself the luxury of pretending she belonged, that she could actively have a life, a bond of some kind with the eclectic mix of peoples that surrounded the Pharaoh and his brother. Then General Barin gasped and sat bolt upright, and the bubble popped as reality once again reasserted itself.

"Your highness." Gripping Ione's wrist, the older man stared wildly around the room, tension draining from his shoulders when he realised Set was gone. "You shouldn't waste your energy on me."

"Your life is no waste," the Princess murmured, patting his arm.

Barin ran a shaky hand through salt and pepper hair and grimaced as it came away streaked with blood. "Was anyone else injured?"

"No." Ione turned dark ocean eyes on Liria, her expression stern. "But the god who dared to threaten me escaped."

The group of spectators turned as one, and Liria barely had time to register the full weight of their attention before she felt the sharp bite of claws deep in her gut. Her knees buckled as the compulsion forced her to the floor, where she bowed so low her forehead kissed the cool marble.

"Your highness," Liria murmured, years of practice keeping the tremor from her voice. "I have failed you."

"*What?*" Raiden's voice was filled with incredulous fury, a whipcrack of sound that echoed in the silence of the room. "No, you didn't."

"I failed to eliminate the threat." Liria kept her forehead on the floor, allowing her eyes to drift closed so that she could better monitor the room with her other senses. "I accept the punishment I am due."

"Now, hang on a minute," Raiden growled. "You faced down a *god*. We're lucky to be alive!"

"Raiden has the right of that," Osiris boomed, his voice shaking the marble against which Liria was pressed. "Defying Set in any capacity is nothing short of miraculous."

The sharp agony in Liria's gut intensified. Ione's skirts rustled as she gained her feet, dainty shoes clicking their way ever closer - until, at last, she had crouched by Liria's side.

"Peace, Prince of Egypt." Ione's fingers lit gently upon Liria's hair. "Rise, my shadow. Though Set was not apprehended, you have kept us all safe this day. No punishment is necessary."

Liria slowly gained her feet, fastening her gaze on the hem of her blood spattered gown. "Your highness is most kind."

"Taos," Osiris rumbled. "Now that my brother is no longer disgracing these halls, won't you make the introductions?"

"Certainly." The Pharaoh stepped forward and cleared his throat. "Osiris, may I present the Princess Ione of Atlantis and her guardian. Behind them is the General Barin, with whom I'm sure you are familiar - by reputation, if nothing else." When Ione held out a hand to Osiris, Taos smiled. "My sweet fiancé, meet Osiris, god of the lands, benevolent ruler of Mu and King of Kings."

"Atlantis has ever created jewels beyond compare, and you are no exception, Princess." Osiris accepted Ione's slender hand in his huge one and bowed atop it. "Welcome to Selekhet, first of the Merged Cities and my personal favourite. I'm glad you are safe from my brother's unusual inclinations."

Ione blushed a soft pink. "Thank you, your grace."

"And you," Osiris released Ione to turn in Liria's direction, the clear blue of his gaze so penetrating she felt stripped to her bones. "Surely you have a name?"

"This is Liria Atlannon, my shadow." Ione's spine stiffened as Osiris held out his large hands in Liria's direction. "If it please you -"

"Brave little shadow," Osiris rumbled, bending almost double to see into Liria's downturned face. "Do you not speak to the gods? I will not hurt you."

Pressing her lips together, Liria said nothing, the clawing bands of Ione's displeasure a vice around her legs and chest. Osiris scooped her limp fingers into the cradle of his own and the moment their skin touched, the weight on Liria's lungs eased and a wave of warm comfort washed over her.

Ione tsked in the back of her throat. "I can answer any questions about my shadow that you may have, King of Kings."

"And yet, I'd like to hear her speak for herself, Princess Ione," Osiris murmured, rubbing his thumb over Liria's palm in a soothing motion. "Humour an old god, won't you?"

"Very well." Ione waved a dismissive hand and turned away. "Speak without fear of reprisal, my shadow."

"It is a pleasure to meet you, King of Kings," Liria whispered.

"I believe," Osiris whispered back, "that the pleasure is entirely mine."

He straightened but did not release her hand, and Liria wondered at the power of a being who could dull the choking weight of her binding with a simple touch. When Ione moved a few steps away to answer a question from her solicitous fiancé, Liria chanced a glance from beneath her lashes. "I pray you forgive my reticence, god of the Earth."

Osiris' hand tightened over hers and he offered a gentle

smile. "There is nothing to forgive, most especially when you were able to deny my brother whatever it is he came here for."

"I could not let him hurt my mistress, your holiness."

"Osiris will do fine," the god chuckled, shaking his head. "I eat and sleep and breathe the same as any other man."

Liria highly doubted that, but her chance to answer was eclipsed by the echo of heavy boots approaching. Raiden's purposeful stride was already familiar, as were the broad shoulders and arched wings that appeared in Liria's peripheral vision. Rather than look his way, she returned her gaze to the floor, examining the immaculate workmanship of the beaten gold cuffs around Osiris' ankles.

"After the fiasco in the grand hall last year, I thought Set couldn't get into the Palace without an invitation," Raiden growled, stopping so close to Liria's side that his restless wings brushed the skirts of her gown.

"That is true." Osiris released Liria and straightened, blue eyes serious as he inspected her face. When the prick of Ione's temper failed to return, the King of Kings inclined his head and turned at last to face the Prince of Egypt. "Considering the people who could offer such an invite are all in this room, I'm forced to admit the wards have either weakened, or Set has found a way around them." Osiris' lips pressed into a thin line. "Either is possible; my brother is chaos incarnate, after all."

"What does he want?" Ione's voice was a blade as she stalked over, vibrating with a combination of anger and fear. "I know of Set only via reputation."

Raiden, who had begun pacing back and forth before the table, stopped long enough to cross his arms over his chest and shake his head. "There's no telling what Set wants in the long term, but for now I'm willing to bet that it's something to do with the more stable relationship this wedding will create between Egypt and Atlantis."

"*More* stable? Our countries have not warred since my grandfather's generation," Ione snapped.

Osiris inclined his head in the Princess' direction. "A mere fragment of time for a god, my dear."

"I cannot bring myself to believe that all of this was simply to cast shadows over an impending wedding," Isis said, materialising beside her husband as the words formed around her. "Whatever his motivations, Set was truly injured in this confrontation."

"And now?" Osiris' rumble turned tender as he wrapped an arm around his wife's shoulders.

"Sleeping in his fortress like a baby." Isis winked. "Amazing how sweet he looks with his eyes closed."

Osiris laughed, and the entire palace shook. "Everyone, this is my most exceptional wife Isis, also known as the Allmother and goddess of life. Isis, this is the Princess Ione of Atlantis, her intriguing shadow, Liria Atlannon, and Theon's favourite General, Barin Dormisculae."

"A pleasure," Isis murmured, a smile in her voice. "Welcome to Egypt. I truly hope Set's sudden appearance doesn't dampen your desire to be here, Princess."

Ione cleared her throat and lifted her chin. "No, Allmother. Set's transgressions have no bearing on my plans to marry your handsome Pharaoh."

"I'm relieved to hear that." Taos inclined his head, expression grim. "However, much as I hate to downplay the importance of my own wedding, I must agree with Isis. Set wouldn't lower himself to meddling in my affairs without a greater motive."

"Greater than war?" Raiden demanded, his incredible, tri-coloured wings beginning to unfurl. Liria drank in the sight, the way he moved with such freedom and vitality, sunlight from the open windows gilding his skin in gold. She didn't have to be told that his helplessness in the face of Set's magic infuriated him; it was written in every tense muscle, in the flashing of his deep golden eyes. "What motivation could Set have that is greater than causing the chaos which is his birthright?"

Isis and Osiris exchanged a loaded glance. "We will think on it," the god-king rumbled. "In the meantime, my sister-wife and I will check the wards and set a watch on Set once he wakes. I will be in touch, Taos. Take care of your lands, your people, and your beautiful new fiancé, and call me at once should things go awry."

"I will," the Pharaoh murmured, his lips tipping into a smile as he looked in Ione's direction. "I had planned to offer a tour of the Palace once breakfast was over, but after this stressful interruption, perhaps my Princess would prefer to see her quarters instead?"

Ione fluttered her lashes, her lips curled into a sultry smile. "An excellent suggestion, my Pharaoh – though, if I may be so bold as to say so, I would very much like to tour this place which will become my home."

"This altercation with Set has not overly distressed you? We did not even finish our meal." Taos waved a hand at the neglected breakfast table.

"I have eaten enough to tide me over for now," Ione assured him, her eyes wide and dewy. "If you insist I rest, then I will accede with grace, but reclining in my quarters pales in comparison to spending time getting to know the man I'm to marry."

"Very well, then." Taos flourished a swift bow, eyes twinkling. His features were smooth and handsome in a cultured way, but Liria found her eyes straying to his brother. Prince Raiden's extra height and breadth, his ruggedly sensual face, made him seem older than Taos rather than several years his junior. Her breath caught as she recalled Raiden swooping between the columns of the room as she'd arrived, dark hair blowing back off his face and expression gloriously alive. His wingspan, too, would eclipse his older brother's, sheer muscle allowing him to power through the air at incredible speeds or twist and turn as nimbly as he'd done that very morning. Liria took a moment to imagine flying with Raiden, baiting him with aerobatics and racing towards the setting sun. As though sensing the direction of her thoughts, the Prince of Merged Egypt snapped his wings shut, the wind created by his action blowing stray tendrils of hair from Liria's face.

Just a passing fascination, she told herself, inhaling the warm sand and burning sunlight of his scent. *That's all it is.*

"A tour of the Palace, then, brother?" Raiden asked. When Taos nodded, he blew out a sharp breath and turned to the female angel behind him. "Yrini, you know the drill."

"Of course." Yrini swept a sharp bow, motioned to her three companions, and together they escorted a dazed General Barin out of the room.

Taos offered his arm to Ione and she accepted, with Liria following the customary five paces behind as the royal couple moved towards a different exit. When Raiden fell into step beside Liria, wings tucked tight to his back and thumbs thrust lazily into his belt, it took everything she had to keep her jaw from flapping like a fish.

"What are you doing?" she hissed, daring to flick him a look from the corner of her eye.

He was already watching her, the deep gold of his gaze sharper than any blade. "What do you think I'm doing?"

Liria stared at Ione for a long second, trying to estimate how deeply she was in conversation with the Pharaoh by her side. When the Princess didn't so much as blink their way, Liria chanced drawing on a trickle of power, using it to muffle the air around them. "I assumed you'd have duties."

"I do." Raiden's voice thrummed through her blood as he took her lead and pitched it lower. "I'm doing them."

A lump formed in Liria's throat, her composure slipping enough that she raised her head to stare at him full on. "You weren't lying when you said we'd be working closely together, were you?"

Raiden's eyes glittered, his smile just this side of predatory. "No, Lady of Shadows, I was not." He jerked his chin at the royal couple ahead. "We're about to become a team, you and I."

"Did you heed none of my warnings?" Liria growled, barely tempering the urge to bare her teeth. "That isn't possible."

"You underestimate me, Liria Atlannon. Or, perhaps, since

we didn't get a chance to finish our conversation yesterday, you still don't quite understand." Raiden leant closer, his voice a furious whisper in her ear. "I have a lifetime's experience in defending my Pharaoh, and nobody and nothing will stand in my way - least of all you."

The rough sandpaper of his proximity rubbed against her skin, and Liria threw caution to the wind to narrow her eyes in the Prince's direction. "Unless you plan to ambush my mistress, then I won't be anywhere near you, *your highness.*"

"Don't take that tone with me," he growled, waving a finger under her nose. "As though I'm some sort of tantrumming brat!"

Dropping the illusion around her head, Liria let the storm-sky blue of her real face show through and sank her fangs into Raiden's clenched knuckles. His temper flashed to astonishment, his looming, overwhelmingly male presence jerking a half step back. Releasing him at once, his blood a warm, decadent pulse against her tongue, Liria resumed the pretence of civilisation and offered a sweet, bloody smile.

"Oh, but my Prince," she purred. "You'll have to do far better than that if you want under my skin."

Raiden's eyes dropped to the perfectly shaped fang-marks across the back of his hand. When his golden gaze settled once more on hers, his smile was dark and threatening in a way Liria didn't quite understand, goosebumps breaking out across her skin and her body heating in places it shouldn't.

"Challenge accepted, Lady of Shadows."

TAKING UP THE GAUNTLET

When Ione professed a desire to change before the Palace tour, Taos showed her to the extensive suite that would be hers until the wedding. After a formal goodbye full of loaded glances and coquettish lashes, the Princess ushered Liria inside and Raiden accompanied his Pharaoh to the royal suite on the next level of the palace. Once they were safely behind closed doors, Raiden accepted the thick glass of honeyed beer his brother offered and slugged it back in one long go.

"I hate that the gods can pin us down," he growled, holding the glass out for a refill. "I hate it with every itching feather on my wings."

Taos merely shrugged, filling Raiden's glass as he sipped from his own. "We are but halfbreeds, brother mine. More than human, perhaps some of us on a level with the pureblood Lemurians, but always will we be less than the gods."

"How can I protect you when I can't even move?" Raiden demanded, taking another healthy swallow. "Set could've torn your wings from your back and excised your heart from your chest while I hung useless."

Squeezing his shoulder with unhidden affection, Taos smiled.

"He did not."

"No, but only because of Liria Atlannon." Raiden growled low and long, spreading his wings as wide as they would go before snapping them shut with enough force to set the curtains flapping. "What did Osiris say?"

Raiden may be the stronger angel of the two of them, a fact they carefully downplayed, but as Pharaoh, Taos had a mental connection to the god who was King of Kings. Coupled with an incisive mind and natural charisma, Taos was an angel who owned his throne through love and honour - a sentiment that was echoed by all the peoples of Merged Egypt.

"When Osiris took the shadow's hand, he breached protocol and skimmed her mind," Taos said. "Rude, perhaps, but he was discomfited enough by Set's appearance he felt it warranted."

"Given Liria clearly didn't notice and nobody is apt to pick a fight with the most powerful of all the gods, I don't think there'll be trouble," Raiden muttered, taking another long draught of his beer. Nothing like the beverages by the same name across the oceans, the sweet, thick drink was filled with nutrients and the low alcohol content helped settle his frayed edges without stealing his wits. "What did Osiris discover?"

"Liria is strong but like us, partly human. Far less human than you or I, however, for her memories show an inability to maintain a fully corporeal form outside of Merged lands." Taos tilted his head to one side, brown eyes thoughtful. "She's power-ful, her heritage from the dark fairies taking full precedence - but whilst Liria is a force to be reckoned with, she should not have been able to defy Set. That particular feat was only possible because she's soulbound to the Princess."

"Soulbound," Raiden frowned, drumming his fingers against his glass. "Liria mentioned the process, but I'd never heard of it before. The Royal Scribe had no knowledge of it, either."

"I can't say I'm surprised - Osiris said the making of shadows is an old practice, one long banned." Taos took a deep drink of his beer and shuddered. "Whomever owns the soul gem can control the soulbound creature's every action, from something as trivial as whether or not they laugh, to how much magic they access, or even if they breathe, blink, speak or fight. Liria's not old enough to have been created before the ban went into place, so someone, somewhere, has broken the laws of the gods - but Osiris found no knowledge of her creators in her memories."

"It matters little the origins of her binding, more the actualities."

"Indeed. Set was unable to compel Liria for the simple fact that she was already held in thrall by a much stronger compulsion: her foremost instruction is to defend the Princess Ione by any means necessary, even should that mean her death." Taos grimaced and shifted from one foot to the other. "Osiris recommends we get the Lady of Shadows on side as quickly as possible. Should Set return, Liria may be the only one who can hope to delay him long enough for Osiris or one of his peers to come to our aid."

"I already asked her to work with us," Raiden admitted, dropping into a chair and bracing his elbows on his knees. "She was not receptive to my overtures."

"Again, I'm not surprised - not if she knows full well how the compulsion can be manipulated against her," Taos answered, his face suddenly sad. "Ione mentioned, during our walk to her rooms, that Liria was a gift when Ione was but a child. From what I could gather, in Atlantis, a shadow is more of a possession than a person, expected to follow their owner around... well, like their shadow."

Raiden grimaced. "It sounds like slavery to me, brother."

"Me, too, but Ione seems to think it doesn't count, since without a soul, Liria isn't a true person - therefore, she cannot possibly be a slave. Getting her to see the situation in a different light may be so difficult as to prove impossible." The Pharaoh drummed his fingers on his glass. "I hope Ione doesn't insist on having Liria in our room when we wish to make love. That would be... awkward."

"I don't imagine Liria would enjoy it, either."

"No, I'd say not."

"You know I love you, brother, but I can't sit idly by and watch someone else be treated with such blatant cruelty and disrespect."

Taos gripped Raiden's forearm, his brown eyes serious. "Nor I. Once Ione and I are married, Liria officially becomes part of our family. We will do what we can to fix this, I swear it."

Raiden swallowed, his next words torn from him. "Can she be freed?"

"Osiris doesn't know. There was nothing in Liria's memories, but he promised to consult the Soulcatcher. Anubis might have more information." An incisive look from one brother to another. "You like her."

Dropping his eyes to his glass, Raiden tilted it back and forth, watching the thick beer slide slowly about. "I... don't know."

"Liar."

"She bit me," Raiden muttered, raising his left hand to show the multitude of fang marks across the back of his knuckles. "Not only does the woman have twelve fangs - twelve! - the bite stings. I think she might be venomous."

"Liria is a dark fairy, so it's possible." The Pharaoh's dark chocolate eyes narrowed on the bite. "If you're still walking, then she held back on the poison - though you'll likely scar."

Oddly enough, Raiden found that idea soothing. He flexed his fingers to determine once and for all that the deep, unforgiving bite proved no impediment to the function of his hand, admiring the shape of Liria's fangs in his flesh. He had other scars on his body, scars far better earnt, but none of them caused the curious satisfaction that these potentially permanent markings did.

"Yes," he murmured at last. "Though we've only known each other a mere few hours, there's something about Liria that draws me."

"Can she use that against you?"

Raiden's lip quirked in a self-deprecating smile. "One, my brother, I don't think she realises that she's snagged my attention in any way, shape or form. Two, I am a soldier first and a man second. No matter that Liria's the most intriguing creature I've ever met, you are my priority."

"I believe you, but it would be remiss of me not to ask." Taos drained his beer and set the empty glass carefully on a side table. "To bring this conversation full circle, we need the shadow to work with us, brother."

"Then we need Princess Ione to modify the conditions of Liria's binding so that she's allotted more freedom." Raiden pushed a hand into his hair and tugged. "I see no other option than that."

"A mission for me, then," Taos murmured, straightening his elegant trousers and long, draped shawl. "For the charm of a Pharaoh."

Raiden stood and crossed the room, whipping the shawl off to reveal his brother's smooth chest. "No; a mission for the charm of a man to his woman."

Taos growled in the back of his throat and stalked to his wardrobe, tugging out a wide collar made from beaten gold plates that hung elegantly from his shoulders but left his abdomen and the lower half of his pectorals revealed. He fastened the collar at the back of his neck, his frown dangerously close to a pout as Raiden used a smear of product to tousle his hair so that he appeared as though he'd just tumbled out of bed. A quick smudge of black kohl, applied with the tip of Raiden's pinky finger, followed by an extra silk sash around Taos' waist to accent the green enamel detailing on the collar and an ornamental scimitar, and they were done.

"Yrini would be pleased," Raiden grinned, taking in his brother's updated look. "The first time she showed me the pot of kohl, I was sure I'd poke your eye out."

"Hmph."

"Come now, you look delicious," Raiden soothed, slapping his brother on the back.

"I do not doubt you, brother. More that I wish to be seducing my fiancé for reasons other than politics."

"It isn't really politics; if the Anarchist returns, he endangers your fiancé as much as yourself. In fact, if Set's words were any indication, it is the Princess Ione who will be in the most danger." Raiden paced away from his brother, hit the end of the carpet and spun on his heel, wings flaring wide. "Though the Princess' instinct will be to keep Liria close - and that is not so bad a thing, in general - we'll be able to protect you both better if she has permission to work directly with me, and for us to make decisions without needing Ione's constant intervention. Don't think about charming the Princess for political reasons - you're charming her because the more she trusts you, the better you can protect her. If you want to have any hope at all of getting the poor woman to fall in love with your useless hide, you'd have to start charming her soon regardless." Raiden donned his cheekiest grin. "She's already known you a few hours. Too much longer and she'll start to realise I'm the better choice."

The Pharaoh laughed, his dark mood lifting as quickly as it had fallen. "I think we know full well that the Princess Ione is a refined lady, and as such has far more delicate tastes than a rough and tumble warrior princeling, my brother."

Raiden bared his teeth, laughed, and walked to the door. With his Pharaoh on his heels, he strode the short distance to Ione's quarters, clenched the fist Liria had bitten and knocked loudly on the polished wood. It opened barely a minute later, silhouetting a slim female form in the doorway - and Raiden felt all the air rush out of his lungs.

Liria had changed into a deep navy dress that clung to the curves her previous outfit had hidden. The bodice cupped breasts that would perfectly fill his hands and hugged close to her ribs and narrow waist, before flaring over slender hips and draping in sleek folds to the ground. Two long slits reached up past mid-thigh, the gown just shy of inappropriate due to the way the outer part of the skirt overlapped the inner panel - and though Raiden knew full well the choice had been made for practicality should Liria need to fight, every step she took would reveal sleekly muscled legs that appeared endless. Her dainty feet were bare, her toenails painted a shimmering Atlantean aqua and she wore a knife strapped to each bicep, as well as a slender sword on an elegant leather belt on her right hip, the hilts of each blade dotted with aquamarines. Indigo-navy hair hung in gentle waves around her face, the tips forming lazy corkscrew curls that brushed the base of her spine. The silver pins which had so elegantly restrained those gorgeous locks earlier were fisted in one hand and her petite brow was drawn into a frown above deep violet eyes.

"Your grace," she said - and though the words were welcoming, her tone carried strain. "The Princess Ione was not expecting you so soon."

"Is she abed?" Taos looked so desperately disappointed that even Liria's stone countenance softened slightly.

"No, your grace," the shadow replied. "She wished another bath, and a change of clothes. Egypt's great heat will take some adjusting to."

Since Raiden was still staring, gobsmacked, at the vision in front of him, the Pharaoh elbowed him aside and stepped a little closer. "The heat? I thought Atlantis was warm."

"It is," Liria inclined her head and then, lips pressing into a line, added, "but my Princess has naiad blood in her veins and there is no great body of water here to sing her blood to soothing coolness. The desert's heat is heavy and dry, where the island of Atlantis has a far more tropical nature." A heartbeat passed, two. "It will not prevent her from performing her duties as a Queen, your grace, merely takes some time to acclimatise to. Bathing regularly helps, particularly since the Princess spent so much power healing General Barin."

So much power? Raiden blinked at the words, trying to force

his blindsided mind into action. The Princess Ione had healed Barin, yes, but his wounds had been relatively minor. If that small display had weakened Ione enough that she needed to bathe to recuperate her energies, then her magic was but a dewdrop in the desert.

"Does the Princess require medical aid?" Taos asked, his face an open book of concern.

Liria softened further, offering a small smile. "No, your grace, just a few more minutes to finish dressing."

"I am ready, my shadow, have no fear." Ione's sultry voice preceded her into the room, her body clad in one of the shorter, lighter, wrapped gowns favoured by many of the women in Selekhet. A bright blue that offset her eyes and dark hair, it emphasised her lush figure and, accented with copious amounts of Atlantean silver, was elegant to boot. Ione's brow creased, however, as she paused in the middle of the room. "You answer the door only partially dressed, then leave the Pharaoh on the threshold? For shame, my shadow."

Liria jerked backwards as though tugged by hidden strings, her eyes widening for a fraction of a moment before she retreated behind an impassive mask and turned her gaze to the floor. "Forgive me, my Princess. After the attack by Set earlier, I worried there might have been another threat."

"There are no excuses for being half naked," Ione snapped, wrapping a hand around Liria's arm and dragging the other woman to her side. "Fix yourself at once."

"It is no worry," Taos assured, nudging Raiden through the doorway and carefully pushing the door closed behind him. "The Lady Liria cares only for your wellbeing - as do I."

Fury clashed with tenderness in the Princess' face, but it was not to Ione that Raiden looked. It was to Liria, who was swiftly gathering those gorgeous, rich curls he wanted to bury his fists in and piling them atop her head in a severe knot - and in that moment, as she shoved her bladed pins in to keep the arrangement in place, he realised why Ione was so enraged.

For all her lush curves and raven tresses, Princess Ione's beauty held not even a flickering candle to the blazing furnace of Liria Atlannon.

Oh, it was carefully disguised by less expensive gowns and unflattering hairstyles, squashed beneath the power of a compulsion that swallowed the fire Raiden had glimpsed in the fairy who'd faced down a god, but he'd seen it now, in that shimmering moment before Liria had lowered her head, curled in her shoulders, and begun to pin back her hair the same way she likely pinned back her personality.

"Do not be overset with Liria, my dear fiancé. This is my fault for being so eager to enjoy our walk through the Palace gardens," Taos said, his voice pitched deep and smooth. "If it would please you, I thought we might also enjoy lunch together afterwards... and perhaps Prince Raiden can entertain your shadow so we might speak privately."

Ione blinked, one hand fluttering towards her throat. "I am rarely apart from my shadow."

"I assure you we will remain in eyeshot, my Princess. After all, our people are here to protect us, are they not?" Taos smiled and it carried every ounce of charisma the Pharaoh possessed. "But I should like to get to know my fiancé better, since she is to become my wife in little more than a week."

Ione tittered and blushed but Raiden didn't hear the response; he was captivated by the sight of Liria's carefully folded gossamer and stained glass wings as she turned her back, picking up a light gauze cape in the same shade of navy as her dress. When she made to lift it to her shoulders, Raiden dared to step to her side.

"Allow me?" he asked, his voice pitched for her ears alone.

Liria froze, her fists clenching in the fabric, and Raiden had the faintest glimpse of the panic that crossed her features before she shook her head the slightest amount. Her words, when they came, were a breath Raiden strained to hear. "That's not a good idea."

"It looks an awkward job," Raiden returned, striving to sound practical rather than breathless. This close to her, his lungs were full of the scent of moon lilies and the clear, cool secrets of dawn. "I can help."

Expecting her to refuse his impetuous request, Raiden thought his heart might stop when, her eyes firmly on the wall in front of her, Liria pushed the cape into his outstretched hands. "Touch my wings and die, Prince of Egypt."

"They're sensitive?" Raiden asked, managing to pin the first side of the cape to the shoulder of her dress without his hands trembling overmuch. "Mine are, in certain places."

She didn't answer, every tendon in her throat standing out in sharp relief as he pinned the cape to her other shoulder and carefully arranged the trailing strips of gauze, strictly avoiding contact with the wings that fascinated him so much. When at last the job was done, he took a half step to the side, his own wings half-spread to shield their faces from the rest of the room.

"You didn't try to touch them," Liria whispered, her violet eyes large and confused.

Raiden raised a brow. "I have no wish to die."

"I -" The Lady of Shadows drew in a sharp breath and lifted her chin in a way he knew instinctively she'd never do where the Princess could see. "It hurts to have my wings touched. Like thousands of knives slicing into vulnerable flesh."

Though he realised she'd tried to trap him in his own arrogance, that wasn't what Raiden focussed on. His hands clenched tightly into fists. "I've seen Ione stroke your wings multiple times since you landed in Selekhet."

"She touches them as she wills."

"Does she know that it hurts you?" he demanded. No answer. "*Liria.*"

"She is a Princess of Atlantis and will soon be Queen of all Merged Egypt." The delicate fairy in front of him turned at last, her face impassive and her eyes dark. "I am just a shadow."

A WALK IN THE PARK

IF LIRIA HAD THOUGHT her glimpses of Selekhet lovely and the interior of the Palace magnificent, it was nothing compared to the sprawling Royal Gardens. Pharaoh Taos and Ione strolled ahead, tall palms and gnarled desert trees providing shade alongside several other, more exotic styles of tree and bush, each plant meticulously cared for. Flowers carpeted the ground at the base of the trees, once again an eclectic mix of hardier Egyptian natives and more delicate foreign blooms. Through it all wound paths of smoothly polished cream stone, delicate mosaics set into the ground at intersections and softly rounded seating areas that featured tinkling fountains and latticed overhangs. Egypt had been singing to Liria since she arrived but this garden was something else, something that threatened to seep into her bones and rub with gentle fingers until she did something dangerous - relax.

The Princess Ione looked lovely, as always, whether framed by hanging blooms or pausing beneath the shade of spreading branches, the Pharaoh's charm in full effect as he pointed out wonder after wonder. For all the royal couple's poise, it was Prince Raiden that Liria watched from the corner of her eye, with his warrior's stride, well-loved twin swords and impeccable musculature. She'd tried to trip him up earlier, letting him have his unusual way by pinning her cape to her shoulders - but he hadn't fallen for the temptation of her wings, hadn't so much as breathed upon their surface and given her the opportunity to cut off his hands.

She really shouldn't be so impressed.

Though the pace Pharaoh Taos set was gentle, they walked for several hours and as the sun pushed into early afternoon, Princess Ione's composure began to fracture. Whether he recognised she wasn't used to such large amounts of exercise or simply because he was chivalrous to the last, the Pharaoh tucked the Princess closer to his side and within minutes they arrived at a beautifully shaded pool, trees encircling a lushly grassed clearing upon which a decadent picnic awaited.

"My brother," Taos turned to Raiden with a barely noticeable inclination of his head, then bowed slightly deeper in Liria's direction. "Lady of Shadows. Will you allow me this next little while to dote upon my most luscious fiancé?"

Liria opened her mouth but Raiden spoke before she had a chance, waving an expansive arm at the large pool of crystal water. "We could walk around the lake, and you'd have your privacy without being truly out of reach. What say you, your royal highness?"

"Oh," Ione managed, her voice just this side of panting. She'd already dropped onto the hand-woven blanket spread across the grass, her posture most un-Princesslike as she sprawled on her back, arms spread wide and lashes kissing her cheeks. "Yes, of course. If I need my shadow, I will call."

Shock curled low in Liria's stomach but she only bowed in her mistress' direction - though with her eyes closed and her chest working to get adequate air, the Princess Ione was oblivious to the courtesy. When Raiden held out his arm she clasped her hands in front of her, set her eyes firmly on the shimmering cream stone that paved their way and began to walk in the direction he'd indicated.

"So suspicious," he murmured as they left the royal couple behind. Raiden's voice was gorgeously rough when lowered, but there was no mistaking the laughter in his tone. "I won't bite - unlike you."

"Perhaps if you didn't make such a tempting target, you wouldn't have been bitten in the first place," Liria returned loftily.

Raiden's shoulders shook and he jammed his fist in his mouth to muffle the sound of his laughter, casting a furtive glance over one shoulder. Liria took advantage of his distraction to examine the fang marks she'd left in his hand; clean but deep, one larger wound with a smaller either side. She couldn't have made a more perfect impression of her darkness if she'd tried - and though it was in no way appropriate, the faintest of smiles tugged at her lips.

"Your bite will serve me right," Raiden said at last. For a moment Liria worried he'd caught her stare, but when he turned back, his wings spreading and then folding against his spine, his face was guileless. "Taos thinks it will scar, and I'll wear your brand forever."

Liria frowned. "Let me see it."

"All right." The Prince of Egypt stopped beneath the shade of a low-hanging tree and held out the hand she'd bitten, the glint in his gorgeous eyes one of pure challenge. Though the soft expanse of his half-spread wings blocked them from sight, Liria drew on just enough magic to muffle their voices before reaching out to grip his wrist.

His skin was warm, the tactile shock of him sending a tingling jolt up Liria's arm and across her chest. Working through the way her breath caught, she stepped closer, turning Raiden's palm to the sky and then to the ground as she checked him over. The perfect indentation of the fangs on the top right side of her mouth were matched by ones from the bottom, scored deep into the flesh between index finger and thumb. It was as well she hadn't managed to get the fangs on the other side of her mouth into play, or his entire index finger would bear the evidence of her temper. Brushing her senses over the wounds, Liria looked up from beneath her lashes to meet the deep gold of his gaze.

"Yes," she admitted softly. "You will bear these marks for the rest of your life, Prince of Egypt." His eyes darkened and Liria swallowed. "If you speak to my mistress, she will see me punished accordingly."

Raiden's gorgeous tri-coloured wings curved more closely around them, though he didn't attempt to hem her in. No, this was more like cupping hands beneath water to ensure none over-flowed, a gentle and almost tender moment that bought them a higher level of privacy.

"I don't want you punished," he said, his voice deepening to a rumble. "Particularly when you acted according to your own instincts - and I was the one who pissed you off in the first place." Raiden flexed his hand, cheeks creasing as she startled away from his coarse language. "Ah, but I can't be expected to be Palace formal for the rest of our lives, can I? You'll need to become accustomed to speaking as a person rather than an ornament if we're to work together, Lady of Shadows."

Liria crossed her arms over her chest. "I told you already, you stubborn, brainless pigeon; that's not possible."

A blink, then laughter poured out of him, warm and loud and deep. Raiden's wing brushed her shoulder as the angel hunched over himself, his mirth a thing of masculine beauty that made Liria's insides tingle. A private part of her basked in the sound, in his sand and sunlight scent as it wafted around them - but the other, far more well trained part of her merely lifted a dark brow and waited.

"I love seeing your real personality make an appearance," Raiden chuckled, knuckling tears from the corners of his eyes. "It tells me you're not so straight laced as you appear. For the record, I remember full well your assertion that we can't possibly co-operate. I chose to ignore it."

"For someone who claims not to be a true Prince, you have

the arrogance of one," Liria growled, flashing her fangs at him. "At least I know your memory isn't as defective as the rest of you. Or maybe it is, and you're just too egotistical to admit it?"

Raiden straightened his shoulders and just like that, his smile was gone and he was a warrior through and through. "You cannot touch or tamper with the soul ring. You cannot attempt to harm the Princess in any way. You cannot speak foully of Ione, even should those words be truth. She can be perfectly horrible, and you'll still stare at your feet or even kiss the floor should that seem necessary." He propped both hands on his hips. "My memory is a steel trap, Liria Atlannon - but this still doesn't explain why we can't work together. I'm not asking you to put the Princess at risk; I'm asking you to help me protect both her and my Pharaoh. I'm not asking you to speak foully of her, even should those words be truth; I've my own keen eyes, can make my own assessments, and will work with whatever information you can provide that's relevant to the situation. Whatever other obstacles there are, we can surmount them together - but I need to know what we *can* do in concert, or you become a chink in the Pharaoh's armour which I will have to deal with in a far less pleasant way."

"I-" Liria paused, brows furrowing as his words sunk in. "Oh."

"Yes, oh." Raiden's jaw tensed to a brutal line. "I don't want to fight you, Lady of Shadows, particularly when we'll be working side by side the rest of our lives to care for the people we love."

Cool, icy knives stabbed into Liria's gut and she groaned, covering her stomach with one hand. "Fold back your wings."

"What? What's wrong?"

"Fold back your wings," she gasped, the sensation creeping down her legs so that they shook and shivered. When the angel made to bend closer, she shoved at the nearest wing, his feathers living silk where they brushed against her palm. *"Raiden."*

He jerked back from her touch as though struck, folding his

wings away as Liria fell to her knees on the soft grass. It took every ounce of her iron will not to change her expression, to carefully lower her face to the ground in submission. Tears gathered in the corners of her eyes and Liria squeezed them shut, exhaling in relief when the sensation cut off as quickly as it had arrived. She was aware of Raiden crouching beside her, one hand flattened in the grass close enough that should she wished, she could have brushed her face against his skin.

"Liria?" he whispered. "Are you all right?"

"Ugh." When he reached out as though to touch her, Liria twitched away. "No, you'll make it worse. Just give me a moment."

A few minutes later, she raised her head and looked across the shimmering surface of the pool. Princess Ione had relaxed back onto her blanket and was chatting with the Pharaoh Taos, who reclined by her side with one wing spread beneath them so that Ione could shyly stroke his feathers. Neither were looking her way, so Liria pushed to her knees and raised shaking hands to fix the few tendrils of hair which had escaped her bun.

Raiden watched with his lips pressed into a thin line and his shoulders tight. "Why?"

"She couldn't see me. Your wing must have blocked the view."

"She'd punish you for that?"

"That wasn't punishment," Liria murmured, smoothing the skirts on her dress. "That was panic." When his brows drew together, she sighed. "Fear is cold, anger is hot. I cannot be clearer than that."

"It still hurts you."

Daring to get to her feet, Liria shook the last few shivers out of her limbs and strengthened the air muffling spell that hung around her and the irritating angel who seemed intent on storming her defences. When she was sure the Princess and the Pharaoh couldn't hear them, she adopted a demure posture while simultaneously glaring at Raiden from the corners of her eyes.

"Why do you care, Prince of Egypt? We've been acquainted barely a day. I am no-one and nothing to you."

"Are we really going to keep having this argument?" Raiden growled, temper making his face even more ruggedly gorgeous than it had been before. "I'm trying hard to be patient, but you're equally intent on pushing me beyond my limited measure." Shoving his wings downward, he created a fierce wind around their ankles that lifted him several inches off the ground. "The Pharaoh's honour guard are not just soldiers. We're like family; we know how each person thinks, how they react, how they dance and laugh and breathe and sleep. We know each other's strengths and weaknesses, their dreams and sorrows, because it means we can function as a unit. A many-limbed creature with a single aim works better than a set of opaque individuals - and for the hundredth time, you and I are going to be working more closely than any of the others. You think you're no-one and nothing, but you're wrong. The moment you stepped off that boat this morning, you became one of my people, and I will fight for you as much as I'll fight with you."

"I can't -"

He swept in and grabbed her biceps, his fingers living brands and the pressure just shy of bruising. "You can. I know you have limits but you can give me something, Liria. *Something.* Don't make me view you as a threat."

Ice froze Liria's throat, hundreds of tiny, pricking claws that threatened her ability to breathe. It gave way almost at once to molten agony in her veins, the vicious heat and stinging barbs so intense that her fingers and toes curled inwards and her teeth clenched so hard she wondered if any would crack.

Then her hand was moving, faster than fast. She stepped into Raiden, inside the circle of his arms, spreading a hand across the draped shawl which was all that protected what she imagined to be a broad, muscular chest. Tipping back her head, Liria stared into those golden eyes as they widened in shock, the knife in her free hand plunging deep into his side. Blood gushed hot and wet over her wrist as Raiden sagged against her, wings drooping.

"I'm sorry, Prince of Egypt," Liria whispered, her voice cut with the echoes of a thousand ghosts and her body a puppet beyond her control. "This is all I'm allowed to give."

JUST A SCRATCH

Raiden woke flat on his back in a bed large enough that his fully spread wings didn't so much as tease the edges of the mattress. He was bare chested and barefoot, with bandages wrapped around his abdomen and his lower body clothed in the loose-woven linen pants he normally wore for sleep. He didn't bother trying to move, staring instead at the detailed mosaic set into the ceiling of his bedroom and allowing his chest to rise and fall in the steady rhythm which had done him well up to this point in his life.

Liria had stabbed him.

On that, his memory was particularly insistent - when Raiden closed his eyes for the fraction of time it took to blink, all he could see was her upturned face, the angle such that he could almost imagine she might've been about to kiss him, except for the cold steel sliding effortlessly between his ribs. He'd felt the hilt bump bone, the blade penetrating enough internal organs that he'd crumpled at once.

Liria had *stabbed* him.

Frowning, Raiden turned his eyes downward, where lengths

of stretched gauze bandage had been wrapped so thick and neat he'd guess it was done by an embalmer rather than a healer, the two professions overlapping when necessity dictated. If he drew in too deep a breath, he felt a sharp ache towards the base of his ribcage, proof in point that his memory did not lie.

Liria had stabbed *him*.

"No."

The single word didn't toll through the room in the deep, bell-like voice with which he'd intended - rather it came out a hoarse rasp, as though Raiden had spent a week in the desert without supplies.

"Your highness?" A young man stepped into view, hands twisting nervously and sleek black jackal's ears poking out of the mess of black hair on his head. "How is the pain?"

"I was stabbed," Raiden muttered. "How do you think the pain is?"

Clear green eyes blinked, and then the kid - early twenties, if Raiden had to guess - lifted one shoulder in a shrug. "I... uh, I'm an embalmer, sir. I can't say as I know, and most of the people I work with are too dead to ask."

That shy admission startled a laugh from Raiden that he immediately regretted. "What's your name?"

"Balai," the youngster croaked, eyes wide and awestruck. At least they were, until he focussed on Raiden's abdomen and frowned, stepping forward to spread capable fingers across the tight wrappings. "Lie still or you'll tear yourself open."

"Bet you don't have to deal with that when it comes to the dead."

Balai tilted his head to the side, his tone absent as he began checking over bandages that didn't look any different to Raiden than they had a moment ago. "Oh, you'd be surprised." He flickered those sleek jackal ears in dry amusement. "I've the touch of the underworld."

"Rare." Raiden forced his eyes back to the ceiling mosaic as the boy fiddled with his wrappings. Whilst embalming was an honest profession many Egyptians worked hard at, a select few of the Merged citizens were born with the powers of a necromancer, allowing them to manipulate the bodies of the dead. To be touched so by the afterlife was an honour beyond price.

"What's it like?"

"Boring, mostly." Balai patted at the tucked-in edge of the bandage and shot Raiden a young man's grin. "It's not like the deceased chat to me while I use magic to re-attach limbs or seal up cuts so their mummies can be perfect - and my superiors get angry if I ask the corpses to dance a jig."

Again, he wanted to laugh - but this time, Raiden worked hard to stifle the urge, settling instead for a snort. "So, since I'm not dead, why are you here?"

Balai hesitated, looking over his shoulder at the door. "I'm meant to wait for -"

A swift gust of cool air swept into the room, closely followed by the creak of Raiden's bedroom door opening. The young embalmer squeaked, bowed and backed out of the way, his face not pale so much as wary and his green eyes on the floor.

"Brother." Taos appeared by Raiden's side first, gripping his hand tightly. "Thank the gods."

"It was our pleasure, Pharaoh." Words both sibilant and seductive preceded a man with charcoal black skin and sparkling hazel eyes to the foot of the bed. Long, straight black hair framed an elegantly pointed face and hung over the chest of the formal black and gold robes he wore, beneath which Raiden glimpsed a well-muscled chest. Black-furred jackal's ears swept up from his hair, and Raiden didn't need to look down to know he walked on a jackal's hind legs, and had a jackal's tail poking out from the hem of his robes.

"Soulcatcher," Raiden said, blinking up at Anubis in surprise. "Am I to die after all?"

"No; thanks to my brother, you will live." Anubis, god of

death and patron of lost souls, waved a hand at the handsome man who came to stand beside him. Not quite as tall as his brother, the newcomer bore soft bronze skin, dark hair and angel wings of grey and black. One of his eyes was brilliant scarlet and the other, an impossible royal blue. "Horus donated his blood to save your life."

Raiden's jaw hit his chest as he looked to Horus, god of the sky and father of all angelkind. "You gave me your *blood?*"

"Rather a lot of it, honestly. Don't look so scandalised," Horus chuckled, his voice throaty and soft. "As if I would let you go without a fight."

It didn't seem so obvious a decision to Raiden. He wasn't the Pharaoh, and the gods had made a point of keeping their blood inside their bodies since the creation of the first Merged people. By the customs of both Mu and Earth, Raiden should be dead, his soul in Anubis' custody for conveyance to the afterlife and his body in the Palace temple awaiting mummification. Furrowing his brow, he looked at Taos. "Explain."

"I saw you go down beneath Liria's knife," the Pharaoh said, his face as grim as Raiden had ever seen it. "Not only did she drive it in, she twisted viciously, making a ruin of your insides. I called for Osiris at once; he was visiting with Anubis and, by chance, Horus was also there. They'd been discussing the abominable nature of Set's intrusion unto the palace and..."

Raiden's conscience immediately cleared. A matter of honour, then, to save his life when he'd so recently been threatened by Osiris' brother, who was also Horus and Anubis' uncle. Returning his eyes to the gods at the foot of the bed, he looked back and forth between them.

"To whom do I owe my debt?"

Anubis shrugged. "I kept your soul inside your shell while Horus poured his blood into your mouth, so I guess that makes it a joint effort. However," the god of death raised a clawed finger when Raiden went to speak, "there will be no debts between us, for by the time the morning comes, you might be cursing Horus and I both."

"I do make a habit of cursing people who save my life," Raiden said, his expression deadpan. "Ask Yrini about that sometime."

Horus snorted; he'd been there, after all. Shifting from one foot to the other, the god of the sky eventually sighed and braced his hands on the footboard of the bed. "What my brother is trying to say is that before this point, you merely carried enough of my genetic code to grant flight, as do all angelkind. Now, however, you actually carry my blood inside you - and it is not idle, Prince of Egypt. You are becoming... more."

"More?" Raiden repeated, a chill shiver working down his spine.

Horus waved a frustrated hand and turned to Anubis, whose eyes had narrowed and begun to glow with a soft blue light.

"Blood of our blood," the Soulcatcher whispered. "You are becoming more of us, less of them. Stronger, faster, better; gaining powers that belong in the strongest inhabitants of Mu. Not just an angel, Raiden. More." Blinking that blue light away, Anubis offered a lopsided smile. "If you survive the night, of course. Your DNA is quite literally being re-written and if I'm right, it'll be mightily painful before too much longer."

Raiden stared from one drawn expression to the other, his fingers tapping a staccato rhythm against the mattress. "That's more than a simple matter of honour. What is it you really want from me?"

Taos immediately blanched, and both Anubis and Horus looked as though they'd been caught raiding their mother's pantry after a drunken binge. It was the young embalmer, Balai, his green eyes lingering on Raiden's bandages, who set his mind flickering to life.

"You need someone in the Palace who can oppose Set," Raiden murmured. "No, that's not it; you want someone strong enough to stand against Liria Atlannon."

Anubis grimaced. "The soulbound have terrible strength, Raiden. This shadow's compulsion makes her strong enough to do things that shouldn't be possible for a dark fairy - or anyone, for that matter - and we can't be on hand to watch her every movement. As Taos' brother, you're ideally placed to protect him best."

"I thought I was already doing that."

"Yes, of course." Anubis hesitated, then added, "But Liria has already overpowered you. If the Princess Ione asks her to, Liria could end even the gods."

"So you made me into a weapon," Raiden breathed, his gut knotting. "You want me to kill her."

Horus and Anubis immediately focussed elsewhere, their expressions such pictures of fake innocence that Raiden would've laughed in any other scenario. He turned to Taos, certain his betrayal was writ clean across his face.

"Right now, Liria is unconscious in the dungeons." The Pharaoh's voice turned hard. "We had to sedate Ione, too, because she wouldn't stop screaming and calling for her shadow. General Barin gave us an Atlantean recipe that won't upset her naiad heritage so we can keep her asleep until we formulate a better plan." Taos let out a shaky breath. "I hate to have her drugged, but Anubis believes the strength of the compulsion might enable Liria to smash through walls to fulfil her mistress' command. Barin couldn't answer either way, but his inability to say such a thing was impossible makes it possible."

Raiden blinked. "That doesn't sound right."

"It isn't," Anubis growled, clenching both hands to fists. "Soulbinding was banned because it turns people into monsters beyond comprehension. Not only does it steal free will, keeping the victim prisoner for the entirety of their existence, it gifts a magical tenacity that drives them beyond normal limits when given a command to carry out."

"That's how you said she was able to defy Set," Taos said, his eyes on Raiden as though being stabbed had stolen his wits instead of his lifeblood. "The compulsion provides a shield not even a god can shatter."

"Yes." Anubis paced the length of the bed and back again, and Raiden wished he were well enough to do the same. After a long moment, the Soulcatcher threw up his clawed hands and made a frustrated noise in the back of his throat. "I've met a few other shadows in my travels - but Liria Atlannon? Never have I seen an enchantment of the strength which binds her. If my senses are correct, she can literally feel Ione's desires, her needs and her instructions. She doesn't need to hear them spoken, she simply knows them and is forced to act."

Fear is cold, anger is hot. I cannot be clearer than that.

The remembered words echoed inside Raiden's head, their meaning suddenly crystal clear.

"Yes," he said. "That's exactly how it works."

"Ione is not only completely dependent upon Liria but insanely jealous of her to boot," Horus put in, his bronze skinned arms crossed over his chest. "Anubis sensed barely a trickle of power in the Princess' veins, in comparison to the monsoon that is trapped inside Liria. She's a disaster waiting to happen - surely you can see that."

"I've both seen and felt it, and it's still no excuse for what you overzealous bastards want me to do," Raiden growled. He made to sit up, and quite suddenly had a Pharaoh, two gods and a young embalmer holding him down. He quirked a brow at the conglomerate of faces above him. "Really?"

"It's starting in earnest," Anubis whispered, hazel eyes flicking to Horus. "Can you feel it?"

The god of the sky shook his head. "Not yet."

"I won't kill Liria," Raiden snapped, straining against their hands. "No matter what you make me into."

Taos stared as if his brother had decided to cover himself in honey and roll in an ant's nest. "Raiden, she tried to kill you - or have you forgotten the knife, the gods, the discussion we've just been having?"

"It wasn't Liria," Raiden asserted. "I saw her face, heard her voice. It wasn't she who stabbed me."

"Brother." Taos rubbed a hand across his forehead. "I watched the knife go in myself. There's no other -" he broke off and took a swift step back, face pale. "No."

"Yes." Raiden spoke through clenched teeth, his muscles tensing one by one until he vibrated on the bed. "Ione."

"No," Taos insisted, shaking his head. "I can't believe she'd order something like that."

Raiden tried to sit again, was shoved back to the mattress by Anubis and Horus, the strength of the gods without compare. "Think, brother. You were all just telling me she was jealous, and we've spent the entire day trying to peel Liria away from her side."

"It can't be." Taos shook his head again. "Ione's sweet. Gentle. Lost and scared without her shadow, but that's understandable given they've been attached since Ione was a child." Expression desperate, he met the gods' eyes. "What reason would she have to make an attempt on the Prince's life?"

"The heart doesn't always think rationally," Horus murmured, his gaze tinged with old pain. "If Ione felt threatened... she might not even have realised what she'd ordered through the compulsion." He sighed. "We cannot condemn Liria until we know for sure."

"You can't condemn her at all!" Raiden sat bolt upright and the two gods staggered back, their faces aghast. Agony speared deep in his gut, as though Liria's knife tore him open all over again. Clenching both fists, Raiden glared around the room. "I won't kill her. I won't. Not without proof."

It was Balai who broke the tension, the embalmer loosing a dramatic sigh as he stepped in to prod at the bandages around Raiden's middle - bandages that were rapidly turning a dark, cherry red.

"Well, I'd say the change has begun in earnest," the kid muttered. "These wrappings are a mess."

"Leave it," Raiden growled, energy punching through his veins with the might of a brewing storm. "I have somewhere to be."

Taos rushed in then, fear sparking in his brown eyes. "No, brother, you have to rest."

"When you want to murder an innocent?" Raiden shook Anubis off his arm, then used that same arm to toss Horus across the room.

"I won't do anything," Taos said, both hands up in placation. "Please, just rest."

Pain began to creep into Raiden's muscles, his vision turning hazy, but he stood his ground. "Swear it."

"On my honour, Liria lives until you've seen her for yourself."

Anubis pushed forward and Raiden punched him on the nose just because he could, his body a discordant symphony of freakish strength and boiling energy. Was this how Liria felt, he wondered as Horus flattened him onto the bed? A tempest leashed by force?

"If you don't stay down," Anubis snarled, baring teeth that were suddenly very much a jackal's, "I will use my powers and *put* you down, angel."

Raw, vicious agony arched Raiden's back and he screamed, the sound broken and ragged as his wings snapped wide and his blood turned to shards of glass. He felt the cool, inexorable shove of the Soulcatcher's energy, some new, infant part of him identifying the kiss of Anubis' power even as it stole his ability to protest. Then Horus the Skywatcher, his energy of the wind and the clouds, reached out to soothe Raiden as only a father, or perhaps a blood brother, could. Their voices murmured softly inside his head, their unfathomable strength curling close around him, gentling, nurturing... binding.

Raiden opened his mouth on a bellowing roar, every cell in his body coming apart and smashing back together again. Magic the likes of which he'd never before felt blossomed in the depths of his soul, clashing in feral rage against the more seasoned power of the gods. He fought their hold with everything he had, everything he was, everything he'd never be - and of course he lost, forcing two of Egypt's most powerful deities to steal his thoughts and send him spiralling into unconsciousness against his will.

ROOM WITH A VIEW

As DUNGEONS WENT, IT wasn't that bad. Atlantis, for example, had a tendency towards slime and the odd confused jellyfish, given that the island's dungeons were well below sea level and featured an entire level of cells specifically for aquatic inhabitants. Liria had also heard that Ur, over in Sumeria, liked to entertain scorpions and snakes in their dungeons, and that the guards had running bets on how long a prisoner would last before getting bitten or eaten. So far Egypt's specialty was little more than eerie isolation; a dungeon full of darkened cells without a single living soul inside them. Instead of clanking chains and grievous moans, there was only dry, oppressive silence.

Liria brushed her fingertips over a carving on the wall. Crudely worked, it appeared to be either a three headed dragon or a goat gone horribly wrong - but it was proof that someone, somewhere, had been here before her. With a lingering sigh, she gave the carving a final pat and returned to the narrow wooden pallet which was the cell's single furnishing. Her room was perhaps six feet square, with iron bars along one wall and stone for the other three. Light filtered in through finger-width cracks spaced evenly across the back wall where it met the roof, letting in just enough illumination during the day to mark the passage of time without actually being enough to see by. Liria's night vision was excellent so the gloom was no issue, and she'd slept in far more chilly places - because for all it was dark, this was still Egypt, and enough heat filtered down through the stones that whilst she wasn't entirely comfortable, neither would she freeze. The floors were clean and dry, as were the walls, the stone blocks plain bar for the crude carving. A small tap and drain in one corner was the only indication of hygiene facilities, but Liria made do without so much as a whimper of complaint.

After all, she'd stabbed a Prince, and a well loved one at that.

Liria dropped onto the wooden pallet, hiding her trembling hands beneath the leading edge of her skirt. Her skin was still stained a dark rust in places, the tactile memory of Raiden's big body slumping against hers playing over and over in her mind. Cold steel in her hand, thrusting, twisting, gold eyes flickering with disbelief a moment before they'd gone dark. Probably forever, if she'd hit as true as it felt she had, particularly when she'd puréed his innards in the time it had taken for the Pharaoh Taos to hit her over the back of the head. Liria had woken in the dungeon stripped of her weapons and had seen no-one since, for all that the flickering hint of daylight said that two days had passed - perhaps more, depending on how long she'd been unconscious. None of the memories, however, held a candle to the flame of agony which licked her heart, threatening to choke off her air and turn her to ashes. If she remained locked in this dark cell forever, it wouldn't be long enough to erase what her hands had done while her soul screamed in helpless torment.

Foolish, really, to be so upset. The Prince of Egypt wasn't the first to fall beneath her hand. Liria had hardened herself to the reality of it long ago, remaining aloof from all others in the hope of preventing exactly the sort of situation that had seen Raiden skewered. It worked for the most part - and when it didn't? Those instances simply served to strengthen her armour and widen the barrier between herself and the rest of the world.

Except for Raiden.

Whether a product of Egypt's more relaxed culture or his own mulish will, the Prince had pushed his nose in where it didn't belong, and he'd paid the price. Yet... the cold distance Liria usually felt was lacking. It didn't matter that she'd only known Raiden a matter of hours; it would have hurt far less to turn the knife on herself.

Not for the first time, she wished she could.

A low, ominous groan echoed through the dungeons, followed by the heavy thud of footsteps. Uneven, as though the owner of those boots was either limping or had a penchant for too much beer, their centre of balance thrown off by a bulging gut. Probably the latter, because what jailor was anything other than a grease-covered, tooth missing ingrate just the right side of the law? Then a silhouette pulled up outside her cell, and Liria's heart shot right out of her chest.

"*Raiden?*" Night vision aside, she'd have recognised the arch of those wings anywhere, the set of his shoulders and the bulge of his muscles burnt into the back of her retina. The angel stood silent, his face in heavy shadow, but his scent tickled her nostrils, warm sand and burning sunlight and... storms? Relief warred with apprehension as Liria stepped closer to the iron bars, nostrils curling. It was hard to pinpoint, but there was something edgier about Raiden's scent, something that hadn't been present before. He shifted his weight and she pulled up short, twisting her hands in her skirts. "How are - I mean - you were - um."

"Stabbed?" His voice was deeper than she remembered, with a reverberation that seemed separate from the echoing emptiness of the dungeons. "You *stabbed* me."

Liria fought the urge to slump, swallowing in a vain effort to soothe the lump in her throat. He had every right to be angry, every right to hate the hand that had hurt him. Still... "I tried to warn you, Prince of Egypt."

A bare rumble of sound, akin to that of distant thunder - and then Liria was scrambling backwards as Raiden, Prince of Merged Egypt and head of the Pharaoh's honour guard, walked through the iron bars of the cell as though they didn't exist.

"What are you doing?" Her breath came out a trembling rush but he didn't stop, backing her hard up against the wall and pressing the electric heat of his body against hers. "Raiden, are you all right?"

Of course he wasn't. Her body had tried to kill him. On that note, how exactly was he up and about? Not only was it a miracle that the Prince had survived, but to be visiting a dungeon? Angel or no, he should be lying weak and pale in bed, not crowding into her personal space.

Powerful fists slammed into the wall on either side of Liria's head, stone chips and mortar puffing around them in a cloud. "Say it again."

"Are you -"

"No," he rumbled, his voice deepening with every syllable. "The other."

Liria couldn't quite catch her breath, her heart a lost rabbit in her chest - but for these few moments her words and actions were her own, and she was determined not to waste them. "Raiden."

"Yes." His big hands fisted in her hair, unbound after whoever had stripped her of weapons had removed the bladed pins which normally kept it contained. "Raiden. Raiden and Liria."

"You shouldn't be here," Liria whispered, tears springing unbidden to her eyes and her lungs working like bellows. He was pressed so hard against her it was an effort to breathe, every sculpted line of his body merciless - and all the gods damn her, but it was the most decadent sensation Liria had ever experienced. Raising trembling hands, she dared to set them on the slope of his bare shoulders. "I hurt you."

"Did you?" Raiden's hands tightened in her hair, tipping her head back so she looked, at long last, into the shocking intensity of his golden eyes. They flickered with a thousand tiny lights, as though a great storm raged beneath the surface. "Did *you* hurt me, Liria?"

Even here, now, with instinct telling her Ione was asleep or otherwise subdued, the compulsion wouldn't let her answer with the truth. Gritting her teeth against the warning shivers, Liria managed, "You were there. You know."

"Yes," he murmured, and there was a hint of something strange in his tone, a fleeting edge that Liria couldn't decipher. "I know."

"Raiden, I -"

"I *know*." And then he lowered his head and sealed his mouth to hers.

Energy arced through Liria's veins, pure, raw lightning that spoke to the most primal part of her. She shook in his arms, tears streaming down her face as he kissed her, lips soft and tender and his body a hot, hard wall. Thunder rumbled - or was that a growl, deep in his chest - and then Raiden was gone as though he'd never been. Heart thumping and face wet, Liria cast about her in dazed confusion, not so much as a lingering hint of scent or the warmth of his touch to say that Raiden had ever existed. When every sense she owned insisted she was alone, Liria crumpled to her knees on the cell floor and sobbed, her hands pressed to her heart as though she'd claw it out.

Her first kiss, and it hadn't even been real.

Desperate not to lose herself to the madness raging deep inside, Liria dashed at her tears, finger combed her tangled hair until it was smooth, and pushed herself upright. A mirage, that's all. They happened, particularly to people who'd had only water for two days and were locked in a dungeon that echoed with emptiness. There was no evidence one way or another to say Raiden was alive, but conversely, nothing to say he was dead, either. Until she knew for certain, she had to stay strong.

A laugh that was part giggle and part agonised hysteria slipping free on that thought, Liria pushed herself to her feet as thunder echoed in the distance. A storm? She sniffed, caught the electric edge in the air. That must have been what she scented earlier, while she was busy hallucinating angry Princes and passionate, soul-melting embraces.

Nodding, she turned towards the back wall... and froze at the sight of two fist-sized indentations spiderwebbing the solid stone.

"Raiden?"

No answer - but the tiny cracks overhead shimmered blue as lightning struck the earth outside with a thunderous crack.

ECHOES OF A DREAMER

COOL NIGHT AIR CARESSED Raiden's skin, teasing him slowly back
to awareness. Someone had left the window in his bedroom open,
the scent of desert rain filling every cell in his battered body. He
tried to shift the arm covering his face, gave up when it proved
both too heavy and too painful.

God of the sky, but he felt awful.

God of the sky, Raiden repeated, flashes of Horus' repentant
face flickering to life in his mind, followed quickly by charcoal-
black skin seen nowhere else on earth. *Soulcatcher. What have you
done to me?*

Besides saving his life, of course. Groaning - or trying to, if
that useless whisper of sound was any indication - Raiden
clenched his teeth and managed to flop his arm out to the side.
Several harsh breaths later, his lashes lifted and he stared up at
the roof, the ceiling mosaic distinguishable in spite of the lengthy
shadows. From the corner of his eye, he spotted gauzy curtains
rippling softly in the breeze, smashed furniture, bloodied
bandages and spilt jars of herbal medicine.

What in the world had happened while he slept?

Raiden tried to move, his body spasming with enough

violence to flop him off the bed and onto the floor with a loud thump.

"Wha?" A jumbled shadow in an armchair came to bleary-eyed life and Raiden recognised Balai, the young embalmer.

"Here," he tried to say, but what came out of his mouth was more like "Hnngarrrr."

The young man was by his side in an instant, all traces of sleep gone from his expression and hands gentle where they hovered over Raiden's shoulders. "Your highness. Are you awake?"

"Yurrrrrr."

"Hmmm. Hold still, now." Brow scrunching with effort, Balai raised his hands and, to Raiden's surprise, his body stood up and got back in the bed without his conscious decision to do so. When it was over, the embalmer slumped against the side of the mattress with a gasp, his brow dotted with sweat. "Well, you're definitely back with us - or close enough as to make no difference. I can feel your life force pushing me away. I won't be able to do that next time you fall out of bed, so if I were you, I'd stay put."

"Uh?"

"Your... transformation? As good a word as any, I suppose." Balai passed a hand over his weary face and Raiden noted the embalmer had an enormous black eye and a split lip. "Your transformation took you into a state beyond life. Once the initial phase passed, I was able to use my power to keep you contained. You feel like all the hells right now because your body has been through significant trauma while it was reborn, and your spirit was temporarily elsewhere."

"Urrr... uh?"

"Dead," Balai said, patting Raiden's cheek in a paternal fashion. "You were a little bit dead, your highness. Not to worry; you feel more alive with every passing moment."

Raiden lay silent while Balai bustled around the ruined bedroom, returning with a chipped mug of what smelt like herb-laced water. Lifting Raiden's head with surprising strength, the young man set the cup against his lips and helped him take several measured sips. Energy and feeling began to return to Raiden's limbs as his body soaked up the nourishment with desperate glee, setting an unpleasant tingling sensation crawling across his skin. With no other choice, he stared at the roof and endured.

"I dreamed," Raiden said some minutes later, pleased when his words came out slurred but understandable. "Impossible dreams."

"You remember them?"

Taking in the young man's awestruck face, Raiden frowned and tried to push his mind back into the strange, lucid state in which he'd found himself. "I thought I did, but now they're fading. I remember..."

Moon lilies and the first tendrils of dawn. Long, dark, corkscrew curls. Rage. Hurt. Heat. Iron?

"Gone," Raiden choked out, letting the impressions go. "Sorry."

Balai sighed. "It would be the utmost of blessings to glimpse beyond the veil, but perhaps that's as it should be."

"Don't you already have the ability to make the dead dance?" With teeth-gritted effort, Raiden reached out to flick one of the young man's jackal ears. "You walk with the blood of Anubis in your veins, Balai. The Kiss of the Soulcatcher is a blessing in and of itself."

Green eyes bright, Balai nodded. "Yes, your highness, you're right, of course. Not all of the Merged are so fortunate as I."

"Humility does you well." Raiden nodded. "Now help me sit up."

"I'm not sure that's a good idea."

"You want me to piss in the bed?"

"No!" Balai leapt forward, and with one arm slung over the embalmer's shoulder, Raiden made it to the facilities without incident. Given there was little the young man hadn't seen, he cajoled Balai into helping him shower - though Raiden drew the line at being dried, wrapping the towel around his own hips and managing a few jerky flaps of his wings to blow off the worst of the water.

His strength returned in fits and starts, allowing him to stagger back to his room, but deserting him halfway through attempting to pull on clean pants. Taos arrived as Balai was trying to pick Raiden up off the floor, the embalmer's magic no use now that Raiden was 'too alive.' Together, the two men hoisted Raiden back onto the bed, where Taos proceeded to laugh mercilessly while he dressed him.

"When I can control my limbs," Raiden growled as his older brother tied a scarlet sash around his waist, "I'm going to pummel you."

Taos grinned, then winced, raising a hand to his jaw. "You already did, you brute."

"I hit you?"

"You weren't in your right mind." Taos pulled him into a sitting position and draped a matching scarlet shawl around his shoulders, securing it in place with a gold pin that had seen better days, but was Raiden's favourite. "Besides, I'm not worried. I might've copped a whack on the jaw, but you beat the ever-living shit out of Horus and Anubis, my dear brother."

"I *did?*"

The Pharaoh grinned, looking to Balai for backup. The embalmer nodded at once. "Ever-living shit, your highness."

"But they're *gods.*"

"Probably why they're still alive - though they were cursing both you and each other by the time you finally... uh..." Taos trailed off, his gaze skittering away.

"Died?" Raiden growled, hands clenching to fists.

"Collapsed," the Pharaoh corrected, his finger lifted and his smile broad - but it didn't reach his eyes, the deep brown glittering with the echo of old pain.

Raiden dragged his older brother into a tight hug. "I'm sorry I scared you."

In that moment, they weren't matured adults but young teens, sharing the grief of burying their parents and their younger sister far too early. Whilst they'd always been close, from that day Taos and Raiden had become inseparable, swearing vows of honour to each other as both brothers and as the newly minted Pharaoh and Prince of Merged Egypt.

"How long was I out?" Raiden asked, releasing his brother more because his arms stopped working than because he actually wanted to let go. "A day?"

"A few," Taos answered. When Raiden's jaw dropped open, he shrugged. "Yes, I know, I've survived without you for three whole sunrises. Astonishing, isn't it? I was worried at first, but Yrini's jokes are better than yours."

Raiden forced a smile. "Liar. My humour is impeccable."

Taos grinned, held out a hand and pulled Raiden upright. His legs held, his arms held, and when he tried to spread his wings they obeyed, opening as far as they could go within the confines of his room. Closing them carefully, Raiden took a cautious step forward - then another, and another, until he was out in his living area doing cautious laps.

"Ione?" he asked, when his bones felt more at home in his skin.

"Still asleep." Taos' face pinched with worry. "General Barin has taken Liria's place as her guardian for now."

"And Liria?"

The Pharaoh hesitated, smoothing both hands over his dark green silk trousers. "In the Kirrilakh."

Raiden stared. The blood in his veins ran cold, then hot, and though he was aware his Pharaoh was still speaking, he could hear nothing through the roaring in his ears. The Kirrilakh. Egypt's most secure dungeon, accessible only by those who could navigate the many deadly traps, both natural and otherwise, that kept it isolated.

Rejection a pulse in his soul, Raiden turned on his heel and was out the open window before he'd finished deciding to make the jump. His wings spread wide, muscles protesting the strain of exercise so soon after his near-death experience. At the precise moment he began to wonder how many bones would break when he smashed into the ground, Raiden's feathers caught the air just right and he swept upwards, his knees brushing against the uppermost fronds of a palm.

He cast a glance backward and saw Taos framed in the window, but his brother didn't follow - and for once, Raiden was glad.

Dawn was a wash of orange and violet on the horizon as he flew, the many beautiful facets of Selekhet spread out beneath him. Lights flickered in windows; tradesmen and craftsmen beginning their work long before Ra's chariot drew the sun into the sky. Tantalising smells wafted from street stalls and morning cafes, the odd snatch of laughter or conversation drifting on dew-fresh air. Moisture darkened several streets, as well as a couple of scorch marks that had Raiden raising an eyebrow - whatever storm had struck had been recent, close and violent, leaving several trees split and even cracking the stone on some of the houses.

Before long Raiden passed out of the city proper and into the residential areas, their smoothly paved streets dotted with elegant houses and well-manicured gardens. Beyond, farmland, and to the left, the port, complete with squealing gulls, laughing fishermen and traders whose language turned the air blue.

The further Raiden flew the better he felt, the ache in his muscles turning to the fierce sort of exhilaration which always accompanied him when he took to the sky. Holding his body straight like an arrow, the result of an angel's genetic musculature and a lifetime's practice, Raiden winged through the still air with enough speed to create his own breeze. When he hit Selekhet's farthest edge, the desert sprawled lazily beyond, he turned towards the squat mountains in the near distance. At the foot of those mountains ran a deep, natural canyon, the sides of which were heavily carved and pockmarked with tombs, each one accessed through a series of carefully crafted scaffolds and ramps. Beyond the mountain rose the first of the Great Pyramids of Selekhet, two long lines of incredible edifices that aligned perfectly with the stars wheeling above and created an excellent runway for approaching aircraft.

Passing directly over the top of the squat mountain, Raiden made sure to keep outside the line marked by the pyramids whose interiors held shops and guest houses. With tops of shimmering crystal that caught both the sunlight and the running lights of airships so that nobody crashed in the dark, the pyramids were a perfect melding of beauty and function. Raising a hand to the sleek passenger liner on approach, Raiden swung west and raced the sunrise across sweeping desert dunes.

Ten minutes on, the first morning rays nipping at his heels, he entered the leading edge of the perpetual sandstorm which surrounded the Kirrilakh. Built into the desert as much as atop it, the prison was almost completely covered by the raging sands, an endless spiral of magic keeping the storm viciously contained. Anyone attempting to navigate said storm would be brutally battered and beaten, thrown to the dunes which sucked them in and down, down, down unto eternity - unless, of course, you were of royal blood or had the attendant clearance to pass through.

With both those permissions to his name, Raiden had no problem flying in the storm, the tips of his wings cutting trails through the grit and dust. As boys, he and Taos had once snuck outside while on a royal visit and flown in the sky for over an hour, creating fancy trails in the storm with their wingtips. Eventually they'd been busted by their parents and the prison warden - who'd all joined in the fun, their laughter snatched away by magic winds and stinging sands.

Today Raiden felt neither joy nor the inclination to linger, dropping through the storm until the Kirrilakh's upper reaches came into view. Carved with the blessings and magics of the ancient Lemurians who'd worked side by side with the first

Merged citizens to create the structure, Raiden fancied it would be truly magnificent should the building ever be revealed in its entirety. As it was, the glimpses he could see were incredible; each sweeping line and furrow as fresh as the day it'd been chiselled into the desert-gold stone. Tucking his wings in tight, Raiden dropped into the eye of the storm, landing on the prison's roof with a hefty thump and a thorough shake of wings and hair.

"You're more dog than angel," boomed a voice from nowhere and everywhere at once.

Raiden lifted both middle fingers into the air. "And you're more ifrit than jann, you grumpy old bastard."

A tiny dust devil began to form, the stilled grains of sand at Raiden's feet lifting and swirling until they coalesced into the shape of a man who was very much flesh and blood. With skin of pale desert gold and sleek auburn hair, he stood eye level with Raiden's six feet four inches, but was easily twice as wide in the shoulders. Dressed in muscles, muscles and more muscles, the djinn cut an imposing figure with eyes like chips of obsidian and beaten pewter cuffs encircling wrists and ankles.

"Prince Raiden," the djinn rumbled. "You feel different."

Raising a brow at that ambiguous statement, Raiden said, "I'd say the same, Kadir, but that would involve putting my hands on your naked hide - and that, I can live without."

Throwing back his head, Kadir laughed deep and loud, the perpetual sandstorm pulsing in time with his mirth. "You make my sacred duties all the more amusing, young Prince. Do you go inside?"

"If you don't mind."

"Be my guest." Kadir waved a lazy hand and the carved roof began to reshape itself, forming a set of stone stairs leading down into darkness.

"Is she..."

"Alone," Kadir inclined his head. "Top floor."

Raiden thumped a hand over his heart and bowed. "Thank you."

Kadir waved his hand again and dissolved, his flesh and blood body absorbed by the wind. Turning his back on the powerful creature who guarded the Kirrilakh, Raiden descended the stairs into the prison proper.

Torches lit by themselves as he hit the first landing, illuminating a well-appointed receiving room complete with cushioned settees and a table of food and water. Raiden bypassed the display to push through the heavy wooden door on the far side, gritting his teeth as the hinges groaned and wailed.

"By the gods, Kadir, it gets worse every time," he muttered, and was rewarded with a faint huff of air across the back of his neck and the barest hint of laughter in the space beyond his ears.

The Kirrilakh's top floor was the gentlest and best maintained, with tiny cracks at roof level that let in glimpses of light and floors swept meticulously clean by Kadir's magic. Elegant braziers on curling iron legs flared to life as Raiden approached, marking a very specific path through row upon row of empty cells. Each was much the same; three stone walls, the fourth made entirely of iron bars, with not a single door in sight. Some bore the stamp of previous inhabitants in the form of scribbles and carvings but Raiden paid them no mind, focussing instead on keeping scrupulously to the route laid out by the lit braziers. He walked for many long minutes, every passage identical to the last and the gloom absorbing the heavy tread of his boots until a trio of crackling braziers illuminated a cell just like any other.

"Liria."

She knelt on the floor inside, head bowed so that her dark curls hid her face and hands clasped in her lap. Her cape was gone and her gossamer wings glinted in the firelight, the refractions throwing bruise-coloured shadows on the walls. She'd been stripped of her weapons, leaving only the dress he'd last seen her in, the fabric stained with grime and Raiden's life blood.

Raising her head at the sound of his voice, Liria locked her violet eyes to his and frowned. "Raiden?"

It was the first time she'd said his name like that - as though he were a man, rather than a biting insect - and it sent a shiver down Raiden's spine that curled deep in his gut and hung on tight. Stepping up to the bars, he crouched so they were eye to eye.

"Are you all right?"

"Am *I* all right?" she repeated, eyes wide with incredulity. "Are you even alive?"

Rather than challenge the odd question, he put his arm through the bars and held it out straight. After a tentative glance in his direction, Liria sidled forward and took hold of his wrist, her fingers pale against his bronze skin.

"Pulse," she murmured, "but you had one before, too."

Then Liria Atlannon, shadow to the Princess Ione, yanked hard enough on Raiden's arm that his head clanged loudly into the iron bars.

"Fuck!" Bouncing off hard enough that he ended up on his backside, Raiden raised a hand to his abused forehead. "What in all the hells was that for, you maniac?"

She merely blinked. "You're real."

"Of course I'm real," he growled, glaring at her through the bars. "First you stab me, now you try to knock me out? Do you *want* to stay in there forever?"

Liria's face went white and her lashes swept down. Raiden's irritation turned quickly to shock when her lower lip trembled and the faintest sheen of silver appeared at the corners of her eyes.

"Kadir!" Raiden called, rolling to his hands and knees. The iron bars fronting the cell drew apart like a fringed curtain, and he crawled through to tug her into his arms. "Liria?"

She curled into a ball in his lap, buried her face against his chest and began to sob loudly.

What did you do to her? Raiden snapped the thought out like a sheet in the wind.

Laughter, low and lazy, preceded Kadir's reply. *Nothing, as per orders - but perhaps you should ask her what **you** did, Prince of Egypt.*

Raiden waited until her sobs had faded, then tipped up her delicate chin with one finger. "Liria? What happened?"

"I thought you were - I thought that I'd -" she choked, grief and pain clouding her expression as her jaw clenched and her hands curled to fists against his chest.

"Don't fight the compulsion," Raiden ordered. "It's hurting you."

"You don't own me," Liria growled, baring teeth at him which were suddenly fanged. By the time he blinked, they were human again, and she looked horrified. "Um."

"There's no need to hide yourself from me," Raiden murmured, fisting his free hand in her hair the way he'd longed to do since he first saw it down. When Liria flinched, he let go. "Did I hurt you?"

"No, I just... do you remember anything? From while you were hurt?"

Raiden frowned. "I've been out of it for days, sleeping the sleep of the partially dead. There's nothing to recall." An acute sadness clouded her features and he had the inescapable feeling that he'd let this fascinating woman down somehow. Casting about for something to say to fix it, he ended up with the truth. "I dreamed some, but the memories faded as soon as I woke."

Rather than help, Liria looked in more pain than ever before. Closing her eyes, she lent her head against his chest - then swept her lashes wide an instant later. When she gasped and scrambled backwards off his lap, Raiden let her go, not sure whether to be amused or offended by the retreat.

"What are you doing here?" she asked breathlessly. "I stabbed you."

"Ione stabbed me," Raiden corrected, watching her face. "Didn't she?"

Liria's jaw snapped shut with an audible click, the muscles in her throat working to produce sound. Holding up a hand, Raiden shook his head and she subsided.

"So you can't answer certain questions, even if Ione's asleep and some distance away from you?"

"Some tenets of the binding are set in stone," she answered, her words coming out measured and careful. "They do not require conscious thought to activate."

"Hmm." Raiden leant back on his hands and stretched his legs out in front of him while Liria trained her eyes firmly on the stone floor at her feet. "You don't have to lower your head to me, you know."

That same head jerked up in surprise. "You're a Prince."

"Not with you," he replied. "Alone, we're just Raiden and Liria."

Echoes of emotion washed over her face and after a moment's hesitation, she settled more comfortably onto her knees and met his gaze. "All right."

"Really? I thought I'd die before you'd ever agree to that."

"You almost did."

How was he the only one who could sense the agony in her voice, the screams she was forced to swallow? Knowing he needed to ease her guilt were she to trust him, Raiden said, "I know it wasn't you. I saw it in your eyes, Liria, and I will defend that knowledge to the death. What I *do* need to know is if Ione targeted me specifically, or if there's something else going on."

Again her teeth clenched, her dainty hands curling into fists. Finally, Liria released a deep breath. "General Barin knows all about my wondrous Princess."

"So he can tell me what you can't? Clever." Raiden grinned, got the ghost of a lip twitch in return. Letting his grin fade, he offered a hand. "I don't want to be your enemy, Liria. That hasn't changed, no matter what happened."

"Why?" She turned her face away, her question filled with an aching loneliness that snagged at Raiden's heart. "Why would you care?"

He blew out a breath, shifting his wings against the stone floor with the soft whisper of feathers. Up until the moment Ione and Taos were married, Liria remained, officially, loyal to Atlantis and therefore the truth remained a risk; but Raiden believed in both honesty and honour, and had learnt to trust his gut as a young teen supporting his older brother - also still a teen - as he took on the role of the Pharaoh.

"Taos and I believe in family," he said quietly. "We were raised in a palace full of life, laughter and love. We rely upon each other as brothers as much as royalty, depend upon those in our honour guard for friendship as much as a warrior's skill. As I said before, whether you like it or not, when Ione marries my brother, she becomes my sister and *both* of you are drawn into our family." A pause. "And I will fight to the death for the people I care about."

Liria, to her credit, didn't falter - though a blush started at the base of her neck and crept slowly across her cheeks. She flexed her fingers, then smoothed her palms across her thighs. "The marriage... is it in danger now?"

"Potentially. After all, whether or not Ione ordered the attack intentionally, an agent of Atlantis attempted to murder the Prince of Egypt." Raiden grimaced. "Taos witnessed the attack, and several of the gods were forced to intervene to save my life. If we cannot work together, your Princess will likely be sent home before the sun has set this evening - the only reason it hasn't happened yet is because Taos promised to wait until I was recovered."

"The *gods* got involved in this?"

Raiden nodded, watching her reaction closely. "Anubis and Horus worked hard to keep me here, Lady of Shadows."

"What was the price?"

"Spoken like a woman who understands payment."

"Spoken like a shadow sold before she ever got to become a person," Liria returned, her voice just as firm. "There's always a price."

"In this case, the price was power." In quick sentences, Raiden gave her the run-down on what he knew of his ordeal. "I don't know what I'm capable of yet, but Horus' blood has made me into a different version of myself."

"You shouldn't tell me these things." Liria held both her hands up, palms out, as though to ward him off. "I can be used against you more than once."

"I know." Raiden stared at her across the cell, watched her face shutter more with every passing second, and knew he was losing. *Kadir.*

Why this one, little angel? Why does she matter so?

I don't know.

A long silence, the stones pulsing beneath Raiden's spread palms. *What you're asking goes directly against your brother's parting instructions.*

I'll handle Taos. Raiden paused, digging his fingers into a crack in the mortar. *Something huge depends on this, Kadir. I can feel it deep inside - we need this fairy.*

The royal we, or you, little angel? Be careful you're not wearing rose coloured glasses.

She stabbed me, you noxious jann.

Laughter threaded through the space between Raiden's ears. *Where I come from, that's courtship of the highest order - but very well, Prince of Egypt. Your wish is my command.*

Raiden fought the urge to roll his eyes, instead fisting his hand around the wickedly curved dagger which pushed up out of the stone floor. Sitting up, he flipped it over so he held it by the blade and offered the hilt to Liria.

"What's this?" she gasped, leaning away from the dagger as though it were venomous. "What are you doing?"

"Trusting you," Raiden answered, his voice even. "Here, Lady of Shadows. Carve out my heart, if you can."

DECIDE

Liria accepted the dagger, hiding the way her fingers trembled by flipping it into a reverse grip and clenching tight, the flat of the curved blade cool against the bare skin of her forearm. The weapon felt good in her hand; a trifle heavier than might be expected for her frame but perfectly balanced and with a slick curve that meant the swell of the blade stuck out enough to do deadly damage with little effort on her behalf.

Raiden watched in silence as she adjusted and readjusted her grip. With his posture relaxed and his wings spread gloriously across the floor behind him, he looked lazy and sensual and Liria wanted nothing more than to crawl back into his lap and beg him to kiss her the way he'd done the night before - except he didn't remember the incident at all, proving without doubt the entire scenario had been a figment of her fevered imagination.

Why, of all people, had it chosen this gorgeous, infuriating creature to dwell upon? Hadn't Liria endured enough torture? Surely she had... and yet there was no denying the pull she felt to the Prince of Egypt, the desperate, wild hope in her chest that said he *saw* her, that he wanted her trust as more than a tool to access and control Princess Ione.

But if Raiden hadn't been real, why were the imprints of his fists set into the back of her prison cell wall? And if he *had* been here, why hadn't he mentioned it? Shaking her head in a vain attempt to clear it, Liria turned just enough that she could look up at the cracked stonework overhead.

"Do you know what these are, Prince of Egypt?"

Golden eyes narrowed as Raiden stared long and hard at the markings, the tiniest furrow appearing between his dark brows. "I... I don't think so."

"You don't *think* so?" Equal parts hope and disappointment poured through her, pure and bright and entirely her own in a way her emotions hadn't been her own in a long, long time. "Try harder."

Again he stared, his profile clean and sharp and his knuckles turning white where his fingers pressed into the floor. Moments turned to minutes, Liria's stomach sinking when Raiden at last shook his head.

"I'm sorry," he murmured. "There's something whispering in the back of my mind, but... it won't hold."

A single tear escaped the corner of Liria's eye to trace a damp line over her cheek. He'd dared her to carve out his heart but the return, it seemed, was to be true.

"Why did you come here?" Decades of pain and resentment bubbled in the back of Liria's throat and she clutched desperately at the hilt of the dagger. "*Why?*"

"I already told you," Raiden answered, his tone carefully measured and his body relaxed. "I will fight for the people I care about."

"You don't care about me." Liria pointed a finger at him, horrified to notice that her skin had faded to the stormy blue-grey that was her natural colouring. Try though she might, she couldn't calm herself enough to change it back to the pale cream Ione insisted she wear. "I tried to kill you."

Whether or not she'd wanted to was irrelevant; this might be her last chance to make Raiden understand that the true function of a shadow was to be forever crushed beneath their master's heel. He had to see that she was nothing, a puppet who could never truly follow through on thoughts or feelings of her own. She wasn't Liria, but an empty shell that might, once, at some point, have had the potential to be Liria.

The potential to be worthy of a man like Raiden.

Liria flinched from that wayward thought, pressing her back to the cell's wall out of raw, feral instinct.

"I tried to kill you," she said again, lifting her chin. "I'd have done it, too, if not for the gods."

Raiden reached up to the pin at his shoulder, fiddling a moment before it and the scarlet shawl covering his chest fell away, revealing sculpted pectorals and mouth-watering abdominals. As with all angelkind, there was no hair on his chest, the stunning vista of his musculature broken only by dark nipples and a smattering of scars that enhanced his rugged, warrior's aura.

"Here you go," he said, rolling his shoulders back to present an even clearer target. "Finish the job. I won't stop you."

Liria hefted the dagger, testing the weight of it in her hand. Ione had forced her to strike the first time, but if she did this, when so clearly acting under her own steam, it would make Raiden hate her once and for all. And if he hated her, he'd be safe - history had shown that to be truth. So she stared deep into his golden eyes, listened to the steady thump of his heart and took careful aim at a spot that would wound, but not kill him so quickly that whoever staffed this prison couldn't summon help. She could do this. She *would* do this.

In a motion made smooth by a lifetime's practice, Liria cocked her wrist and threw.

Raiden didn't move, not so much as a hair out of place as the dagger sailed past his ear and disappeared into the darkness with a muffled clatter. Liria screamed, a sound of depthless grief and fury, baring her fangs and clenching her taloned hands so tightly that blood slicked her palms.

"I can't do it. I don't want to kill you," she whispered, lowering her gaze to the floor. "I would never willingly choose to do so."

His body slammed into hers, Raiden's superior weight taking them to the ground and stealing the breath from her lungs. Liria's head cracked against the cell floor hard enough that she saw stars, one forearm braced against his naked chest in instinctive defence.

"You care," he murmured, his voice so deep it vibrated through her very bones. "Don't you?"

"Of course I care!" Her voice broke, and Liria pressed her lips into a thin line until she felt more in control. "But caring is dangerous, Raiden. The compulsion has the capacity to destroy anything I show an interest in."

Raiden shifted against her and Liria tried not to notice his warmth, the hard lines of his body pressing decadently against hers. He narrowed his golden eyes at her... then he grinned, wide and bright and boyish. "I knew it."

Liria spat a curse at him in her native language, her taloned fingers flexing against his flesh without conscious thought.

"Fuck!" Raiden jerked back, straddling her knees as he slapped a hand to the puncture wounds she'd made above his right pectoral.

"Are you all right?" Liria sat bolt upright and grabbed his wrist, tugging at his hand. "I'm sorry; I forgot I had my talons out. I should never -"

"Liria, stop." Amusement erased the pain from his features. "It's not serious; you just took me by surprise."

"Show me."

"It's fine."

"Show me!"

Raiden sighed and allowed her to pull his hand away. Two of her talons had pierced the skin near his armpit, the holes jagged and, judging by the blood staining her first knuckle, deeper than he'd let on. Liria frowned. "Your blood is thick... like molasses."

"That's new." He craned his head to try and see better. "Must be the gods' interference. At least we know I'm not in danger of bleeding out from your tender ministrations."

"This isn't a joke," Liria hissed, baring her fangs at him again. "Don't you see how dangerous I am?"

Raiden rolled his eyes. "You've really had the ever-loving confidence beaten out of you, haven't you? I know you're dangerous, Lady of Shadows. I like you dangerous." He reached out to prod her in the shoulder. "And you may not have seen it yet, but I'm dangerous too. Danger does not frighten me."

"Then you're an idiot," Liria snapped.

The Prince of Merged Egypt threw back his head and laughed, while blood bubbled from his wounds with the slow, ponderous persistence of treacle.

"You're not the first person to say that," he admitted, regarding her with an almost feline amusement. "Seriously, Liria, don't worry about it. I'll wear my shawl like a bandage and get the healers to check things later."

"No - the wounds could get infected by then. I'm as clean as I can be, but I've also been in this cell without a proper bath for several days now. There's no telling what was on the end of my talons." Liria took a deep breath, her lungs shuddering, and strove for courage. "There's another way."

"There is?"

"I can remove any potential infection and stop the bleeding," she admitted, barely daring to look at him from beneath her lashes. "Nobody... nobody knows I can."

The angel's golden eyes went wide and his body oddly still. "You're trusting me with your secrets?"

"This one, yes. Consider it penance." She swallowed heavily, her heart a rabbit in her chest, and took a leap more dangerous than anything she'd ever done before. "The others will depend on how you handle what happens next."

Raiden shifted into a better position across her knees and relaxed his shoulders. "Do your worst, Lady of Shadows."

Liria stared at the wounds on his chest and chewed on her lower lip. Redemption may yet prove impossible for one such as her, but while she was as free from Ione's influence as she would ever truly get, she could do this one small thing. For once, instead of destroying something, she could fix it. Bracing her hands on Raiden's thighs, Liria lowered her head and drew her tongue across the closest of his open wounds. She heard the sharp intake of his breath, felt the fine tremor of his muscles, but refused to look up, concentrating instead on the slow, methodical movement of her lips and her tongue as they danced over each cut. His blood was honey inside her mouth, thick and sweet and the most perfect thing Liria had ever tasted. Energy flooded her starved cells and tingled deep in her gut but she refused to succumb to the heady sensations, focussing solely on the task at hand. The natural healing agents in her saliva cleaned each of the jagged wounds before encouraging the flesh to knit and when she leant back a minute later, Raiden's chest bore nothing more serious than a tracery of pink against darker caramel skin. His breathing had turned jagged, his spine ramrod straight and his eyes like saucers - but his discomfort was a small price to pay for the knowledge that he was, for now, safe.

"So, Prince of Egypt," Liria's voice came out husky, the unique flavour of his blood yet coating her throat. "It seems you will live."

"I..." Raiden paused, the sound of his heavy swallow loud in the bare cell. "I didn't know you could heal."

She couldn't resist looking at him from beneath her lashes again, well aware he'd see the bright sparks of power in her violet eyes. "I can't heal; not the way you're thinking. Dark fairies can survive on a variety of things, one of those being blood. My fangs carry venom to paralyse prey and my saliva possesses the power to clean and seal any wounds I make should I choose to feed that way."

"That makes sense." Raiden lifted the hand she'd bitten, turning it back and forth to examine the deep marks - now partially healed - that her fangs had left in his skin. "I didn't feel paralysed the other day."

"Probably because I didn't use the paralytic poison."

"You secrete more than one type?"

Liria's eyes narrowed. "I only promised you one secret, Prince of Egypt."

His grin was unexpected, and so bright she fought the urge to lean back and avert her face. Whether seeing or sensing the change in her through some other mysterious angelic method, Raiden's face softened.

"I won't betray your secret, Lady of Shadows." Taking her blue-grey fingers in his, Raiden brushed the barest of kisses over the back of her knuckles. "Thank you."

Heat crept over Liria's face and this time she did turn away, tugging her fingers from his warm grip before all reason deserted her and she started screaming at the injustice of her existence.

No, she scolded herself. *Justice and injustice are terms applied to people, and you're not a person. You're a shadow.*

Settling herself with a few long, deep breaths full of Raiden's sand and sunlight scent, she chanced a quick study of the angel who fascinated her so. His breathing had settled into a more normal rhythm, his pallor flushed with health and the torchlight flickering off eyes that were clear rather than glazed from the shock of her ministrations.

"What now?" she managed, trying not to think further on his body, his blood, or how good either of them tasted. "Have you come to fetch me for my execution?"

"That depends on you," Raiden returned. "I think we can get this whole fiasco back on track, but you'll have to trust me. Not as a Prince, but as a man named Raiden who cares for his brother and wants to see him happy. And you'll have to work with me, not as the Lady of Shadows but as Liria, the dark fairy of Atlantis who's about to become part of the Egyptian honour guard. No titles, no bullshit - apart from whatever we need to do to work around your compulsions - just Raiden and Liria."

"Raiden and Liria," she echoed, her heart pummelled by the memory of those same words on his lips in this very cell. "Can I tell you another secret?"

"Of course."

"I hated living in Atlantis."

Raiden barked a short, sharp laugh. "Oh?"

"Yes." It had been a beautiful prison for the entirety of her life. "When I heard we were to come to Egypt, I was glad. This place... even as a shadow, bound to my mistress, there's a freedom here that Atlantis can never offer me. A freedom I covet."

"And will you fight for that freedom, Liria?" He tipped up her chin, leaning forward until his breath was a warm puff on her cheeks and his eyes filled her entire world. "Will you trust me? Trust us?"

His hands in her hair, his body hard and hot, his lips soft, the air electric.

Memories pushed in from every side, perfect and painful - and not a one of them reflected in the deep gold eyes that threatened to swallow Liria whole. *Mistake,* a tiny voice inside her shrieked. *This is a mistake.*

It didn't matter. Mistake or otherwise, there was only one answer, and she gave it without an ounce of regret.

"Yes."

DIG DEEP

Raiden led Liria out to the prison's foyer, then stood over her and glowered while she ate as much food as he could convince her to stuff into her mouth.

"My body has different requirements to yours," she said, shaking her head when he pushed a plate of pickled vegetables her way. "Between the blood I took from you and what I've already eaten, it's enough."

When her beautiful stormy skin began to fade to cream, Raiden dared lay a hand on her slender shoulder. "Don't."

"What?" Liria blinked, and though she flinched at his touch, she didn't pull away.

"I like your real skin." The words were out before he could stop them, and Raiden leaned over to snag an apple lest she see his cheeks colour. "It suits you."

Silence met his words, and he turned back to see Liria's jaw clenched tight, her taloned fingers digging into the wood of the table. Raiden opened his mouth to tell her not to fight when abruptly she gasped and stepped back, words popping out like a cork from a bottle. "I can wear my normal skin until we return to the Palace, but after that I must endeavour to look normal."

She's a fighter, this creature. The pain of the compulsion is incredible, and I'm only getting it second hand.

Have you been eavesdropping the whole time, Kadir?

Bit hard not to - you're inside my walls, Prince of Egypt, and they have ears.

"Normal," Raiden repeated aloud, watching Liria's face and sorting through possible translations of her sentence. "Are there not all kinds of skin tones among the Merged citizens of Atlantis?"

Liria's stance relaxed instantly, relief in every line of her body. "Not in the royal family."

"Ah." Raiden nodded, his stomach souring. "Yes, gods forbid you outshine anyone with a crown on their head."

Surprise flashed in the depths of those violet eyes and he fought the urge to rage, for if there's one thing he'd learnt in their brief acquaintance, it was that Liria Atlannon had been taught she was nothing, both inside and out. And though it was an insanity, Raiden knew he wouldn't stop trying to prove otherwise, because she was the most fascinating and astonishingly beautiful woman he'd ever met. If he had his way, she'd wear her real skin forever, the blue-grey an exquisite contrast to the warm brown of his hands as he stroked them over her -

Chomping viciously into his purloined apple, Raiden closed his eyes and chewed mechanically. Now was not the time to start down that line, not when Liria had so recently offered a trust he knew, in his heart of hearts, she expected him to shatter at the earliest opportunity.

It wasn't going to happen.

Refusing to examine his reasoning for that particular sentiment too closely, Raiden finished his apple, disposed of the core and dusted his hands on his thighs. "Ready to go?"

"Yes."

"You don't sound ready."

"I..." Liria blew out a long, slow breath, then shook her head. "I cannot explain it to you."

Raiden took in the tension in the line of her jaw and nodded. "Okay."

"Okay?"

"Sure." He shrugged. "There are some things the compulsion won't let you say. We'll find a way to work around it. In the meantime, how well do you fly?"

Indignant rage suffused her delicate features and caused violet eyes to flash bright. "Better than any feathered upstart, that's for certain."

"Oh?" Raiden gave her a toothy grin. "Come on, then."

He led her up the stairs and out onto the roof, which was now level with the shifting dunes. Liria's head craned back in wonder, eyes wide as she took in the perpetual sandstorm lashing the desert around them. When the few grains at her feet began to twitch and twirl, she took a cautious step back - and gasped when the sand coalesced into a very naked Kadir.

"Pants," Raiden growled.

The djinn laughed and snapped his fingers; his lower body was immediately covered in a loosely wrapped shendyt, the traditional skirt made from white linen and tied in a knot at one hip. Kadir offered Raiden a mocking bow. "Will this do, your highness?"

"Liria," Raiden snarled, "this is Kadir, Warden of the Kirrilakh."

"A jann," Liria murmured, holding out her hand. "A powerful one, too."

"And a dark fairy who knows the different types of djinn," Kadir returned, his pale gold skin a delicate contrast to Liria's stormy blue-grey. "I'm so glad to finally meet you in person - though I'd hoped you'd make our dear Prince pay a little more for his insolence."

Liria flushed and Raiden frowned, his mind flashing back to the twin marks on the wall of her prison cell. His body tightened as it had when she'd first asked about the marks but his foggy memory refused to give him more than that, no matter how he tried. Pushing the image away before he embarrassed himself, Raiden glowered at Kadir.

"Just hand back her weapons and we'll be out of your hair," he grumbled. "Liria can extract whatever payment she thinks necessary from me later."

Kadir laughed his deep, booming laugh while Liria flushed darker, pressing both hands to her cheeks and looking decidedly scandalised.

"Oh, little angel, if only you knew," Kadir snickered. He snapped his fingers again and the stone roof extruded a small pile of weaponry. "Here you are, my Lady Liria."

"Just Liria," she muttered, dropping to one knee. "I am but a shadow."

"I know what you are," Kadir boomed, his voice vibrating with power. "And you are just a shadow as I am just a jann."

Raiden's brow quirked. Though Kadir was bound to the Kirrilakh and oversaw its protection, he was a king among his kind, with far more power than the average djinn ever dreamed of possessing. Raiden opened his mouth to stop Kadir from teasing Liria any further - only to pause, realising at long last the Lady of Shadows hadn't so much as blinked at the announcement.

"We all have our secrets," she said mildly, twisting her hair into a knot atop her head and securing it with her jewelled silver pins. "One day, if we are ever freed, we'll share a drink and talk of things better left unsaid."

Kadir dropped to one knee beside her, black eyes glittering as he stuck out a hand. "Deal."

Liria shook without a second thought, then set about secreting an astonishing number of blades upon her person without so much as a glimpse in either Kadir or Raiden's direction.

Oh, little Prince, I like her, Kadir purred.

Back off, or I'll feed you to a ghul.

Kadir's laughter echoed inside Raiden's skull. *Best not make a mess of this then, hmmm? Because I can be quite charming, should I choose.*

That, Raiden had no argument for; he'd seen it with his own eyes. When Liria was finished covering herself in knives, daggers, darts and other things he'd barely had time to glimpse, she stood, adjusted her blood-stained dress, and spread her wings. "Shall we?"

It was rude to stare, even ruder not to answer, but Raiden did both. His jaw felt like it bounced off his chest as the meagre sunlight which carried through the Kirrilakh's protective sandstorm caught the full beauty of her gossamer and glass fairy wings. Coloured shadows spread over the stone, shifting like a kaleidoscope when she moved. Here, a hint of plum. There, a hint of ocean blue. Ever changing, glistening with a gorgeous oil slick sheen, Liria's delicate wings were truly magnificent.

"How do they work?" he managed, taking a half step forward and drawing up short. Sensitive, he reminded himself, her wings were sensitive - and he'd not touch what he'd not been invited to touch. "They seem so fragile."

Raiden spread his own wings in emphasis, the tri-coloured feathers plain and boring in comparison. Liria frowned, examining the shape and structure of his body with an intensity that threatened to make him blush all over again.

"Your wings are like a second set of arms," she said at last. "They come from a shoulder, have an elbow and a wrist, and contain fingerlike bones to support muscle, flesh, blood and feather. I've seen you use them like arms, too - they wave around when you talk, shade your face from the sun, encircle you when you need privacy, and support your weight when needs demand it. Correct?"

"Yes."

"Mine are... not like that." Liria frowned, fisting her hands on her hips. "They are far less sturdy in a physical sense, and open and close much like a fan; though that is, in itself, partially due to the magic.

The stiff wings of a butterfly do not fold, but a fairy's certainly do. However, what I lack in physical strength and structure, I make up for in other ways. I will never tire while aloft; I could literally fly every moment for the next one hundred years without needing to land. I flutter where you flap, meaning I'm far more nimble in the air, and the way my magic works means I don't need to pay heed to air currents, updrafts or other things that normally affect flight."

As Raiden watched, her wings indeed began to flutter, not with the erratic gait of a butterfly but with movements more akin to a hummingbird. Where he needed to launch into the air in a burst of pure muscle or fall from a height, Liria's feet lifted off the ground as though she were floating.

"Incredible," he murmured, watching the play of light and shadow across the prison roof.

"It's been many a year since I've witnessed a fairy in flight," Kadir rumbled. "I was intending to grant a pass through the storm, but perhaps I'll accompany you in person."

The jann's body dissolved from the waist down, becoming a swirling maelstrom of sand that trailed out behind him in a long tail. Liria grinned as Kadir dipped and wove around her, his body propelled to dizzying speeds by the magic that kept him aloft. Raiden watched them rise with a clenched jaw, never so impatient to be airborne as in that moment - and as soon as they were high enough, he bent his knees, bunched his thighs and launched skyward in a rush of muscle and feathers.

He'd never felt more ungainly in his life.

Wings working in strong, measured motions - because he was a warrior, and despite Liria's thoughts otherwise, *never* flapped - Raiden caught his companions just as Kadir parted the sandstorm, guiding Liria through with a teasing smile and a sparkling wink. Once they were out in the desert proper, the djinn bid them a polite goodbye and watched as Raiden led Liria towards the sweeping outline of Selekhet.

Raiden's body cut like an arrow through the air, sleek and straight. Liria fluttered along at what was almost a forty-five degree angle, leading with her head and chest while her legs floated gracefully along behind her as though she were an immaculately carved figurehead on the prow of a ship. The delicate motions of her wings, the awkward posture that promoted drag and the serenity in her face meant she should have been screamingly slow.

She wasn't.

For every strong, pounding beat of Raiden's wings, Liria's whizzed so fast he could barely track the motion, and she kept easy pace beside him. He pushed himself to top speed, racing her over pyramids, canyons, farms and houses, and never once did she drop back from his side. And when he landed on Princess Ione's balcony, sweat beading his brow and muscles burning from the exercise, Liria touched down beside him with the grace of a floating leaf, not so much as a hair out of place.

"God of the sky," Raiden murmured, pacing around her in a swift circle but being careful not to touch. His reward was to have Liria fan her wings ever so slightly, allowing him the full effect of the sun through their stained glass surface. The faint breeze she created brushed across his sweat-slicked skin like the gentlest of caresses but he crushed his instinctive shiver lest it startle her, and smiled instead. "You're incredible."

Liria shot him a smile so wide it was full of fang, her face brighter than the morning sun for the fraction of a moment the expression held. Then one hand rose to knead at her breastbone and her face turned serious. As she folded her wings against her back, her skin turned from stormy blue-grey to pale, delicate cream and she interlaced her fingers in front of her skirts. If not for the blood on her dress or for the wild joy he'd just witnessed, Raiden would have thought her carved from ice.

They slipped through the sleek chiffon hangings that cloaked the room from view whilst still letting in light. Ione's sitting room was a study in peace and tranquillity, except for the grim-faced General Barin who stood against the closed bedroom door in full Atlantean aqua, shimmering silver chain mail poking out from beneath the half sleeves on his tunic. He relaxed perceptibly when Liria inclined her head in his direction and entered her chambers across the way, closing the door with a soft snick.

"Prince of Merged Egypt," Barin murmured, his voice roughened by the scar tissue from an old battle wound. "I thank you for your mercy."

"A mercy that should have been unnecessary," Raiden returned, his voice flat. "Once my brother arrives, I'll have some questions for you."

Barin's lips pressed together but he nodded with a military precision that said he'd been expecting such. Raiden lounged against the arm of a chaise, adjusted the way his shawl was pinned at his shoulder - and the chamber's outer door opened as Yrini ushered the Pharaoh Taos inside.

"Leave us," Taos murmured, and as Yrini shut the door behind him, he strode across the room to enfold Raiden in a fierce embrace. "My brother. I am sorry."

"The Pharaoh does what he must," Raiden replied, squeezing once before they both stepped back with a smile. "And a brother forgives."

Barely had he finished speaking than Liria's door swung open and the Lady of Shadows stepped out in an elegant floor length gown that started off a deep blue and ended up black where it brushed the floor. A matching cape hung from the thin shoulder straps, and the dress was cinched below Liria's generous bust with a simple silver cord. Her hair had been brushed and fixed back into its customary knotted twist, the jewelled blade pins again in place, but Liria had left a few curls free to whisper around her face. Catching the skirt in dainty fingers, she sketched an elegant curtsey.

"Pharaoh Taos," she purred, "I thank you for your mercy."

Taos took the ritual thanks in stride, offering Liria the slightest dip of his chin. "It is the Prince of Egypt you must truly thank, Lady of Shadows, for he alone was your champion in this matter."

Liria's posture didn't change but her eyes flickered and after a moment, she lowered her lashes. "Indeed, I am in his debt."

"General Barin." Raiden turned from Liria's discomfort and felt more than saw her relief. "I would ask your honesty, and in turn I'd give you mine."

The older man's eyes narrowed the slightest fraction, but he assumed a military rest position and cocked his chin. "I'm listening."

"You must be aware that the Lady Liria's actions put the marriage contract in danger," Raiden began. "Up until this very moment, I'm the only one who believes that the Princess Ione was the driving force behind her shadow's regrettable actions. Unless you can shed some light on this situation, I'll be forced to make decisions based only upon the information I have available."

Barin's steely grey eyes narrowed, his hands drifting towards the well-loved sword strapped to his hip. "You would so openly accuse a Princess of Atlantis?"

"I will do whatever I think necessary to ensure that this marriage is a legitimate joining of hearts and not an underhanded attempt to weaken Egypt and dethrone the Pharaoh," Raiden snapped.

"In that case, you have only to look at the facts." Barin pointed a scarred finger in Liria's direction. "The shadow stabbed you. She will accept any punishment due this crime, as is the duty of a shadow."

Raiden quirked a brow. "Even if the crime is not hers?"

"Not hers?" Barin laughed, though the sound held no humour. "She is a shadow, your highness. She has done what we say she has done, whether or not she has actually done it."

Taos' gasp was sharp, his soft brown eyes wide. "By the gods, my brother was right. Ione *did* order the attack."

Barin's face immediately turned to stone, his shoulders tense, but he said nothing. Raiden tried to catch Liria's eye but she too stood silent, her eyes on the floor in front of her, posture not so much relaxed as resigned. She'd known, he realised - she'd known they would throw her to the wolves to be torn apart, the compulsion which kept her bound removing her ability to defend herself.

"Brother," Raiden rumbled. "What is your will?"

Pain blanched the Pharaoh's features but when he spoke, his voice came out steady. "Arrange an audience with King Theon. I will terminate the marriage contract as per the traitor's clause, and summon him to collect his daughter post-haste."

"What?" Barin paled.

"Furthermore, send a message to the Warden of the Kirri-lakh." Taos raised his voice to be heard over General Barin's spluttering. "We shall need the Princess and her entourage safely contained while we await the King's arrival."

"You would imprison a Princess and drag the King of Atlantis here over such a trivial matter as a shadow?"

Taos at last turned to face the General, who, to his credit, managed not to flinch from the Pharaoh's fury. "No, General. I would demand the King of Atlantis' presence that he may learn of the treachery of his own blood, and so that I may see in his face if this action was undertaken against his knowledge, or if I should be sounding the drums of war."

"*War?*"

"An agent of Atlantis attempted to murder the Prince of Merged Egypt," Raiden pointed out, flattening one hand over his chest. "You're older than both my brother and I, General Barin. You know that constitutes as an act of war." He turned to the Pharaoh and pasted a considering look upon his face. "Mayhap contact the King of Kings too, brother. Osiris may lend us the aid of the gods to help expunge this insult."

Taos' eyes lit up. "Oh, yes. If I can persuade him to part with Ra, Horus, Anubis -"

"Stop!" Barin took a step forward, his military calm gone and his brow dotted with sweat. "Please. There is another way."

Raiden bit his lip to hide his smirk, and settled more comfortably on the arm of the chaise. "Speak, then, General - and if I were you, I'd make it good."

General Barin snarled under his breath, running both hands through closely cropped hair that was more silver than black. After a long minute, he glanced over his shoulder at Ione's closed door. "Will she remain asleep? It would not do to be overheard."

"Ione's sleep is based in the potion you gave us, but strengthened with enchantment. She will not wake until the Soulcatcher chooses to wake her," Taos murmured.

Barin grimaced, then nodded, and Raiden wondered idly how many times the General had tried to wake his Princess over the last few days. Stalking to the sideboard, the Atlantean poured himself a glass of Egyptian beer and took several long, steadying swallows.

"As you may or may not know, Queen Coranna has a naiad mother," he began at last. "Her father, however, is Vasilios, King of the Naga. He once kept Coranna's mother and his children under strict lock and key, but when King Theon of Atlantis snuck into his grotto to retrieve an item once stolen from his grandfather, he discovered the prison and was able to free those inside."

Raiden didn't bother masking his astonishment. "A human against the naga?"

"He was not alone. We were fools," Barin acknowledged, "but Theon had been visited by a seer and given the information he needed to succeed, and Coranna herself gave us aid. Vasilios was in a rage when he discovered what had happened, and in a bid to avert war, Theon called upon Poseidon to mediate the matter. The story is long and complex but in the end, Coranna opted to marry Theon to escape her father's dominion. As payment for the loss, Vasilios demanded the sixth child of Coranna come to live in the naga domain in place of the daughter who had left. Poseidon decreed it a fair request and the bargain was sealed with the presentation of the shadow Liria Atlannon, who would watch over Coranna where her father could not."

"Coranna was the sixth child of Vasilios?" Taos guessed.

"Just so." Barin nodded. "Theon and Coranna determined that as long as they never had more than five children, there would be no need to worry. However... they suffered a stillbirth between their second and third child."

"Meaning Ione was not the fifth child but the sixth," Raiden murmured. "How long before Vasilios found out?"

"Ione was five years old," Barin said. "Vasilios kidnapped her in the dead of night."

Raiden could only imagine the young Princess' terror. "Naga are not known for their humanity."

"And Vasilios is the least human of them all." Barin's eyes tracked to Liria and he took another deep swallow of his beer. "Liria was only a youngling when she was gifted to Coranna, but by the time of the kidnapping, she was... perhaps twelve?"

"Fourteen," Liria clarified.

Barin blinked. "Eh, the years run together, they do. Either way, Coranna knew she'd receive no support from Poseidon should she make a formal appeal; after all, by technicality, Ione was the sixth child that she had agreed to provide and Queen Coranna had tried to conceal that fact from the world in an attempt to avoid the bargain. So, knowing there would be no divine help, she sent her shadow to fetch the Princess back instead."

"She sent a fourteen year old child into the depths of the naga infested ocean?" Taos demanded. "Fleets of grown warriors won't even go there!"

"There was little choice - and besides, Liria didn't count as a child. She's a shadow."

Raiden tried to hold in his growl and failed spectacularly. He was off the chaise in a moment, reaching for his khopeshes, when Taos stepped in front of him.

"Brother, no."

"It is *slavery*," he snarled, baring his teeth. "No living being should be seen as a commodity!"

Taos slapped both palms against his chest hard enough to garner Raiden's full attention. "It is slavery, and it is immoral. I, too, am enraged - but that does not change the past. If you cannot get a grip, we will never get to the bottom of this situation and I'll be forced to sentence Liria accordingly."

Raiden's chest rose and fell in discordant rhythm, the temptation to take Barin's head riding high in his blood. Then he caught sight of Liria, fingers interlinked and gaze downturned, awaiting her own condemnation with cool resignation, and his temper turned to determination. He'd promised to fight for her, and executing one of Atlantis' most well-known Generals in a fit of rage would only make matters worse.

"I'm all right," he told Taos, forcing himself to return to his previous perch on the chaise. He glared at the Atlantean General across the room. "Keep talking - but I want it noted that slavery of any kind is not tolerated in Merged Egypt, and from now on, you will accord Liria the manners she deserves as a member of Ione's guard, or I'll take it as a direct insult to the honour of Selekhet."

"As you wish, your highness. I assure you, no offence was intended." Barin eased his hand away from his own sword and took a deep breath. "Shall I continue?"

"Please," Taos nodded. "As I recall, you'd just finished explaining that a young Liria was sent alone into the heart of naga territory."

"Indeed." Barin shrugged, but the tension in his jaw gave lie to the casual nature of the gesture. "I know not the details, but two months later, Liria returned to Atlantis with Ione in hand. Coranna and Theon expected a war with the naga to follow shortly after, but nothing happened. Whilst our nation was relieved, Ione was terrified by her ordeal. She would speak to no-one, look at no-one, touch no-one - except for the shadow who had brought her home."

Raiden passed a hand over his face; he knew what was coming. "Coranna gave Liria's soul ring to a traumatised child."

"She did." Barin shrugged again, seemingly unconcerned. "With a faithful shadow dogging Ione's every movement, the Princess began to relax, and with her, the court."

"And Vasilios?"

"Nothing," Barin answered. "To this day, not a word has come from the naga grottoes, either hostile or friendly. No trade, not so much as a sighting at sea. It is as though they disappeared into the depths forever."

The Pharaoh frowned. "I've had no dealings with the naga, but I'm well versed in their reputation. They are not a race who simply forgive and forget - Vasilios least of all."

"Indeed." Barin thinned his lips, glancing again in Liria's direction, but the shadow said nothing. "As to the present day, Ione may present a cultured front, but she has lived a life of terror. She's heavily dependent on her shadow and panics instinctively if anyone gets too close. There were... incidents in Ione's teenage years where servants who were spotted speaking to the shadow, or touching her, ended up mysteriously deceased the next morning."

"None recently?" Taos asked.

"No," Barin shook his head. "I do not believe the shadow has spoken to anyone of her own accord in the ten or so years hence."

Raiden's gut clenched. "Lonely."

"She is a shadow." The general spread his hands. "I do not wish to offend Egypt's sensibilities, but the customs of Atlantis are clear; Liria is soulbound to the Princess Ione. She exists purely to fulfil her wishes and keep her mistress safe. There is room for nothing else."

"Ione cannot protect herself?"

Barin crinkled his nose. "Her magical abilities are the least of all her siblings, and tend towards healing. She bears no interest in the arts of war, and with her shadow by her side, has no need to do so."

"So, let's get this straight." Taos drew himself up to his full height, face grim. "Ione ordered Liria to attack my brother because he spoke to her, perhaps touched her, and therefore threatens her purported ability to protect?"

"There would have been no conscious order given," Barin said quietly, his face drawn into mournful lines. "The shadow is bound tightly to the Princess and would have been forced to act based purely on the instinctive panic and rejection Ione felt. Should you ask her, the Princess would have no knowledge of her part in these actions."

Raiden rubbed a hand across his jaw, considering his new information from as many angles as possible. "Queen Coranna and King Theon accepted the marriage contract with such grace because they think Ione will be safer here than in Atlantis."

"And not just because of the distance between our two nations," Barin agreed. "Once Ione is married to the Pharaoh Taos, she becomes a citizen of Egypt and Vasilios' claim is no longer valid. If he were to steal her from under your nose, he would have not just Egypt but all the gods turned against him, including his own - and Vasilios is not so foolish that he would try such a thing."

Taos' eyes narrowed until they were nothing but slits of brown in his golden-skinned face. "I dislike being misled in such a manner, General - and before you deny such a thing, remember it is your country's silence that almost saw my brother murdered."

General Barin finished his beer, set his glass on the table, and bowed so deeply his nose almost brushed his knees.

"You are right, esteemed Pharaoh. I can only beg your forgiveness on behalf of my King and Queen," he murmured. "They were afraid."

"Hmph." Taos planted one hand on his hip, his gaze focussed off into the distance. "I have spoken to Osiris, and he has in turn reached out to Anubis. Ione will wake in the next few minutes - and Liria will fetch her to my quarters within the hour, that we may settle this once and for all. If she is so much as a moment late, I will terminate the marriage contract at once. Is that clear?"

"Yes, Pharaoh." Barin bowed again.

"Come, my brother." Taos shot Raiden a look that brooked no argument. "We have much to discuss while we await the Princess."

Raiden tried to catch Liria's eye but she was staring with grim determination at the hem of her dress. With a sigh, he pushed to his feet, bowed in her direction and followed his Pharaoh out the door.

A CRACK IN THE GLASS

Princess Ione's eyes snapped open, her breath already indrawn for a scream - a scream that cut to a squeak as her eyes focussed on Liria. With a strangled sob, the Princess tackled her shadow to the mattress and held on tight.

"Your highness," Liria murmured, slipping her arms around Ione as best she could. "Are you well?"

"What happened to you?" Ione demanded, her face buried in Liria's shoulder. "Why did you leave me? Where did you go?"

"I stabbed the Prince of Merged Egypt, your highness."

"You stabbed the Prince?" The Princess lifted her face to stare down at Liria in astonishment. "Why would you do that?"

The compulsion pulsed in Liria's temples, and she lowered her gaze. "I was not myself, your highness, and can only beg your forgiveness."

"It's a bit late for that now, isn't it?" Ione's eyes welled with tears, belying her tart tone. "They might have killed you!"

"They did not wish to make any decisions until the Prince regained his senses, so I was imprisoned within the Kirrilakh, under the guard of a black jann."

"*Black?*" Ione's breath caught, her eyes impossibly round. "Are you certain?"

"Yes, your highness. Though he concealed himself behind golden skin and a charming smile, his eyes did not lie - nor did his power." Liria swallowed a grunt as Ione's grip tightened around her chest, crushing her wings against her back. She closed her eyes against the sharp agony of the contact and concentrated on breathing until Ione's grip relaxed. "Prince Raiden came to fetch me as soon as he was healed."

"I called for you," Ione whispered. "I called and you didn't come."

Tendrils of icy cold spread through Liria's body, thousands of tiny knives that pricked and slashed. Drawing a deep breath, she managed, "I was unconscious at first, your highness, and then beyond that I believe the djinn was able to muffle the call. The Kirrilakh is far from here, and surrounded by thick enchantments."

Ione pouted. "They put me to sleep."

"For your own safety," Liria soothed, running a gentle hand across the Princess' back. "By the order of the gods."

Ione shuddered, and the ice in Liria's lungs melted away. When the Princess at last unlocked her arms, Liria positioned herself demurely on the side of the bed as though the desperate embrace had never happened and this were any normal morning. Ione wore a light sleeping gown but retained her bustier and underwear, leading Liria to believe General Barin had likely changed her before tucking her into bed. Ione's raven-dark hair had been set free, and it tumbled becomingly across the pillows, highlighting softly tanned skin and the dark blue eyes which were the only nod to her naga blood.

Vasilios' eyes had been the same colour, before Liria had carved them out.

"What do we do now?" Ione asked, running a trembling hand over her face. "I'm supposed to be planning a wedding, not sleeping several days away."

"As to that, your highness." Liria paused, choosing her words with care. "The Pharaoh has summoned you to his chambers within the hour, to negotiate whether the marriage contract will be terminated or not."

"He *what?*" Ione sat bolt upright, her jaw slack. "What do you mean?"

"Attempting to murder the Prince of Merged Egypt has been construed as an act of war," Liria said quietly. "Under the traitor's clause, Pharaoh Taos can summon your parents and have them remove us to Atlantis."

"But... but I didn't stab anyone," Ione whispered, skin pale and eyes impossibly large in her face.

"No, but I did, and as far as Egypt is concerned, we are as one." When Ione just stared, Liria gathered her courage and took a risk. "What do you dream of, your highness?"

"Freedom," Ione answered at once, her eyes turning to the window. It was closed, delicate metalwork casting curlicued shadows on the floor, but Egypt's cerulean sky was clearly visible beyond and if either of them stood, Selekhet would be spread out below in all her vibrant glory. "I want to be free, my shadow. I want to be Queen, a power unrivalled by any other, that I may never be commanded again."

"And marriage to the Pharaoh Taos?"

"More important than you can possibly imagine. Without Taos..." Ione shuddered. "I won't go back to Atlantis. I won't."

"Then you may need to fight for your place, your highness," Liria murmured, her heart thumping in the base of her throat.

Ione's eyes, dark as the bottom of the ocean, settled unerringly on Liria's face. "What do you mean?"

"Recovering from... an incident like the one that happened with Prince Raiden... may require a great deal of compromise." Liria's breath came in sharp pants, words poking at the solid wall of her binding until they found a way to tumble out. "Taos values his brother highly, and if we are not careful, the Egyptians will either exile us or execute us."

The Princess' perfect, coral pink lips pursed. "None of this would be necessary if you'd stayed your blade, my shadow."

Frustration soared, but Liria clamped it down. She longed to be free of Atlantis as much as her mistress, and the only way to achieve it was to convince Ione to hold her ground - that, and to co-operate with a certain ornery Prince. Isolating herself may have worked well enough in the past, but Raiden had the right of it when he'd appealed to her in the Kirrilakh; there was no way to keep their lives separate when Ione and Taos were to be married. And while working with Raiden was dangerous to the extreme, if it meant that she'd never see the idyllic tropical shores of Atlantis ever again, Liria would gladly work alongside the infuriating Prince of Merged Egypt for the rest of her days.

"I can only throw myself upon your mercy, your highness," Liria gurgled, clenching her hands to fists lest she claw at her tightening airways. "If I could take back my actions, I swear I would do so."

"Of course." Ione smiled and the pressure in Liria's lungs eased, allowing her to gasp a welcome breath. "I may not under-stand the lapse in your thoughts, but you would never knowingly endanger my future, my shadow. You have ever fought for me."

Liria inclined her head, left it down so that Ione could run trembling fingers across the surface of her hair. When the Princess drew her hand away, she chanced a glance from beneath her lashes. "If it please you, your highness, we have but half an hour to get you dressed and to the Pharaoh's door, or your chance to fight will be taken from you."

"You are right that Taos values his brother's life," Ione mused, slipping from the bed and stretching. "I suppose it makes sense - after all, the Prince is a consummate warrior and his chief bodyguard. To be without such a tool would be a most unpalat-able prospect."

The love between the Pharaoh and his younger brother was a bright, unshakable bond, but Liria wasn't suicidal enough to remind Ione of her stilted relationship with her own sisters by saying so. Instead, she helped the Princess bathe and dress, brushing her hair and setting strings of silver and Atlantean aquamarine amongst Ione's sleek raven tresses.

They knocked on the Pharaoh's door with ten minutes to spare, the royal suite outwardly unguarded - though Liria could sense several figures on the other side of the thick wood which swung open at that moment. The man framed in the doorway had skin of a deep, dark chocolate, with black hair cropped close to his head and eyes almost the same shade. His muscles were lean but well defined beneath the tight, sleeveless tunic and leather pants he wore, and his expression was decidedly unfriendly.

"Shadow," he growled.

"Daywalker," she returned.

The daywalking vampire - the politically correct term for a Merged vampire with enough human blood to stand the sunlight - frowned and flashed fangs that were barely sharp enough to be considered more than teeth. "Watch it, little one. I bite."

Liria smiled broadly, allowing him a clear view of her very human teeth. It gave her immense satisfaction when the vampire's superior smirk froze on his face as she dropped the illusion concealing her fangs, the longer canines framed either side by the slightly shorter, but no less deadly, extra fangs that were a peculiarity of her family line - or so she'd once been told, never having met a blood relative in person. When she'd asked King Vasilios, he'd said her family was dead. Given she'd been carving out his kidney at the time, Liria had believed him.

"I bite, too," she purred, stepping forward. "Want to find out how deep?"

To his credit, the Daywalker stood firm, though his adam's apple bobbed as he called, "My Prince?"

"Ah, Lady of Shadows." Raiden appeared in a sweep of half-spread wings, wearing the same scarlet shawl and billowing linen pants as he had an hour earlier, though he'd added a khopesh to either hip. "Princess Ione, how delightful to see you up and about. Excuse Gallin's manners - I do believe he skipped break-fast this morning." Grabbing the daywalking vampire by the back of his sleeveless tunic, Raiden shoved him aside - and then blinked in surprise as the muscular male sailed through the air to crash against the wall on the far side of the suite. "Oh."

"Feeling a little stronger than usual, your highness?" Liria asked, her voice dripping innocence. "Perhaps Gallin's so gruff because you ate his breakfast as well as your own."

A long, low snarl echoed from the depths of the room and Raiden laughed, waving them in on the deep, rich sound. No sooner were they inside than Princess Ione dropped the Prince of Merged Egypt a deep curtsey, her face flushed. "Your highness - I must offer my most sincere apologies for what happened. I fear my shadow has completely lost her mind. Whatever punishment you deem necessary, she will gladly accept as recompense for such a grave insult to your person."

Liria gaped, glad she was out of Ione's line of sight. If Raiden was as astonished as she, he gave no sign, simply bowed deeply in return and then stepped forward to capture both of Ione's hands in his.

"There are bound to be misunderstandings in any new life, your highness," he murmured, as though being stabbed and almost dying were as trivial a thing as polishing his sword. "I fear it is not me, however, who is the most upset."

Ione waved a hand and tittered nervously. "My shadow will bleed for whoever requires appeasing."

"Blood and violence are not the way to my brother's heart, nor will they appease his temper. He is not the kind of monarch - or man - to derive pleasure from such things."

"Oh." Ione's shoulders drooped. "Then how else do I fix this, Prince of Egypt?"

Raiden's expression softened, his fingers gentle as he tipped the Princess' chin upward in a way very few in Atlantis would ever dare. "Do you truly wish to marry my brother?"

"Yes." Ione lifted her chin and squared her shoulders. "More now that I've had the chance to spend some time with him. He's gentle and kind and strong, a great Pharaoh beloved by his people and a man of integrity who gives freely of his affection and is obviously adored by those close to him. I... I should like to be part of that world, Prince of Egypt."

"Then I suggest, rather than offering spilled blood and broken bones, that you speak from your heart unto his." Raiden dropped his fingers from the Princess' chin and cut a glance over one shoulder. "There is no need for formality amongst family - only love, honesty, and respect."

Liria stepped back as an inner door opened and Taos strode into the room, his golden-bronze hair tumbled as though he'd been running his fingers through it and his deep brown eyes swamped with sorrow.

"My brother," Raiden flourished a half bow. "Your guests are here, as requested."

"Princess Ione." The Pharaoh's voice was a rasp, his hands clenched to bloodless fists. "I -"

Taos cut off as Ione threw herself into his arms, her sobs loud and not the least bit princess-like. Liria shot a look in Raiden's direction and saw him scowling at his older brother, miming wrapping his arms around an invisible person until the Pharaoh, rousing from his shock, cradled the Princess close and buried his face in her hair. When Raiden jerked his chin in the direction of the balcony, Liria and the glowering Gallin followed him outside at once.

The gauze curtains and floor to ceiling folding glass doors provided little to no privacy in a visual sense, but when Raiden closed those glass doors behind him, the Pharaoh and his Princess were safe from being overheard - and Ione, should she look up, would have a clear view of Liria only a few paces away.

"A clever test," Liria murmured, moving to lean on the carved stone balustrade. "Though you might have been better to strip me of my weapons first, Prince of Egypt."

"There are two of us and one of you," Gallin pointed out, his tone one step short of murderous. "What have we to fear from a fairy?"

Raiden chuckled, bracing his forearms on the balcony on Liria's left and settling one of his wings across her shoulders. "Oh, Gallin, if I didn't like you so much, I'd let her show you exactly what you have to fear."

Liria lifted her hands to shove off Raiden's wing, but the infuriating angel merely tightened it around her shoulders until it swept down her arms and back like a warm, silken feather cloak.

"Do you *want* to die?" she snapped, gripping the elegant swirl of a vine etched into the balustrade's surface. "Testing the Princess' resolve is one thing, but inviting your own death is entirely another."

"You tried killing me already. Didn't we agree to work together from now on?"

Clenching her teeth so hard her jaw hurt, Liria shook her head. "You know my co-operation can only go as far as the Princess will allow."

"For now. Look out there," Raiden nudged her shoulder with his wing, bronzed arm gilt by the sun as he pointed over Selekhet. "The rooftop markets are open."

Frowning, Liria followed his gesture. Several of the low, flat roofs surrounding the colourful market district now had shaded stalls atop them, thickly woven rugs providing soft places for angels and the occasional other winged creature to land.

"There are so many angels here," she murmured, enchanted in spite of herself. "So much flight."

"Egypt - Selekhet in particular - is the birthplace of the angels," Raiden returned, flexing his wing against her bare shoulders. "When the gods first met with Egypt's Pharaoh and signed the agreement to merge our two worlds into one, it was here in Selekhet. Though the other Merge sites soon saw the benefits and followed suit, we were exposed the longest, began exhibiting signs of blended Earth and Mu energies before anyone else."

"Your gods were also the first to step in and help shape those energies, so people weren't mutated in a debilitating way but accepted the merging with less pain and suffering," Liria murmured, nodding. "Horus' energy took quickly and thus the angels became the first Merged species that was neither truly human nor Mu, but a perfect blend of both." She smiled at his startled expression. "I may not have been given my own formal education, but I was present for every one of Ione's lessons."

"Then you know that the merge sites began as a spot only a few paces across and have been growing ever since, and that eventually our entire two worlds will be as one."

"Yes. I also know the gods control the merge to prevent the two worlds destroying each other in a chaotic smash of opposing forces," Liria answered. "Though it means that those with too much Mu in their veins cannot venture outside Merged land, it prevents wide scale death and destruction."

Raiden's grin was bright and breathtaking. "Indeed. And it is the job of those who rule Merged sites to ensure that things run smoothly on our side of the fence, while the gods of Mu do the same on their side."

"Of course." Liria examined Raiden's profile, studiously ignoring the daywalking vampire who'd drifted closer to her other side. "What I don't know is why you felt I needed a history lesson."

"Oh, I think you do." Golden eyes crinkled in the corners. "As I've been saying since you lit upon our shores, Lady of Shadows, you're about to become part of the Pharaoh's honour guard - an honour guard I'm responsible for. I need to know what you know, what you can do, and who you are underneath that alabaster facade."

Liria squashed the urge to smile, but she couldn't quite squash the curious thrill that arose when making him work for the answers he sought so doggedly.

"Can you fly in Earth skies, Prince of Egypt?"

"All angels can - though I confess I've not tried since my injury." Raiden frowned. "With Horus' blood remaking me...

perhaps I carry too much of Mu inside me now. What about you?"

"I came here, didn't I, across un-Merged oceans?" Liria quirked a brow. "It is difficult, however. I cannot maintain a corporeal form; I become as a ghost, my powers a whisper."

"So Anubis told us." Raiden nudged her with his elbow and Liria realised with a start that he'd used his wing to draw her so close that a solid inhalation would cause their arms to brush. The ridiculous angel winked. "Though I much prefer hearing the news from your own lips, Lady of Shadows."

Icy knives shot through Liria's system, stealing her pithy response and causing her to double over in pain. Rather than step away, Raiden used his wing to scoop her closer, swinging her into his arms and turning to face the full length glass doors. The agony shredding Liria's veins increased and she groaned, but Raiden didn't try to walk inside, nor did he release her. With her head lolling uselessly against his chest, Liria could see his jaw set in a brutal line, golden eyes flashing with fire.

"What's wrong?" Gallin demanded, his surliness replaced with surprise.

"Liria's compulsion is punishing her." Raiden's wings spread wide before they returned to cradle Liria in a tender echo of his arms. Her body spasmed and her teeth snapped together but he held firm, ensuring she didn't accidentally injure either him or herself with her body's thrashing about.

"My shadow?" Ione's voice preceded hurried footsteps and a breathless gasp. Raiden's wings lowered enough for the Princess to lean in close, her cool hands brushing over Liria's cheeks. "The Pharaoh - he says I'm doing this to you. That I'm hurting you. Is that true?"

Liria groaned, spots dancing in front of her eyes as competing instructions clashed deep inside.

"You're killing her," Raiden growled. "Give permission for her to answer or I'll have Gallin knock you out cold."

Ione gasped. "Permission! I give my shadow permission to answer my question with utmost honesty and no fear of reprisal."

The ache in Liria's head eased and she panted in relief, heart hammering and tears gathering in the corners of her eyes. How long had she hoped for Ione to realise the intensity of the emotions leaked down the compulsion? How many years had she yearned for the freedom to say the one word that the icy daggers of Ione's panic had stuck in her throat?

"Shadow." The Princess' dark blue eyes sought Liria's, her tone brooking no nonsense. "Answer me. Now."

"Yes," Liria croaked. The singular response felt like razors in her mouth, the compulsion punishing her for speaking hurtfully about her mistress even as it forced her to answer with the truth. "Every time."

The Princess jerked as if slapped, and Taos caught her with gentle hands. "*I* did this? I made you stab the Prince?"

"Yes."

"And... the others? All those years ago?" Tears glimmered at the corners of Ione's eyes as the awful truth sunk home, and Liria wished, for the first time ever, that she didn't have to speak the truth that had rubbed her the wrong way for so very long.

"Yes." Her teeth clenched as the icy clawing inside her ribcage intensified - and then abruptly melted away as Ione's knees buckled, her lashes fluttering closed. "Your highness?"

"She's fainted." Taos swept the Princess into his arms and shot a sharp look at Gallin. "Food. Drink. Now."

The daywalking vampire bowed from the waist, turned, and vaulted over the balcony, disappearing from sight. The Pharaoh didn't so much as blink, merely nodded once in Raiden's direction and swept back inside his chambers with the Princess Ione in his arms.

"Are you all right?" Raiden murmured, lowering his head to speak directly into the shell of Liria's ear. She shivered and he raised his wings, shielding them behind a wall of soft, silken feathers. "Liria?"

The scent of warm sand and burning sunlight filled her lungs, chasing away the lingering frost in her blood. When Liria pushed at the wall of Raiden's chest, the Prince of Merged Egypt set her carefully on her feet - but he didn't retract the barrier his wings provided.

"I'm fine," she said, trying desperately to contain the blush that threatened her cheeks. "It's gone now."

"Do you want to fly? I could take you to the gardens, or the market?"

Liria closed her eyes so she wouldn't have to look at him, his proximity and the tender concern in his voice threatening her fragile equilibrium. For her own sake, she needed to rebuild what his single, spectral kiss had destroyed - and she needed to do it at once. He was, after all, a Prince, while she would only ever be a shadow.

"No," Liria said quietly, pleased when her voice came out smooth. "I should stay where Ione can see me when she wakes. Whilst I understand your need to test her resolve, I do not wish her tipped over the edge."

Raiden tilted his head to the side, brow furrowed. "Taos has a little courtyard around the corner which attaches to his bedchamber. Will you sit with me? If they need us, we'll be less than three paces away."

Liria smoothed her hands over her gown to settle the wrinkles, noting with a start that her colouring had bled to mottled blue-grey all the way up to her elbows. Frowning, she forced her skin back to the creamy nothing shade that Ione preferred and fixed the tendrils of hair that had escaped her elegant updo. Through it all, Raiden waited patiently, hands balanced on the hilts of his swords and the sun gilding his skin with gold.

"Three paces," she repeated, drawing a deep, settling breath. Raiden nodded, holding out an arm. After a moment's hesitation, Liria touched her fingertips to the back of his wrist. "All right. Lead the way, Prince of Egypt."

LET'S TRY THIS AGAIN

Taos' private courtyard had been their mother's sunroom, once, until he and Raiden had worked day and night for two weeks straight to transform it. As grieving teenagers the manual labour had given them an outlet, and as budding rulers, a place to plan and think that was private from the rest of the court.

Most of the ceiling was gone, the remaining section changed to thick panels of hand-made glass that refracted rainbows across the crudely done mosaic set unevenly into the floor. The walls had been removed down to hip level with the exception of the roof supports - even in the sections where there was no roof. Instead, a thick carpet of creeping plants draped from every column and beam, creating a sense of privacy whilst still leaving the courtyard open to the air.

A daybed was tucked into the most protected corner, with a latticework screen behind it and a tumble of rust and green cushions on top. In the bowl of the courtyard, a wonky round table with a scarred surface and a scattering of mismatched chairs looked out towards Selekhet, the vibrant capital of Egypt framed by chipped masonry and delicate greenery.

Liria stood in the centre of the space with one hand flattened over her chest and the other trailing down the leaves of a passionfruit vine, the deep midnight to black ombré of her dress adding a soothing, peaceful note to the chaos of bright colours the little retreat boasted.

"It's beautiful," she breathed, her voice thrumming with emotion.

So are you, Raiden thought - but bit his tongue before he spoke the words aloud. Instead, he berated himself thoroughly for noting the way her slender figure curved beneath the gentle fall of her gown, and flung himself on the daybed with his wings spread wide across the mattress.

"I'm glad you like it," he said, examining the wisteria blooming overhead. "When our parents died and Taos took the throne, it was... difficult. Creating this space was cathartic in many ways."

"*You* did all this?"

"Taos and I, yeah." Raiden snorted a laugh, lacing his hands behind his head. "What, you thought that crappy mosaic was done by one of Egypt's master craftsmen?"

"Crappy?" An indigo brow arched. "Your tone changes from palace formal to street casual from one moment to the next."

"As a Prince serving his Pharaoh, I speak the way etiquette dictates. As a man, in my own time, I speak the way I'm comfortable. I've far worse words than 'crappy' in my repertoire."

"Hmm. I suppose I'll become accustomed to the constant fluctuation as time goes on." A moment's silence, her words soft. "For the record, the mosaic isn't crappy; it's wonderful. And I can tell at a glance which bits were yours, and which were Taos'."

"You can?" Raiden sat up, intrigued in spite of himself. Liria had dropped to a crouch, delicate cream fingers brushing wobbly grouting and wings spread behind her in a glorious display of gossamer and stained glass. He swallowed and forced his gaze to the tile work. "Go on then, enlighten me."

A flash of violet eyes that said she'd recognised the challenge in his tone, then Liria returned to her contemplation of the mosaic. An ankh took pride of place in the centre, with a pair of angels' wings spread wide behind it. One of the wings was picked out in shades of white, grey and tawny rust, while the other was a blend of chocolate and white. Above the ankh, two eyes watched over the scene, one red and the other blue.

"You tiled Taos' wing," Liria murmured, stroking her hand down the tiles which echoed the Pharaoh's deep brown and white feathers. "And he yours. You shared the ankh, and these eyes... I do not know the significance, but you did the blue eye and he, the red."

Raiden watched her caress the tiled copy of his left wing and fought a shiver. "Both eyes belong to Horus, god of the sky. The blue eye symbolises the moon and the red, the sun. As for the work, you're correct. How could you tell?"

A tiny, barely visible smile crept over Liria's face, as though she held safe the secrets of the world. She placed her hands in the centre of the ankh and lowered her face until her forehead bumped gently against the eternal symbol for life in all its many facets. When she raised herself up, she drew a single finger down the centre of her brow, kissed the fingertip and pressed it to the tiles below. Raiden longed to ask the meaning of the gesture but couldn't find the words, unable to shake the feeling he'd witnessed something private, something inescapably Liria, rather than the mask she wore as a shadow.

"Your work is like your personalities," Liria murmured at last, that secret smile still curling her lips. "Taos, accurate and orderly with delicately cut tiles and slender, meticulous grouting. And Raiden, haphazard and strong, making the pieces fit together with ruthless determination and lumpy, uneven grouting that's nevertheless undertaken with the same devotion he applies to everything in his life."

Her words fell like stones, and Raiden was forced to slump back on the bed lest Liria look up and see what she'd smashed apart with the quiet force of her observations. Gods, had he really only known her a few days? It felt like a lifetime; so easily could she peel open his skin and slip inside.

"You were always meant to come here," he whispered, staring again at the wisteria overhead. "You were always meant to be part of this." When she didn't answer, he turned his head and saw Liria's chin tilted to the side, her gaze turned inwards and one hand spread across her abdomen. "Liria? What is it?"

"The Princess..." Liria blinked, and to his surprise, her cheeks began to colour. "Um."

Raiden rolled to his feet, arms crossing over his body as he reached for the hilts of his swords - and then he stopped, at last picking up the very faint sounds filtering out of Taos' bedroom.

"Oh." He cleared his throat. "Well. Looks like they're not waiting for their wedding night."

"Raiden," Liria's voice had turned husky and when she looked up at him, her pupils were dilated. "I..."

"God of the sky, you can feel what she's feeling?" Raiden crinkled his nose as her breathing started to turn jagged, and turned his attention inwards, guided by an instinct he'd not possessed before waking with the blood of a god in his veins. *Soul-catcher.*

Prince of Merged Egypt. Anubis' voice rang like a bell in his head, thick with both surprise and delight. *Well, well, this is unexpected. Why call me, instead of your blood brother?*

Again guided by that tiny, inner voice, Raiden opened his mind's eye to the god of the dead and shared his memory of the previous minute. *What do I do?*

Well, there's a rather practical solution, Anubis chuckled, *but something tells me your shadow might be embarrassed come the morning.*

I don't want her in my bed as the result of a compulsion driven by my brother's cock, Raiden snapped, propping his fists on his hips. *This is as much a violation as the pain and I'll not add to it. Can you help?*

Not without Ione's permission - and I'm not appearing in the middle of your brother's bedroom right now to ask her, Anubis replied. *However, I'd wager the effect on Liria will lessen with distance.*

Thank-you, Soulcatcher.

You're welcome, Prince of Egypt. I look forward to discovering what other interesting abilities your transformation has gifted you.

Raiden growled and cut the connection as the jackal god howled with laughter. He reached to tug Liria to her feet but pulled so hard she flew through the air, thumping soundly against his chest.

"Don't," she gasped, staggering back from him with sweat beaded across her forehead and horror writ in the depths of her gaze.

"You're safe," he held up both hands, palms out, masking his hurt that she'd think him capable of forcing her. "I know you wished to stay close, but Anubis says if we put distance between you and Ione, the effect will be lessened."

It was a measure of Liria's discomfort that she didn't argue; merely turned and flung herself into the sky in a flurry of midnight cloth.

Raiden hunted down replacement guards and left a note for his brother in the Pharaoh's outer chambers, doing his studied best to ignore the sounds coming from the bedroom the entire time. Though he'd played wingman for Taos on a number of occasions, his cheeks were still flagged red by the time he launched skyward, beating his wings hard to work off the lingering embarrassment while he went in search of Egypt's only shadow.

He found her at the rooftop market, eyeing off an ice-cream cart with the same focus one might apply to setting explosives. Raiden circled in the sky, keeping to an easy glide while his newly sensitive ears caught snatches of the polite greeting Liria exchanged with the cart's owner before moving on. When she was out of sight, he landed by the ice cream cart in careful silence, bought two cones, and threaded through the crowd in her wake.

"Jewellery?" Raiden queried, draping one wing around Liria's shoulders and using it to angle her towards him. As she turned, eyes wide and fingers reaching - most likely for a weapon - he slid one of the ice cream cones into her outstretched hand and smiled. "I didn't picture you as much of a jewellery person."

Liria stared down at the ice cream and then back up at Raiden, and he had the distinct impression she was trying to decide whether or not to mash it into his face. The lure of the frozen treat won out, however, and she ran her tongue over the chocolate ice cream with a shiver of delight that did strange things to his insides.

"I don't know if I'm a jewellery person or not," she said absently, investigating the butterscotch underneath her scoop of chocolate in such a way that she ended up with ice cream on her nose. "I've never been allowed it. I was looking with Ione in mind - for the wedding."

"She didn't bring her own things?"

"Of course she did," Liria replied, then rolled her eyes when he still looked confused. "It's tradition in Atlantis for family to give presents on a wedding day, to augment what the bride or groom already has. Since Queen Coranna and King Theon won't be present, I'm to provide something in their stead."

Raiden shook his head, buying time to answer by taking a large bite of his ice cream. In the end, he couldn't find a nice way to phrase his question, so he just asked it. "Didn't they give you something to pass on before you left?"

"No," Liria said softly, her eyes passing back over the arrangement on the table. "They didn't."

And quite suddenly Raiden was sure beyond doubt that Liria was looking at jewellery not because the King and Queen of Atlantis had asked her to, but because they'd deliberately not supplied anything and Liria didn't want to see the Princess Ione hurt by the lack of care.

"Why?" he asked, as she picked up a silver hair comb set with dark sapphires the colour of Ione's eyes. "With everything she does to you?"

The dark fairy sighed, licking up a section of her ice cream that was starting to dribble down the side of the cone. "The compulsion makes that difficult to answer."

"Try."

"Do you not... look after your family... no matter their temperament? Ione... goes into any situation with... the best intentions."

Raiden narrows his eyes. "Just because she doesn't know she's hurting you doesn't excuse the behaviour. Her jealousy is petty and her panic is something that should have been addressed in her youth."

Liria smiled, her eyes and face sad, and ate more ice cream.

"You want that?" The store owner demanded, waving at the comb.

"Yes," Liria answered, handing it to him. "But I have no money. Do you barter? I could perhaps kill someone who has wronged you?"

The burly human blinked. "Uh..."

"I think not." Raiden swallowed a laugh, reaching into his pocket to tug out a thick gold coin. "Here. Keep the change, my friend."

"My Prince." The store owner bowed deeply, deftly wrapping the comb and smiling as he pressed it back into Liria's hands. "Take it with my thanks, Lady."

Liria frowned up at Raiden as they stepped into the crowd. "Now I owe you a service, instead of him."

"No," he shook his head. "Nothing is owed between us, Liria."

She looked down at her ice cream, frowned, and took a large bite. Judging from her expression, she preferred the smooth flavour of the chocolate to the sweeter butterscotch - information Raiden filed away in the back of his mind alongside all the other astonishing things he was learning about this petite fairy with a hidden soft side.

"This place is strange," she mused, looking out over the market. "It will take some getting used to."

"Why don't you have any money?"

Another frown. "I'm a shadow."

"Which means?" Raiden shook his head. "You keep saying those words as though they will magically make sense."

They meandered between stalls in silence, Liria's gaze turned inward as she methodically demolished her ice cream - and then, to Raiden's secret delight, licked her fingers clean. He was careful not to direct their wanderings and at first she seemed confused, but after a while the exotic sights and scents drew Liria from one stall to the next and he followed as she darted to and fro. A couple of hours later, Raiden bought them hot, sweet pastries from a vendor and coaxed her into a quiet nook created by the overhang of a nearby roof.

"As has been explained to you already, shadows are not people," Liria said at last, biting into her pastry and staring in surprise at the custard filling. "This is good."

"And as has been explained to you already, Egypt doesn't tolerate slavery. So the statement 'shadows are not people' is not the catch-all phrase you seem to think it is."

The look she shot him said that she was rapidly reassessing how many brain cells he owned. In a slow, clear voice, Liria said, "A slave is a person in chains, a person who can be freed to claim a life of their own. A shadow qualifies as neither."

"Why not?"

"Because a shadow has no soul, Prince of Egypt. They are an empty husk... a ghost... a pale mockery of the real thing." With an elegant hand, she gestured at where his own shadow stretched long and thin across the ground. "A shadow cannot be a real person, because their only function is to always follow where their master leads."

"You..." Raiden stared, his own pastry forgotten in his hands. "Liria, you don't cast a shadow."

"No soul," she said, shrugging as though they were discussing the weather. "No shadow. I *am* the shadow."

How had he not noticed that she didn't cast a shadow? The

answer came at once - because Liria made a point to fade into the background, the same way that any real shadow did. Nobody noticed, because nobody noticed *her*; and even Raiden, who had been trying to pay attention, had overlooked this most critical fact. He bit into his pastry. "You like this?"

"I said I did. It's delicious."

"So you have opinions, thoughts, feelings. Like everyone else."

"Of course; but they are secondary considerations for a shadow when it comes to what the master wants, thinks or feels. A shadow's desires are, like the rest of them, paler echoes of the real thing."

Raiden shook his head, opting for a change of subject rather than bending his brain any further. "You offered to kill someone for that storeman."

"Is that not the traditional form of barter here?" Liria asked, peeling off a loose flake of pastry and slipping it into her mouth.

"No!" Raiden laughed in spite of himself, the sound soft and without humour. "There is very little death in Egypt, Lady of Shadows. Selekhet is, by and large, a peaceful place."

"Huh. Then what do I..." she went pale.

"No," Raiden said again, his tone gentle this time. When she didn't look up, he used the bony edge of his wing to tip up her chin. "Never that, Liria. That's not a form of currency here."

A sigh of relief. "If I have no money, I have to be able to offer something."

"Once Ione is married and you're formally part of the honour guard, you'll get a wage," Raiden answered, keeping his tone soft. "You'll have money."

"I'm not allowed -"

"You *are.*" He clenched his teeth, forced out a breath, deliberately modulated his tone. "You are a person. Your soul might not be in your body, but you have one, or you'd not be bound."

"It's not that simple."

"It is, and I'll prove it to you or die trying," Raiden growled.

Liria blinked, and then smiled. "Admirable, Prince of Egypt, but unnecessary. I've already agreed to give you whatever I have the capability to give."

Not in the way he wanted, she hadn't. Still, something freely given had far more worth than a thing forced - and Raiden was starting to suspect force was all Liria knew. He watched her finish her pastry and waited until she looked up at him. "What did you like best?"

"The chocolate ice cream." Liria grinned and the sight of her perfect human teeth irritated Raiden; it meant she was still hiding, still masked. Next to him, but not truly present.

A shadow.

Raiden shifted on the bench and forced himself to smile back. "And here I thought I'd win you over with the butterscotch."

"Unnecessary." Liria looked out towards the market and inhaled, her violet eyes spangled with glittering sparks. "Egypt won me over the moment I saw her on the horizon."

"And me?" he asked, unable to hold back the words. "What of me?"

Liria looked down at her hands, sticky from the pastry, then up at the sky. "I... What is that smell?"

"What?" Raiden sat up straighter and took a deep breath. "Your nose must be more sensitive than mine. I can't smell anything odd."

"You're still settling into your powers," she said absently, her brows creased into a neat frown. "Your energy's been in constant flux since you came to me at the prison." Liria pushed to her feet. "It smells like... sour milk. And..."

Raiden caught her arm as she spread her wings, the long strips of her cape falling neatly to either side. "Liria?"

"Blood," she said, her feet already lifting from the ground. "This way."

He ran to keep up, following her across the roof and leaping off the edge without a thought for who might be watching.

Instead of rising into the sky, Liria dropped into the narrow alley below and Raiden twisted sideways as he fell, flaring his wings at the last moment to soften the impact on his knees as he slammed into the ground.

"Shh," Liria scolded, crouching to run her fingers through a dark puddle. She straightened to show Raiden her stained fingertips.

"Blood," he murmured, fisting both hands. The alley was empty, shaded from the afternoon sun by the buildings either side and, with the exception of some neatly stacked wooden crates, empty. "No way to tell from whom, or where they went."

Liria raised bloody fingers to her mouth and flicked out her tongue. "Human and feline blend," she announced. "The sour milk smell isn't in the blood, so I'm assuming it belongs to the attacker." She tilted her fingertips towards his face. "Confirm?"

"No." Raiden caught her fine-boned wrist and fought the urge to grimace. "I believe you. Human and feline... Bast's temple is just over the way, and her priests and priestesses often visit the market on their breaks."

Still hanging on to Liria's wrist, Raiden jogged down the alley and into the main thoroughfare. This late in the afternoon it was clogged with people either heading home from work or rushing to finish off last minute errands. Rather than attempt to brave the mess, Raiden bunched his thighs and launched into the air, beating his wings twice to clear the road before landing softly in the manicured gardens of Bast's temple.

"Do you plan to drag me around all day like a dog?" Liria snapped, tugging at his grip. "I'm not about to flee, my Prince."

"Don't call me that," Raiden muttered, releasing her arm even though it was the last thing he wanted to do. "Just Raiden."

For some reason the words inflamed her temper and she hissed between her teeth, then turned and stomped towards the thick greenery that grew alongside the temple. "This way, *just Raiden.*"

As they stepped into a well-kept herb garden, Raiden was

assaulted with all manner of scents. He went to his knees on the gravel path, his lungs full of lemon, thyme, tomato, basil... blood and rot.

"Gods above," he croaked, turning his face into his own armpit in an effort to find some relief.

Liria didn't answer, her wings tucked close to her back as she leant over a slumped shadow on the ground. Raiden's vision blurred as he watched her, his focus sharpening to painful clarity before bleeding to a blurred haze. The cycle repeated with such swiftness that his stomach churned, threatening to return the pastry and ice cream he'd eaten at the market.

"Are you all right?" A soft voice, a cool hand on his shoulder. "Let me help you."

The cloying odour of moon lilies shoved into his nostrils and it was all Raiden could do not to gag as he struggled to his feet. "When you said my energies were fluctuating, you weren't kidding."

"I rarely do such things as jest," was the quiet reply. "Come now, my dear Prince. Let me ease your pain as only I can."

Huh? His pain? Raiden shook his head, every breath full of moon lilies, her soft voice like running water in his ears.

No. Liria's voice was husky, filled with the notes of crushed gemstones, her scent overlaid with the crisp freshness of dawn - not cloyingly sweet, with a voice like honeyed poison. He opened his mouth to say so but his tongue felt thick in his throat and only a gurgle emerged.

"It's all right," she purred, smooth fingers sliding up his bicep. "I live to serve, after all."

She really didn't, but before he had the chance to protest, her lips covered his, slick and full and seeking. Raiden groaned as Liria's fingers tunnelled into his hair, tilting his head to better their angle.

Oh, yes. At last.

He froze as that cold, clinical voice ignited a vivid memory; heat and lightning, a pliable body squashed against his harder one, Liria's heart a trapped bird against his chest. His fists, slamming against stone. His voice, vibrating in the gloom, her scent igniting in his lungs, filling him, urging him to more.

This kiss... it was nothing like that one.

This woman... was not Liria Atlannon.

The taste of rot slipped into Raiden's mouth on the edge of her seeking tongue, a tongue that was a touch too long, a touch too purposeful. He tried to pull back but that tongue curled around his own, holding so tightly that Raiden had no choice but to endure. His eyes flicked open and he blinked rapidly but couldn't focus; he caught the faintest impression of pale skin and dark hair but the image shifted like a desert mirage.

It didn't matter. She was wrong. *This* was wrong.

With a growl of deep, dark fury, Raiden drew his dual khopesh swords in a brutal, scissoring motion. The woman who'd been latched to his tongue gasped, her body going slack and then falling to the ground in two pieces.

Able to draw a breath at long last, Raiden turned his head to the side and vomited into the nearest bush.

SNAKE IN THE GRASS

LIRIA WOKE FROM HER shock as the woman who'd been locked in a passionate embrace with the Prince of Merged Egypt separated into two neat pieces. She reached Raiden's side before the body of his attacker hit the ground, catching both khopeshes as they dropped from his nerveless hands. Blood-soaked steel said the encounter hadn't been an embrace at all, but an ambush - not that the fissure in her heart cared for the distinction. The image of Raiden with his eyes closed and his lips pressed against another's was emblazoned on the back of her brain and Liria knew when next she had a nightmare, that's what she would see.

"My Prince?" She set the twin swords on the ground, laying a hand against the small of his back as he retched noisily.

"Just -" more vomit "- Raiden -" a gurgle "- dammit."

She couldn't. Not with the vision of dark hair and pale, willowy limbs so fresh in her mind. Crouching down, Liria dipped her fingers in the meal he was so heartily regurgitating and lifted it to her nose for a sniff.

"Gods, Liria, you did *not* just smell my puke," Raiden groaned, hands braced on his knees and wings arched as though he didn't know whether to take to the skies or cover his face.

"Poison," Liria said quietly. Wiping her hand on her skirt, she straightened just enough to grip Raiden's chin and pop his mouth open with a subtle clenching of her fingers. "Snake venom, to be precise. You live, I'd wager, because of your new blood."

While the Prince of Egypt stared in shock, his tongue and lips dark with the lingering effects of the poison, Liria crossed to the bisected body on the ground; a woman who was no longer a woman but a frightful, serpentine caricature of humanity. Hauling the severed torso up with one hand twisted into wiry black hair, Liria yanked open the dead creature's mouth and watched as a long, forked serpent's tongue lolled out. Behind her Raiden gagged and retched again.

"Make sure to wash your mouth out," Liria said absently, leaning close to the dead body to sniff the creature's throat. While she maintained a cool facade, she was highly aware of Raiden sheathing his swords, moving to the trough built into the side of the temple and scooping running water into his mouth. When he'd finished, his face yet pale, she said, "This is the woman who killed the Priestess of Bast."

For a long moment, his face was blank. "Priestess?"

Dropping the dead snake-thing on the ground, Liria led him to the first body; a diminutive female with a cat's ears and tail. Her throat had been punctured with sharp viper's teeth but she'd struggled - just enough to create a wound that had dripped blood into the street. The wounds on her neck were marked with the same dark discolouration Liria had seen in Raiden's mouth and her face had been painted with hieroglyphs of blood.

The Prince of Merged Egypt stared at the glyphs with a furrow between his brows. "It says 'heavy heart.'"

"Heavy heart?"

He bent slightly, double checking the complex glyphs whose meaning could be changed with the slightest alteration of an accent. "Yes."

"Does that mean anything to you?"

"I..." Raiden ran a hand over his pale face and drew a deep

breath. "It is said that when Anubis takes a soul to the Duat, before they can enter the afterlife, their hearts must be weighed against the feather of Ma'at. If the heart is lighter than or equal to the feather, they have lived a virtuous life and are permitted to pass to the afterlife proper. If the heart is heavier, the soul is damned. The heart in which it resides is given to Ammit, the devourer of the dead, who binds the unsavoury character to the less palatable areas of the Duat for all eternity."

"Is that really how it works?" Liria asked, curious in spite of herself.

Raiden shrugged. "Anubis is notoriously tight-lipped on the subject, which means the stories are only that - conjecture and no more. To see 'heavy heart' written here, however... I would guess it a reference to a soul who has been damned."

Liria studied again the dead woman, taking note of the unevenly written glyphs that repeated over and over across her face, then turned to glare at the serpentine corpse behind her. "Is it the woman here who is damned, or that creature?"

"I have no idea." Raiden shuddered, angling his body away from the serpent who had turned his kiss into an attack. Golden eyes roved the garden, and his frown deepened. "Where is everybody?"

"I hope you're not expecting an actual answer to that." Liria snorted. "I know naught of Selekhet's temple regimes."

"There is a break in the early evening for the temples, but there should still be guards," he muttered. "Particularly here."

"Particularly here? Why?"

"The Temple of Bast is Selekhet's primary place of healing," Raiden answered. His wings flared for balance as he moved unsteadily towards a door set into the side of the Temple. "It's attached to the Temple of Sekhmet, where many of our warriors are trained."

Liria's brows shot up. "A hospital attached to a military facility?"

"The goddesses Bast and Sekhmet are twin sisters. Both are

warriors, but one is a protector and healer, the other a master of weapons. They appear to be opposites but work arm in arm in all things - each of our healers has a warrior partner, and they toil together for the greater good." Raiden wrapped his hands around the heavy door handle and yanked it open. "Come on."

The temple's foyer was nowhere near the grand affair Liria had anticipated. The vaulted ceilings and swathes of marble were present, but it was a place that was functional as much as it was elegant, with comfortable waiting areas, private consultation rooms and a single, central desk which, though she couldn't read the hieroglyphs carved into the sign overhead, was clearly meant to be the temple's information hub. Cleansing incense hung in the air, along with a sense of peace unlike any other hospital Liria had ever visited.

A human woman looked up from the desk as they approached, wearing simple robes in the same gentle olive green as the two dead women outside. Her smile widened as she saw Raiden and she raised a hand to smooth back her sleek blonde hair.

"Prince of Merged Egypt," she greeted him, bowing in her chair. "How may I be of service?"

Raiden's wings flared wide, then shut with a snap. "I need the High Priestess and her partner. Now."

The woman's eyes had followed the movement of his wings; now they widened. "Of course."

Liria watched as the woman turned to one of the many screens on her desk, tapped a few of the glowing glyphs, then laid her palm flat on the surface. The humming machine chimed a gentle response. The woman smiled again at Raiden, her expression a little more tentative, and relaxed visibly when he nodded.

"Sit with me," the Prince murmured.

Though Liria wished to be anywhere other than close to Raiden in that moment, she could see the fine tremor in his muscles. Should another attack occur, there was no telling if he'd have the energy to defend himself - so she inclined her head and led the way to the empty waiting area, deliberately choosing a backless chair that would suit only a single occupant. If Raiden noticed, he gave no sign, slinging his body across a chaise lounge and closing his eyes with a sigh.

Liria clasped her fingers in her lap, adjusted her wings more comfortably behind her, and waited. The temple remained peaceful, the woman at the desk bending her head to her work and the soft tinkling of running water harmonising with the sound of Raiden's breathing. His chest rose and fell rhythmically but Liria could hear his blood swishing urgently in his veins, vanquishing whatever remained of the poison he'd ingested with the serpentine creature's kiss.

Though he'd been the victim of an attempted murder, Liria found her temper sparking. Why in the world had he let that strange woman seal her lips to his? Was he in the habit of passionately embracing every person he came across? Was it some strange Egyptian custom she didn't know about? Liria frowned. She knew too little of the culture to say for certain, and the only person she felt comfortable enough to ask was Raiden - at least, before she'd seen him with another woman's hands tight in his hair, his head tilted for intimacy and his lashes dark across bronze cheeks.

Stop it, she scolded, unsheathing her talons just enough to dig into the backs of her hands. *Nothing good will come of this line of thinking.*

Yet her eyes burned as she examined the way his wings draped across the back of the chaise and spread over the floor, her jaw clenching in an effort to keep her breath from hitching in hurt. Stupid to remember how he'd cradled her against that broad, muscular chest. Stupid to think how warm he'd been, how delectable the hard lines of his body had felt fitted against her softer ones. Stupid to dream of his lips, warm and demanding against hers in the cool loneliness of her cell. In that moment, Liria didn't need the Princess Ione's compulsion - she wanted to kill Raiden of her own accord.

His life was saved by the musical creak of a door, the swish of robes and the murmur of low voices. The Prince of Merged Egypt opened his eyes, their deep gold focussing on Liria's face. She pretended not to notice as she stood, smoothing skirts stained with blood and vomit, her gaze trained on the marble floor as Raiden rolled to his feet at her side. When he stepped forward, Liria stayed quietly in his shadow, listening to the exchange of pleasantries whilst cataloguing what her other senses divulged.

The first newcomer was a woman, tall and slender and beautiful, with mahogany skin, pointed black cat's ears and a slinky black cat's tail. Deep brown hair in an elegant yet functional braid fell almost to her knees, and she watched the world through slitted cat's eyes the same olive green as her Temple gown. Beside her stood a man with skin of an even darker shade, his close-cropped black hair highlighting tawny lion ears and his warrior leathers matching the tawny yellow of his tufted lion's tail. Magic cycled constantly from one to the other and back again, creating an aura of strength and peace that permeated the atmosphere around them.

"Liria, meet Vargon and Hetessa, the High Priest of Sekhmet and the High Priestess of Bast." Raiden's wing slid behind Liria's shoulders and swept her forward so that she stood at his side. "This, your Holinesses, is the Lady of Shadows, Liria Atlannon. She has come to us from Atlantis with the Princess Ione, and will be joining the Pharaoh's Guard once the Princess is your Queen."

"An honour." The two spoke in unison, their voices in perfect harmony.

Liria smiled her well-practised court smile and curtseyed, eyes on the floor by their feet. "The honour is mine."

"How may we be of service to you, Prince of Merged Egypt? Do you require aid?" High Priestess Hetessa raised her hands, palms out.

Couldn't she sense the way Raiden's body shimmered with fever as it threw off the last of the poison? She was a healer, after all. Liria fought the urge to curl her lip - or worse, to slap Hetessa's hands away.

"I'm fine," Raiden answered, his wing tightening around Liria's shoulder as though he sensed her irritation. "I'm wondering why your gardens are so empty."

"Oh? It's ascension day," Hetessa replied, chuckling. "All acolytes are preparing for their vows, and the rest of the staff - of both Temples - are setting up the ceremony and the feast."

Vargon's warrior eyes were narrowed on Raiden's face. "Something is wrong."

In quick, succinct sentences, Raiden explained what lay outside in the garden. Hetessa gasped, her fingers curling into her partner's - who promptly raised her knuckles to his lips and kissed them with the ease of long-term familiarity. The High Priestess relaxed at once and Liria's curiosity spiked. These two were partners in every sense of the word, it seemed.

Vargon wasted no time summoning four pairs of partnered Priests and Priestesses, those of Bast in their olive robes and those of Sekhmet in the same tawny leathers as the High Priest wore. Together, they followed Raiden outside, giving Liria an excellent excuse to melt to the back of the garden, watching as the small gathering examined both dead bodies.

"Excuse me... Lady of Shadows, isn't it?"

Liria turned to the woman who'd stepped up beside her. She wore olive healer's robes and had a pair of soft grey cat's ears poking out of mousy brown hair that had been braided into a coronet atop her head. Her eyes were a pale blue, just light enough to be remarkable without drawing too much attention. She didn't seem much older than Liria but wore a distinctly maternal smile, her face softened by years of love and care.

"That is the title your Prince insists upon giving me," Liria answered politely.

"I am Safiyah." The woman's smile lit her eyes, her face turning from pretty to lovely in a heartbeat. Gentleness seeped out of her every pore, and Liria wasn't sure if she wanted to protect the woman, or ask her for a hug and a cookie. "Welcome to Selekhet."

"Thank you."

"You're guarding the Prince while he's unwell?" Safiyah asked, watching as Raiden waved both his arms and his wings while he spoke animatedly with Vargon.

Liria blinked. "So, a Priestess whose healing gift is active. I'd begun to wonder."

It wasn't a polite response, but Safiyah laughed gently and patted Liria's arm in a maternal fashion.

"My brethren are conserving their energies for tonight's celebrations." The woman's eyes twinkled. "Unfortunately for me, I cannot switch my senses off."

"You won't be at the celebration?"

"No, I'm excused. I have a daughter waiting for me at home," Safiyah said, her chest swelling with love and pride. "My partner - my sister - will go in both our steads."

"So not all partnerships here are romantic?"

Safiyah laughed softly. "Oh, no, though it does happen, as you can see from the High Priest and Priestess. Mostly we're friends, sometimes already blood relatives." The healer's shoulders drooped as she looked upon the dead bodies. "These two were due to ascend tonight. So young."

"They were partners?" Liria asked, looking from the dead priestess to the serpent creature and back again.

"No, no. Partners are one healer, one warrior, never two of the same." Safiyah's lips firmed. "They were friends, however, and spent a lot of time together. I don't know how Thissish could go through with such a horrid thing."

Liria narrowed her eyes. "Will you tell me about Thish... Thissssshhi... I'm sorry, I do not think I can pronounce a name that sounds like it needs two forked tongues to manage."

"Thissish came to us claiming to be predominantly human with mild ties to Sobek - the crocodile god of healing and protection," Safiyah added, smiling at Liria's confused expression.

"Though I recognise her body, she did not look like that during her time here."

"In my experience, crocodiles do not have forked serpent's tongues."

"No." Safiyah frowned. "We will need an embalmer to confirm, but I'd wager she carries the blood of Apophis, the serpent demon."

"A demon?"

The healer nodded. "Yes, a great serpent hidden in the depths of Mu. He thrives on the dark and has made trouble for Ra, the god of the sun, on multiple occasions. Set was sent to dispatch him years ago and though the serpent hasn't been seen since, rumours have crept across the Merged lands that the god of war and chaos didn't kill Apophis, but kept him for himself."

"How does a demon make merged children?"

Safiyah's mouth twisted. "With the help of a god, of course."

Set. Liria stared at the dead serpent creature and shivered. Though Safiyah's chatter had been pure conjecture, the words settled like stones in Liria's gut. Thanking the healer for her time, she gathered her skirts and strode to Raiden's side. When she tugged his arm, he bent so she could set her lips against his ear and curled his wing around them to further shield the conversation.

"How soon can we get an embalmer to examine the creature's body?" Liria asked quietly.

Raiden's smile was little more than a thin curling of the corners of his mouth. "As soon as I snap my fingers."

"We need someone discreet."

"I agree." He chewed his lower lip a moment, then nodded. "I know someone. Young, but strong in his skills."

"Tell him to look for the blood of Apophis."

"Apophis?" Raiden blinked, then his eyes went wide. "Set."

"It could be a coincidence."

"I've never believed in those." The Prince of Egypt rumbled deep in his chest, gold eyes narrowing. "How sure are you?"

"I know nothing of Apophis himself, but I know rot when I smell it." Liria jerked her chin towards the dead thing on the ground. "This was no person but a puppet of evil, sent here with one purpose: death and chaos."

Raiden raised his fingers to his lips and swallowed. "I believe you."

TAKING THE CROWN

Raiden stood on the private balcony outside his bedroom and fumed. He should be getting ready for Taos' wedding - Yrini was due to fetch him in less than half an hour - but instead, he stood in the cool moments before dawn with a towel wrapped around his hips, water from the shower trickling down his chest and his wings half spread as though he was about to launch into the air.

Three days had passed since his visit to the rooftop market with Liria. Three days in which she'd done her level best to avoid seeing him more than absolutely necessary, and been largely successful at managing it.

Upon returning from the Temple with both dead bodies in tow, Raiden had wasted no time summoning Balai and the embalmer had promptly ensconced himself in the sacred chambers below the Palace to do what he did best. Liria had been subdued when they returned to the Pharaoh's suite to find Taos and Ione deep in conversation with Anubis. When Ione announced that she'd given permission for the Soulcatcher to research ways to lessen the crippling demands of the soulbinding, Liria had barely even blinked; merely inclined her head and murmured her thanks, then excused herself to shower and rest -

leaving Raiden to tell the tale of their adventures while his Pharaoh, the Princess and the god of death had listened in astonished silence.

Liria had been given leave to train with the honour guard and she'd done so, turning up to every session like clockwork, putting in the effort required, and then somehow managing to slip away whilst Raiden was distracted with one of the others. Whenever he went looking for her, she was either with the Princess Ione or General Barin, going over details for the wedding. Once, he'd cornered her in Balai's rooms downstairs, but the embalmer had interrupted to give them what little information he'd gleaned from the dead bodies - and whilst Raiden had dutifully conveyed that information to Anubis and Horus via the new and somewhat terrifying divine mental highway, Liria had taken her leave and disappeared. Again.

Raiden snarled and slammed his fists down on the carved railing of his balcony. Tiny chips of stone flew every which way and when he lifted his hands, there was a clear indentation where his blows had landed. That, too, had been plaguing him the last few days - almost everything he touched, he crushed, smashed, cracked, shattered or pulverised without meaning to. His senses had finished their torturous sliding and settled; far more sensitive than he was used to. It had taken over twenty-four hours to learn *not* to hear every heartbeat in a three-room radius and he'd almost passed out twice from subconsciously holding his breath to lessen the impact of scenting... everything. His vision had been the easiest to handle, once the blasted blurring and the motion sickness it created had subsided, but he'd developed a rather frustrating habit of being distracted by fine details that had been unnoticeable before, like the sparkling flecks of silicate trapped in the sandstone of the Palace, or the individual fibres which twined together in the woven carpet on his bedroom floor.

"My Prince?"

"What?" He spun around in time to see Yrini flinch and jerk away. "What is it?"

The other angel rubbed her eyes. "Gods, I... you're so fast. I didn't even see you turn."

Yes, he was something other now. Something that made even his closest friends startle, watching out of the corners of their eyes as though he'd combust at any moment. Thunder rumbled in the far distance and Yrini's eyes flicked nervously to the sky before returning to Raiden's face.

"I brought you some breakfast," she said slowly, as though he might have gone deaf. "Our Pharaoh was worried you'd forget to eat before you join him."

"Fine."

Yrini opened her mouth, closed it, opened it again. "Should I go?"

Raiden looked her up and down. She was already dressed in ceremonial leathers, her weapons polished to a sheen and her pale blonde hair elegantly coiffed. Her wings, predominantly white with a hint of pale grey at the outer edges, were held tight to her back and her pale blue eyes shimmered with concern.

"You can stay if you're not going to stink of fear when I throw my breakfast at the wall," Raiden said at last.

Yrini, an angel he'd played with as a child and a woman he'd considered a friend as well as a sister in arms, blanched and took another step back. "My Prince... you haven't been yourself lately."

"I know."

"I don't... I'm not sure..."

"Just go, Rin." His anger left him on a sigh, and Raiden turned to stare back out at the approaching dawn. It reminded him of Liria, which only served to make his melancholy worse. "And for what it's worth, I'm sorry."

Combat boots rang on the smoothly polished stone floor, her scent a swirl of delicate floral perfume as Yrini closed the distance to lay a gentle hand on his arm. "No, Raiden. It's I who should apologise. Being given the blood of the gods wasn't your choice, and these reactions while your new body settles are not your fault. It's just..."

"Terrifying?"

"Yeah." She huffed a humourless laugh. "What do you need?"

Like he was going to admit to anyone out loud what - who - he needed. Drawing another deep, calming breath, Raiden muttered, "Coffee."

"Get dressed while I make it - if you're a good little angel, I'll even hold the mug so you can drink it without breaking something." Her teasing was tentative, but there was no fear in her scent and when Raiden turned to look down, Yrini's blue eyes were laughing.

He growled, making sure the sound was good natured, and stalked back inside to get dressed. After all, brooding didn't solve anything and his brother was getting married in little over an hour. Once that was done, Raiden's time would be his own... and he and a certain shadow had some unfinished business to resolve.

Yrini made coffee as promised, though he didn't let her hold the cup - instead, Raiden set it on the kitchen bench and drank through a straw without using his hands, while his friend laughed herself stupid. After she'd watched him eat his omelette - which he ended up doing with his hands after ruining two forks and a spoon - Yrini gave him a sisterly kiss on the cheek and left to meet her husband and the rest of the honour guard, while Raiden swept next door to collect the Pharaoh.

Taos looked resplendent in billowing cream silk pants cuffed at the ankles with beaten gold, a matching belt and ceremonial khopesh on his hip. His collar was made of gleaming golden panels set with emeralds and accented by enamel in shades of green that ranged from a gentle new grass right through to deep forest. Upon his head he wore the double crown that had been their father's, two circlets of gold with a large ankh in the centre and a pair of golden angel wings on either side.

"I've not seen that in years," Raiden murmured, raising his

hand and then snatching it back at the last moment. The last thing he needed was to crush a family heirloom with his unpredictable strength; particularly on the morning of his Pharaoh's wedding.

Taos brushed self-conscious fingers down the ankh that sat heavy against his forehead. "I thought perhaps it was time."

"Yes. It will be like he's standing beside us." Raiden swallowed and though his next words hurt, he forced them out. "Will you give Mother's to Ione?"

"No." Taos shook his head. "I had something made for her. Mother's crown... I thought you might wear it, my brother."

"*Me?*"

Taos looked up from beneath his lashes, brown eyes vulnerable in the flickering light of the torches that lined his room. "We both know that I've never ruled alone. Today, of all days, I want you beside me in both roles."

Raiden choked back his instinctive denial, his heart hammering in his chest as Taos fetched the golden crown which was a smaller, but no less impressive, replica of their father's. "I'm already Prince of Egypt."

"As my heir, yes - but now you carry the blood of the gods. Once this hits your head, you are both my heir and a ruler in your own right - and I think we both know it's time."

"I..." Raiden stared down at the green velvet pillow which cradled his mother's crown and swallowed hard. "And when Ione is crowned Queen?"

"She will be equal to you in authority, with the two of you below me." Taos took a deep breath, blew it out slowly. "I'd like to make her my partner in all ways, but for all I care for Ione, I don't truly know her. There must be balance for our people, above all else."

And if Raiden accepted this official crown, cementing his title as Prince of Merged Egypt in an official capacity on the same day Ione accepted hers, they became a triumvirate whom the people could depend upon - and Taos would never have to walk alone.

"I don't want to lose the honour guard," he whispered. "If I do this, I won't become a figurehead."

"I'd not dream of taking them from you; besides, Liria will become part of their number, allowing you to lead from the front without losing a member."

"All right." Closing his eyes lest his brother see how much this new burden weighed, Raiden inclined his head. He'd fought for years to stay in the background, but the truth of his new blood hung between them; if Taos didn't do something to acknowledge - and claim - Raiden's power for his own, rumours about the Prince's allegiance would start to swirl.

"By the power vested in me as Pharaoh of Merged Egypt and Avatar of the Gods, I, Taos Horushood, crown you, Raiden Horushood, as the true Prince of Merged Egypt and bestow upon you the title Prince of the Skies." Cool gold settled against Raiden's forehead, the double crown shifting with its own innate magic to fit over his head as though made for it. "May you rule with wisdom and grace, brother."

Tears spangled Raiden's lashes when they opened, and he saw the same reflected in his brother's eyes. "I shall endeavour to make you proud, my Pharaoh."

"You do so every day." Taos stepped forward and they exchanged a tight embrace, faces turned into each other's necks as their tears fell in unison. "I would not be the Pharaoh I am without you by my side."

"Thank you." Raiden stepped back, knuckling away the last of his tears. "Why Prince of the Skies?"

"Horus is god of the sky and you carry his blood, do you not?" Taos smiled, using a rag to dab at his tears lest he smear the thick kohl around his eyes. His brow furrowed. "You've not done your makeup."

"I forgot," Raiden admitted. "It's been a strange few days."

Taos waved a hand and Raiden immediately dropped to his

knees, flaring his wings for balance. He held still while his older brother applied kohl to the top and bottom of both eyelids, followed by a smudge of dark green that gave his golden eyes a smoky backdrop. When Taos finished, his hand lingered on Raiden's jaw, his gaze tracking up to the crown which was no longer their mother's but his own.

"I see her every time I look at it," Taos murmured - and though there was grief in his voice, there was also a cautious joy. "They are both with us today."

"And every day from now on," Raiden muttered. "It's bad enough you've forced one crown on my head - I'll not be forming a collection."

Taos laughed, and just like that, they were as they'd always been - brothers, united against the world. "Will you scold me as Mother did, too?"

"Likely." Raiden grinned and resumed his feet. "Come now, Avatar of the Gods. It's time for your wedding."

LIVING MEMORY

LIRIA STOOD WITH A nervous Princess Ione in a luxurious antechamber in the heart of the Temple of Osiris. Her strapless dress was a deep, Atlantean aqua, the skirts a shimmering fall of elegant silk scarves and the bodice a tight, low-necked confection that Ione would never have condoned were they still in Atlantis. The cape which normally hid her wings was conspicuously absent, the decision made by a Princess who wanted a pair of wings to showcase in opposition to those of the angels, even if they were only the wings of her shadow. With her wings out and her hair piled atop her head in a delicate bundle of curls, Liria Atlannon had never felt more exposed.

The only consolation was that Ione shone brighter than sunlight on the ocean, her dress a pale aqua lace over puffed silk skirts that made her look like walking sea foam. Her ebony hair hung in thick, soft waves down her back, with the comb Liria had gifted her set above one temple. An elegant silver chain graced her throat, from which dangled an enormous pearl - one Ione had found herself upon the shores of Atlantis when she was but a child, and the only personal item she'd brought with her from her homeland.

General Barin looked equal parts resigned and refined in his Atlantean chain mail and a silver-embroidered tunic the same colour as Liria's dress. He'd combed his salt and pepper hair neatly and exchanged functional weapons for more ornate ones, his spine stiff and his bearing that of a warrior who found formal occasions wearing at best and deadly boring at worst.

"My Princess," he murmured, holding out a hand as someone knocked on the door. "It is time."

Liria dutifully scooped up the train of Ione's dress and followed her into the temple, keeping her head bowed and her eyes on the floor while her senses spread through the cavernous room. The main section of the Temple of Osiris had three open walls supported by carved columns, with lush garden beds flowing across the floor in a way that invited long walks and contemplation. The domed roof above was a living mural, with a team of artists working daily to alter it in accordance with the seasons and the weather, reflecting the many facets of Merged Egypt and the god-king who watched over them all.

Osiris himself, tall and broad and divinely handsome, stood atop a dais with his wife Isis at his side, each of them resplendent in white and gold, their black hair liquid silk and their eyes bright with joy. The crowd at the base of the dais spread out into the streets as the entirety of Selekhet tried to gather close enough to see the ceremony, regardless of the fact that Lemurian technology was broadcasting the wedding on every available wall, screen and surface throughout Merged Egypt.

Murmurs ran through the crowd as Ione appeared, and though Liria couldn't see, she sensed Taos and the unmistakable, crackling aura of Raiden approaching from the opposite end of the dais. She shivered, wondering how nobody else was reacting to the energy swirling around the Prince of Egypt, energy that carried the tang of an oncoming storm and reached to caress Liria's skin from halfway across the room. Why hadn't he been taught to control it?

Ione stiffened ahead, and the murmurs in the crowd became

more pronounced; even Osiris' face flickered with surprise. Liria had to wait until she was able to step into her allotted place slightly behind and to the side of the Princess to see - Raiden wore the double crown of Merged Egypt upon his brow, albeit a smaller version of the Pharaoh's.

"My avatar," Osiris boomed, his voice causing the walls of the Temple to tremble. "Have you talked your brother into a crown at long last?"

"I have, King of Kings." Taos swept a bow that was elegant without being subservient, his face wreathed in a smile. "May I present to you my brother, Raiden Horushood, Crown Prince of Merged Egypt, newly titled Prince of the Skies?"

"Prince of the Skies!" Osiris' delighted laughter shook the earth around them, and his hand clapped like thunder as it landed heavily against Raiden's shoulders. "A perfect title for the pinnacle of angelkind."

"Your divine grace is too kind," Raiden rumbled, his voice rich as rolling thunder as he bowed his head. He wore billowing silk pants in Selekhet's palm frond green, with an elegant gold belt and his two favourite khopesh swords in sleek golden scabbards. The long, draping shawl he usually wore was absent, his chest a breathtaking sculpture of muscle decorated with a golden collar reminiscent of his brother's, though far less ostentatious. With the golden double crown of Merged Egypt atop his dark hair he appeared handsome, strong, and so far beyond Liria's reach it hurt to look at him.

"Welcome, Prince of the Skies," Isis said, her soft, rolling voice no less audible than her husband's. She stepped forward and pressed a kiss to Raiden's cheek. "Blood of my blood, you are the link between worlds."

A gasp went through the Temple and Liria knew that before the day was done, rumours about Raiden's new powers would triple as people tried to work out the exact meaning of Isis' words. If the Prince of Egypt cared, he gave no sign, simply brushed his lips to the goddess' cheek.

"Mother of my bloodsire," he rumbled. "You honour me."

"Now," Osiris raised both arms, as though to embrace the whole world. "We are here for a wedding, are we not?"

Raiden grinned and stepped back as the Pharaoh and the Princess Ione were ushered into the centre of the dais. He tried to catch Liria's eye, separated as they were by only a few feet of space he could have easily covered should he extend a wing - but Liria kept her eyes on the hem of her skirts and the Prince of Merged Egypt kept his wings uncharacteristically still. When she didn't react to his presence, Raiden turned his eyes forward and something inside Liria wilted. Relief, she told herself; it was relief.

The wedding was wonderful and elegant without being ostentatious, ending with the groom placing a delicate golden crown on his bride's head, coronating his Queen as she became his wife. Nobody, least of all Ione, missed the fact that the crown was a match for Raiden's rather than for the Pharaoh's.

"I now pronounce you man, wife, Pharaoh and Queen," Osiris cried.

Cheers flooded Selekhet as Taos took Ione's face in his hands and kissed her, the tension in her shoulders melting in the face of his unhidden affection. Liria closed her eyes and drew a trickle of power around herself, muffling the onslaught of sound - and when she noted that Raiden's body trembled, she extended the shield to him, too.

The Prince of the Skies startled and began to turn in her direction - and then stood firm as he was supposed to, the muscles in his face tight. Liria's heart thundered unnaturally loud in her chest as the Pharaoh and his Queen began to descend from the dais, arm in arm, and Liria moved to lay her hand on Raiden's wrist as custom dictated. While they followed the royal couple, he leant down close enough to whisper a gentle thank-you in her ear.

Throat tight, Liria managed the barest nod.

Somehow, she made her way through the organised chaos of

the elegant reception without standing on anyone or getting stood on in return. She picked at her meal just enough to be polite, participated in the remaining rituals and blessings as was required, then retreated gratefully towards the edge of the garden when the celebration moved outside. Guests threaded to and fro, glittering gowns and shimmering weapons no impediment to the good cheer that permeated the gathering. Liria bumped into a tall warrior with dusty teal skin and the biggest sword she'd ever seen, keeping her gaze downcast as she murmured an apology and sought deeper cover. She'd be far happier if she retired to her bed but duty dictated she keep Ione in sight until her new husband whisked her away, so she found a quiet, shady spot beneath the broad boughs of a foreign fruit tree and settled in to wait.

"You're a hard woman to catch, Lady of Shadows."

The voice was a low, rich rumble, sinking into her bones. Liria sighed. "Your energy is so thick it's impossible for you to sneak up on a blind, deaf old man, let alone a shadow, Crown Prince of Merged Egypt."

"Oh?" Raiden stepped out of the garden behind her, pressing a tall, cool glass into her hands and sipping from his matching one. "Faugh. Dessert wine."

Liria sipped and smiled. "It's lovely and sweet."

"Honeyed beer is better."

"I've never tried Egypt's unique beer, so I have no data with which to compare." She glanced off into the distance. "Congratulations on your ascension, my Prince."

"Don't," he growled, the rumble turning dark. "I never wanted it."

"If I were you," Liria murmured, lowering her voice so that it were barely audible, "I wouldn't say that where the Queen can hear you."

"She's mad?"

"Furious." Liria sipped her wine, examining the muted impressions that were filtering through the compulsion. Drawing a deep breath, she said, "Ione is filled with both anger and hurt. She came to be Queen, and she is not."

"She is," Raiden answered. "Queen of everyone but myself and Taos."

"You know what I mean, Prince of the Skies."

Raiden grimaced. "I do, but what would you have of us? Taos likes Ione, wants to love her, I think - but he doesn't know her. To hand her equal power over Egypt would be a fool's move. This way, we are equal at his side."

"Even so, no-one likes to be so thoroughly shown their place, particularly at their own wedding."

"Taos forced the crown on me because I now carry the blood of a god," Raiden growled, flexing his free hand. "Being his heir is no longer enough - if he didn't put some sort of very public and very ceremonial leash on me, it would cause rumours that I might threaten his power. If Ione can't see that, she's more petty and jealous than I thought."

Liria paused, swallowing her instinctive reply to consider his words. "Damn. You're right."

"Damn?" He blinked, then offered a lopsided grin that threatened to cut her open. "Did you just say damn?"

"I know all sorts of interesting words; I just rarely use them." Liria rubbed a hand over her brow, melancholy stealing through her bones. "I wish that I could leave this party."

Storm clouds raced across the Prince's expression. "So eager to be rid of me?"

"Pardon?"

"You - and everyone else - have been running from me for days," Raiden muttered. "I'm starting to think I must smell."

"You smell -" Liria cut off, sipping her wine to hide the jump in her pulse. No matter the pain in him, no matter that it reached out to her, she needed to keep her distance if she had any hope of surviving in this new place, this new life.

"What?" Raiden turned to her so fast that wine sloshed over

the rim of his glass and dripped down the back of his hand. "What do you smell?"

For the first time in days, Liria raised her eyes to his. Deep, beaten gold, sparking with a power that had been absent when they'd first met - and filled with fear and uncertainty. Vulnerability. With a word, she could cut their relationship off completely, set him free forever, protect herself behind the walls of ice his very presence threatened to destroy.

Gods help her, but she couldn't do it.

"Warm sand and burning sunlight," she whispered. "You smell of the desert, the sun, and the slightest hint of a brewing storm."

"Is that bad?"

"It's what you usually smell like, with a little more intensity," Liria hedged. She wanted to tear her gaze from his, couldn't. "The storm edge comes and goes. I'd hazard a guess it's contingent on your energy levels."

Raiden went to run a hand through his hair, discovered his crown in the way, and bared his teeth in irritation. Liria watched his glorious chest work itself into deep, calming breaths, his voice once more a low rumble as he said, "Why have you been avoiding me?"

"I've been busy with my duties."

"Don't bullshit me, Liria," he snarled, wings shifting restlessly. "I walk into a room, you walk out of it. Ever since that damned serpent creature tried to kill me with her poison mouth..." Raiden's eyes went wide. "That's what it is. You're mad because she touched me."

"No."

"I don't believe you."

"Irrelevant." Liria closed her eyes tight. "You may kiss whoever you want. It is none of my business."

"Fuck." His voice was rough with a thousand things she didn't understand. "Liria, my body went haywire in that temple garden. I couldn't see or hear or smell properly. That creature, whatever it was, emanated some sort of magic that mucked with my head. I couldn't think straight, much less anything else - and she kissed me, not the other way around."

Temper sparked, temper born of pain and a memory that was Liria's alone. Her eyes snapped open. "You could have pulled away."

"I tried. This is going to sound ludicrous, but she held me down with her tongue."

No, no, no, she couldn't think about that. Swallowing deep in her throat, Liria crossed both arms over her chest and went with the safer topic. "Your body's still not working properly, is it? I can feel the power crackling under your skin, building with every moment. If you don't learn to control it, it will boil out of you when least expected."

"Power?" He frowned. "You mean magic?"

Liria shrugged. "Power, magic, energy; choose your term. It's all the same in the end."

"Am I dangerous?"

"Since nobody but me seems to have noticed? Definitely." Liria wafted her hand through the air between them, so thick with energy that the hairs on her arm stood on end. "Unless you've been very good at hiding the evidence, we have no idea what form your new powers are going to take. Anything could happen."

"What about you?" Raiden asked. When Liria quirked a brow, his wings hunched closer to his body. "Now that Ione and Taos are married, you're part of my honour guard. We'll be working far more closely together than we have so far, closer than any of the other members. Am I dangerous to you?"

Oh, yes, but not in the way he thought. Liria forced herself to breathe, though his scent was all around her, causing her straining heart to tremble. "Nobody is dangerous to me, Crown Prince of Merged Egypt. I'm a shadow. From what I can measure, we could fight all day and all night and all day again, and neither one could kill the other. I'm not afraid of you."

The glass in his hand shattered, but Raiden's eyes were closed and his face so relieved Liria knew he hadn't noticed. She used a quick sweep of power to banish the fine shards of glass, frowning at the cuts in his skin. His blood welled thick and dark, mingling with the wine he'd spilt, and she knew even before she did it that she was about to do something hugely, incredibly stupid.

Setting her glass aside, Liria blurred their bodies with magic, lifted Raiden's hand in both of hers and licked her tongue across his bleeding skin.

He'd frozen at her first touch, his breathing turning more ragged with every movement of her mouth against his palm, but Liria didn't stop. He could be revolted later; now, she was going to heal him, and enjoy every single drop of his powerful, alcohol-laced blood in the process.

"Liria," he said as she closed the final cut. "I have a confession."

Her task finished, she rested her forehead against his wrist so he wouldn't see the torture in her eyes. "What?"

"That serpent creature... whatever spell she wove... I thought she was you." He cleared his throat. "Before the attempting to kill me part, that is."

Liria looked up, blinking. "Pardon?"

"You heard me." Golden eyes blazed into hers, the buildup of magic making them slightly luminous. "If what you saw hurt you, I'm sorry."

"I..." What now? Liria straightened slowly to her full height, shock thick in her veins. Still, he'd guessed the truth - there was little point hiding it. "Thank you. I accept your apology."

"I have something for you." Raiden reached into the pocket of his trousers and pulled out a small box. "May I?"

No, her heart said. This was too much, too soon, and it was all too confusing, too raw. Say no. "Yes."

"I saw this and I thought - that you might like it." The words tumbled out of him, his cheeks flagging pink as he flipped the box open.

The rings inside were simple, a stack of three silver bands which fitted together like a puzzle to form the shape of one of the eyes Liria had seen tiled onto the Pharaoh's courtyard floor.

"Oh," she murmured.

"This is one of the eyes of Horus," Raiden whispered, fingers trembling as he took the trio of silver rings from the box and slid them onto her left index finger one at a time. "It goes on your left hand because it's the left eye. This symbolises the phases of the moon, her healing energy and protective abilities... but mostly, it just makes me think of you."

Tears pricked Liria's eyes as she stared down at the neat stack of rings, the silverwork so intricate and elegant she knew it had been done by a master. She tried to step away, to gain some space, but the trunk of the tree was solid at her back, preventing escape.

"Why?" she whispered. "Why are you doing this to me?"

Raiden stepped in close, his body pressing hers into the bark of the tree, his lines hard and hot against her softer ones. The air around them crackled with electricity, his warm sand and burning sunlight scent filling her lungs. Thunder rumbled in the air - or was it his chest - and Liria could look nowhere else but into the burning intensity of his face.

"Because," Raiden murmured, very carefully placing his hands either side of her head and bending until his golden eyes were all she could see, "I wanted to."

Liria wasn't sure if her heart was going to burst or break. Tears streamed unbidden down her cheeks, her voice a rasp. "The Crown Prince of Merged Egypt should not give presents to shadows - and I have nothing to offer in return."

"Consider it an apology. My second, and most important apology for today."

"What? Why?"

"I forgot," he said, leaning so close his breath fanned her cheeks. "And it hurt you. I'm sorry."

"My Prince, I -"

"No. My name is Raiden. Just Raiden... and I remember everything."

Then his lips were sealing over hers, his hands tearing the pins from her hair until it cascaded over his hands. Liria melted, clinging to his shoulders as he pressed closer, heat and light and glorious life. Raiden's hands fisted in her curls and tilted her head for better access, his tongue teasing her lips until they parted for him to sweep inside. It was as good as she remembered - better, her heart slamming against the cage of her chest and her body screaming for the angel who held her with both incredible strength and tender care. She swept her tongue over his teeth and he shuddered, groaned; and all at once Liria realised her licking his wounds hadn't revolted him at all. In fact, if the pressure against her abdomen was what she thought it was, he was very, *very* pleased at this precise moment. He wanted her, and more importantly, he'd remembered their kiss in the cell.

Giving in to the honey in her blood, Liria slid her arms around his neck and kissed Raiden for all she was worth. Though she had no skill in the area, he didn't seem to mind. In fact, he growled into her mouth, thunder rumbling in his chest as his kisses turned desperate, one hand sliding down her ribs to press her lower body impossibly closer to his. Lost in the glorious sensation, Liria twisted her hands into his silken hair and bit down on his lower lip.

Lightning struck, shearing the tree behind her in two.

BLOOD AND WATER

Screams filtered through to Raiden's ears as though he were deep underwater. The sensation might have been disconcerting if his attention wasn't consumed by the woman in his arms, his wings curled around her in a protective embrace. When the lightning had struck, his only thought had been to keep her safe.

"Liria?" Raiden whispered, pulling back just enough to look down. "Are you all right?"

He was expecting confusion, perhaps fear, but their time apart had made him forget the sort of woman he was dealing with. Liria snapped her head up at the sound of his voice, violet eyes glittering with flecks of brighter purple and her skin no longer pale cream but gorgeous, stormy blue-grey.

"I told you what would happen if you didn't learn to control it," she growled, fangs flashing. "But did you listen? No, you had to go and blow up your brother's wedding."

"What?" Raiden started to straighten, froze when she sagged in his loosening grip. "Liria?" Taloned fingers scrabbled weakly at his formal gold collar and Raiden swept her into his arms. "Are you hurt?"

"No, just used a lot of magic." She sighed, resting her head against his shoulder. "At least this has taken the edge off your energy."

What in the name of the Merged worlds was she talking about? Raiden folded back his wings to assess the situation, brows drawing into a frown. "My eyes must not be working. Everything is fuzzy."

"Your eyes are working fine. That's my magic, blurring our image so nobody can see us." Liria took a deep, slow breath. "I don't have enough energy to completely disguise my true nature; you'll have to hide me somewhere."

Raiden growled deep in his chest. "I won't."

"Raiden, I'm a monster," Liria snapped. "You can't take me over there."

He still wasn't sure where 'there' was, but he flared his wings in a show of temper and glared down at her. "I can't speak for Atlantis, but Selekhet is full of strange and wonderful creatures. Let go the illusion, Liria. You're no more a monster than I."

"Queen Ione will be angry."

"Fuck Ione."

Her eyes went wide, and then Liria laughed. "That's supposed to be your brother's job. All right, Prince of the Skies, have it your way - but don't say I didn't warn you."

"Just Raiden." He lifted her body even as he lowered his head, coaxing her lips with soft, suckling kisses. "You don't kiss someone and then call them by some stuffy, royal title. In fact, every time you use one of mine, I'm going to kiss you until you scream my name - my real name - and I won't care who's watching. Got it?"

Liria's eyes widened even further, growing impossibly large in her fairy face. Her bone structure lengthened, cheekbones becoming more pronounced and her chin pixie-like while the points of her ears sharpened where they poked through her unbound hair.

"And now?" she murmured. "Now that you see me without so much as a hint of the transformation Ione requires?" Her gaze tracked down to his lips. "Do you still wish to kiss me like this, Crown Prince of Merged Egypt?"

Raiden growled and claimed Liria's mouth for his own, holding her close. Carrying her meant he couldn't fist his hands in her hair or stroke her as he longed to do, so he settled for clenching one fist in her skirts, the other splayed down the length of her ribs as his wings curved tight around them.

"Gods, Liria," he gasped, tearing away before he took her right there on the ground. "You can't do that to me. I won't make it."

"Just checking if it was as good as I remembered." Her fingers reached to trace the line of his jaw, leaving fire in their wake. "I've never kissed anyone else, so there's little data with which to compare."

Something primal inside Raiden rumbled in satisfaction even as another part of him faltered. Her first kiss, in a prison cell, while he'd been a half-mad, half-dead apparition... and he'd forgotten it. No wonder she'd been so angry, so *hurt*. He wouldn't have told him what he'd done, either. Raiden opened his mouth to beg forgiveness - though how he could make up for what he'd done, he didn't know - when the faint but unmistakable sound of his brother's voice filtered in from somewhere far, far away.

"I can feel Ione calling," Liria said at the same time. Her hand dropped from his face, her eyes turning outward. "Brace yourself."

As warnings went, it was succinct, if understated. Raiden flinched as the fog dissipated, arching his wings as though to block the sudden frenzy of sound and scent that flooded in from every direction. He hadn't given much thought to their location, but saw now that they stood less than ten paces from the smoking ruin of the fruit tree, just outside the crowd of wedding guests trying to get a better look at the destruction. Taos loosed a shout of relief as he spotted them, spreading brown and white wings with a snap. Courtiers jumped back in surprise as he pushed out of the throng, covering the distance to Raiden's side in a single, elegant leap.

"Brother," he cried, grabbing Raiden's shoulders and peering up into his face. "Are you all right?"

Raiden couldn't answer; he was too busy staring at the tree. The lightning had struck true, disintegrating leaves and peeling the trunk open like a flower. More astonishing than that, however, was that the blackened ground and flung debris extended three paces out from the trunk in a perfect circle. Smoke curled from the wreckage, caressing the invisible demarcation line but not progressing beyond it. Only one section of the trunk remained, wilted but not destroyed, about the height of the fairy who'd been pressed against the wood as she'd bitten his lip and sent his pulse into the stratosphere.

And in that moment, Raiden knew - *he'd* called the lightning.

"Raiden." Liria's voice, so soft that only he and Taos heard it. When they both looked down, the fairy's face was soft with compassion. Shielded from the rest of the crowd by Taos' body and two sets of angel wings, Liria spread her hand across the hollow of Raiden's throat. "It wasn't your fault."

"Brother? What does she mean?" Taos asked, keeping his voice low.

Liria's eyes flickered, but she kept them trained on Raiden's face, deep pools of violet with brighter, glittering sparks. "The Pr - Raiden's transformation is complete, my Pharaoh. He has manifested the power of the storm. I was attempting to teach him to control his energy at a safe distance from the guests when his magic overflowed and called the lightning down upon us." Gentle fingers stroked the base of Raiden's throat again, sending a shiver down his spine. "Your brother whisked us away from the damage and I used my magic to control the explosion so that nobody was hurt."

"*I* got us away?" Raiden shook his head. "Nobody is that fast."

"We are," Liria said simply.

"My shadow!" Ione's voice, filled with panic, preceded some very non-Queenlike shoving as she forced her way between Raiden and Taos. Ocean dark eyes snapped with fury as she stared at the three of them, focussing finally on Liria. "What have you done? Why are you so exposed?"

"My love," Taos soothed, "your shadow defused a magical incident. She has done us a great service."

Ione shook her finger under Liria's nose, the scent of her fear spiralling swiftly into fury. "This is my *wedding*, shadow. You have no right to ruin it. Put your skin back on at once."

The slender fairy in Raiden's arm went stiff, her jaw clenching tight with pain. Slowly, so slowly, her skin and facial features began to change, her body shuddering with effort.

"Stop," Raiden said. "You're hurting her."

"My shadow knows the rules," Ione hissed, her eyes narrowed to slits. "There are *no* excuses." The Queen watched until Liria's change was complete, then gasped and snatched up her shadow's left hand. "What is this? I gave no permission for you to wear jewellery."

When the Queen made to slip the stack of rings from Liria's finger, Raiden shifted his grip to catch Ione's wrist. "I gave them to her."

"She is *mine*," Ione growled, her fury so palpable that Liria's body arched in Raiden's arms and then went limp, her lashes closed. The Queen let out a noise of frustration. "Now look what you've done. Release her at once."

"No."

"My love," Taos put his hand over Ione's, carefully drawing it free of Liria's skin. "Your shadow has fainted. Let Raiden take her to a healer, while we return to the party."

"She will wake as I command," Ione snapped, eyes flashing, "and she will remove those rings and give them to me. Shadows own nothing, particularly the artisan work of a master. Those trinkets are mine."

"*No*," Raiden growled, curling Liria's body closer to his chest.

Taos shot him a searing look. "My brother is well within his rights to gift Liria a token in honour of her entry to the honour guard, who will be responsible for protecting both of us. That is what the rings symbolise, my sweet wife - protection. As you are stepping into a new life, so Liria must adapt. What she wears on her finger will be proof of that. Doesn't it warm your heart to see her accepted among our people?"

Ione's nostrils flared, her chest rising and falling swiftly. "Liria is *mine*. Her duty is to *me*."

"And now you are part of me, and of Raiden - so her duties must expand." Taos' voice was gentle, his hands soothing as he cupped Ione's chin and lifted her face to his. He kissed her, a gentle coaxing of lips. After a long, stiff moment she relaxed into him, and Raiden examined the curls of the destroyed tree while his brother distracted the Queen with hints of teasing passion. Taos drew back and spoke in a velvety, bedroom tone, his gaze intent on Ione's. "Didn't we agree that this was best? For us and for Liria?"

A flicker in Ione's gaze, but she sighed. "Very well. Take her to a healer."

"Raiden?"

"It will be done." Raiden inclined his head to Taos, but not to Ione. After all, they were equals, and it was best he make that clear from the start.

"Thank you, Prince of Egypt," Ione said, her voice light - as though the altercation never happened. Leaning forward, she placed her lips to Liria's pointed ear and whispered something so soft Raiden couldn't catch the words. Pressing a kiss to the shadow's cheek, she curled her arm through Taos' and allowed him to lead her away.

Gallin appeared by Raiden's elbow, followed closely by Zsil, the sand sprite. As members of Taos' honour guard, they wore the same ceremonial leathers that Yrini had chosen for the wedding, their expressions warrior stern - though Zsil couldn't quite hide the sparkling merriment that was a sprite's true nature, his startling green eyes dancing in his serious face.

"Stay with our Pharaoh and his Queen," Raiden murmured, fixing each of his warriors with a firm look. "I'll come and see you when I can."

The two men bowed and fell into step behind the royal couple, Gallin with his vampire grace and Zsil with a cheerful spring in his step. Raiden strode to the edge of the crowd, trading a loaded look with Yrini as he went. She nodded and raised her glass in his direction, taking over his role without the need for long explanations.

Bending both knees and spreading his wings, Raiden threw himself into the air, Liria clutched tight to his chest. With a few strong downward strokes he was high above the Palace, Selekhet spread out below. The city nestled in the gentle embrace of the Nile river, with the glimmering ocean in the distance and the beating heat of the desert brushing the edge of the fertile farm-land that bordered the city's outskirts. While several of Selekhet's buildings were tall, the Palace rose above them all, a glittering triumph of both Lemurian and Egyptian effort, built by the first Merged Pharaoh on the very spot that contact was made with Osiris, god of the Earth and King of Kings. That sacred piece of Merged space still existed, deep beneath the heart of the Palace; no longer a meeting place between Egypt and Lemuria but a sanctuary of healing and peace.

It was toward this heart that Raiden flew, sweeping past open windows and inviting balconies to land in an immaculately mani-cured courtyard. Lush greenery cradled a wide, intricately mosaiced path leading to an ornate set of double doors set into the side of the Palace, perpetually thrown open in welcome. Tucking his wings close, Raiden shot through the doorway to land in the Sacred Heart of Selekhet.

The round chamber where gods and humans had once met was an elegant blend of carved columns and soothing artwork, with a shallow fountain in the centre marking out the exact size of the original Merge space. What had once been guest wings surrounding the chamber had been transformed; on the east side stood the Palace healing temple, and on the west side, the embalming temple.

Raiden strode straight to the sacred fountain and stepped over the edge, dropping immediately to his knees. The water in the Merged Fountain was not just sacred; it carried the joint energies of both Earth and Mu and was used in healing, embalming, and blessing, carrying the heady magic of two worlds becoming one. It was chock full of raw energy and if anything stood a chance at replenishing exhausted reserves, he figured it would be this, the wellspring from which Merged magic had sprung.

Liria's hair spread around them in a halo, the deep aqua of her dress swirling like seaweed in the gentle current. The fountain itself wasn't large - only three paces across with a central pillar that kept the water flowing - but Raiden arranged his body so that he knelt with the dark fairy in his lap, his wings curved against the fountain's edge and water lapping at his waist.

A soft gasp pierced the silence and he glanced up to see a male figure silhouetted in the doorway. Raiden began to growl a warning as the figure hurried into the light, but swallowed the sound when he recognised the young embalmer, Balai.

"My Prince," Balai hurried to his side, hands stretched to hover above Liria's forehead and chest. "She lives."

"A healer," Raiden managed, his voice rumbling in such a way that it echoed through the chamber. "Please."

"Of course." Balai's jackal ears twitched, his brow furrowed - and then he was gone, his slippered feet silent on the stone floors.

Raiden shifted his grip to cradle Liria closer to his chest, using his free hand to cup water in his hands and lift it to her mouth. Her lips stayed firmly closed, even when he dribbled the sacred liquid over her chin, painting it across her lips with a trembling fingertip.

"Gods above us!" A female voice this time, a woman in olive

healing robes with mousy hair and grey cat's ears appearing with Balai at her side. "Prince Raiden, are you injured?"

"I'm fine," he growled, pushing his left wing lower in the water to make room for the healer to lean over Liria. It would have been simpler to let her go and move away, but he found he couldn't bring himself to give her up. "This is -"

"The Lady of Shadows," the healer interrupted, nodding. "We met at the Temple of Bast, though I never caught her name. I am Safiyah."

"Her name is Liria," Raiden answered, his eyes narrowing. "You were at the Temple of Bast?"

"Most everyone was, given the ceremonies," Safiyah answered, pale blue eyes unfocussed as she examined Liria with her healer's senses. "But I normally work here, at the Palace."

Raiden forced himself to relax. He didn't know every Palace healer by name, but her scent carried the truth in it - and he trusted Balai.

"What happened?" The young embalmer asked, both hands on his hips as he studied them both. "Did she try and kill you again?"

"No." Raiden snorted a humourless laugh. "My new powers chose a rather inconvenient moment to rear their head and Liria saved my life - and probably countless others."

"She's not injured," Safiyah announced, "merely exhausted. She'll wake in a few days."

"That won't be soon enough for the Queen," Raiden said quietly.

Safiyah's lips pressed together. "In that case, the Lady of Shadows needs an energy infusion."

"I tried giving her the water." Raiden scooped a handful and let it trickle between his fingers. "Her mouth is clamped shut."

Safiyah frowned, leaning over his shoulder to poke and prod at Liria's jaw. "So I see."

"Does she get energy any other way?" Balai asked. When both Raiden and Safiyah stared up at him, he shrugged. "She's more dark fairy than human; I don't know much about their biology but I can think of several other creatures who draw energy from multiple sources. If she won't open her mouth for the water, she might open it instinctively for something else."

Raiden blinked, understanding blossoming deep in his gut. "I know what she needs."

"I can fetch it," Safiyah began, pausing when he shook his head.

"No, that won't be necessary - though I think Liria would appreciate some privacy. Could you organise a room?" Raiden waited for Safiyah to bustle off, then looked up at Balai. "News?"

Balai's jackal ears flickered again, and he bent so his mouth was close to Raiden's ear. "It took me a long time to decipher the secrets, but that creature was made of dark magics and demon flesh."

"Apophis?"

The embalmer shrugged. "I'd need to see the demon serpent himself before I could say for certain; contrary to popular opinion, we don't have those sort of samples just lying about. But, yes, it's highly likely."

"Have you analysed the dead creature's venom?"

"Yes, and in a large concentration it would be highly toxic," Balai answered, tapping his nails against the edge of the fountain. "However, in smaller doses it would make you... open to suggestion."

"So did she seek to control me, or kill me?" Raiden shook his head. "And for what purpose?"

Another shrug. "Only her master could answer that, my Prince. If the creature had a soul, it's long gone by now."

"A soul," Raiden mused. "Do you think the Soulcatcher might have ideas?"

"Perhaps. Shall I contact him?"

"No, I'll do it when I'm finished here." Raiden grinned as the embalmer startled back a step. "Yeah, there are lots of fun new things going on inside me right now. Don't go far, will you? If Anubis shows, he might want you in on the discussion."

"Of course. I'll be in the embalming temple if you need me." Balai bowed, drifting away as Safiyah re-entered the chamber.

"I have a place," she said softly.

Raiden rose from the fountain on a wave of water, shaking his wings dry as he followed the healer down a corridor to a set of identical looking doors.

"Do you need anything?" Safiyah asked, hovering by an open doorway. The room was simple; a thick-woven rug over the polished stone floor, a soft but practical bed large enough for two angels with their wings spread, and a bathroom behind a half-height wall. A stack of cube shelves held blankets, towels and basic robes, and a discreet cabinet to one side contained all the supplies a healer might require.

"Not right now," Raiden said. "I'll call you if I do."

"Should I..."

He pinned the gentle healer with his stare, biting back his instinctive response in the face of her open concern. "Liria would prefer privacy for this - and so would I. If there's a problem, you have my word that I'll call."

Pressing her fingertips together in the shape of a pyramid, Safiyah bowed over the top of them and backed out of the room, closing the door behind her. Raiden strode to the bathroom and got into the enormous tub, settling Liria between his legs and curving his wings around them both. With one arm supporting her head and shoulders, he used his free hand to brush gentle fingertips across her chin, feeling the tension in her clenched jaw.

"The healers said you need energy," he murmured, stroking her hair back from her face. "And you won't drink the water. This is the only other thing I can think of that might help, Liria. I hope I'm right."

Taking his hand from her face, he slid the khopesh on his right hip just far enough out of its scabbard to bare part of the blade and used it to slash his wrist. The pain was clean and bright, Raiden's blood thick and dark as it welled. The blood of an angel mixed with a god - blood that had been brimming with energy barely a half hour ago. It had boiled out of him in the gardens, calling down lightning to pulverise the fruit tree against which he'd pressed this gorgeous fairy he wanted with a ferocity that, at the time, had terrified him. Now, the only thing that terrified Raiden was that he'd burnt off too much power and his blood wouldn't be strong enough to rouse her.

He held his wrist to her mouth, blood oozing across his skin like honey to stain Liria's lips. It should have been macabre, but something deep inside Raiden tightened and thunder rumbled in the room. He jerked in surprise and it cut off - not thunder, but the sound of his own voice echoing in his chest.

What had he become?

The question rolled around inside his head but was quickly forgotten as Liria's nostrils flared. Her jaw relaxed, lips parting just enough that his blood dribbled inside. Raiden pressed his wrist against her mouth, letting her head tilt back so that gravity would work in his favour. After the longest minute of his life he saw Liria's throat flex, an instinctive swallow. Then another. A third.

Her eyes flew open, bright violet and glittering. Pale cream skin faded to stormy blue-grey, face sharpening and ears lengthening as Raiden watched. Taloned fingers tightened, the silver stack of rings he'd given her shimmering in the steam-muted light. When he saw her tongue slide out, he shook his head.

"Don't heal it," he whispered, his voice a rasp. "Drink."

"Raiden?" Her lips moved across his skin and he shuddered, electricity turning his blood hot.

It wasn't just him, either - steam rose from their wet clothes, clouding the bathroom and cocooning he and Liria in damp intimacy. Heat and a longing unlike anything Raiden had ever known crushed his body in a fist.

"Please," he managed, leaning down to brush his lips over her cheek. "Please, Liria."

Raiden wasn't even sure what he was asking for; he just knew that if he didn't have it, he might die. Liria's chest rose and fell in a jagged rhythm, her trapped wings fluttering against the arm that supported her. His wrist was still poised over her mouth, his blood trickling down her throat, but it wasn't enough.

"Raiden." Her tone carried a hint of warning; a final chance to change his mind.

"Yes."

Closing her eyes, Liria tucked his wrist flush against her lips and sank her fangs into his skin.

FIGHTING FATE

THERE WAS NOTHING MORE incredible than the raw vitality of
Raiden's blood inside her mouth. Thick like honey, rich with
magic and more decadent than the finest cuisine, it was everything Liria needed and so much more. Her body tingled with
energy, heat sweeping her veins with every swallow. She pulled
harder on Raiden's wrist and he cried out, arching and shuddering against her as his blood revived her heavy limbs and eased
the labouring of her heart.

It would have been easy to gorge, but Liria lifted her head the
moment her energy levels were back to normal, swiping her
tongue across Raiden's wrist to seal the gash he'd made. He
rumbled deep in his chest, wrapping both arms around her and
burying his face in her neck.

"Raiden?" Liria swallowed, startled to find her voice a husky
rasp. "Are you all right?"

A short silence, and then his body shook in silent laughter.
"You might say that."

"What do you mean?" Liria tried to twist in his arms but
Raiden held her firm. Rather than break the hold, she waited

until he lifted his head, brow damp and cheeks flushed with colour. "Did I hurt you?"

"No," he shook his head, the colour in his face deepening. "Quite the opposite, in fact."

The *opposite?* Liria took in Raiden's embarrassment, the sweat slicking his skin, the way he sagged against her in luxurious satisfaction. She blinked and felt her own cheeks heat in response. "Oh."

"Is that..." he cleared his throat. "Normal?"

"No!" Liria yanked free of his grip and scrambled backwards. She made it as far as the other end of the tub before Raiden's weight crushed her against the fine porcelain.

"Liria," He rumbled, his body hard and hot against her back. "Don't run from me. Not now. Please."

"I'm not sitting in the bath with you while you think I'd... I'd... why are we in the bath, anyway?"

"We were wet."

"Why?"

"Because I sat in a magic fountain."

"Okay, that's it. First you insult me, now you're spinning tales." Liria let out a long, warning hiss. "Move, or I'll move you."

"Fine." One of Raiden's arms braced against the rim of the tub, the other slid around Liria's waist and flipped her so she faced him. "There. I've moved. Now will you listen?"

"No." Liria shoved him in the chest but the Crown Prince of Merged Egypt didn't so much as flinch. Steam clouded the room, damping his dark chocolate hair so that it hung across his forehead in tousled clumps. And overhead... those wings, feathered in white and grey and tawny rust, moisture beading on the surface in crystalline drops. Liria's next shove stalled, and she raised a hand to catch one of those drops on her fingers. "We're making the steam," she murmured. "The energy transfer. How much did you give me?"

Raiden didn't answer, so she spread her hands across his

chest. The formal gold collar he wore was cool beneath her palms, the metal preventing an accurate reading. Liria growled and reached for the clasp but their angle in the bath made it difficult to locate. After a frustrating few seconds she drew back and snapped her fingers, summoning a surge of storm-touched energy. The collar disappeared amidst a shower of sparks, revealing sculpted bronze pectorals beaded with moisture.

"How did you - oh, god of the sky," Raiden moaned, long lashes drifting shut as she flattened her blue-grey hands against his hot skin. "Liria."

"Shhh." Blinking droplets from her lashes, Liria concentrated the full weight of her senses on the angel atop her. His energy sparked not only inside him but inside herself, lingering while her dark fairy metabolism converted it for use. Until the process was complete, she had an unparalleled view into Raiden's powers, cataloguing and assessing with a combination of instinct and practice. "Prince of the Skies is the wrong title for you," she muttered, smoothing her fingertips over his flesh. "It should be Prince of the Storm."

"We'll change it," Raiden panted, dropping more of his weight onto her palms. Liria was all-but supporting him now, and he groaned as her talons pricked his chest. "What in the name of the Merge are you doing to me?"

Liria opened her mouth and paused, feeling the faintest frisson of warning go up her spine. The compulsion didn't allow her to lie, and though she'd become adept at spinning the truth in a way to suit her purposes, the flat out 'nothing' on the tip of her tongue wouldn't come. Examining the response more carefully, Liria tested the boundaries of her compulsion and blinked up at the man sagging against her hands. "You may be suffering some blowback sensations as a result of my body's attempts to accept the energy in your blood. What are you feeling?"

Raiden gave a weak shake of his head, breathing harsh and pulse visible in his throat. "It's like you're touching me, deep inside."

"It hurts?" Liria twisted her shoulders to brace against the bath better. "If you knock me unconscious, the sensations should lessen."

"No." Raiden caught her wrists and yanked her hands from his chest, the full weight of his body slamming down onto Liria's. It was instinct to catch his muscular form in the cradle of her hips, her knees sliding either side of his thighs so she didn't accidentally jab him somewhere vulnerable. It wasn't until Raiden's body lined up against hers, his face so close they shared breath, that Liria realised how vulnerable *she* now was, particularly to the hard, hot protuberance wedged against her abdomen. Raiden's hands shook as he caressed her face, stroking back the hair which had fallen into her eyes. "No, Liria, it doesn't hurt at all."

This time, when his lips settled against hers, Liria tilted her chin to meet him halfway. One of Raiden's hands slid behind her head, supporting her neck as he kissed her, his movements tender but no less passionate than the previous kisses they'd shared. Liria whimpered into his mouth, their tongues brushing in a soft, sweet dance. Her fingers drifted over his bare back, caressing the sculpted lines of his shoulders before shifting south to the dip of his spine, where pants and belt prevented further exploration. Everywhere she touched, she felt tingling echoes in her own body, the shared energy in their blood reflecting the sensations from one to the other and back again. Raiden kissed his way along her jaw and down her throat, rumbling deep in his chest as Liria arched against him. His long, warm fingers caught in the neckline of her strapless dress and she wondered why she'd ever worried about how low it was, if it meant she could feel the burning path of Raiden's lips, tongue, and teeth as he made his determined way down her sternum to lavish attention on the swell of her breasts.

"Liria," he whispered against her skin, breath hot and kisses wet. "I want to..." his fingers tugged ever so gently at the neckline of her dress, power and strength contained as he asked for permission - this incredible angel who was perhaps the only person in Liria's living memory who'd asked her thoughts, her opinions, or her permission for anything.

"Yes," she managed, her hands tangling in his hair. "I want you to."

Thunder rumbled against her, Raiden's voice sinking deep into her bones as he peeled the top of her dress down with a reverent touch. It meant lifting his body from hers, but Liria was rewarded with the heady sensation of skin on skin as he bared her breasts and lowered back down, cupping the soft mounds in his hands and sucking one nipple deep into his mouth. They growled together, electricity arcing between them as heat burned a straight path from Liria's breast to her belly. Her pulse began to beat between her legs, a strange, hollow feeling causing her thighs to clench, but Raiden's hips were in the way and prevented the movement. He seemed to understand, shifting his own hips until the rigid length of his arousal settled against the place where she ached. Even through their layers of clothing, the pressure of his erection caused Liria to cry out in surprised delight. Raiden immediately slid up her body to claim her mouth again, swallowing her exclamation with his kisses, muscles flexing and contracting in a way that made Liria shudder against him, her hips pressing closer to the thick, delicious heat he'd positioned between her thighs.

"If you shout," he rumbled, nipping at her lips, her cheeks, her ear, "the healers will come running to see what's the matter."

"I didn't mean to," she whispered, words hoarse and taloned fingers clenching in his hair. "I've never felt anything like that before."

Raiden lifted his head, golden gaze glittering with heat and his expression decidedly smug. "I know."

Uncertainty caused her heart to stutter. "If you... if you want me to conjure the humanity illusion, I... have enough magic now."

"If you think I'd prefer a lie, then you don't know me half as well as I thought you did." Raiden pushed his erection harder into that wonderful ache, drawing a gasp from between her lips. "In case you can't tell, I like everything about you." He spread his wings over the lip of the bath and used them to lever upward, smoothing his hands over stormy skin until he cupped her breasts again. "Ione is insane, wanting to hide you away. You're perfect."

Liria kept silent, negating the compulsion's ability to restrict her speech by not attempting to speak at all. Instead, she traced her fingers over Raiden's face and smiled when he turned into her touch, pressing a kiss to her palm. His deep golden gaze burned with heat but a second later turned glassy, long lashes fluttering and brow drawing into a furrow.

"What is it?" she asked, spreading her senses wide. They were alone in whatever rooms Raiden had secured, but beyond she sensed a healer with a familiar energy signature and two darker powers that spoke of the cool, soft darkness of the grave, one significantly stronger than the other.

"Anubis is coming." They spoke in unison, Raiden sitting back on his heels and drawing Liria upright with a firm grip on her ribs. When she reached for the bodice of her dress, he caught at the fabric instead, taking a moment to press a tender kiss to each of her breasts before tucking them back inside.

Lowering her head to hide the way her cheeks burned, Liria watched him step from the bath, shaking his legs to settle his pants - mostly dried, now - before offering a large hand in assistance. She didn't need it, and they both knew that, but still Liria slid her fingers into his and allowed Raiden to support her weight as she gathered her layered skirts and slid out of the tub. While the Prince of Storms adjusted his crotch, muttering under his breath as he tried to disguise what was, now she was getting a better look at it, a rather impressive bulge, Liria went to the mirror to ensure her clothes were straight and her unbound hair didn't look as though a devastatingly handsome angel had been tangling it in fisted hands.

Wearing a pained expression and an oddly positioned sword

belt, Raiden pressed a kiss to the side of Liria's neck, smiling against her skin as she shivered.

"Take what time you need," he murmured, then left to answer the swift rap at the door.

Liria stared down her reflection, breathing deeply as she sought the impassive expression she'd worn at the Atlantean court for so many years. When the worst of her hair was finger-combed into submission and the excess colour had faded from her cheeks, she straightened her skirts and stepped around the corner.

Raiden had perched himself on the half height wall that separated the bathing area from the sleeping space, muscular arms crossed over his naked chest. Anubis stood in the centre of the room, his charcoal skin seeming to absorb the light that filtered from wall sconces and his bright hazel eyes an exact match for the shade of loose trousers that hung low on his hips. He, too, was bare-chested, long, straight black hair cascading over powerful shoulders to brush the base of his spine. A double-ended scythe was strapped to his back and his jackal's ears rose tall and pointed until they almost brushed the roof.

"Lady of Shadows," Anubis purred, his voice carrying the soft whisper of the place beyond death. "I'm glad to hear you are well."

"Soulcatcher." Liria offered a polite bow. "I was never unwell, merely exhausted. I've not yet been able to ask what all the fuss was about - I'd have woken on my own in due time."

"The Queen wanted you awake as soon as possible," Raiden rumbled, an impending thunderstorm thick in his tone. "Given today is her wedding day, I volunteered to take the task in hand."

Liria raised an eyebrow, but kept her face cool. "That makes sense, I suppose. Ione could have roused me, but I'd have been no use to her, which would only have increased her distress." She spread her hands, inspecting the mottled texture of her stormy skin. "Raiden was kind enough to revive me with his blood, which even now fizzes inside my veins."

"A clever trick, one that will likely serve you both well as the years go by." Anubis gave a short, sharp nod, then settled a hand on his hip and turned to Raiden. "I got your message, Prince of the Skies. I have spoken briefly with the embalmer, Balai, and wish to examine the body of this creature you killed, but I'd like the story of the encounter from you first."

"Prince of the Storm," Raiden said quietly.

Anubis blinked, then frowned. "Oh, yes, I see it now. Thunder and lightning in your heart, the power of the wind and the rain in your lungs. An angel blessed by the god of the sky, manifesting the power of the storm. Yes, indeed." The god of death grinned. "I'll have Osiris change the title."

Raiden inclined his head, then settled himself more comfortably and began to recount how he and Liria had followed the scent of blood from the rooftop market to the Temple of Bast.

Liria drifted to a side table, where someone had set a jug of water and several glasses. Pouring one for each of the men and herself, she sipped, closing her eyes as the rolling timbre of Raiden's voice wrapped around her. Each syllable echoed in her blood - or rather, his blood, in her veins - and she cherished the sensation while it lasted. What had been a near overwhelming vibration in the tub was now a whisper, her body faithfully converting the wild energy into dark fairy magic. And once it was gone... reality would come rushing back, and she'd be forced to deal with the repercussions of Ione's panicked rage. She could feel it already, simmering in her gut, curling up the back of her throat and creeping through her skin; a backwash of twisted emotion and the faint, muffled whisper of words.

"What's burning?" Anubis lifted his nose and sniffed, the action more animal than human. "It smells like raw meat."

"It's me," Liria answered, lifting her left hand. Smoke curled from beneath the stack of rings Raiden had given her, the flesh of her finger emitting a soft hissing sound. "Raiden's blood is almost fully absorbed and the compulsion is returning to full strength."

"Why are you - Ione." Raiden was at her side in an instant, grabbing her wrist and reaching for the rings. "Take them off."

"No." Liria slapped his hand away. "I cannot."

"You can," he snapped, reaching again. "We need to remove them before the damage is serious."

Catching his fingers in hers, Liria tipped her head back to meet his gaze. "No, Raiden. You're not listening. I *cannot* take them off."

Anubis was the first to catch on, his face creasing into a forbidding scowl. "Repeat her command word for word. You can do that, can't you?"

"Keep them, my shadow," Liria whispered, her voice taking on the cultured iciness Ione favoured. "Let those rings burn your skin as you have burnt my heart with your betrayal. Let them fuse deep into your flesh, never to be removed. Pretty trinkets may be Egypt's right to gift, but you will wear them by my word, and whenever you see them, you'll be reminded that no matter what, wherever you go and whatever you do, you are *mine*."

The two males stared intently at the burning skin while Liria breathed through the slowly mounting pain. Raiden's face twisted and he slammed his clenched fists against the wall beneath him.

"Don't try to tell me she's a frightened little girl this time," the Prince spat, "because that is nothing but cruelty."

Liria merely stared, her jaw clenched tight, the pain from her finger spreading over her hand and up her arm.

"Perhaps not a frightened little girl, but certainly one capable of having a spoilt brat's tantrum." Anubis bent close, nostrils dilating as he sniffed at Liria's singed skin.

"Ione is jealous," Raiden growled, tendons standing out in his neck. "Jealous, hateful and petty."

Thunder rumbled in the room and the Soulcatcher grabbed Raiden's shoulder in a punishing grip. "Control it."

"I don't know how!"

Liria set down her water glass and stepped between them, laying her palms flat on Raiden's bare chest. She looked up into his golden eyes, the heat of his body washing over her and lessening the severity of Ione's punishment.

"Breathe," she instructed. "Follow the movements of my chest; in, out. Again. Now, in your mind, make a fist and squeeze slowly. You don't want to crush the power and force an overflow, but you must collar it."

Raiden's expression was mutinous but in less than a minute the ominous growl of thunder died away. "I've got it."

"Good." She knew she should remove her hands but his chest was warm, his heartbeat a strong, steady counter to the pain of the rings on her finger. "Powerful magic is both blessing and curse, Raiden. There will be times it leaks no matter what you try, but it is our responsibility to keep it under control as much as possible, lest we hurt someone innocent by accident."

He grunted. "I give a similar speech to novices when they first take up a sword."

"It is the same. Let your emotions rule, and people die."

"You're in pain, and it's my fault," he snapped. "Am I supposed to feel nothing?"

Liria nodded. "Yes. Ione's reaction stems from a deep... a deep..."

"Insecurity?" Anubis suggested. "Mental trauma?"

"She only knows how to be herself," Liria grumbled, frustrated by the lack in her words. Shaking her head, she willed Raiden to understand. "If there is even a hint of an emotive reaction from you, my punishment will be worse."

"So I should sit idly by whilst those rings slice your finger clean off?"

"Now you're being dramatic," Liria growled, pricking his chest with her talons. "I cannot function at optimum levels with a missing finger, can I? This burn is magical in nature; brought on by the compulsion." Liria waved her ringed hand under Raiden's nose. "Once my magic learns the shape of this new restriction, the energy will be accepted and the pain will fade. The process of fusing the silver to my flesh is unpleasant, yes, but I've endured far worse. When this is finished, I won't know any different - and neither will anyone else." She paused, giving him a sharp look. "Unless someone is foolish enough to say something."

Raiden blinked. "The soulbinding shields you from her wrath, even as it hurts you."

"Correct. My primary function is to protect the Princess Ione, and the compulsion will allow nothing to endanger my ability to perform at optimum levels - not even itself." Liria slanted a glance at Anubis, whose fingers still dug into Raiden's shoulder. "I am trusting you both with this; revelation could cost me my life."

"Fear not - your secrets are safe with me. I work for the good of Egypt and the Pharaoh, and you are far more use alive than otherwise, even though you walk in chains." The god of death smiled, displaying pointed canines. "Speaking of chains, Raiden needs to keep you close until he learns control."

"Impossible," Liria responded, tinting her voice with frost. "I know how my Queen thinks, Soulcatcher. After today, she will fill my schedule with duties that keep me far from Raiden's sphere of influence."

"I still don't understand," Raiden growled. He rolled his shoulder to break Anubis' grip, then gently covered Liria's hands with his own, trapping them against his chest. "You are so much more useful to her by working with me."

"Jealousy can be tricky, but in this case I think it's rather straightforward." Anubis dropped onto the large bed, heedless of the weapon strapped to his back as he laced his hands - clawed, like a jackal - behind his head. "I'd wager that Ione expected to receive the full and gushing attention of the entirety of the Palace from the moment the Atlantean contingent arrived in Selekhet. However, from what I've been able to piece together, both circumstances and cultural differences between the two countries have resulted in Liria getting far more attention than she likely ever has before."

He looked to Liria for confirmation, and she inclined her

head. "In Atlantis, I am less than the leavings of the gulls who circle constantly overhead. Most do not notice me - and those who do, look away and pretend they do not."

"Right," Anubis agreed. "Do you see now, Prince of the Storm? Events have conspired in a way that have drawn Ione's insecurities to light, and from my observation alone, there are many." He lifted a hand and began ticking items off on his fingers. "Liria is more beautiful than Ione. Liria is more skilled than Ione. Liria is stronger than Ione. Liria is more intelligent than Ione. Liria is more gracious than Ione. Liria has more magic in her eyelashes than Ione has in her whole body. Liria can fly, while Ione is bound to the earth. Liria doesn't need Ione, but Ione needs Liria." He heaved a dramatic sigh. "I could go on, but suffice it to say that for the first time in her life, Ione is being forcibly reminded of her shortcomings on an almost hourly basis - something nobody enjoys, least of all a Princess who has just become a Queen."

Liria stared. Had the Soulcatcher lost his mind? But no - Raiden was nodding, as though it all made perfect sense. She opened her mouth to argue but the compulsion stole her words, left her making choked noises deep in her throat before her jaw snapped shut and the muscles clenched to keep it that way.

Anubis shot her an amused look. "You don't see it, Lady of Shadows, but I've dealt with innumerable souls over thousands upon thousands of years. I know more about the inner workings of the heart and mind than I care to admit. Trust me - your mistress fears losing you as much as having you turn on her, and has no facility to understand why the royal family of Selekhet are treating you as anything less than a background ornament. Her cruelty is born of ignorance, privilege and dark emotions that should have been nurtured out of her, but clearly weren't."

"The court of Atlantis is a viper pit," Liria said at last, her muscles relaxing as she approached the topic in a roundabout fashion. "There is no kindness there, only survival."

"Coranna and Theon don't police it?"

"Queen Coranna was never the same after I rescued Ione from the naga," Liria said quietly, aching deep inside. "Though King Vasilios never tried to exact vengeance, she was petrified he'd raise the seas against Atlantis and steal her daughters. She saw treachery in every face and became consumed with getting her children married, as that would negate any claim the naga had. Theon rules the kingdom with an icy fist and together, they jump at every imagined ghost. My memories of the court before Ione's kidnapping are vague, but it became a cold, deadly place with startling swiftness." She shrugged. "When Crown Princess Hettalia married a strong Nightstalker vampire, the King and Queen began to relax, but that was only two years ago. It will be some time before true change hits Atlantis - if it ever does."

Raiden's expression turned thoughtful and he shifted his weight, muscles flexing beneath Liria's hands. She tugged at his grip and he let go, watching her retreat to her glass of water as though seeing her anew for the first time.

"So now, under the guise of a treaty, the troublesome Princess has been shipped to us." The Crown Prince of Merged Egypt fisted his hands on his hips. "Are we to expect a knife in the back, then, once Ione is no longer Atlantis' problem?"

"Oh, no." Liria gave a sharp, humourless laugh. "Peace between the two kingdoms is vital. If the naga ever attack, they'll bring all the denizens of the deep with them. Atlantis will need allies if it is to survive such an eventuality - and who better to call upon than Egypt, strongest of all the Merged lands?"

"Damn." Raiden shared a pinched look with Anubis. "I need to warn Taos."

Liria held up a hand as he strode for the door. "Relax. Vasilios isn't coming."

"You seem sure," Anubis murmured.

"I am." She smiled, baring her triple fangs. "The compulsion forbids me from giving details, but if nothing else, you may trust me on this. We are safe from the threat of the deep."

Raiden's eyes narrowed, but whatever question he'd thought

to ask died on his lips as the ground shuddered, the Palace loosing a loud groan. Liria threw out her arms and spread her wings wide, lifting off the floor as it bucked underfoot. The sound of cracking stone echoed through the chamber and she flinched, but the walls and ceiling held.

"What was that?" she gasped.

"I don't know," Raiden shook his head. "It felt like cannon impact."

"It wasn't," Anubis growled. He was staring at the roof with a furious expression on his face, hands balled to fists and body quivering with tension. "Set is here."

GODS AND WARRIORS

RAIDEN SWEPT INTO SELEKHET'S skies with Liria and Anubis close behind. The furious energy he'd collared only minutes earlier once more strained at the leash, his every cell tingling and his heartbeat echoing in his ears.

Set hovered above the Palace's main courtyard in the billowing black silks and leather armour of a desert warrior, his long, red hair swirling around his face in an unseen wind. Eyes the colour of old blood glittered in the afternoon sunlight, and when he spread his heavily ringed hands in macabre welcome, the gold shone with an inner fire.

"Anubis," he cried, lips twisting in a bitter smile. "Nephew. How good to see you."

"Anarchist," Anubis growled, crossing burly arms over his barrel of a chest. "You're meant to be in bed... recovering."

The god of war and chaos bared his teeth. "As you can see, little one, I'm well and truly healed."

"So you seek to bring the Pharaoh's Palace down around him?" Anubis tilted his head to the side, one black jackal ear drooping. "An illogical decision, even for you."

Set chuckled, large fireballs coalescing in the palms of his spread hands. "I merely seek to return the hospitality I received upon my last visit - it is the Pharaoh's wedding day, after all. Custom demands the gods bring a gift."

Raiden tensed, but instead of tossing the fireballs, Set tipped them from his hands to hover in the air either side of him. The twin maelstroms swirled and grew, unfolding into the shape of two long, winged snakes.

"Wyrms," Anubis growled, his face grim. "You two stop those beasts getting to the Pharaoh. I'll deal with the Anarchist."

"Shouldn't you call the other gods?" Liria asked, her gossamer and stained glass wings a whirring blur. "With help, Set would be easily overwhelmed."

Fine lines tightened around the corners of Anubis' eyes. "He's blocking me."

"He can do that?"

"Set is one of the Ennead; the most powerful gods in all of Mu. He presides over not only war and chaos, but fire, storms, the desert, mischief... the list goes on." Anubis squared his shoulders. "He's a match for entire pantheons by himself. Blocking my ability to reach Lemuria is nothing for a god like Set."

Raiden drew a deep breath, fighting the urge to look behind him, where instinct said his brother, the Pharaoh, was watching. "As soon as Liria and I deal with the wyrms, we'll come to your aid."

"I will likely need it." Anubis offered a sharp, sad smile. "Set has no love for me."

Lack of love wasn't what Raiden saw in Set's face as he looked down on them, one hand on the back of each of his wyrm's heads. No, such passion didn't come from a lack of anything - in fact, had he been a betting angel, Raiden would have laid gold on the idea that the Anarchist felt with such complex intensity it burned hotter than the very fire he'd cradled in his palms moments earlier.

Set's eyes blazed from old blood to bright crimson, and he raised one arm as his lips formed a single word. The language was one Raiden had never heard, the sound reverberating through his soul like the tolling of a deep, dark bell. A weapon materialised in the god's hands; long, like a staff, with a forked base and a strange, bladed top that was something of a cross between a khopesh and an axe.

"I have never seen a thing like that," Liria murmured, her eyes narrowing.

"It is an ancient Lemurian weapon. Set calls it Wasceptre, which translates loosely to sceptre of power. A rare sight, these days, though of course he is a master with it." Anubis tugged his double ended scythe free from the straps on his back. "Do not be fooled by the unwieldy appearance. Wasceptre is deadly."

The two gods stared at each other a moment longer, then Set dropped his arm and the wyrms rushed forward. Anubis rose higher into the sky, threading between the beasts without sparing them so much as a glance. Every instinct Raiden possessed screamed at him to follow the Soulcatcher into battle, but he drew his twin khopeshes and moved to intercept the wyrms instead. Though Set had called them from fire, their bodies had solidified into leathery black hide with burgundy underbellies and eyes that burned like roiling magma. Lacking arms and legs, the crests of their wings were capped with vestigial claws that looked as equally suited to gripping as they did to shredding.

The wyrms opened their mouths in unison, thin streams of fire shooting between razor sharp teeth that were each as long as Raiden's fingers. Twisting into a barrel roll to avoid the gout of flame that came his way, Raiden brushed close enough to one of the creatures that his left khopesh sliced deep into an obsidian flank. Fire shot from the wound, heading on a direct trajectory for Raiden's face - until a familiar weight tackled him out of the way, the heat of the blast raising a line of soot across his skin as it sailed by.

"We need to decapitate them," Liria ordered, turning the two of them right side up. Her pale, human facade was gone, the talons on the ends of her fingers gripping so tight they pierced the skin of his biceps. "Don't let them bite you, either - their saliva is acidic."

"How can you tell?" Raiden belled his wings out as she released him, soaring upward on a gust of air. As he did, he glimpsed a double line of teeth marks across Liria's bicep, the skin burnt away to reveal muscle and bone underneath. "Liria!"

"Do your job, Prince of Merged Egypt," she snapped, moving to intercept one of the wyrms. "And I'll do mine."

She was magnificent, swinging astride the beast and jamming a dagger into the place where the wyrm's wing joined its body. As the wing crumpled and the wyrm began to tumble from the sky, Liria twisted, heaved, and tore the thing's head clean off.

The second wyrm screamed in fury, spraying fire through the air as it dove towards Liria like an arrow shot from a bow. Raiden's arm flung out on instinct, dropping one khopesh to wrap his fingers around the wyrm's tail as it spiralled past. He heaved with all his strength and the creature snapped back at him like a whip, jaws gaping wide and flame pouring between serrated teeth. Raiden ducked, slicing out with his remaining sword as fire brushed dangerously close to the spot where his wings sprouted. For a moment, his gaze locked with the wyrm's, then his blade swept the beast's head from its body and the two pieces tumbled from the sky in a cloud of smoke and ash.

"Messy," Liria commented, appearing on his left. Her hair was in complete disarray, dark indigo blood trickled from the ragged wound on her arm and her dress was a scorched ruin - but her smile was brilliantly wide, showing off her unique triple fangs and emphasising the battle-joy in her violet eyes.

Raiden felt the impact of her wild beauty like a punch in the chest and it was all he could do to smile and shrug. "It worked. Shame about the khopesh I dropped, though. It was my favourite."

"Oh, that?" Liria snapped her fingers and quite suddenly Raiden's missing sword was in her hand. She offered him the hilt with a wink. "Here."

"How did you -" He cut off and shook his head, sliding both swords home in their scabbards. "Later. We need to help Anubis."

Liria tipped her head back, exposing the elegant arch of her throat. "The god of death holds for now, but he labours while Set laughs. Can you reach any of the other gods?"

"I don't know." Raiden closed his eyes and turned his mind inward. *Horus?*

Static, sharp and biting, filled his mind. He pushed harder, seeking a way through the unpleasant sensation, trusting his instincts to guide him - and still, nothing. It was only when he felt talons on his arm that Raiden blinked, realising he'd sagged in the air and Liria was shaking him.

"Stop," she said, her words sounding far away. "It's a trap. Whatever you're doing is draining your strength."

"Set," Raiden growled, thumping hard with his wings to regain the altitude he'd lost. "We need to break his concentration long enough to get a message through."

Liria nodded, her lips pressed into a thin line. When she began to rise higher in the air, he followed - and caught her when she gasped, wings faltering and body curling in on itself.

"What is it?" Raiden demanded. The way Liria's jaw clenched answered his question and he spun to face the Pharaoh's balcony - and the woman silhouetted in the window - a bare ten paces away. "Let her go!" he shouted. "If you want to see tomorrow, you have to trust her." Liria's back arched and she groaned, a deep, soul-wrenching sound. Desperation swept through Raiden, followed swiftly by fury as the compulsion turned his wild, vivacious fairy into nothing more than a limp bag of bones. *"Taos?"*

The silhouette of an angel joined the woman in the window, his hand reaching up as though to cradle her face. The woman pulled away, the balcony doors flung wide and Ione stumbled out, a sheet wrapped around her body and her black hair wild about her face.

"I need her!" Ione cried, terror turning her features stark. "If you take her up there, she could die."

Raiden took a deep breath and levelled the Queen with his best glare. "If you keep her down here, we *all* die."

"Her purpose is to keep me safe," Ione sobbed, her arms wrapped tight around her middle.

Pity stirred, and Raiden forced himself to gentle his voice. "She will. *We* will. But it has to be together, Ione. Please."

Ione screamed, a terrible sound of helpless agony, and turned into Taos' chest. The Pharaoh swept her into his arms, his wings curving protectively around the fractured woman he'd taken as his own. He raised sober brown eyes to Raiden's and inclined his head. "Be careful, brother. Come back to us."

Raiden didn't have time to answer, because at that moment Liria took a great, gasping breath. Her lashes sprung open and she shoved off his chest, shooting skyward like the blast from a laser cannon. Though Raiden's wings were strong and he was among the fastest fliers in Selekhet, he struggled to keep up with Liria as she cut through the air. Set and Anubis came into sudden, sharp focus, their movements faltering as the sky around them turned an unusual shade of stormy grey - and Liria disappeared.

"Soulcatcher! Go left," Raiden shouted, drawing his twin khopeshes and slicing upward with a twist of his shoulders. Anubis complied, catching the bladed end of Set's sceptre against the inner curve of a scythe and giving a hard wrench.

Set laughed as the shaft slid through his fingers. Regripping towards Wasceptre's forked base, he released one hand to draw a scimitar from his belt and deflect the khopesh Raiden swung his way. With breathtaking skill and the flick of a wrist, the god of war tangled his scimitar with the hook on Raiden's khopesh and yanked.

Caught by surprise, Raiden slammed into Anubis' side with bone-jarring force. The impact caused all the weapons to slip and in a shower of otherworldly sparks, Set was free, spinning

Wasceptre in one hand while his scimitar gleamed a dull bronze in the other.

"All right, Prince of the Storm?" Anubis murmured.

Raiden nodded, steadying himself against the Soulcatcher's implacable strength. "My wings still beat and my blood still flows. I can fight."

Anubis surveyed the odd-coloured atmosphere and nodded. His double-ended scythe whirred as he surged forward, buoyed by his own godly power. Set danced out to meet him, and for the second time that day, Raiden felt ungainly in comparison.

"Give it up, Set," Anubis grunted, parrying the forked end of Set's staff with the outer curve of his scythe.

"What for?" Set grinned, ruby hair flying as he bunched his knees and lashed out with both feet, forcing Anubis to jerk back or be kicked square in the face. "We're having fun."

"Are we?" Liria's voice hissed from everywhere and nowhere, and the odd-coloured sky coalesced into the form of the dark fairy. She plastered herself to Set's back, slender legs wrapping around the Anarchist's ribs and one arm looping over his shoulders to grip the god's jaw. Set's eyes went wide, movements faltering as Liria yanked his head to one side and buried her fangs in his throat.

"Now!" Raiden cried, hooking his khopesh around Set's scimitar and tearing it from his slackened grip.

Anubis lowered his scythe and closed his eyes. Set roared, an animal sound out of a human shaped mouth. Sand whipped around his body in a vicious tempest, caught in a heavy wind that battered Raiden aside. As he struggled to stay aloft, Set reached over his shoulder, fisted a hand in Liria's hair and tore the shadow from his throat. Dark blood oozed over the Anarchist's smooth golden skin, his face suffused with rage as he landed a solid blow to the side of her head.

Ice gripped Raiden's heart as Liria slumped. He threw himself at Set's whirling sand barrier without thought for the consequences, the fine grains slicing his skin like razors. The god of war and chaos laughed, tossing Liria into the air and catching her by the throat. Eyes the colour of old blood locked with Raiden's as Set began to squeeze.

"Anubis!" Raiden shouted, shoving harder at the swirling sand only to be thrown emphatically backward. "Hurry!"

The god of death's reply was slow. "I'm almost through... just a little longer."

Liria didn't have a little longer; any moment now Set's fingers would crush her windpipe and snap her spine, and none of Raiden's experience as a warrior or a prince would be enough to help her. Not against a god, particularly one as powerful as Set.

Blood of our blood, his mind whispered, the words creating a deep pool of stillness inside Raiden's spirit. *Not just an angel.*

Prince of the Storm, Liria had called him, her eyes twinkling with violet light.

Prince of the Storm. Son of the Skies. Weapon of the gods.

Raiden burrowed deep inside himself, searching for the crackling aura of energy that surrounded his warrior's heart. He'd never been able to maintain the calm, almost meditative state that made Taos such a good Pharaoh, but he did understand finding focus during a battle, knew how to seize the fierce clarity needed to fuel his body when duty called. The frenzy of emotion inside him bled to silence as Raiden drew that warrior's calm on like a cloak, the snapping energy of the storm sweeping through his blood and echoing in his ears. He laid his hand against the swirling sandstorm protecting Set and let the energy overflow.

Thunder rumbled in the cradle of his palm and the sand protecting the god of war and chaos trembled. The sky above grew dark as clouds began to gather, thickening with every breath Raiden took, every inch of space he claimed as he pushed deeper into Set's shield. When his arm was buried wrist deep, he clenched his fist and snarled. Lightning struck, arrowing down from the clouds overhead to smash through the sandstorm and strike Set between the shoulders. The sandy shield dropped as the

Anarchist arched backwards, electricity shivering down his arms and wrapping around his legs.

As quickly as it had begun, the lightning cut out.

"Is that it?" Set laughed, raising his head to pin Raiden with blood-red eyes alive with energy. "I, too, claim the power of the storm, angel. And unlike you, I've had millennia to perfect the use of it." The Anarchist grinned, revealing perfect white teeth and pointed canines. "I wonder what happens if I send all that lightning you just gifted me into this rather intriguing little fairy? Shall we find out?"

Set lifted Liria until she dangled above his head, limbs slack and head lolling. He flexed the fingers of his free hand and Wasceptre reappeared, blood-coloured lightning crawling up and down the shaft and caressing Set's skin like an old friend. Raiden drew both his swords and lunged forward, but the god of war and chaos handled Wasceptre like an extension of his own arm, his expression smug as he defended himself. Every time Raiden's blades struck the sceptre, a sharp jolt shot through his body, making his teeth ache and his eyes water - until, all of a sudden, Set flinched. With a flick of the hooks on the tips of his blades and a well-practised twist of his shoulders, Raiden tore Wasceptre from Set's grip and sent it spiralling away.

"What..." Set coughed and spat blood, the arm holding Liria beginning to tremble.

The dark fairy's eyes swept open, blazing with violet light. She wrapped a taloned hand around Set's wrist and peeled his fingers from her throat, wings whirring into blinding motion to keep them both aloft - for Set was sagging in the air, his body turning limp and his face a mask of disbelief.

"Arrogance," Liria said quietly. "A crime which is its own punishment."

Set's mouth worked like a fish. "You were never trying to drink my blood. You poisoned me."

"Yes." Liria bunched her shoulders and spun, swinging the Anarchist like a pendulum. He came to an abrupt, fleshy stop, impaled through the abdomen in two places by Raiden's twin swords.

Raiden grunted, shifting his grip to take the weight of the god who was now almost in his arms. "A little warning would have been nice."

"He'd have used it against us." Liria's grip tightened, her talons digging deep enough into Set's wrist to reveal a flash of bone. Bending down, she set her lips to the Anarchist's ear. "I have your scent, god of war and chaos. I have your taste. There is nowhere in this world, nor the great, magical construct of Mu, that you can hide from me, should I choose to follow. Remember that."

Set groaned, face pale as he lifted his head. His eyes had begun to turn glassy, limbs twitching of their own accord, but still he managed a hollow, rattling laugh as his gaze locked to Liria's.

"I like you," he said, and disappeared.

Raiden jerked at the sudden loss of weight and Liria caught the arm that came towards her, deflecting his khopesh with a smooth twist of her wrist.

"Sorry," Raiden muttered, returning both swords to their scabbards.

Liria merely raised a brow. "For what?"

"For... never mind." An odd popping noise sounded and Raiden worked his jaw as the atmospheric pressure eased.

Horus appeared amidst a clap of air, large wings beating steadily and mismatched eyes blazing. Isis and Osiris appeared beside him, hovering in the air much as Set had done.

"Father." Anubis floated upward to join them, scythe once again strapped to his back. "I could not hold him."

"Don't blame yourself," Isis purred, smoothing a comforting hand over Anubis' sweat slicked shoulder. She flicked a glance to her husband. "I suggest we find him, though, my love."

"Agreed. Soulcatcher. Skywatcher. Go," Osiris commanded. Anubis and Horus inclined their heads, linked their hands, and disappeared.

Raiden pinned Osiris with a look he'd never have dared even a day previously. "You're late, King of Kings."

"We came as soon as the barrier allowed." Isis slid a hand around her husband's waist and smiled, as though floating in the sky in the wake of a battle with a god was commonplace.

"Will Horus and Anubis alone be enough?" Liria asked, her eyes on the spot where the two gods had been. "That encounter was a gross mismatch of strength."

"They will likely not engage," Isis replied, "but have no fear. Anubis is unable to use his powers in Selekhet, so he was at a significant disadvantage - but that is no longer true, now that they have returned to Mu. Should it come to blows, Set will find himself in deep water."

"Anubis cannot use his powers in Selekhet?" Liria's voice was sharp. "Why not?"

Isis turned, green eyes bright and face luminous. "He is the god of death, little one. Would you unleash those sort of energies above a city full of innocents?"

Liria raised a brow, but said nothing. Raiden cleared his throat, drawing both gods' attention back to him. "On behalf of the Pharaoh, I thank you for coming."

"Diplomatic, Crown Prince, but unnecessary." Isis watched Liria with a contemplative expression. "It seems to me like you had him in hand."

"Appearances can be deceiving," Liria replied smoothly. "Though delayed, your appearance is likely what drove Set away."

"Whatever the reasons, he is gone - and believe me, I am as frustrated by this situation as you," Osiris rumbled, the very air around them trembling with his displeasure. "Something is afoot and I should very much like to know what it is."

"Set said he was here for the Pharaoh," Liria returned. "He conjured wyrms to attack the Palace."

Isis' face pinched into an elegant frown. "How unusual. Set adores Selekhet - he helped build it, even has a temple here, though it's wild and long overgrown. He laid many of the stones of the Palace with his own two hands."

"*Set* helped build the Palace?" Liria demanded, her jaw dropping open.

"We all did." Isis smiled. "We came to Egypt as desperate rulers of a dying people and a lost land, looking for an anchor. We had little to offer in exchange for a second chance at life besides our technology and our strength - yet the Pharaoh accepted us with open arms. Accepted that the blending of our two worlds would change his people - and eventually, all people - into something new, something other, forevermore. He greeted us with love and a faith that, to this day, steals my breath." She shook her head, face misty with memory. "Building Selekhet was more than a sign of equality and trust between the gods and the people of Egypt; it was gratitude, pure and simple. We vowed to protect this land and her people and we laid every ounce of that intent into each stone that was laid both here, in the Palace, and through the city at large. Set was a huge part of the undertaking; he was passionate about ensuring we paid our dues."

"We all were - and still are," Osiris murmured, his gaze locked on the gleaming sandstone walls of the Palace. "Selekhet, and most particularly the Palace, was a labour of love for everyone involved."

"If Set loves this place as much as you say, why would he threaten it?" Liria lifted bloodied talons to her lips and tasted the blood still lingering there. "I don't sense any toxins in his system besides my own. He was in his right mind when he came here."

"A distraction," Raiden said suddenly, his heart kicking hard in his chest. "He wanted Anubis away from the Palace and having Liria and I join the battle merely added to the spectacle."

A feral light dawned in Osiris' expression. "Meaning that with all Selekhet's eyes trained on the sky, Set's real goal could be carried out with minimal fuss and, perhaps, entirely unnoticed."

Raiden had already turned towards Taos' balcony, his heart

in his throat - and sagged in relief to see both the Pharaoh and his Queen framed in the open balcony doors. "Not Taos."

"No," Osiris agreed, tapping his chin with a finger, "but that brings me no reassurance, Crown Prince of Merged Egypt. Come, let us join your brother. We must find out what Set was after, and we must do it quickly. He is not called the god of chaos for nothing."

SPACE TO BREATHE

Liria touched down on the balcony in front of her Queen and
went immediately to one knee. Still dressed in only a sheet, which
she'd knotted over her breasts to prevent it slipping, Ione dropped
down alongside her shadow and dragged her into a fierce
embrace.

"You must never do that to me again," Ione demanded, her
tears smearing across Liria's skin. "I thought we agreed on this."

The Queen's tight hug pressed agonisingly on Liria's ravaged
arm, but she pushed the pain aside with a strength born of practice and smoothed a hand over Ione's tumbled hair. "It is my
primary function to protect you, your grace."

"A job best done from beside me," Ione returned, her voice
cracking. "Right beside me."

"I wish it were as simple as that, but we both know it is not,"
Liria said gently. "But I have never failed to return, have I? Not
then and not now."

It was a risk, bringing up the secrets only she and Ione
shared, but in this instance, the Queen's tension left in a rush and
she sagged, dropping her head to Liria's shoulder. Her strangle-

hold loosened and after a moment Ione sighed, smoothing a hand over Liria's spine and down the length of her closest wing. The sensation bit deep, sharp knives that slashed and tore, but Liria clenched her jaw and rode it out, patting her mistress' shoulder while Ione began to hum, settling into the long, almost ritualised process of soothing herself with the presence of her shadow.

"Stop that." Raiden's voice preceded a sharp jerk, and Liria blinked as Ione toppled backwards onto the cobbles with an indignant shriek. The Prince of Storms stood over the Queen, her hair spread out in disarray and her seductive curves barely disguised beneath the loosening bedsheet. Raiden seemed not to notice, hands on the hilts of his twin swords and his words a breathless growl. "Liria's already injured; don't make it worse."

Ione's ocean-dark eyes flashed and she scrambled upright, clutching at her breasts as the sheet slid dangerously south. "How dare you? She is *my* shadow. Her care is my responsibility, not anyone else's."

"Oh?" Raiden jabbed a trembling finger in the air, and Liria fought the urge to flinch. "Look at her! She just fought a god for you. *Bled* for you. Is still bleeding for you - and you step in to torture her for your own benefit? What sort of care is that?"

Liria's stomach sank as Ione's brow furrowed. She made to get to her feet but was stalled by a gentle touch on her elbow, and looked around in surprise to find the goddess Isis kneeling beside her.

"Hush," Isis murmured, lifting Liria's arm to inspect the wyrm's vicious bite wound. "You do Ione no favours by protecting her ignorance - she must learn the truth, little one. Sit with me here, and let me tend this hurt for you."

"Torture?" Ione shrieked, her voice rising so high it creaked with effort. "What torture do you speak of?"

Liria looked at the beautiful goddess who probed her raw flesh with gentle fingers. "You don't understand."

"Yes, I do." Isis smiled, the expression maternally indulgent. "I am the Allmother, my sweet child. Goddess of life, fertility, love, magic, healing... so many, many things. I've lived more lifetimes than you can comprehend and have been a Queen, wife, lover and mother for most of them. The only being on this balcony who doesn't understand is your mistress - and that, no matter how painful, must change if either of you are to have a life here in Egypt." She laid her hand flat over Liria's open wound and shushed softly, as though anticipating a pained outcry. When it didn't come, Isis chuckled. "So much strength in you. So much love, with no place for it to go." Bright green eyes flicked up at Raiden. "Or perhaps not?"

"No," Liria shook her head, clutching desperately at the lie of her denial. "I can't."

"Oh, my dear." Isis leant in to brush a kiss to Liria's cheek, and as she did so, gentle energy flowed from her body into Liria's. "Did you not listen to the list of things over which I preside? It is already too late for you; I can see it with my own eyes."

"I can't," Liria hissed, then snapped her mouth shut as Raiden cut off Ione's shrieking tirade by the simple expedient of slapping his hand over her mouth. The compulsion immediately tried to drag her forward to protect her mistress but Isis' gentle grip held her firmly in place, the goddess still humming softly under her breath.

"You can," Isis whispered. "Now watch, and trust me."

Trust a goddess she didn't even know? Liria wanted to scoff, and yet... Isis' reputation was untarnished, the love and respect she garnered stretching from all corners of the world. Not only that, whilst the goddess' grip on Liria's arm was far from painful, it was implacable. Breaking free would require effort and likely make the situation worse, so Liria inclined her head in silent acceptance.

"You are so caught up in your own little world that you've been blinded by it," Raiden snarled, shaking his brother off when

Taos tried to separate him from the Queen. "You see only what you wish, hear only what you desire, and stomp your feet like a child when circumstances don't go your way. Who gave you the right to touch Liria's wings like that?"

Ione wrenched from the Prince's grip, her face pinched with a fury that should have been melting Liria's nervous system into a puddle of goo. The fact it wasn't mystified Liria until she realised Isis was still humming, the goddess' energy flowing over them like a gentle river. Not even the compulsion, it seemed, could cause a hurt the Allmother couldn't heal.

"What are you talking about?" Ione panted, tying her sheet back in place with a vicious jerk. "She is my *shadow*. She belongs to me, and I can touch her as I please." The Queen waved a hand at Raiden's feathered pinions. "People touch your wings all the time; I've seen it with my own eyes. Your brother has hold of one right now. Why should that be different with Liria?"

"Because touching my wings doesn't cause me debilitating agony," Raiden shouted, spreading those wings wide in his agitation. Taos hung wide-eyed several inches off the ground for a moment before releasing his grip and dropping to the floor, the sound of his bare feet slapping the pavement the only thing which interrupted the perfect silence on the balcony.

"Touching Liria's wings doesn't hurt her," Ione said at last - but her voice was wobbly, her expression uncertain. Wide, dark eyes turned in Liria's direction. "Does it?"

Liria stared at the stonework in front of her until Raiden, his tone filled with exasperation, snapped, "You have to give her permission to speak."

"I..." Ione swallowed. "I grant permission for my shadow to answer my questions honestly for the duration of this discussion."

Isis nudged Liria gently. "Well? Come on, child - we have much more to sort out, and it cannot be done until this hurdle is surmounted."

"It hurts," Liria croaked, examining the neat way the paving stones were set against one another. "Anyone touching my wings hurts. The sensation is akin to being cut by a hot knife."

Ione let out a strangled cry, clapping her hands to her mouth. "Why didn't you ever tell me?"

"I cannot," Liria snapped, her temper twisting as the Queen's eyes went theatrically wide. "The compulsion forbids me to speak ill of you, mistress. I am not allowed to protest."

She dared lift her gaze to Ione's and saw horror there, as the Queen no doubt recalled the myriad times over their long years together where she'd stroked Liria's wings as she willed it, sometimes for hours in one go, if her panic had needed the extra time to settle.

"But I..." Ione trailed off, and then turned desperately to Taos, tears welling in the corners of her eyes. "I didn't know. I swear it, I didn't know!"

"Hush," the Pharaoh soothed. He opened his arms and Ione tumbled into them, sobbing against his bare chest. Though his expression was soft, his words came out firm. "There is much about your shadow that you do not know, kept from you by the compulsion that binds her to your side. You have been taught to see her as a thing, when I can assure you, she has far more value as a person." Tipping up her chin with a gentle finger, Taos kissed the tip of his Queen's nose. "Do you truly wish Liria pain?"

Ione was already shaking her head, the motion wild enough to set her hair swinging. "No, no! I love her." The Queen's voice broke, then, and she began to tremble violently. "I need her." She sniffled, a fresh wave of tears silvering her pale skin. "Stroking her wings brings me comfort. What will I do if I can't touch them?"

Raiden made a snarling sound deep in his throat, and Taos' head whipped around. "Enough," the Pharaoh snapped. "You've made your point, brother. Leave her alone." Taos nuzzled Ione's hair, his next words gentle as he curved his wings to shield her from view. "You can stroke my wings instead, my sweet wife. As long and as often as you like. I know they're not the same, but their comfort is yours."

The Prince of Egypt looked like he wanted to say something more, his face as dark as the clouds gathering in the sky overhead, but Osiris clapped a hand on his shoulder. "Breathe."

"Hmm," Isis said, her voice a gentle hum that Liria strained to hear. "I think we need our Soulcatcher back, my husband. Now is as good a time as any, don't you think?"

Osiris, his handsome face inscrutable, gave a short nod and disappeared. Raiden immediately strode to Liria's side and she lowered her eyes to the hem of her dress, tattered and stained after the altercation with Set. Since Isis didn't seem interested in releasing Liria, she stayed kneeling, and after a long moment Raiden knelt before her, ducking his head in an attempt to catch her gaze.

"Liria," he rumbled softly, when she turned her face away. "Don't. Please."

"You are meddling with things you don't understand," Liria whispered, shaking her head. "The tumult you are creating will scour me to the bone far deeper than if things had been left to lie as they were before. You think you're helping, but as soon as the Allmother retracts her hands, I will be the one paying the price for your scathing words."

"No," Isis said softly. "It is time for that to end, Liria Atlannon. What has been wrought upon your soul is no fault of Ione's but it is a crime nonetheless and we, as the gods of Lemuria and guardians of all in our care, cannot let it stand."

In a display of timing so perfect Liria might have believed it contrived, if not for the open honesty on Isis' face, the god-king Osiris reappeared with both Horus and Anubis at his side.

"We could not find him, Mother," Horus said, the handsome face which reflected his parentage drawn with disappointment. "Wherever Set has gone, he is beyond our reach."

Isis shrugged. "Set has ever been fickle; he will show up eventually. Don't berate yourself, my sweet boy."

"Anubis," Osiris' voice boomed across the balcony, causing everyone bar Isis to startle. "It is time."

The Pharaoh Taos lifted his head, one wing drooping slightly to reveal the Queen's pale face. "Time for what?"

"I believe I can alter the mechanics of Liria's soulbinding," Anubis announced. "If I am able to handle the soul gem, I can -"

"No!" Ione shrieked, clenching her fists tight to her chest. "You will not take her from me!"

Anubis held up a hand, his expression pained. "Peace. Whilst it would be easier if you gave the ring up, it isn't necessary. I only need to touch it, and that can be done easily enough while it's still on your finger."

"What will you do?" the Queen demanded, her eyes snapping fire. "What will you steal?"

"Nothing that isn't yours to keep," Anubis snapped. "As the god of death, the reaper of souls and the guardian of the spirit, I can influence the original spell which was used to bind Liria's essence into the crystal. It means you will no longer hurt her with your emotional overflow, nor accidentally compel her to do something neither of you consciously wish done." The Soulcatcher paused, his hazel eyes turning to Liria. "I cannot free you from the stone without causing your death, nor can I lift the basic core compulsion to protect whosoever owns the gem with your life. But, after much research, I believe I possess enough knowledge to make your existence more comfortable."

Liria said nothing, her stomach a twisted knot in her gut. The choice was not hers, and would never be hers - once again, her fate rested in the hands of Ione, her life not her own. She let her lashes drift closed, Anubis' words a hollow echo inside her mind, and waited for the axe to fall.

"My sweet -" Taos began, only to fall silent.

"No," Ione whispered. "I need no convincing, my husband. It is one thing to walk in ignorance, quite another to keep things as they are when I know it causes pain to my shadow. I see the way you look at me; the cruelty which you must think I possess." She cleared her throat, her voice growing stronger. "I will prove to you I am not that person. I *will.* I am not too proud to say that I tremble at the thought of life without my shadow sharing every breath, but perhaps, with my new husband by my side, I can learn new ways to do things. Better ways. Soulcatcher, I grant you my permission. Please help my shadow."

HIT THE GROUND RUNNING

WHILE RAIDEN STARED IN a stupefaction that was surpassed only by the open astonishment on Liria's face, Anubis stepped forward, took Ione's extended hand, and covered it - and the soul ring - in both of his.

Liria made a choking sound deep in her throat a moment later, squeezing her eyes as tightly closed as she could and leaning unashamedly against the goddess Isis, who curled a maternal arm around the shadow's shoulders and pressed a tender kiss to her hair.

Me, Raiden thought, clenching his hands to fists. *That should be me.*

But it wasn't, and Liria had made it clear she didn't want Ione thinking there was more than professional courtesy between them, which meant Raiden could do nothing but watch Anubis murmur under his breath in an unknown language while Liria's chest worked like a bellows, her body slicking with a fine sheen of sweat.

"There," Anubis announced, stepping back after little more than a minute. "It is done."

Ione stared down at the ring, turning her hand back and forth to admire the dark, fathomless facets. "I feel no different."

"I should think not," the Soulcatcher returned. "You weren't the one upon whom the changes were wrought." He released the Queen's hand, his expression stern. "It is time to start thinking of your shadow as a person. Liria Atlannon is bound to protect you, but she is sentient, with thoughts, feelings and a life of her own. If you truly wish to be Queen of Merged Egypt, you must embrace that life, and in doing so, give Liria the freedom to embrace hers - and the new role that comes with it."

In a desperate attempt not to laugh at the shock on Ione's face, Raiden focussed his entire attention on Liria, offering a hand to tug her upright. Isis let her go, this time, and the Lady of Shadows leant heavily on his strength while she tested her legs and ran a shaky hand over her sweaty face.

"Are you all right?" Raiden asked. He thought the question had been soft, intimate, even, but was suddenly very aware they had the attention of the entire balcony.

"I..." Liria stared down at her arms, turning them back and forth as though seeing them for the first time, then bent her head to examine the rest of her body. "I feel so different. Empty, and yet full at the same time. Strong. Light." Her voice hushed with wonder, and her violet eyes were wide when they at last lifted to Raiden's. "Free."

She wasn't truly free and they both knew it, but whatever Anubis had done caused Liria to break into a broad smile that was more beautiful than Selekhet's finest sunrise. Raiden wanted to kiss her more than he'd ever wanted anything in his life - but he would not violate the tentative trust he'd earnt by going against Liria's wishes simply to indulge the chaotic need inside him.

"My sh - Liria?" Ione's voice trembled with uncertainty, her fingers clenched tightly around the supportive edge of Taos' wing. The Queen's face was paler than Raiden had ever seen it, fear turning her expression stark. "Have I... have I lost you?"

In a move that demonstrated with alacrity the depth of Liria's heart, the dark fairy crossed to Ione with open arms. The Queen shoved away from Taos to meet her halfway, the two women locking tight to one another, Ione's face buried in Liria's unbound hair.

"I'm sorry," Ione sobbed, her voice broken. "I'm so sorry."

Liria tucked Ione gently closer and Raiden saw, in that moment, not a master and a slave but a young child who'd been stolen, and the woman who had brought her home and kept her safe ever since.

"You have not lost me," Liria said slowly, her words a deep, powerful thrum. "But you must accept, my Queen, that you never really knew me, and that what you thought you had was a fabrication of the compulsion. Do you remember what I said to you, when we first arrived?" She paused, and Ione nodded against her. "Never has that statement been more true than in this moment. These people are not our enemies - they are our family now, and we must fight to keep them, even if that means uncertainty and change."

Ione stepped back, and as she did, her tears dried and her countenance firmed. She was a mess of tangled hair, tear-stained cheeks and a rumpled sheet, but Raiden saw a hint of fire in her eyes, a determination that surprised him.

"You are right," the Queen declared, and she turned to Taos with a shy smile. "The Palace of Selekhet is filled with light and love and I have always wanted a family like that."

"It will require education and patience," Osiris said, his deep voice contemplative, "but it can be done. You are not your birth, Ione, or your past. You are who you choose to become."

Ione lifted her chin. "I chose to become the wife of a Pharaoh, and I stand by that. I will learn to be the Queen that Merged Egypt deserves."

"Even if that means your shadow must act autonomously?"

"Yes, King of Kings." Ione's fingers twisted anxiously in her bedsheet dress, but she nodded. "I won't fight any longer; Liria is free to move as she wishes within the honour guard, and go wherever her duties take her." She shot a narrow-eyed glance in Raiden's direction, the look so quick it might almost have been imagined, then smiled. "I trust Taos to take care of me."

Taos grinned, and swept Ione into his arms. "In that case, since it *is* our wedding day, I should very much like to start taking care of you, right now." When the Queen blushed, he dropped a tender kiss to her lips. "Brother?"

"Go," Raiden answered. "I can handle our kingdom in your absence."

Taos went without looking back, his bare heel catching the balcony door and slamming it shut behind him.

"Let us go from here," Isis murmured, turning to her husband. "They have earnt their privacy, and there is much to be done."

"I'll check the Palace, and the people," Raiden volunteered.

Anubis nodded. "Since I initially came here to view the dead serpent creature and speak with your embalmer, I shall return to the heart of the Palace to do just that."

"Excellent," Osiris boomed. "Horus, my son, will you continue to search for Set? Your mother and I have some things to attend in Lemuria."

Horus inclined his head and the three gods disappeared without so much as a goodbye, leaving only Anubis. Raiden followed the Soulcatcher to the edge of the balcony, Liria at his side, and together they dropped towards the courtyard in front of the Palace, where Set had managed to destroy two of the ornamental fountains that bordered the Palace's front steps. A contingent of Egyptian soldiers had cordoned off the area from curious onlookers and two of the Pharaoh's honour guard stood amongst the wreckage, one with a furious frown and the other hefting enormous pieces of masonry about as though they weighed nothing. Anubis lifted a hand in greeting to the few citizens who called his name, then floated off around the side of the Palace.

"Gallin, to the Pharaoh's chambers. Assist Yrini in guarding the door," Raiden called, landing amongst the wreckage with a thump and a gusty backdraft from his wings. "Dyrian. Report."

Dyrian dropped the sculpted head of a sphinx into the murky waters of what remained of a fountain and wiped a hand across his brow. His skin was a pale brown brushed with gold, his hair and eyes so dark as to be almost black, and his bared chest and arms almost entirely covered with an intricately swirling tattoo reminiscent of whispering winds. His musculature was deceptively lean, as was that of most vampires, and he squinted in the bright afternoon sun as he dusted his hands against one another.

"My Prince," Dyrian's smooth voice was cultured and bore the lyrical accent of Sumeria, the land of his birth. "I'm glad to see you well after the altercation with our Anarchist." Dark eyes slid to Liria, taking in her blue-grey skin, overlarge eyes and pointed ears. "This must be the Lady of Shadows I've heard so much about."

"And you must be the final member of the honour guard that I've yet to meet," Liria returned equably.

The vampire bowed and offered his arm. "Dyrian. If I'd known how beautiful you were, I might've protested being on opposite training rotations."

"Liria." The dark fairy clasped his arm and held on, her cheeks darkening at the compliment. "I'll admit that I'm surprised to find two Daywalkers in the Pharaoh's honour guard and no Nightstalkers."

"Nightstalker vampires are often seen as better than their daywalking kin because they have a higher concentration of vampire DNA, but the Pharaoh's honour guard must be able to work in any environment, at any time." Raiden gestured at the sky high above. "And Egypt, as you may have noticed, is persistently sun drenched."

"Meaning the advantages of a Nightstalker's superior speed and strength are moot, because they can't go outside," Liria murmured. She retrieved her hand from Dyrian's grasp and gave him an assessing once over. "You're borderline."

The vampire shifted uncomfortably, but eventually nodded. "Daylight is an effort, but not deadly."

"I know the feeling." Liria lifted a hand to her eyes, and offered Dyrian a smile that made Raiden's heart give a jealous thump. "I've learnt to function well enough in the day, but prefer the dark." She bent to inspect a shattered piece of the fountain, her brow furrowing into a frown. "Why would Set smash these? They're no more than decoration."

"I've been wondering the same," Dyrian admitted. "It's why I began shifting rubble; in case there was something hidden here. If you wish my report, my Prince, it is that this whole area is nothing more than shattered sandstone and sullied water." He kicked a piece of broken statue, sending it flying across the ruined courtyard. "The Anarchist has lost his mind."

Raiden shoved a hand into his hair and tugged as he surveyed the damage, using both a lifetime's familiarity and his strange new senses to try and fit the pieces together. If their theory that Set attacked the Palace to cause a distraction held true, then something more was afoot. But then... why the fountains, specifically? Why these two? Or was it no more than random chance, the god of war and chaos goading them into searching for reasons when there was none? Raiden tugged at his hair again and growled. His skin felt raw, his nerves as though someone were running sandpaper over them, and his thoughts sluggish. Every breath was an effort, the air thick and heavy and the sky darkening as the clouds which had sprung up whilst they stood on the Pharaoh's balcony closed in, blotting out the sun.

Dyrian, working close beside Raiden as was often his habit, paused with his arms buried wrist-deep in rubble and squinted up at the sky. "Two unusually intense storms in less than a week. I wonder if it's an omen?"

"You Sumerians and your omens," Raiden muttered; but he looked up at the sky, too, at the strange, boiling clouds that were a deep grey, tinted with flickers of bronze and gold. "What sort of storm is that?"

"If it's like the last, one with raindrops as large as your fist and lightning tinted with gold that's strong enough to shake the ground and score the Palace walls." Dyrian's dark eyes narrowed on the writhing storm front and he raised his face to the air, sniffing in that way only vampires could. "Though, this one smells like it might bring strong winds, so it's apt to be worse."

Raiden stared around at the shattered fountains, some of the fractured masonry pieces big enough to take off his head. They stood in twilight now, the approaching cloud thick enough to block the sun and create long shadows and indistinct shapes from the wreckage of the fountains. Snapping out his wings, Raiden launched himself across the courtyard to where an angel in Palace colours stood in the thick of her soldiers, the golden breastplate she wore marking her as an officer in the Pharaoh's army.

"Issue an urgent storm warning," Raiden said as he landed, wings still partially spread and knees bent for take-off. "I want everyone currently airborne grounded, buildings locked down and people secure. Once that's done, put out a call for anyone with enough supernatural strength to assist in moving this debris; if it's left here and the winds are strong, we're in trouble."

The angel offered a short bow and spread her own wings. "I'll see to it personally, my Prince. You can count on me."

Raiden interlaced his fingers and offered her his cupped palms. The angel set a foot into his makeshift step without protest and allowed him to boost her skyward, his newfound strength sending the woman soaring in moments. With a swift downward shunt of his own wings, he was back at Dyrian's side, the Daywalker already beginning to organise rubble in anticipation of a clean-up crew.

"I'll handle it, my Prince," Dyrian said with a sharp nod. "Do what you need to."

Raiden clapped his friend on the shoulder. "I'll ever be thankful for your sharp ears, Dyrian."

The vampire blinked, then one corner of his mouth twitched

ever so slightly. "I don't think you realise how your voice sounds now, my Prince. That short speech you made rolled through the courtyard like so much thunder - see? The people who were gathered at the gates are already dispersing, passing word to others, and the storm horn hasn't sounded yet."

Unease slithered down Raiden's spine but he swallowed the urge to shiver, clapped Dyrian on the shoulder and began to cross the courtyard in search of Liria. He'd last seen her inspecting one of the broken fountains but realised with a start she was nowhere to be seen, the sudden lack of her presence smacking him in the breastbone with the force of a warhammer. Still, she was both dark fairy and shadow, ideally suited to blending into the murkiness of the oncoming storm. Perhaps she'd moved to check the other fountain? Rubbing absently at his chest as though that would ease the pressure inside, Raiden had almost reached the second fountain when the dust and smaller pieces of debris around his feet began to tremble and swirl. A moment later, a man's head and shoulders extruded from the sandstone paving. Startling green eyes sparkled in a handsome face whose lines were made for laughter, the man's skin the colour of Egypt's desert and his hair two shades darker.

"Zsil," Raiden dropped to a crouch, wings half spread for balance as he met the sand sprite's unusually serious expression. "What is it?"

"Anubis sent me, my Prince. He says to tell you he could not call the usual way -" Zsil tapped his temple, "- because he's otherwise occupied."

Raiden shifted in irritation. "Can it wait? A fierce storm is on the way, and I've lost our Lady of Shadows."

"No," the sand sprite shook his head, mouth pressed into a line. "I can take over your search for the Lady, if you wish, but Anubis needs you at once. The body you recovered from Bast's temple has disappeared, your highness, and the young embalmer Balai teeters on the brink of death."

CAUGHT IN THE RAIN

Liria pasted her back to the smooth, sun-warmed outer wall of the Palace and peeped around the corner. The scent which had drawn her from the courtyard lingered faintly in the air, igniting every one of her predatory instincts even as it threatened to turn her stomach.

Sour milk, and the cloying sweetness of rotting flesh.

This side of the Palace bordered the kitchens and was an elegant mixture of functional pathways and lush gardens. Liria scuttled down an aisle between several different types of tomato plants, stooping almost double to ensure she didn't present an obvious target to anyone who might be watching - though her natural skin tone blended so well with the shadows it would take more than a casual glance to spot her, even whilst moving.

The scent trail led through a forest of enormous fired-clay pots from which grew towering pumpkin vines, the long stems coaxed to grow around wirework frames. Further along, an arching trellis covered in climbing beans provided shade for a small herb bed overflowing with parsley and basil. Whoever owned the scent had come through swiftly, attempting to mask their passage with the stronger odours of the plants - but Liria had the unique blend of sour milk and rotten meat in her lungs, in her blood. If even the slightest hint were to linger, she could follow it anywhere, including the bottom of the ocean.

The talent was one Coranna and later Ione had bade her keep to herself, stifling her instincts unless they were needed; but whatever Anubis had done to the soulbinding had caused Liria's abilities, her *self*, to coming roaring to life in a way she'd never before experienced. Magic flooded her body, her senses lit with impressions, and most wonderfully of all, Ione's constant mental presence was gone. For the first time in her entire existence, Liria felt like the person Raiden insisted she was.

Pulling at her magic, Liria blurred her body from sight and hurried past the open porch that marked the Palace's kitchen door. The faint scent took her past beds of vegetables that were low to the ground, so she kept her cloaking spell active and picked up the pace, her bare feet soundless on the well-swept path. Too bad about her dress which, like every other dress she'd worn since her arrival in Selekhet, was torn and stained. Liria's blood heated as she recalled how Raiden had peeled down the bodice to feast on her breasts, his golden eyes dark and his face etched in reverent longing. As much as Liria feared to admit it, Isis was right; it was too late. Raiden Horushood, Crown Prince of Merged Egypt and Prince of the Storm, had wormed his way into the cavity of her chest and lodged there permanently. The easing of the soulbinding hadn't cooled the feeling - rather, it was exacerbated, pumping through her blood with every beat of her heart until Liria wondered if, should she listen hard enough, the rhythm would pound out the letters of his name.

The soft snap of a stick caught Liria's attention and her head lifted, thoughts of Raiden slipping away to leave her cool and focussed. The kitchen gardens had given way to gentle, mani-cured lawns and, ahead, a heavily forested section of the Palace gardens which looked to provide a natural buffer for whatever lay beyond.

Drawing a deep breath into her lungs, Liria spread her wings and lifted silently from the ground, nothing so much as a zephyr of air stirring to mark her passage. With her toes only inches from the grass, she followed her nose over the lawns and into the cover of the trees beyond, a fascinating mix of hardy desert breeds and gentler specimens from across the seas. The soft rustling of fabric had her drifting to the left, every cell in her body straining to interpret the mixture of sounds and scents that curled their way through the impromptu forest. Such a place was good cover for someone wanting to hide, but the noises making their way between bough and branch weren't those of someone hiding. Likewise, this back corner of the garden made an ideal cover for someone trying to flee, but the sounds Liria struggled to interpret weren't those of escape, either. They were...

Feeding.

Liria faltered as the trees thinned around a delicate gazebo complete with wrought iron curlicues, paintwork just shabby enough to be charming, and a carved wooden daybed. Spreadeagled on the daybed was a young woman, eyes glassy and limbs slack. Bent over her was a figure shrouded in a heavy blanket, the fabric rustling in counterpoint to the slurping sounds someone might make when enjoying a hearty meal. The woman being eaten was already dead, something Liria counted as a small mercy - having one's internals consumed whilst still alive was one of the more horrific ways she could think of to leave this plane of existence for the next.

Keeping her magic close about her, Liria made her way soundlessly into the gazebo. The scent of sour milk and rotten flesh grew stronger with every passing moment, until it was all Liria could do not to gag by the time she arrived beside the daybed. Whatever was under the blanket didn't notice, hunched as they were over their dinner's abdomen, but the position also meant Liria had no way to get a clear view of what she was dealing with; not without giving away her presence, at any rate.

Thunder rumbled overhead but the covered figure didn't so much as flinch, so deep in their feeding frenzy it was likely Liria could sneak into the Palace, gather backup, and return to find her quarry in exactly the same position it was now. It would be the sensible course of action, particularly if what Liria guessed to be under the blanket was true - but as she made to step back from the daybed, the gorging creature jerked her meal and the young woman's arm bumped against Liria's leg.

She stared down at the limp fingers, her heart twisting. If the girl had still been alive, the way her hand lay against Liria's thigh would give her an ideal position in which to grasp Liria's skirts, to tug at them in a desperate plea for help. But she couldn't beg for rescue, because she was already dead; her life stolen and her body in the process of being desecrated. Her glassy eyes weren't yet filmed, her flesh still tinted with enough of a flush that Liria knew should she lay her hand on the body, it wouldn't yet be cold. The expression on the woman's face was one of terror, her final moments full of the crushing knowledge that she was trapped, with no way out.

In that instant, Liria knew that no matter how foolish it might be, she couldn't leave this poor young woman to be eaten piece by piece, her glorious life reduced to nothing more than a late afternoon snack. Liria had never had an opportunity to fight for herself - now, she did, and she'd use it to fight for this nameless young woman's chance to be mourned, to be remembered. To be loved.

Liria reached out a hand and snatched the blanket away. The creature underneath startled upright with a hiss, blood and gore dripping from a gaping serpentine mouth. A forked tongue flicked out to taste the air, the creature stretching to reveal a long neck coated in emerald and lime serpent's scales topped by a feminine, if monstrous, head. The olive gown of Bast's temple hung in shreds from a frame which, though it didn't display any obvious outward signs of rot, bordered on emaciated. Eyes so dark a red as to be almost black glittered with a predator's cunning as she examined the area around her. Liria didn't give the snake-woman a chance to lock onto her heat signature; she twisted the blanket in her hands, looped it over the creature's head and yanked down hard.

The thing's face slammed hard into the side of the daybed and she let out a piercing shriek, the discordant sound shredding Liria's blurring spell and echoing inside her head until she staggered back with her hands over her ears. She'd barely had time to register blood on her palms when the cold, unforgiving weight of the monster slammed her out of the gazebo. Liria hit the trunk of a tree and bounced off, grappling with claws and teeth as the serpent female tried to pin her to the ground. What had this woman's name been? Liria tried to think, her head throbbing and her memories a scattered mess. Something with thick syllables, that had been almost impossible to pronounce. Something like...

"Thissish," Liria gasped, slapping the serpent hard across the face. "Thissish, stop."

The creature hissed, spittle dripping from her jaws to splatter over Liria's collarbone. There was no life in it, no warmth, only a slimy chill that was echoed by Thissish's dark red eyes. Whoever this woman had once been, she was gone, nothing more than a re-animated corpse.

Liria raised her hands as the monstrous head struck, catching Thissish by the sides of the face and digging sharp talons into the creature's eye sockets, gouging her eyeballs out with one smooth motion. Thissish howled, and Liria took advantage of the distraction to roll them over, pinning the creature with her knees. With the serpent woman thrashing beneath her, Liria changed the angle of her clawed fingers and thrust a hand through the creature's eye socket to bury wrist-deep in her brain. With the suddenness that can only come from a swift death, Thissish's struggles ceased and she flopped back against the grass.

"I'm sorry," Liria whispered, extracting her hand and shaking off the gore. "You did not deserve the end you were given. May your soul find peace in the otherworld."

As though in answer, a raindrop the size of Liria's fist splattered onto the creature's forehead, sending blood streaming off the side of Thissish's scaled face as though she were crying. Another raindrop fell, then another, and by the time Liria staggered to her feet she was drenched, one arm raised in an attempt to shield herself from drops that were heavy enough to leave bruises. Keeping to the relative shelter of the nearby trees, Liria made her way back to the gazebo and the ruined carcass inside it, sheltered from the rain by the thickly tiled roof.

"Sleep now," she whispered, using the barest touch of her taloned fingers to sweep the girl's eyelids shut. "I'll take you home."

The promise was far from practical, but seeing it through had become vitally important in a way Liria wasn't sure she could explain, even to herself. She eyed the girl's shredded abdomen critically, then tore several strips from the bottom of her dress - it was ruined anyway - and began to bind the body. There wasn't much left of the girl's internals, but what there was, she'd honour in the Egyptian way. By the time the young woman was wrapped from hip to armpit, Liria's skirts barely covered her backside and the lashing rain splattered against her exposed legs. Tucking now-cool arms over a bandaged middle, Liria scooped the body into her arms, cradling it against her chest as one might a child. Securing the girl's head against her shoulder by resting her cheek on top of her tangled hair, Liria stepped from the gazebo and froze.

Thissish was gone.

UNHAPPY COINCIDENCE

RAIDEN STARED DOWN AT the bruise forming on the side of
Balai's face and let out a long, calming breath that did nothing
whatsoever to calm him. With every passing second, the pressure
in his chest built and he crossed his arms and leant against the
door jamb in a futile effort to hold it in.

The embalming room where Balai had been working seemed
relatively undisturbed, but the embalmer himself was laid out on
the floor, skin waxy and lashes closed. Anubis knelt opposite the
healer, Safiyah, one large hand spread at the base of Balai's
throat and his lips pressed into a thin line.

"Well?" Raiden snapped. He wanted to spread his wings,
wave his arms, *something* - but he fought the urge lest he buffet the
delicate embalming equipment laid out on the bench.

"Patience," Anubis muttered, closing his eyes. "Holding a
soul is no easy task, and Balai already carries the touch of the
underworld - keeping him in place is like trying to hold off a
wriggling mermaid intent on giving me a kiss."

Raiden blinked. "That happens often?"

The Soulcatcher growled deep in his throat, his jackal's ears
flattening against his head. With a sigh, Raiden took to making

228

laps of the room - eight paces by ten - and looking for signs of who might've attacked the young embalmer and stolen the remains of the serpent-demon-female. Simply thinking of the creature conjured memories of her lips, cold and slick, followed by the wrenching of muscle and bone as Raiden cut her in half at the waist. He picked up a fine hook for removing brains and shivered as he turned it back and forth. Not only had the demon-spawn's kiss made him violently ill, it had hurt Liria; something that had rapidly become unacceptable to Raiden, both as a Prince and as a man.

Gods and goddesses, what was happening to him? He'd almost blame the dark fairy for casting some sort of snare that he'd unwittingly wandered into, but she'd been trying to warn him off or shut him out since the moment they'd met. Why he was so determined to get under her skin, he couldn't say - but the first glimpse of the furious tempest that boiled behind her cultured facade had him hooked in a way that was entirely unprofessional at best and blisteringly intimate at worst. Perhaps he should've been gentler with her, rather than his usual, blustery, strong-arming self. If he'd channelled his brother's charm, maybe found smoother words to offer... but then, that man would've been a lie, and a poor one at that. A more cultured approach meant they'd not have clashed so delightfully, not have struck sparks until Liria dropped her defences to respond.

It was a measure of his growing insanity that despite being stabbed, receiving otherworldly powers, facing off against a god and almost ruining his brother's wedding day with an errant lightning strike, Raiden didn't regret a single moment. In fact, if he were being brutally honest with himself, he'd do it all again, just to have Liria near.

Gods, I'm an idiot. His heart softened as he remembered the feel of Liria's lips on his and their bodies pressed tight together, surprised hunger sparking in those deep violet eyes. Heat curled low in his body as he called to mind the moment she'd given him permission to peel down the bodice of her dress, to lay his hands on her skin in a way nobody had ever done before. Raiden carefully set the hook back on the shelf and drew a long, slow breath. Now was *not* the time to be wandering about with a tent in his trousers.

A weak groan issued from the floor and Raiden turned to see Balai open his eyes, their clear green swimming a moment before he focussed on the faces above.

"Soulcatcher," he rasped. "You... why?"

Anubis ruffled the young man's hair affectionately. "We need you, little one. Your work is not yet done."

"But..." Balai licked his lips and grimaced. "You broke the rules. I felt the pull - I should have died."

"They're my rules." Anubis shrugged. "I'm not a god of death, I'm *the* god of death; the others all answer to me. I'll break the rules if I think it's necessary." He gave the embalmer an amused look. "Are you going to tell on me?"

Balai tried to shake his head and groaned again, raising a hand to his bruised face. "No, Soulcatcher. I'm surprised, not stupid."

Anubis let out a loud guffaw, helping Balai into a sitting position while Safiyah fussed over his bruised face and ran her hands down the rest of his body. Her healing energy was soothing and Raiden drifted towards it, his chaotic tension calming somewhat by simply standing in her aura.

"What happened?" Raiden asked, dropping to a crouch. His wings slid out behind him on the floor, the cool stone helping to soothe his agitation even further. "Did you see who attacked you and took the body?"

"You might say that," Balai replied. He opened his mouth and paused, looking around curiously. "Where is the Lady of Shadows?"

Raiden growled, and just like that, his equilibrium was shot. "I don't know. She went missing moments before Anubis summoned me to guard your hide."

"Missing?" The echo came simultaneously from god, healer and embalmer, their faces mirroring their shock.

It was Anubis who recovered first, shaking his head so that the gold beads braided into his hair clicked and clattered. "Why didn't you say something?"

"Oh, I don't know," Raiden snarled, "Maybe because you were *busy?*"

The Soulcatcher's eyes hardened, but Safiyah laid a gentle hand on his arm. "Peace. The sooner Balai tells his story, the sooner we can search for Liria."

"Good point." Anubis snapped his fingers, and a glass of water appeared in his hand. He offered it to Balai, who sipped with the reverence of one whose throat was as dry as the desert beyond Selekhet's border.

"I was working on our demonic snake-woman," Balai said at last. "I'd finished taking samples and removing organs for analysis - much easier when the victim's already been cut in half, I might add - and was ready to start the mummification process. I used my skills to seal her body back together into a whole, and she opened her eyes."

"She *what?*" Raiden stared open-mouthed. "Didn't you just say you'd removed her organs?"

Balai nodded, his expression rueful. "Quite. No brain, no heart... there was nothing inside that creature at all. Still, she opened her eyes and before I could do more than think 'well, shit,' she attacked."

"Did she try and bite you?" Anubis asked, his eyes narrowed.

"At first." Balai shuddered. "She had a lot of teeth, all sharp - but she got a couple inches short of my face and stopped. When I tried to take a step back, she struck me an enormous blow to the head, heaved me across the room and..." he spread his hands. "That's all I remember."

Anubis nodded as though it all made perfect sense, but Raiden was still trying to get his head around the part where a corpse, an *empty* corpse, had hopped off the embalming table and fled.

"Your magic, embalmer, is what saved you," Anubis said quietly. "The creature sensed the touch of the underworld and knew it could be used to control her." He tapped a long finger against his chin. "She couldn't have gone far - undead like that need to eat to replace what's been lost, and their energy reserves are limited."

"Why -" Balai shivered and swallowed. "Why didn't she just eat me?"

"Again, the magic." Anubis waved a hand in the air around them. "The touch of the underworld makes you dangerous to the undead in many ways, little one. Taking your flesh and blood would hurt her further than she is already."

"Lucky for Balai," Raiden growled, "but where is this undead serpent creature now? What if it catches someone else?"

"She may already have done so," Anubis replied softly. "I've sensed nothing, but that is immaterial; a creature such as this consumes both body and soul for sustenance. Being able to camouflage oneself from the death gods is a rare skill - but if our undead friend is made from Apophis, it is entirely possible she has it."

Safiyah gasped, pressing both hands to her chest. "What a terrible fate! Can the soul not be saved?"

"If the creature is killed, I can extract the souls and cross with them to the Duat," Anubis replied, shrugging one shoulder. "We have to find it first, though." His face twisted. "Your Lady of Shadows would be useful here, Raiden. She's tracked this crea-ture before and might retain the scent profile in her memory."

Liria. A chill swept through Raiden and he jumped to his feet. "Blood of the gods, we have to find her."

"I did just say -"

"No, Soulcatcher. Think!" Raiden snatched a wide swathe of brown linen from a nearby shelf and draped it around his bare shoulders, using an embalming pin to secure it the way he'd normally pin his shawls in place. "Liria is missing, this creature is missing - and I don't know about you, but I don't believe in coincidences." He settled his khopeshes better on his hips and gave Anubis a sharp look. "Now that you're no longer concentrating on being godly, you can guard the embalmer yourself. I'm going to find Liria."

The god of death opened his mouth to reply, but Raiden didn't wait; he yanked open the door and strode out.

STORM FORGED

THE RAIN WAS FALLING in earnest by the time Liria stumbled onto the manicured lawns that separated the overgrown garden from the back of the Palace. Fierce winds tore at her hair, her clothes, and though instinct said to keep low and hope the shadows hid her from prying eyes, after less than a minute of being pummelled with fist-sized globes of water she conjured an energy shield to protect her precious burden and straightened her spine.

The unnatural rainfall sheeted down like a curtain, thumping heavily against the ground and streaming off Liria's protective bubble in silver rivulets. It made visibility almost nil and forward progress slow, but there was nothing to be done short of remaining alert and moving forward.

A presence pinged Liria's senses and the ground shivered beneath her feet. She danced back a pace, clutching the dead girl's body closer to her chest as a man's head and shoulders popped out of the ground within licking distance of her bare toes.

"There you are," he said, clear green eyes sparkling with mischief and mouth curled in a cheeky smile.

"Zsil, you idiot!" Liria widened her weather shield as the sand sprite emerged from the ground, his grainy image firming into flesh and blood on a sweeping wave of energy. "If this rain catches you in sand form, it'll smash you to pieces. Have you no thought for your own safety?"

"Why, Lady of Shadows." Zsil slapped his hands theatrically to his chest. "If I didn't know better, I might say you cared."

Liria glowered, and the sand sprite howled with laughter. He was handsome, in a sweet, boyish kind of way - though the honed muscles on his body and the seasoned tone in his energy were proof that Zsil was anything but a youth. Liria took advantage of his distraction to inspect his naked body in a way she'd never done with a man before, noting smooth hollows and sleek planes that, while attractive, only made her wonder what Raiden would look like in a similar state of undress. Zsil was syrupy and inviting, much like a dessert - but Raiden? No. He wouldn't be smooth and sleek but rich and decadent, a little rough around the edges with a heat just shy of burning. Realising Zsil had gone quiet, Liria lifted her gaze to find him watching her with one eyebrow quirked and his eyes full of amusement.

"Never seen a naked man before, my Lady?"

"Not one like you," Liria answered, tilting her head in consideration. "Usually they're in pieces."

"In that case..." The sand sprite gave his body a self-deprecating wave. "What do you think?"

"Pretty enough, but you're too clean cut for me. Although," her eyes dropped to the juncture of his thighs, where his penis hung from a nest of dark gold curls that matched his hair. "I'm not entirely sure why people make such a fuss over *that*. It's in an incredibly inconvenient location, seems incapable of defending itself and isn't remotely aesthetically pleasing - unlike the rest of you. I rather liken it to the promise of the ocean's finest treasure, only when the wrapping's removed, all you've got is a sea cucumber."

The sand sprite howled with laughter, wrapping both arms tight around his midriff and bending double in his mirth. Rolling her eyes at his antics, Liria angled to cross the lawns towards the Palace and Zsil, in spite of his all-consuming amusement, managed to stagger along close enough behind that he was in no danger of leaving the safety of her protective shield.

"What have you got there?" he asked eventually, appearing by one elbow.

"A lost soul," Liria answered, tilting her arms to show the pale face of her charge.

Zsil made a strangled sound in the back of his throat. "That's Jedda; she's a nurse at the Palace healing centre."

"Jedda," Liria murmured, tucking the young woman's face back into the safety of her chest. Something flickered at the corner of her vision and she paused, examining the open lawns. They appeared alone, but... "Can you feel that?"

"Feel what?" Zsil lifted his face to the air, boyish good humour fading into a warrior's watchfulness. "Rain plays havoc on my senses; I'm all-but blind out here."

Irritation curled along Liria's spine. "Why did you come, then?"

"Because Raiden couldn't," Zsil answered, lifting one shoulder. "Anubis summoned him instead. He was pissed as all hell, so I volunteered to look for you in his place."

Something warm curled deep in Liria's gut and she hid her tiny smile in Jedda's soggy hair. The cool weight of the young woman's body pressed back, reminding her there were more important things to be done than moon over the Crown Prince of Merged Egypt.

"If your senses are at a disadvantage, then stay close to me." Liria picked up her pace, squinting at the blurry curtain of heavy rain that pummelled her spellshield. "We're not alone."

"Oh? Any clues as to what exactly is keeping us company?"

"I don't know your Egyptian word, but in Atlantean, the term is vrykolakas - though even that isn't an accurate description." Liria caught the hint of a dark shape to her left but when she spread her senses that way, she found nothing. "Perhaps the closest equivalent you have would be a ghul."

"A flesh eater?" Zsil shivered. "Djinn, demon or undead?"

"Undead demon."

Zsil barked a sharp laugh. "God of the sands, you sure know how to make a guy feel better."

"What would make me feel better," Liria growled, lifting her face to the sky, "is if Raiden would stop with this cursed weather."

"Raiden?" Zsil's head whipped around, his clear green eyes wide. "What makes you think Raiden can -"

The rain stopped.

In its absence, Liria looked out upon a field of grass crushed flat by the sheer impact of the water, some of the lower sections shimmering in the gloom with shallow pools. The wind died, leaving the Palace gardens somewhat bedraggled, with limp boughs and squashed flowers taking the place of verdant shrubs and cheerful blooms. A prickling between Liria's shoulder blades had her turning left, where a slouched figure blocked their progress to the Palace proper. Slitted nostrils dilated and a serpentine head tilted, dribbling second-hand rain and brain matter onto the grass.

"Allmother save us," Zsil whispered. "What happened to her eyes?"

"I gouged them out to get to her brain. I hoped it would be enough to keep her down."

"Undead," Zsil reminded her, swallowing audibly. "We need fire."

Thissish let out a long, low hiss, her head darting from side to side as she slunk closer. Her forked tongue flicked out of her mouth, tasting the air.

"Take the dagger strapped to my thigh," Liria whispered, pressing her body against Zsil's.

His fingers patted at her leg before sliding carefully around the sheath strapped just below the hem of her criminally short dress. "Please don't tell Raiden I did this; he'll kill me."

"I can kill you myself if I'm worried."

Zsil palmed the dagger and barked a short laugh. "True."

Thissish lunged, swiping clawed hands. Liria jerked aside with a quick flutter of her wings and Zsil ducked, slashing a long line across the serpent's ribcage as he went. Thissish shrieked and struck back, her aim true and her whole body behind the blow. Her talons should have dug hard and deep into Zsil's chest, but instead his torso shattered into a million particles of sand, reforming after Thissish's attack had passed through. Blocking the backhanded strike with his forearm, the sand sprite stepped in close and buried Liria's dagger in the undead creature's heart. He twisted the blade viciously and Thissish collapsed with a sigh.

"Keep it," Liria said, when he offered the hilt of the dagger back to her. "In case she wakes before we can incinerate the body."

Zsil gave the undead creature a considering look. "How long have we got?"

"Not long; I turned her brain to mush and she disappeared the moment my back was turned." Liria took a careful step away from the serpent woman. "Don't take your eyes off her."

The sand sprite nodded, his face tight. "I don't suppose fire is one of your many talents?"

"No. Luckily for us, however, we've the next best thing on hand."

As though on cue, thunder rumbled overhead and the thick clouds fractured, spilling golden lightning to the earth. It struck a bare four strides away, shaking the ground and leaving dark scorch marks on the grass. Liria turned her eyes skyward, watching the curling, boiling cumulus as it flickered and sparked with golden light.

"Don't move," she said, her words echoed by another crack of lightning, this time behind them. Magic hung heavy in the air, caressing Liria's skin and raising the hairs on the back of her neck as lightning began to strike over and over, a near-deafening display of primal, elemental fury. When Zsil made to step closer to Liria, she shook her head. "I mean it - be still, if you value your life."

Lightning slammed into the ruined body of Thissish and Liria watched as flesh turned to ash, ash to dust, dust to nothing. The world was a chaos of light, heat and cacophonous sound, but still she knew the precise moment a man stepped from the shadows around the Palace, his burning sand and warm sunlight scent mixed intrinsically with that of the storm.

"Raiden," she whispered, and though it was impossible for him to have heard with such a great stretch of lawn between them, he turned his head unerringly in her direction. Golden eyes glowed with power, his skin burnished copper by the energy that turned his blood to liquid light.

"Liria?" Zsil's voice echoed with warning and she blinked to see she'd begun gliding over the grass towards Raiden even as he moved to her.

"Can you get out of here safely?"

He hesitated, testing the ground with one foot. "If I use one of the lightning strike sites, probably."

"Go, then." Liria drifted past him, her eyes locked on the angel whose wings flickered with sparks of golden energy.

"But -"

"*Go.*" She didn't look back but felt him leave, his essence sinking into the sandy earth and heading in the direction of the Palace.

Raiden came to a halt almost halfway across the lawn, fingers flexing and face blazing with power and sensuality. Liria drifted to a stop in front of him, her darker energies stirring in response to the invitation he presented. Magic leached from them both, raising the hairs on Liria's arms and tinting the air with the taste of the desert at dawn.

"Liria," he murmured, and it was a rumbling of thunder, a wild promise. "I thought I lost you."

"No," she replied, hearing the thick, slick darkness in her own voice. "I'm right here."

Something stirred against Liria's chest and she looked down. Jedda's lashes fluttered, then lifted to reveal irises turned the colour of dark, dirty blood. "Help me," she said, looking from Liria to Raiden and back again. "Please."

Raiden reached out a hand to cup the young woman's face, his thumb feathering over her cheekbone. "Why did Set send his creatures here?"

"She... we... there was no sending," Jedda answered, her limbs beginning to twitch. "We... escaped. We wanted... to be free. To go home."

"We'll set you free," Liria whispered. She looked up at Raiden, her heart clenching at the emotion etched deep in his expression. "Use the lightning."

"I don't know how."

Jedda shifted again, turning her face into Liria's throat. "Please. Help me."

Liria bent to press a kiss to the dead girl's chill cheek. "Close your eyes, little one. Sleep well."

"Liria," Raiden warned, thunder growling all around them. "I don't know how."

"Trust me?" she asked, catching at his linen shawl with a finger. It was awkward to get a proper grip whilst still holding Jedda close but Liria managed, and Raiden bent closer when she tugged softly.

"With my life," he said, his breath caressing her cheeks.

Liria tipped her face up and let her lashes drift closed. Raiden crossed the final space between them, his kiss a questioning caress. She parted her lips in invitation and he surrendered with a rumbling growl, his arms sliding around her waist as his wings curled around her shoulders. Liria expected the sensation of his feathers sliding against her gossamer wings to hurt but shivers of ecstasy rippled down her spine instead. She gasped into his mouth, pressing closer so that Jedda's weight was crushed between them. Their tongues tangled and Raiden's power surged, bursting out of his chest on a wave of light and heat that crackled in the air around them with a sound like shattering glass.

The slender burden Liria carried turned to ash, to dust, to nothing. Raiden's hands tightened as their bodies slammed together with enough force to make them both gasp.

"Jedda's gone," Liria managed. "We did it. She's free."

"I can't stop," Raiden panted, raining kisses across her cheeks and down the line of her jaw. "I can't reel it in."

"Don't try; let it out." Liria tilted her head back and he took the invitation, his kisses wet and hot as he moved down her throat. She twined her arms around his neck, fisting both hands in Raiden's dark, silken hair as he nipped the skin above her racing pulse.

He pulled back a fraction, golden eyes wild and face stark with hunger. "Liria, I -"

"I told you before, we're evenly matched." She slid one hand to his jaw and lifted the other for his inspection. Tendrils of dark, smoky power trailed from her stormy skin, wrapping around the Prince of Storms even as his heat and life burned over them both. "You need to empty this overcharge that's inside of you, and I've the strength to keep it contained. You *can't* hurt me, not even if you tried."

"I want - I want to - I need -" he swallowed, thick lashes cresting sharp cheeks. "Gods, Liria, I need you."

"Yes," she whispered, nipping at his lips. "I know."

SURRENDER

Raiden scooped Liria closer and threw himself into the sky. She could fly herself and well he knew it, but the press of her body against his was the only thing keeping him sane, and if the way she tucked against his chest to reduce drag was any indication, she understood.

He flew without conscious aim, winging to the back corner of the Palace gardens where a secluded grotto had been carved from rocky earth. Tall, broad-leafed palms arched overhead, shading the crystal pool from prying aerial eyes and the blistering Egyptian sun. Polished marble stepping stones lounged in the lush green grass, and several close-growing trees hid a small, pyramid-shaped cottage made of smooth sandstone.

Raiden landed on one of the stepping stones beside the steaming pool and, though it was almost physically painful to do so, released Liria from the circle of his arms. Rather than look around in wonder at the environment, or even scold him for absconding with her so readily, Liria spread her hands across his chest and closed her eyes. Cool darkness spread through him, tickling and nudging at his rowdy energy until Raiden clenched his jaw in a brutal effort not to pace, or jump up and down on the spot, or whip out one of his khopesh swords and do a quick training session. Overhead, the sky continued to growl and snap, the golden lightning which had populated the gardens not so long ago gilding the dark clouds with streamers of light.

"Let it go," Liria whispered, digging her taloned fingers into the linen covering his pectorals. The sharp tips poked through the rough weave of the fabric and Raiden hummed in the back of his throat, pushing into the sensation. His reward was a flash of violet from beneath long, curling lashes, and a raised indigo brow. "Your power is one step short of dangerous right now. Let it go, Raiden."

"I don't know how. I don't know how to do any of the things you've been asking of me."

She chewed her lower lip a moment, then said hesitantly, "I could show you."

"Yes."

"It means..." Liria cleared her throat, her eyes seeking the grasses by their feet. "It means letting me in."

"Yes." Raiden didn't know what she meant, but he didn't care. Anything to draw out the exquisite torture of having her near, her entire attention focussed on him while the world ticked away in the distance. "Tell me what to do."

She took a step back, twisting to examine their surroundings. Liria's indigo-navy hair hung long and wet over her shoulders, the remains of the soft dress she'd worn to Taos' wedding clinging valiantly to curves it wasn't prepared to handle. Her skin, a storm-tossed blue grey, faded to darker tones at her fingers and toes, and at the tips of her pointed fairy ears. Half turned away as she was, Raiden had a spectacular view of her shoulders and the elegant gossamer and stained glass fairy wings furled against her back. He lifted a hand to touch and caught the caress at the last minute, choosing instead to lace his fingers through those of the hand Liria had left partly outstretched behind her. His eyes, however, would not be held responsible for their actions and they drank in the deep violets, purples and plums of her wings, tracing the veinwork that was only visible up close and savouring the oil slick sheen of the light as it moved across the surface.

"We need somewhere you can relax," Liria murmured, then froze when she turned to find him staring. "What is it?"

"You." His voice came out a rasp. "You're so beautiful."

Colour suffused her cheeks and she dropped her gaze, tugging free of his hand. "And you're power-drunk. What about the water? It's a hot spring, right? Let's get you in."

"Liria." He caught at her wrist. "I mean it."

She shook her head, the colour on her cheeks spreading down her neck. "Get in the damned water before I push you in."

Narrowing his eyes, Raiden released her arm and dragged off his sword belt, dropping it in the shelter of a nearby bush. Boots and socks followed, then his makeshift shawl. When he dropped his hands to the waistband of his formal silk trousers, however, Liria drew in a sharp breath and he stopped. Diverting the motion to scratch at his abdomen instead, Raiden moved to the edge of the pool and crouched to test the water, wings spread on the grass behind him.

"It's perfect," he commented, then slid in feet first, letting the water close over his head. The pool enveloped him like a warm hug and for a moment Raiden choked on memories of bright sun and brighter laughter - but when he surfaced and found Liria sitting at the edge of the pool with her lower legs in the water, those memories evaporated like mist in the sun. "Are you coming in, too?" She looked reluctant, so he added, "You're covered in blood and dirt."

After a moment's more silent indecision, Liria nodded once. "I just need to get rid of my weapons."

Raiden watched with a slack jaw as, from a dress that was shorter than his arm from neckline to torn hem, she removed a thin dagger in a waist sheath, an empty thigh scabbard for another dagger, three tiny throwing knives and what appeared to be a clothes pin but, from the way it was handled, was clearly far more dangerous.

"Is that all?" he asked, as she slithered into the water.

Liria flicked him a glance from beneath her lashes. "For now."

The warning was barbed but he grinned, and her blush deepened in response. Raiden settled himself on a ledge that had his head and shoulders above the water, letting his wings float on the surface and the heat of the pool soak into his muscles. He sensed Liria slip into the water and then hesitate, so he opened his mouth and let the words tumble out as they would.

"This spring has been a retreat of the royal family for generations. My parents used to bring us here when we were kids, and pretend to be irritated when we showed my sister how to fold her wings in and bomb the water."

"You have a sister?"

Raiden squeezed his eyes shut. "Had. She died."

"I'm sorry." Liria's voice drifted slowly closer. "Will you tell me about her?"

"She was wild, bright, and cheeky. Ran circles around her two older brothers, even as she wrapped herself around our hearts. We'd have done anything for her." He sighed. "She and my parents were killed on a diplomatic visit to Petra. There was an earthquake, and over half of the caves collapsed. The city was ruined so badly the people who survived had to relocate. Taos and I had elected to stay here in Egypt, but Jianne wanted to see the carvings and my parents... well, there was no reason to say no."

"You lost them all? In one go?"

Raiden nodded. "And Taos became Pharaoh at seventeen."

"A tough beginning for any monarch." The words were almost in his ear, and Raiden lifted a single eyelid to find her hovering less than a pace away, studying his face as though it held all the secrets of the universe.

"Yes. It hurt - it still hurts - but Taos and I had each other. We were lucky, in that way."

Silence filled the grotto, and though his body screamed at

him to swim laps of the pool or bench press a tree trunk, Raiden forced himself to be still.

"I always wondered what it would be like to have a family," Liria said at last, her voice so quiet it was almost lost in the music of his pounding heart.

"Well, be prepared to find out, because now Egypt has you, we won't let go so easily." Something whispered against Raiden's thigh and it took him a moment to realise it was Liria's fingers, easing gently across his trousers until she was supporting her weight on his leg. When he didn't complain or back away, she edged closer, appearing more siren than fairy with her violet eyes and clinging dark hair, the steam from the pool clouding around her face.

"Just Raiden," she murmured, and it held the lilt of a question. "Just Liria."

"Yes."

She swallowed, and a second later she was straddling his thighs, the movement sloshing warm water up his neck and sending his pulse skyward. "To help release your magic, I need to be able to feel it. I..." Her breath hitched. "I'll need to be connected to you."

Raiden resisted the urge to catch her hips and drag her hard against him by curling his fingers around the rocky ledge on which he sat. "How?"

"I know of a couple of ways, but blood is the easiest option." She hesitated. "A little like when you gave your blood to me before, only this time, the intent isn't to revitalise but to form a bridge." He opened his mouth and she pressed two wet fingers to his lips, her gaze serious. "Wait. You have to understand; you'll need to lower every barrier you have, let me into your deepest self and trust me not to strip you bare. This process... it's very intimate, Raiden."

He turned her words over in his mind. "How many others have you done this with?"

"None." She worried her lower lip with her teeth. "But it was done to me, once upon a time."

The tone of her voice told him all he needed to know. "I'm sorry."

"Control is necessary. Once this is done, I can assure you it won't be an issue afterwards." Her gaze dipped, and Raiden watched her struggle with some internal demon. "I will endeavour to make sure none of my thoughts or impressions impinge upon your consciousness, but I cannot promise. Inside my head... it's not a nice place."

"I'm a warrior," he reminded her.

Liria's smile was unutterably sad. "I'm not."

"I'll take that risk." Anxiety fluttered in his chest. "Whatever powers Horus gave me with his blood, I feel like they're tearing me apart and making me into someone else. Someone I don't want to be. If you can stop it, it's worth whatever you think I might see."

Her sad smile remained in place but she nodded, and he sensed the final reluctance drain from her body. Liria's hands smoothed up his bare chest, over his collarbone and then around his throat and into his hair, coaxing his head to one side. She shunted forward on his lap, set her mouth to the curve where shoulder flowed into neck, and nipped at his skin so that he jumped.

"Here," she murmured, pressing closer. "You need to bite me, as I bite you. There must be blood, Raiden. My blood in your mouth, and yours in mine, to complete the circuit." She hesitated. "I know it's unpleasant, but you don't need much."

"Is my blood unpleasant to you?" he asked, unable to resist running firm hands up her back. Liria's breasts pressed against his bare chest, the fabric of her dress a dull abrasion he longed to do away with. The curve of her spine was taut with muscle, her body shivering where he stroked. Raiden lowered his head to the place she'd indicated, licking his tongue over her skin. "Do I taste bad?"

The sharp prick of her longest fangs settled against his shoulder. "No. But blood is normal for me."

Raiden longed to tease her a little more, but his body was wound so tightly he could barely think. So he grazed his blunt, human teeth over her flesh and muttered, "This is going to hurt you. My teeth aren't sharp."

"They're sharp enough."

Then, as though she sensed he was stalling - or perhaps she was - Liria sealed her lips to his skin and sank all twelve of her fangs deep.

The shock of pain was a whipcrack to the senses and Raiden bit down instinctively, his fingers pressing into the flesh beside Liria's spine even as his teeth dug at her stormy skin. In the back of his mind, a thready voice begged him to stop, repulsed by the idea of causing her pain - but it was drowned out by the mechanical way his body craved, his far blunter teeth forcing themselves harder and harder into her skin until it broke. Liria's blood wasn't sharp and coppery but cool and dark, with a bittersweet edge akin to treacle. It coated Raiden's tongue and trickled to the back of his throat, forcing him to swallow, to take her essence into himself.

The pool, the grotto, the garden beyond - it all ceased to exist, his eyes filming over until there was nothing but feeling. Power surged, a violent storm that pounded against the walls of Raiden's body. Flashes of memory crackled overhead the way lightning had crackled in the clouds, pure and raw and merciless. The core of who he was, Raiden Horushood, angel and Prince, brother and son, glowed in a tiny, golden ball in the far distance, slowly shrinking beneath the chaotic pressure of the magic that rampaged through his system.

"The problem," Liria's voice purred, "is that you're fighting it. This is part of you now, and you'll never achieve control until you accept it, jagged edges and all."

Her presence loomed to his left, the suggestion of a dark shadow that twirled and twined about him like smoke. Raiden took a step towards the maelstrom and hesitated. "I like being me."

"You'll still be you, Raiden." A gentle press in his back, urging him forward again. "You'll just be... more you."

The words echoed the ones he'd first heard upon waking, confused and altered in his bed. "What if you don't like it?"

"Me?" She stopped, and her presence flickered. "You're worried about what *I* think?"

Memories coalesced in the lightning overhead, the conversation between himself, Taos, Anubis and Horus, right before he'd thrown himself out the window to seek Liria at the Kirrilakh.

"You need someone in the palace who can oppose Set," Raiden murmured. "No, that's not it; you want someone strong enough to stand against Liria Atlannon."

Anubis grimaced. "The soulbound have terrible strength, Raiden. This shadow's compulsion makes her strong enough to do things that shouldn't be possible for a dark fairy - or anyone, for that matter - and we can't be on hand to watch her every movement. As Taos' brother, you're ideally placed to protect him best."

"I thought I was already doing that."

"Yes, of course." Anubis hesitated, then added, "But Liria has already overpowered you. If the Princess Ione asks her to, Liria could end even the gods."

"So you made me into a weapon," Raiden breathed, his gut knotting. "You want me to kill her."

"Ah," Liria said, and there was no censure in her tone, only grim acceptance.

"I won't do it," Raiden snarled, jerking back against her. "I won't become their weapon."

Liria was silent a long moment. Her dark essence twisted around his ankles, slid up and down his back, but never did she move in front where he could see her.

"I'm a weapon already, Raiden," she said at last, her tone a hiss of brittle edges and rattling scales. "I warned you of that from the beginning. If anyone is to stand against me - if anyone is to be wrought to a blade that would bring about my end - I want it to be you." A brief caress down his cheek, the soft suggestion of moisture against his throat. "Only you."

An almighty shove sent Raiden spinning into the heart of the storm. At first he panicked, a novice warrior with his first wooden sword in the ring against a seasoned veteran. Then Liria was there, spreading around him, over him, through him, her dark power guiding his hand so that he knew where to reach, where to touch, how to grip the lightning and mould it back into himself. The raw power burned him inside and out but Liria never faltered and so Raiden kept on, dragging and snatching at the boiling fury the gods had gifted him and smoothing it flat, drinking it in until he began to grow and change with it.

"Softly, now," she said, and he obeyed, keeping calm because she was with him, her cool touch instructive but not forceful, supportive rather than overbearing. Liria showed him how to accept the lightning, the clouds, the wind and the rain, helped him embrace the changes in his body so that they enhanced him instead of overwhelming the man he'd spent so many years becoming. Horus had given of his blood, but it was Liria Atlannon who made him, her cool energy stroking over his, teaching him not only how to handle his new power, but how to turn it against her.

Through it all, their essences mingled, and Raiden caught snatches of her life as she caught flashes of his. He experienced muffled echoes of a young child, frightened, cold and in pain. Glimpses of faces - mostly naga, then Coranna, to whom Liria was gifted as a mere babe. He watched her grow in the naga caves and then the Atlantean court, experienced the bone deep dread when a young Ione was kidnapped and Liria was compelled, still a child herself, to mount a rescue. Raiden witnessed her terror, returning to that place, so dark and cold and crushing at the bottom of the ocean. He saw her discover Ione, stood by her side as she, driven by Coranna's command, visited the vengeance of Atlantis upon the kingdom of the naga. He bathed with her in arterial spray, felt the tear of flesh, the snap of bone, the squish and squelch of innards. He got lost with her in the echoing screams, the chanting of spells, the magic chains she used to shackle what remained of King Vasilios to his throne of polished shells. He felt her distress as she collected a wide eyed, bloodied Ione and returned to Atlantis, felt her despair as Coranna, overcome with horror at what had been done on her own instruction, bound Liria to the Princess Ione with the darkest, strictest compulsion magics she could find. His lungs ached as she struggled to breathe beneath the pressing weight of another's needs, another's desires, another's fears and hates and insecurities. He witnessed Liria mature into a woman, powerless to stop the traumatised young Princess who used her to lash out, both consciously and unconsciously, at anyone and anything that got too near. He lived for years in cold, terrible isolation and then he saw... himself. Not the way he saw himself in the mirror, but as Liria had seen him that first day; tri-coloured wings spread, golden eyes dancing, dark hair tousled by the wind. Gloriously alive in a way she'd never been, brimming with an innate warmth that called to her even as she flinched from the burning vivacity of it.

Liria eased her energy from his as she lifted her lips from his shoulder - but not before Raiden caught the sharp slash of her longing, the deep pull of her uncertainty, and the howling emotion he'd sparked as he kissed her in the Kirrilakh. He licked his tongue across her skin, eyes squeezed shut as his mind resettled inside his body. The frayed restlessness which had plagued him was gone, and he no longer felt as though his body and soul would fracture apart at any moment. Instead, strength beat in his veins, every single part of him vibrating with the incandescent joy of life.

The glorious woman in his lap shifted and he drew back slowly, pressing a kiss to the side of her throat as he went. His blunt teeth had left a mark on her shoulder that was already bruising but the bleeding had stopped, the tearing punctures he'd created little more than slits upon the surface of her skin. Raiden smoothed his hands up to cup her face, tilting Liria's chin until her violet eyes lifted to his.

"Thank you," he murmured.

She sat docile across his thighs, her hands slipping from his shoulders to twist together in her lap. "You're welcome."

Liria's voice was thick and distant, her gaze tracking away from his. Raiden frowned. "What's wrong?"

"Nothing." She tried to tug from his grip but he held firm, newfound strength making her eyes widen in surprise. Giving up her attempt at distance, Liria instead made a show of inspecting what she could see of him above the waterline. "You look better. How do you feel?"

"I feel fine - but I'll be even more fine when you tell me what's wrong. Did I hurt you somehow? Besides the bite, that is."

Giant, violet eyes blinked. Raiden wanted to throw himself into them, to drown in their depths and never come out, but instead he brushed a thumb across her cheek and waited patiently for a response.

"I'm fine," Liria said eventually. "You didn't hurt me." She chewed her lower lip a moment, and Raiden ached at the vulner-ability in her expression. "Sorry about... whatever you saw. I tried to keep it in, but the constant mingling of our energies makes it difficult."

Raiden opened his mouth to ask what she'd hidden, if that was just the overflow, and stopped at the resignation he saw in her face. She was waiting for him to judge her. To reject her.

"Oh, Liria." Raiden slid one hand into her hair and wrapped the other around her hips, drawing her body tight against his. "You've quite literally rebuilt me from the inside out, and you think I'll throw you away? Have you not listened to a thing I've said, since the day we met?"

Temper chased the bleak light from her eyes, and a second later her hands pressed flat against the wall of his chest. "Trust you. Learn to work with you. Become part of the team." She flexed her fingers, her talons digging into his skin. "I've done it."

"Not those things," Raiden purred, leaning more of his weight against her. When she pricked at him a second time, he hummed deep in his chest. "Gods, do that again."

Liria's jaw went slack. "Have you lost your mind?"

"No." He caught her gaze with his. "My mind is in perfect working order, thanks to you. Do you remember when I asked you to trust me, not as a Prince but as a man? As Raiden?"

"I remember."

"You said yes, then. Do you still?"

Liria swallowed, her fingers flexing against him until he fought the urge to groan like a teenage boy confronted with his first taste of paradise. "Yes."

"Good, because when I say this, I want there to be no doubts between us." Raiden teased her lips with soft kisses until she began to relax against him. "As sure as the sun rises and the waters of the ocean lap at the shore, you have stolen my heart. All that I am is yours, if you'll have it. I love you, Liria Atlannon."

HOLD TIGHT AND DON'T LET GO

"You can't," Liria gasped. Raiden was all around her, his golden eyes shimmering with banked power and his warmth threatening to melt her from the inside out. "Raiden, we've only known each other nine days."

"I don't care." He shook his head, his dark hair spraying water. "There's something in us that matches, something that clicks. I knew it before, but what we just shared? Gods, Liria, if you say you don't feel it, you're a liar." Raiden shivered, his face cut with a need that softened his rough words. He swallowed, his hand clenching harder in her hair. "I. Love. You."

Liria's heart faltered in her chest, something deep inside her twisting and crying out as she attempted to stuff it in, to protect Raiden however she could.

"I... I..." Her breath hitched. Now that her compulsion was eased somewhat, she should be able to lie, but the words wouldn't come. Her mind echoed with the intensity of his declaration, backed by a weight of emotion she'd felt during their connection. His honesty demanded her own, and Liria began to tremble in his arms. "I'm not a whole person."

"What you are, what there is, I want it."

"But I'm a shadow!"

Raiden growled deep in his throat. "You feel, Liria Atlannon. I know you do. Your soul might be bound, but your heart is your own - and so help me, I'll do whatever it takes to earn it."

"This is dangerous," Liria whispered, wilting in his grip.

"I'm not afraid."

"I am."

"I won't let you down. *I won't.*"

No, he wouldn't; that was a truth she felt to the very depths of her soul. Tears gathered in her eyes and Liria blinked to clear them, captivated by the burning intensity of Raiden's gaze, all the more piercing now that his powers were under control and his natural energy shone through. The Crown Prince of Merged Egypt, the most beautiful angel she'd ever seen and the most wonderful man she'd had the opportunity to know... and he loved her.

"Take me," he whispered, leaning in to kiss the tip of her nose. "Take *my* heart. It's got your name on it, now and always."

A gift. Something and someone for her and her alone, something nobody could take from her, no matter what they tried. Liria's trembles became shudders as she tore down her last remaining barriers and gave him what they both needed. "I love you, Raiden."

He groaned, deep and long, and then she was crushed against his chest, his lips urgent against hers. His wings slid through the water to wrap around them, a tight cocoon of silky heat that dripped springwater onto their heads and down their faces. Feathers tickled at the gossamer and glass surface of her own wings and Liria broke the kiss with a gasp.

Raiden froze, then immediately spread his wings with enough force to send a wave of water out of the pool and onto the grass. "Oh, shit, I'm sorry."

"Wait." Liria took a deep breath, then another, followed by a third. Her voice came out hoarse, as though she'd just spent three days in the desert with no water. "It didn't hurt."

"What?"

"It didn't hurt." She swallowed heavily. "Close them again. Slowly."

Reluctance etched into the lines on his face, Raiden carefully tucked his wings back around them and tightened the cocoon until his feathers again brushed the delicate surface of her fairy wings.

"Oh," Liria whispered, clutching at his shoulders for support. "It... it tickles."

"It *tickles*?" Raiden watched open-mouthed as she shifted her wings under his, gossamer sliding against silk. "How?"

"I... I don't know." Liria's heart thumped unevenly and she bit her lip. "Touch them."

He lifted a hand, hesitated. "Are you sure?"

"Raiden, I swear upon whatever god you care to name, if you don't touch them I'll - *oh.*"

His hand smoothed over the leading edge of her wing, the caress warm and soft. The contact shot tingles of sensation deep into her body, a strange, tickling kind of feeling that fizzed through her blood and pooled in her middle. When Raiden paused uncertainly she growled at him, spreading her wing as much as the cocoon of his feathers allowed.

"You like that?" he murmured, repeating the movement.

"Oh. My. Sweet. Darkness," Liria breathed, shivering as something deep inside her began to twist into a knot. "I don't... it's..." her hips hitched, her body twitched, and suddenly she was too hot, her skin itchy and ill fitting. "Raiden," she panted. "I need... something."

Golden eyes darkened, and a slow, wicked smile wreathed his face. "Yeah?"

"Your touch," Liria pressed a fist to her pelvis, her knuckles brushing Raiden's abdomen beneath the surface of the water. "I can feel it here."

"Mmm hmmm," he nodded, his wicked smile widening. "How about now?"

Shifting his grip, Raiden spread his hands across her shoulder blades and skimmed them down the surface of both wings simultaneously. Liria cried out as sensation flooded her body, arrowing through her cells to congregate on the strange, aching emptiness between her thighs. She tried to squeeze her legs closed but Raiden's body was in the way, so she shifted against him, angling her hips to rub over the firm bulge in the front of his trousers. The acute pleasure that shot into her veins from the simple motion made Liria see stars, and she gasped out her shock and delight against the soft skin of Raiden's neck.

"Gods, Liria," he groaned, seeking her mouth for a desperate kiss. "I want you so badly it hurts."

"Do it," she whispered against his lips. "I want to know you every way there is to know you."

Raiden flared his wings and with a mighty downward sweep they were out of the hot spring, streams of water trailing from their limbs as he set them down out the front of the pyramid shaped cottage. The sandstone structure was barely tall enough to accommodate the arching wings of an angel but when Raiden opened the door and ushered Liria through, she gaped in astonishment.

It wasn't a little cottage at all; rather an open plan house whose bottom two thirds, like an iceberg, were hidden beneath the surface. They stood upon a square platform looking down at a sunken floor covered in thick carpets, soft cushions and, beyond, a canopied bed large enough for a family of angels to share. Liria was struck by the notion of Raiden as a child, curled amongst the bodies of his siblings and parents on that very mattress, basking in the love of his family.

"This place is too special," she gushed, balking at the edge of the platform. It hung over space without guardrails or stairs, the house a sanctuary built for those with wings. "We can't."

"Why?" Raiden's deep voice filled the space, snuck through the gaps in Liria's sundered armour and wrapped around her innermost self. "Because you're just a shadow?"

She opened her mouth on an affirmative, but just like she'd done in their shared vision earlier, he shoved her in the back and she toppled forward. With no other option but to splatter on the floor, Liria spread her wings and hovered in the centre of the pyramid, her heart beating out of time as she noted the casual wealth in the space. Raiden dominated the area like he owned it - and he was, after all, the Crown Prince of Egypt - but his gaze was trained on Liria, not on the silk curtains or marble bench tops or the sinks gilt with gold. She *was* just a shadow, but they had a promise between them, a promise which superseded all other commitments and was the basis of a love that consumed her like nothing else had ever done in her life.

"Just Liria," she whispered. "Just Raiden."

"Yes."

It was enough. It was more than enough; it was everything.

Liria closed her eyes and spread her arms, calling the darkness which was her birthright. It slithered through her soul, ignited her blood, set her senses tingling. Magic, dark as midnight and thick as sin, swept through the pyramid that was a monument to the light, bringing with it a floral breeze. When the soft wind died and Liria opened her eyes, she and Raiden were both dry and naked, and the inside of the cottage was thick with the scent of a night-time garden.

The shock on Raiden's face did nothing to detract from his fierce masculinity. Wings spread wide and strong from his back, feathers of white and grey and tawny rust providing an ideal backdrop for the man between. His body was a breathtaking expanse of muscle, every dip and ridge caressed by smooth bronze skin which begged to be touched. The scars of his warrior's life intrigued Liria, turning him from artistic impossibility to a rugged perfection that sung to every part of her nature. The thick, dark brown of his hair swept across his forehead, almost cloaking bright golden eyes which would forever shimmer with the promise of the storm. Liria swallowed as her gaze tracked downward, halting at the thick erection which pointed straight at her, thrumming with sensual promise.

"I've never seen one like that before," she said, then slapped both hands over her mouth.

Raiden, who'd been perusing her naked body with similar intensity, erupted into laughter. Then he was on her, tackling her onto the enormous bed below, his laughter vibrating through the chest that was pressed so gloriously against her own.

"A cock in general?" he asked, his grin wide. "Or one that was standing at attention?"

"Attention," Liria replied, fighting the blush that bloomed over her cheeks. She lost, and Raiden tracked the sweep of colour with a hungry gaze. "I never thought them particularly enticing before, but I like yours."

Huge wings spread wide overhead as Raiden braced his arms and bumped his erection against her inner thigh. "I'm glad, because he's pretty partial to you, too."

"Oh." Liria arched into him, wriggling against the bed in an effort to get that warm weight where she wanted it. Raiden dropped more heavily against her, crushing her to the bed and preventing further movement. "Raiden!"

"You're rushing," he murmured, trailing a line of hot, wet kisses along the angle of her jaw. "I don't want to rush; I want to make this perfect. I want to love you."

She panted underneath him, her senses in a whirl. "I've never
-"

"I know." His lips moved down her throat, suckling and nipping until Liria's eyes crossed and she clutched helplessly at his shoulders. When he scraped his teeth over her collarbone, she all but lifted off the bed and Raiden paused. "You like that?"

"*Yes.*"

He chuckled and repeated the motion over the upper curve of her breast, digging his teeth in a little harder. "I don't want to hurt you."

"You're not," she gasped, thrusting her breasts into his face and catching at his silken hair. "Bite me, Raiden. Please."

He groaned, dragging a hand over her ribs to cup one breast in his palm. He nipped gently at the underside, stroked his tongue up over the curve, then sucked her nipple into his mouth. Liria cried out as his teeth grazed her skin, his tongue a heated lash that had her writhing against the weight of his body. Her hands clenched to fists in his hair and she tried to temper her strength but it proved impossible as he lavished attention on her needy flesh, moving to the other breast to provide the same exquisite attention to detail.

Just when Liria thought she could take no more, Raiden lifted his head. His eyes had turned molten, his smile a wicked slash in a flushed face. He slithered backwards over her stomach, dropping nibbling kisses across the expanse of her ribs and then dragging his teeth over the curve of a hip. As had happened in the bathtub - was it really only a few hours earlier? - Liria's legs dropped apart to cradle him between her thighs, only this time it was his chest that slid over her most sensitive place, his breath a hot intimacy.

"Liria?" He swallowed. "Can I -"

"Yes." She had no idea what he was asking, but she wanted it, wanted *him*, with an intensity that was overwhelming. Deep in her bones, the knowledge that Raiden would never hurt her echoed in time to the thunderous rhythm of her heart. "Whatever you want."

He slid his hands under her hips and angled them upward, his gaze never leaving her face. "Are you sure?"

"Very."

A breathtaking smile, and then he began kissing his way through the thick curls at the juncture of her thighs. Liria had time to draw a shocked breath before his tongue sought her tender flesh, and then his entire face disappeared as he bent himself to the task of feasting on her. The world rocked on its axis - or was that the way her head thrashed across the pillow - as pure, unbridled pleasure shot through Liria's veins. She scrabbled desperately at Raiden's hair, his shoulders, was rewarded with a deep, throaty laugh that vibrated against her skin and intensified the tingling ecstasy that had her crying out in her native language. His wings curved down and inwards, smoothing across Liria's shoulders and giving her a warm, silken mass in which to bury her face while her hips tried to buck them right off the bed.

"Raiden," she gasped, digging her talons into his shoulders just enough to garner his attention. "I need... I need..."

"It will be easier for you like this," he murmured, pressing another long, drugging kiss to the bundle of nerves between her thighs.

Liria bucked against his mouth, but she was already shaking her head. "I want it to be you. The first time, I just want you."

His fingers clenched around her buttocks and he groaned - but he moved his kisses to her thigh, then her hips, then her abdomen, sliding his wings to the mattress either side of her shoulders and bracing his weight against the strong joint that formed the topmost arch.

"For the record," Raiden growled, pressing a kiss to her sternum and then pausing to nip the underside of each breast, "you're driving me crazy. What if I hurt you by accident?"

Liria reached to cup his face as he made his slow, inexorable way back up her throat until they were at last sharing breath. "I'm a virgin, not a china vase, Raiden. I don't break."

He opened his mouth to respond but she slid a hand between their bodies and curled it around the steel and velvet of his shaft. Raiden froze above her, his pulse pounding in his temples and his eyes glazing over. She'd never touched a man like this before and the sensations were as intriguing as they were erotic, ratcheting her desperation up another few notches even as she debated exploring his body as he'd explored hers. His skin was hot and soft, while beneath it his erection was hard and thick and long. The hair around the base was a riot of curls that tickled against her fingers as she slid through, cupping the warm weight of his testicles beneath before easing her hand back upwards.

"Liria," he grunted, his jaw tight with strain. "If you keep doing that, I'm going to embarrass myself."

Delighted and emboldened by the declaration, she tipped her face up to nip at his chin and stroked her fingers lightly over the tip of his cock. "You carry the blood of a god, Raiden. I'm sure you'll recover in the blink of an eye."

He tried to glare, but failed spectacularly as Liria shifted her grip on his shaft and smoothed her hand back down the length of it, earning a rumbling growl. "Dammit, I'm serious."

"So am I." She released him, though, and slid her arms around his back to caress the place where his wings sprouted. "I want to feel you pressed up against me everywhere."

Those wings flexed in response, bringing him closer so that Raiden could capture her lips with his. His kisses were deep and drugging, his chest hot where it pressed against hers. He settled into the cradle of her thighs, caressing his way over her hips and tugging with his fingers until Liria got the idea and wrapped her legs around him. She'd never felt more exposed, more vulnerable; but Raiden was there with her, his lips as demanding as his touch was reverent. His erection bumped at the entrance to her body and she gasped into his mouth, her fingertips digging reflexively into his back. He shifted his hips and then the long, hard warmth of his shaft was pushing slowly inside. Liria cried out as he stretched her, filled her, one glorious moment at a time.

"Don't stop," she gasped, dragging at his hips in an effort to pull him in faster. "Don't stop, Raiden."

"I -" he hesitated, groaning as she hitched against him, sweat dotting his forehead and eyes wide where they locked with hers.

"It feels good," she whispered, her own voice a throaty rasp. "It feels so good."

He bit his lip and his lashes fluttered, as though he fought the urge to clench them shut as he continued to fill her. The pace was agonisingly slow, her body a burn that was somewhere between incredible pleasure and stretching discomfort. Raiden watched her face the entire time, and when at last he was buried to the hilt, his hips flush against hers, he fell still.

"Are you okay?" he whispered, his body trembling with strain.

Liria managed a nod, almost her entire attention focussed on the place where they were joined. "I... it... you're... so..."

Despite the way he was obviously holding himself together by sheer willpower, Raiden cracked a grin. "Yeah?"

"Yes." Liria swallowed. The muscles in his back shifted and she clenched her arms and legs tighter, suddenly fearful he was going to try and leave. "Wait -"

"Shhh." Raiden dropped kisses on her lips, her cheeks, her eyelids. "Trust me."

Heart in her throat, Liria forced herself to relax. His muscles shifted again but instead of leaving as she'd feared, Raiden drew his hips back a few inches and then slowly pushed forward again. The odd burn of his initial entry dissipated as heat and pleasure flooded through Liria from the contact, and she gasped, pushing her hips harder against his.

"You like that?"

"Yes. Do it again," Liria commanded. Raiden chuckled, the sound rapidly turning to a groan as he pulled out a little more than before, then pushed just as gently back inside. It felt better than the first time, especially when he didn't stop and check on her but repeated the motion, drawing out even further before returning with a warrior's strength and grace.

Liria's body rose to meet his, chasing his hips with her own in instinctive understanding. The rhythm was like a dance, a beautiful symphony of movement that delivered not only pleasure but a sense of connection and belonging she'd never dreamed possible. As though with every thrust, Raiden pushed himself not just into her body but deeper and deeper into her heart.

"Raiden," she gasped, not entirely sure what she was asking for, what she needed. But he knew, taking her mouth with desperate passion while his thrusts kicked into a higher gear - still smooth and graceful, but with the promise of so, so much more. His body undulated in such a way that he rubbed against her clitoris with every movement, and Liria broke their kiss to shout, "Harder!"

"Fuck," Raiden growled, and then he slid his arms beneath her shoulders, locking them tighter together, and gave her what she wanted.

Fire zipped through her veins and though Liria's hips did their best to arch with every stroke, the way Raiden filled her, gave to her even as he took, shook her to the core. In the end, all she could do was hang onto him, safe in the knowledge that as she unravelled completely, so did he. Their cries echoed through the room in unison, their bodies grinding and reaching, the pleasure ratcheting up and up until Liria thought she might die. Her body began to tighten impossibly further and she scrabbled at Raiden's back for purchase.

"Yes," he growled, lowering his face to the hollow beneath her jaw and laying a kiss against her thundering pulse. "Gods, Liria, yes. I'm going to - you have to -"

A scream barrelled up Liria's throat as he bit her neck, the sensation of his teeth against her skin pushing her off the precipice of their joining and into a world of brilliant ecstasy. There was no up, no down, no earth and no sky, only incredible, blinding sensation and Raiden, his scent in her lungs and his body shuddering in her arms as he, too, lost his grip on reality. And together, for those few glorious moments in time, they were one.

SHIMMERING DAWN

RAIDEN LOST COUNT OF how many times he worshipped Liria through the evening and well into the night. When they finally collapsed in laughing exhaustion, she curled in close and Raiden fell asleep with his limbs tangled and his heart full.

He woke to bright sunlight slanting across the bed and Liria's face pressed into his chest. One gossamer wing was spread over his torso, his own wings draped over the top like a living blanket. Raiden traced a reverent finger over the smooth perfection of one blue-grey cheek, brushing errant strands of hair back from her face. Liria sighed and shifted against him, long lashes tickling his bare skin as she burrowed deeper into his embrace.

Gods, she was so beautiful. His cock twitched to life, but Raiden was in no rush to indulge it; the feel of Liria completely relaxed in his arms was too good to cut short. He'd never forget the moment she'd used her magic to banish their clothes, head back and arms wide in a sensual invitation he couldn't have refused if he'd tried. Full breasts, flared hips, petite waist - all fairies, both light and dark, were built appealing and Liria was certainly no exception - but it was her inner fire that drew him most. The sharp tongue powered by an even sharper mind which had captivated him from the very first. Now he had her, and she him, and every physical and emotional fantasy he'd tried to ignore since they'd met had come to screaming life.

She shifted again, grumbling into his skin. Her left hand smoothed over his bicep and across his shoulder, the bright silver rings on her index finger shimmering in the sunlight as she curled her fingers against his sternum. He frowned down at the skin around the bands as her lashes drifted open, revealing violet eyes still hazy with sleep.

"Raiden?" Voice husky in a way that made his cock all the harder, she blinked muzzily up at him. "What's wrong?"

"Your finger," he said, catching her hand and rubbing his thumb over the rings. "It looks healed, but the rings are embedded in your skin."

Liria yawned, displaying her triple fangs, then tilted her hand so she could inspect it herself. Lazy and soft in a way he'd never seen - and was completely undone by - she shrugged against him. "Yep."

"Dammit, Liria -"

"Don't start, Prince of Storms," she grumbled, shoving her ringed hand against his face and closing her eyes. "I told you that would happen. And before you ask, no, I'm not sorry; they're mine, and I wouldn't take them off even if I could, because they came from you, and I love you. Now shut up."

Astonishment and delight warred in Raiden's heart and he captured her wrist, turning her hand to bite the side of her palm. "Don't you remember what I said about my title, lover mine?"

"Of course I do." Talons flexed against his ribs, and Liria lifted her head to pin him with her violet stare. "Crown. Prince. Of. Egypt."

Rumbling deep in his chest, Raiden dragged her up his body to claim her mouth in a passionate frenzy. He kissed Liria until he couldn't breathe, and then he nipped at her jaw and ground against her until she was just as breathless as he was.

Someone knocked on the door.

Liria rolled off his chest and Raiden's jaw dropped as her arm disappeared into a pool of shadows beneath the blankets and emerged with a curved dagger in hand. Held down the length of her forearm in that strange reverse grip she favoured, the blade's curve flowed off her skin in such a way that a single blow would remove an enemy's limb.

"Where did you get that?" he demanded, watching the sun play across her skin as she leant into the same shadow and pulled out a throwing knife. "Liria!" When she flicked him a look out of the corner of one eye, he shook his head. "It's just Taos."

"I know who it is," she muttered, her features drawn into a frown. "Distract him, will you?"

"Why? Liria, what are you -"

She disappeared.

Grumbling under his breath, Raiden rolled upright, gave himself a shake, then flew up to the front door.

"What?" he barked, yanking it open and glaring at his older brother.

The Pharaoh, clad as casually as he'd ever get in loose silk trousers and a palm green shawl, blinked deep brown eyes in surprise. "You're naked."

"And?" Raiden turned to Ione, who wore a scandalised expression and a toga-style wrap. "You can both swim without banging the door down, you know."

"I just thought it would be polite to warn you of our intent," Taos replied.

"Don't know why," Raiden muttered. "You'd be out there, and I'd be in here, and never the two need to meet."

Ione recovered enough to draw herself up regally. "Do you always speak so to your Pharaoh?"

"We're brothers first," Taos and Raiden said in unison - and then shared a small smile.

"Where's your escort?" Raiden rumbled.

"I knew you'd be here, so I didn't bring one." Taos tried to peer into the cottage, his smile widening to a grin when Raiden blocked the doorway with his body. "Where's Liria?"

Ione made a scoffing noise deep in her throat. "In her rooms, where she belongs, of co -"

"I'm here," said Liria.

Taos and Ione turned with a gasp, and Raiden choked on the laugh that had been bubbling in his throat. Liria hovered beside the hot spring, still gloriously naked. In one hand, her dagger dripped ichor and in the other she held a short, fat snake.

"My shadow," Ione gasped, both hands fluttering to her throat. "Fix your appearance and cover yourself at once!"

Liria's violet eyes moved over Ione and Taos and settled, at last, on Raiden. She flew slowly closer, touching down to the grass to cross the final few steps to the cottage on foot.

"Liria?" Ione's voice was breathless as she jumped out of her shadow's path. "Liria Atlannon, follow my commands at once!"

Instead, Liria came to a halt in front of Raiden, their bodies so close he could feel her heat against him. She held up the short, fat snake - which, now that it was closer, Raiden realised was actually *half* a snake - and dipped two fingers from her opposite hand in the dark blood.

"I only know the naga way of doing this," Liria whispered, "but the sentiment is the same as any other culture."

"Liria!" Ione took a half step forward. "Stop."

"No." With the dagger still folded back against her wrist and her violet eyes boring a hole into his very soul, Liria raised her fingers and painted a bloody stripe on Raiden's cheek. When he didn't move, she did the other cheek, re-blooding her fingers to paint a set of parallel lines the length of his sternum. "*Writtlakka,* Raiden."

Ione had begun to make odd, choking noises, but Raiden didn't move his focus from the dark fairy in front of him. He didn't understand the significance of the ritual but he knew from the set of her features it *was* significant, important in a way he couldn't fathom but would never ignore. When she tilted the severed snake in his direction, he dipped his fingers in the blood and ran the smooth, sticky liquid in a line across each of her cheeks. Something deep in his chest began to burn, the heat increasing as he re-bloodied and set two fingers against the top of her sternum. Gods above, had she felt this too? Was she still feeling it?

Swallowing as the burn became a blaze, Raiden dragged his fingers down between her breasts so they wore matching designs. His lungs felt too tight, his heart set to catch fire as he opened his mouth and tried to wrap his tongue around the word she'd used. "*Writtlakka,* Liria."

Liria's serious face broke into a smile so wide it displayed her triple fangs to full effect. Her wings whirred as she lifted off the ground until they were the same height, and then she dropped the snake and dagger, pressed her bloodied body against his, and kissed him.

The burn in Raiden's chest turned near-lethal, spreading into the areas where he'd been painted in blood - but then Liria's tongue slipped into his mouth and the fire turned sweet, the burn into a drugging pleasure. He groaned and wrapped both arms and wings around her, deepening the kiss as though he'd climb inside and take up permanent residence there. Someone was shrieking in the background, but he didn't care; he knew only Liria's body against his, her scent twining with his own, her cool, dark energy bolstering his bright, electric one. Something clicked deep inside him and he shuddered, Liria echoing the motion as though she'd felt it too.

Drawing back with a gentle nip at his lower lip, Liria took a deep breath and cleared her throat. "By the ancient laws of the naga court and in front of witnesses, I claim this man as mine. Written in blood and bound by magic, he has accepted the gift of my heart."

"No!" Ione cried. "No, I forbid it! You are *my* shadow!"

Liria pressed a hand to Raiden's chest and he released her, his mind a spinning top of confusing sensation. Leaning against the door jamb for support, he could do little more than watch as Liria picked up the dead snake and tossed it on the ground at Ione's feet.

"As long as you wear that ring, I am your shadow and my soul is yours," Liria said quietly. "But my heart is mine to give as I wish, and I have given it."

"Take it back," Ione whispered, clenching her hands to fists in her dress. "Take it back, put back your skin, dress and return with me to the Palace. Undo this, and you will be forgiven."

"No." Liria tilted her head to the side. "I'm to be treated as a real person now, remember? Real people can make their own choices."

"Nonsense. I own you," Ione hissed, brandishing the fist upon which Liria's soul ring glittered. "You are *mine*."

"I am," Liria nodded. "Now, I am also Raiden's, and his claim is equal to yours. You must learn to share."

The wail which tore from Ione's throat was an unearthly sound the likes of which Raiden had never heard. A moment later, she fainted, and Taos just barely caught his Queen before her body tumbled into the hot spring.

"Liria," Raiden rumbled, stepping forward to curve an arm around her waist. "What just happened?"

She released a long sigh, and waved a bloodstained hand. Raiden blinked as a set of loose linen trousers appeared on his body, closely followed by a matching pair for Liria, and a halter neck top that hugged her figure and left several inches of abdomen on display.

"My apologies, Pharaoh Taos, for your Queen's distress," Liria murmured. She flicked a glance at Raiden. "I knew once Ione saw us together she would figure out what had happened. I had to make a choice: hide what we had done, or act." Her shoulders squared and she lifted her chin. "I chose to fight for what I wanted."

"But what did you do?" Taos asked, curling Ione closer to his chest. "Why did she get so upset?"

"Because I gave Raiden my heart."

Raiden shook his head. "I don't understand."

"It was a spell... a ceremony," Liria corrected. She chewed on her lower lip a moment. "It binds my heart to Raiden. He has a claim on me now, as much as Ione does - it means that she cannot order me away from him, nor to harm him."

"You bound your heart to me?" Raiden demanded, jaw dropping.

"Yes. If you put your hand to your chest, you'll feel the echo."

"The -" Raiden slapped his hand to his heart, breathing turning ragged as he noted that behind the thumping pulse of his own heartbeat, there was indeed an echo, with a different rhythm. "*Why?*"

Liria's gaze dropped to the ground, and her body seemed to shrink inwards. "You said you wanted it, and it's all I have to give."

Raiden swallowed, and it felt like crushed glass. The hurt pulsing from Liria was almost visible, the expectation of his rejection written in every line of her body.

"I do want it," he choked out. "Gods, Liria, of course I want your heart. I just - I didn't realise you meant to give it to me literally. The thought that I have some sort of hold over you, like the soul ring does, I..."

"No," Liria said quickly. "No. You cannot compel me, Raiden. It's a gift. One that means you'll be able to find me wherever I am, and..." she cleared her throat. "Um."

"And what?"

Liria flicked a glance at Taos and fidgeted with the bottom of her top. "Links my life force to yours."

"Your life force? So, if I die... you die?"

"Yes."

Raiden shoved both hands into his hair and tugged. "That's what you meant when you said Ione couldn't force you to harm me - because that would kill you, and suicide goes against the primary directive of your compulsion, which is to protect the wearer of the soul ring at all costs." He shook his head at the enormity of it, what she'd done to try and keep him safe. "Liria."

"You told me were to work as a team," Liria said, her tone brisk though her eyes swam with emotion. "To protect Ione and the Pharaoh. Now you are the Crown Prince and though you wish it otherwise, you must be protected as well. I am the best chance you have, Raiden." She flicked Taos a sharp look. "And as for the dangers a dark fairy in your court may pose, be at ease, Pharaoh. This claim is only one way - should I step out of line, Raiden can kill me with impunity. Should Set or one of the gods strike me down, it will mean nothing for your brother."

"It would mean everything," Raiden growled, wrapping his wings around her and burying his face in her neck. "I love you. I'd break."

"But you'd live," Liria murmured, threading her fingers through his hair.

"And if I die? What then? Who protects Egypt when my death takes you with me?"

"The same people who were protecting it before I got here." Cupping his face, she nudged his chin until he raised his head. "Should you die, there would be nobody else left save the gods who could strike me down. You were made to stand against me, and I'm glad. This is my heart. My life. My choice."

"Liria, I -"

"Brother," Taos interrupted, moving to stand beside them. His wings settled over Raiden and Liria's shoulders, drawing the four of them into a shared embrace. "Liria is right. In the time I have spent with Ione, I... she has many deep scars. I hate to admit it, but now that she knows you and Liria are in love, she may indeed have tried to move against you."

Raiden stared from the deep, sad brown eyes of his brother to the violet ones of his lover and back again. Liria smoothed her hands down the side of his neck, talons pricking his shoulders as she massaged gently.

"Ione grew up in a place of fear. The naga were not kind to

her - they are not known for their kindness, in general - and her upbringing in the Atlantean court was cold and lonely. She was the youngest Princess, spoilt because of her trauma and over-looked because she is the weakest in both magical ability and political power. She craves love, but doesn't understand how to come by it honestly. She is selfish and sheltered and completely lacking a moral compass, but she's not evil - just lost, lonely and afraid." Liria turned a sad look on the Queen cradled in Taos' embrace. "I believe, truly, that with guidance, she can be helped."

"You love her," Taos murmured.

Raiden watched his fairy turn that statement over in her mind, frowning. "I suppose I do," Liria said at last. "At times, though, I also hate her."

"Hah!" Taos' grin was suddenly wide, and he winked. "That is what it means to have a brother or sister, young fairy."

"I'm older than you," Liria muttered, but her lips twitched in response. She glanced at the Pharaoh from beneath her lashes. "You're not angry that I laid hands on your brother?"

Taos blinked. "What? No! Though I'm astounded to think you've both fallen in love in the short time you've been in Selekhet, I cannot deny what I see written plain across your faces. Love is love, Liria Atlannon, and it is worth sacrificing everything for." He looked down at Ione, and something tortured flitted across his face. "I'm happy you have found joy. You both have my blessing."

"Brother..." Raiden trailed off as Taos shook his head and stepped back, wings spread for flight. "Where do you go?"

"I'll take my Queen back to our chambers and stay by her side until she wakes." Taos flipped golden-bronze hair back from his face, his bearing suddenly every inch the Pharaoh. "You should know that Balai collapsed shortly after you left his side yesterday, and there was a scramble to heal him all over again. He's safe, and woke earlier this morning - but he asked to see you, when you're ready."

Raiden inclined his head. "I'll take Liria with me, if you don't mind."

She stirred in his embrace, but subsided when Taos nodded. "Yes. The two of you are a team, now more than ever; Yrini will attend Ione and I while you focus on this mess with Set. It must be concluded before the god of war and chaos does any real damage."

The Pharaoh of Merged Egypt launched into the air, his Queen in his arms. Raiden watched until they were out of sight, then turned back to Liria, whose brow was tight with a frown. "What is it?"

"In the light of what happened last night, I'd almost forgotten Set." She shook her head. "Also, did you notice..."

"That Taos and Ione are very much not in love?"

She pressed her lips together and nodded. "I do not blame him, but I'm sad for them both."

"There's time yet," Raiden replied, but his own heart ached. "It's only been ten days."

"It was long enough for us."

He drew her closer, capturing her lips in a hot, wet kiss. "Yes. It was."

THE OTHER SHOE

Liria rubbed a hand over the warmth in her chest as she watched her lover towel himself dry. She'd known the basic mechanics of what they'd done, but until Raiden had held her in his arms, she'd never understood *why* anyone would be interested in doing it. Now, a large part of her thoughts were consumed with watching the bunch of taut muscle under smooth, bronze skin and wondering when they could do it again.

Jedda's face swam before her mind's eye and she flinched.

"What is it?" Wrapping the towel around his hips, Raiden caught her chin and bent to stare into her face. "What's wrong?"

Liria fought a short internal debate and lost. She'd promised him honesty, after all. "I was feeling guilty."

"For?"

"Wasting time showering off sweat and snake blood when people are dying." She dropped her gaze to the floor, then chanced a look up from beneath her lashes. "Thinking I'd rather ignore Set in favour of licking you from head to toe."

He blinked rapidly, then grinned. "Really?"

"Or having you bend me over the kitchen bench, and -"

"Gods, Liria. Stop, or I will." Raiden adjusted the tent

forming in his towel and gave her a hot look. "I like this new side of you."

"Good. I was worried that when the compulsion was lifted, my personality would be unattractive to you."

"Is your personality unattractive to *you*?"

She shrugged. "I don't know. I haven't suffered the full depths of my own thoughts and desires since I was fourteen, and that was... a long time ago."

Raiden hooked his fingers in the towel she'd knotted over her breasts and used it to drag her against him.

"Be clear, Liria Atlannon, there is nothing about you I dislike - and I've seen inside your memories, so I should know." He pressed a hard kiss to her lips. "Whatever your personality is, it's yours, and that's good enough for me. Although... we might have to work on your cultural mores. Offering to murder someone in return for goods isn't how we do things in Selekhet." Heat flooded her face and Raiden laughed, kissing her again. "As for the guilt, I suppose we'll have to share it, because I'd much rather ignore Set and lose myself in you instead."

Liria shivered, feeling a curious mix of giddiness and shame swirl in her gut. "I don't understand these new emotions. They're too strong."

"They're normal," Raiden corrected. He searched her face, his own expression soft. "Set is a knotty problem. He's causing havoc and putting people in danger. Stopping him is, and should be, a priority. The thing is... there will always be a problem that needs solving. Always someone in danger, needing protection, or a wrong that must be righted. Surely in Atlantis, that was the same?"

"Of course. I just don't know how to offset it against what I feel for you."

"Give yourself time, and remember that life is about balance. There's nothing wrong with taking refuge from the darker moments in the arms of a loved one, or dinner with friends, or a long flight over a moonlit beach. It's the freedom to do those things that keeps us going when times are rough."

She frowned. "I suppose that makes a certain sense."

"Good." Raiden leant down to nip at her lips. "I will never feel guilty for being with you, Liria. Ever. If that makes me a bad person, so be it."

When he released her, she leant back against the vanity, trying in vain to catch her breath as he strode from the room. Once her knees felt able to support her weight, Liria followed.

"I don't feel guilty for being with you," she told him. "I've never dared to dream before, but if I did, it would have been of you. It's just that all this..."

He paused by the end of the bed and nodded. "Yeah. I know." A flash of a grin. "If it makes you feel better, I don't know what I'm doing, either."

"Oddly enough, that does make me feel better." She let her eyes rove his scarred torso, making a note of which blemishes she'd like to lick at the next available opportunity - and then, the indulgence complete, drew herself up to her full height. "We should, however, make good on our word to your brother before we worry about anything else."

"Indeed." Raiden flipped open a clothes chest and began to hunt through it. "If you don't mind borrowed clothes, I have some of Yrini's things here - all the Pharaoh's guard keep spares in the places we frequent most often." He held up a bundle of black cloth and frowned. "Unless your entire wardrobe is made of magic?"

"No, it isn't. Until my compulsion was loosened, I couldn't use my magic for conjuring clothes or weapons without Ione asking me to." Liria accepted the pile and shook it out to reveal a pair of wide-legged pants in tough black linen, black underwear and a backless black tank that tied with a sash at the waist. "I've never seen the Pharaoh's guard in black before."

Raiden shrugged, returning to the chest to rummage some more. "Yrini went through a phase."

Liria tugged on the underpants. They were a little tight, but after a bit of wiggling she settled them well enough. The pants came next - too long, something she remedied by adjusting the drawstring ties at the waist and each ankle. Finally she tugged on the backless top. It had built in support for a woman with a far less ample bosom, but Liria managed to stuff her breasts in, using the adjustments on the straps to make herself as comfortable as possible. The thick sash went under her wings and wrapped around her waist, crossing over several times before Liria tied it closed at the small of her back. She looked up to find Raiden watching her with a predatory gleam in his eye, and flushed.

"I seem to be shorter and wider than your Yrini," she muttered, tugging self-consciously at the neckline of the top. "She's slender and long limbed while I'm..." she trailed off and made an exaggerated hourglass shape with her hands. "Bumpy."

"It's your fairy blood," Raiden answered, stepping close. "Flared hips -" he cupped them in his hands, "- nipped waist -" his hands slid up to frame the waist in question, "- and these." He moulded her breasts in his palms, bending to place tickling kisses along the upper curves.

"I've never met another fairy," Liria said, her tone breathless as she pushed helplessly against his mouth. "I don't know what they're supposed to be like."

"They're like you - beautiful predators, particularly the dark ones." He grazed his teeth over her collarbone and then straightened. "I've only met a couple, and no two are ever truly alike, but one thing I can promise is that all fairies are built for seduction. It's how a lot of them hunt." Raiden lent back and passed an appreciative look down her body. "You shouldn't be self-conscious - you're exquisite. Those clothes Ione had you in mostly hid your frame."

"Of course," Liria muttered, pulling away to rub her arms. "I got tired of having to kill anyone stupid enough to look. It was easier to keep my distance."

"You couldn't keep your distance from *me*," Raiden rumbled, his expression settling into one of masculine satisfaction.

Liria propped her fists on her hips, trying to affect a stern countenance as he dragged on a pair of beige linen trousers and tied them off with a dark mustard sash. His sword belt went over the top, each khopesh settled lovingly into place at his hips. That done, Raiden pulled a palm green shawl from a pile of identical palm green shawls on a nearby shelf and draped it around his neck and shoulders with the ease of long practice, securing the garment in place with the clothes pin he'd used the night before.

"You didn't let me keep my distance," Liria said, running her eyes over the perfection of his rough edges and smooth hollows. "I was furious with you, and terrified of what I'd be forced to do. After the stabbing, I..." She blew out a long breath. "I expected to be executed, but instead, you fought for me. I thought you were crazy."

"Maybe I am." His deep voice curled around her like a caress, and she itched to run her fingers through his shower-damp hair. "Perhaps you scrambled my brains."

She opened her arms and he stepped into them, pressing his chest to hers while his hands took a commanding grip on her backside.

"If this is insanity," Liria whispered against his lips, "then we have found it together - and I never want it to end."

Raiden squeezed his eyes shut and ground his teeth. "We need to go see Balai."

"Yes."

"We promised."

"Yes."

"I want to kiss you."

"*Yes.*"

Her mouth was open already, and they met in a clash of teeth and tongues. Liria hitched her legs around Raiden's waist and held tight as he tried to meld them into one person.

"Balai," he gasped, breaking the kiss. "Set. Selekhet. Egypt."

Liria groaned and kissed his throat, rubbing her core against the bulge in his trousers. "Is it always like this?"

"The passion or the need to save the world?"

"Passion."

"Gods, I bloody well hope so."

"Wait." Liria lifted her head, frowning into his flushed face. "You've never..?"

"Not like this," Raiden answered, squeezing her buttocks. "Never like this."

Liria draped her arms around his shoulders and turned that notion over in her mind. After a long minute, she smiled, broad and true. "Good."

They stared at each other, then Raiden's lashes lowered and he dropped his forehead against hers. "We can't."

"There will be other opportunities at some point, surely." Liria nipped playfully at his nose and was rewarded with a chuckle.

"Move into my quarters and we can make opportunities whenever you like."

"What?"

He leant back slightly, golden eyes shimmering with power. "You don't have your own quarters yet, as far as I know. Taos intended to let you keep the suite Ione was in, since she's now in the royal chambers with him, but that was before we... I mean, I know this is fast, but you did just give me your heart. Surely sharing a bed on a nightly basis is only logical?"

"I... I..." Liria's head spun and she swallowed. "I'm allowed to do that?"

"You can do whatever you want, Liria." Raiden raised a single dark brow. "Besides, I'm the Crown Prince of Egypt. Who's going to stop us?"

Madness. It was all madness. And yet... she'd never felt so at home as she did in Raiden's arms, never felt so whole as she had in those moments they'd been joined. Liria swallowed. "All right."

The radiance of his smile lit her entire world, and Liria blushed as Raiden lowered her back to her feet. He brushed his lips across the warmth of her cheeks, then adjusted his pants with a grimace. "Let's go, before this gets any worse. Do you need shoes?"

Liria shook her head, heart warming when he took her at her word and returned to the bed, sitting down to tug socks and then boots onto his broad feet. They left the cottage to the warmth of mid-morning, flying in easy synchronicity back towards the Palace. After a quick detour to the kitchens for a breakfast of honeyed oat cakes, Raiden showed her the interior route to the sacred heart chamber where the embalmers and healers kept their temple.

"Welcome, my Prince." An older man with a generous belly and a cheerful face met them by the fountain, hands clasped over the top of his olive healer's robe. "You're here to see the young embalmer, then? Our Pharaoh sent word to expect you."

Raiden nodded, his smile easy. "Thank you, Nurus. Yes, we're here for Balai, if he's awake."

"He is." The healer turned to Liria, his gaze curious. "You must be the Lady of Shadows. My name is Nurus Venethite, senior healer at the Palace Temple."

"Liria Atlannon," Liria replied, inclining her head respectfully. She shot Raiden a glance out the corner of her eye. "But I must warn you, good healer, I'm no Lady. There's been an error in my titling."

Nurus laughed, his blue eyes twinkling. "Oh, no, my dear, I don't think so. If our Pharaoh and our Prince say you are the Lady of Shadows, then I'm afraid you are, indeed, the Lady of Shadows." His eyes glowed for a fraction of a second as he looked between her and the angel by her side. "Besides, whatever your previous role, you'd be a Lady no matter what, now that the Crown Prince is on your arm." He proffered a deep bow. "It is an honour."

"I..." Liria took a step back, but was prevented from escaping by the warm wing that Raiden curled around her shoulders. "What?"

"Oh, I see I may have spoken out of turn." The healer bowed again, but the amusement in his expression made the gesture anything but sincere. "This way, if you will - our young Balai is waiting."

Liria spun to face Raiden even as he used his wing to scoop her against him. "What did he mean?"

"Nothing. He's a meddling old busybody who cannot keep his opinions where they belong," Raiden rumbled, his voice carrying across the room to where Nurus had opened a door. "And he forgets that I'm a man grown, who's well able to manage his own life."

Nurus chuckled and disappeared down the hall. Liria glared up at the Crown Prince of Merged Egypt and poked him in the chest. "Stop prevaricating. What did he mean?"

"I'm not trying to avoid the topic, but we're hardly in private." Raiden waved a hand at the chamber. "Do you really want to have this discussion here?"

Liria narrowed her eyes, using her magic to blur their forms and cut off all exterior sound. "Yes."

"All right." Raiden hesitated, then shrugged. "Nurus has been the senior healer here for as long as I can remember. Longer. He knew my parents and after they died, took it upon himself to offer unsolicited advice to two young angels he deemed woefully unprepared for the roles in which they found themselves." A smile tugged the corner of Raiden's mouth, but his face remained serious. "One of the first things he preached - and what he was angling at just then - is that Taos and I can never forget, most especially in matters of the heart, that we're Pharaoh and Prince of Merged Egypt. A casual encounter is one thing, but to take a lover makes a statement... and gives that other party a power they wouldn't otherwise have attained within the court."

Something cold worked through Liria's gut. "But you said... you said we were just Raiden and just Liria."

"We are, and nothing will ever change that." He hesitated, then grimaced. "What Nurus was pointing out, however, is that our claim upon each other has certain... side effects. Like ripples in a pond after a stone has been dropped in; the stone itself remains the same but the environment around it is altered."

Liria dropped her gaze to the floor, and it was only a lifetime of practice that kept her from loosing the scream crawling up her throat. How could she be so foolish? She'd been born into the naga court, had spent years in the Atlantean one. There was no such thing as 'just Liria' and 'just Raiden,' because he was, and would always be, the Crown Prince of Merged Egypt... while she was just a shadow. And to be his lover, his partner, his *heart*, she'd be stepping out of those shadows and into a very public light.

"No," she whispered. Her feet took her backwards, but once again, Raiden's wings hemmed her in. "I can't do that. I can't be that person. Gods, Raiden, I'm a monster, and you'd march me around the throne room like a fancy trinket?"

Storms clouded his expression. "I'd have us standing side by side, because I love you. Nothing else matters."

"Nothing else matters? You're the Crown Prince! If something happens to your brother, you ascend the throne." Liria clutched at her stomach, bile rising in her throat. "You'd need a Queen. *Heirs.* How can you ask me to stand by and watch that happen?"

He flinched as though struck, then growled deep in his chest. "You think I'd put you aside and take someone else? Never."

"So, what? You think to make me Queen, instead?" Liria shook her head, the pain in her heart dragging her to her knees. "No, no, no. Sharing a room is one thing, but this? It's not possible. I'm just a shadow. I can't."

The world rocked, and it took her a moment to realise that lightning had struck the ground outside. Fighting the yawning maw of despair inside her, Liria wrapped a hand around Raiden's ankle and dug her talons into his skin. He jumped, but the crackling energy around them immediately dissipated as he re-established control between one heartbeat and the next. With-drawing her hand, Liria tightened the magic which shielded them from view and curled into a ball on the floor.

What a fool she had been, to believe their love could ever be just between them. But now, having claimed Raiden in front of not only Ione but the Pharaoh, how could she go back? Particularly when she'd sampled his love, his heat, and craved more of it? She was trapped, all over again. A strange sound escaped her throat and it took a moment to recognise it as a whimper.

"Liria." Warm arms gathered her close, the scent of warm sand and burning sunlight filling her lungs. "Gods, don't cry."

The words seemed to unlock something ancient deep inside Liria and before she knew it, she'd buried her face in his linen shawl and was crying in great, wrenching sobs. Raiden smoothed her hair and kissed her face, his lips catching her tears and his wings surrounding them in protective comfort.

"Please, Liria," he murmured. "I don't understand."

"You're a P-P-Prince," she managed, "and I'm a-a-a-a shadow."

"I'm a man who loves a woman," he replied evenly. "I don't care about the rest."

"I'm not even a real person! I don't have a soul!"

"You do."

She thumped a fist against his chest. "Ione has it."

"So we get it back."

"We get it *back?*" Liria shook her head, burrowing harder against him even as she wanted to tear off his limbs. "She'll never give it up, Raiden. And watching you make me into a... whatever you think I'll be? That will tear Ione to shreds; it's not how she views the natural order of the world. It's not the way her life works."

He growled again, his fury vibrating through her frame. "Fuck Ione. What about your world? What about your life? I don't want to make you anything other than you already are - I just want you, with every fibre of my being. You gave me your heart, Liria. Does that mean so little?"

"Of course not." She sat up straight, horror warring with temper. "It's all I had to give. It's all of me."

"Then why won't you fight for it?" Raiden shouted, then immediately flinched. "I'm sorry. The storm..."

Liria sighed, dropping her head against his shoulder. "I know. It's all right."

Warm lips pressed against the shell of her ear, Raiden's hands kneading the muscles up and down her spine. How long they sat that way, Liria couldn't tell, but eventually she found herself relaxed against him, curled into his body like a kitten seeking warmth.

"I love you," Raiden said at last, and his voice trembled with emotion. "It's only ever been just me and just you, Liria, from the moment we met. But if it's important to you, then, yes - to be with me, you'll no longer be just a shadow." He blew out a long breath. "Taos and I have been calling you Lady of Shadows since you arrived, so the title will likely stick, but it would have done that anyway; as part of the Pharaoh's guard, you'll be more in the limelight than you have been before. Being my lover will intensify the attention, but that doesn't mean you have to become an entirely new person. Egypt doesn't work that way. Taos and I don't work that way. Surely you know enough of us by now to believe that's true?"

"I'm sorry," Liria whispered. "I'm not used to this. I don't know how to... be what you need. And I..." She swallowed, forced the words to come. "I cannot give you an heir. The soul ring forbids it. I should have told you before I offered my heart, but -"

"I don't care," he said fiercely, his grip on her tightening. "All I ask is that we face the future together."

Liria forced herself to breathe, to speak as calmly as she knew how. "Think for a moment, please. I'm a weapon, an ugly one, and without the compulsion to keep me in check I may not be...

appropriate at court. You should know those things before you commit to having me stand at your side. I've given you my heart, and I will ever love you, but you... be sure, Raiden. Once you let me in, I... I fear what I would do to stay there."

"You're already in, Liria." Raiden took her hand and slid it under his shawl to press against his chest. "It's too late for both of us. You're branded on my every breath, and I will never let you go."

SLEIGHT OF HAND

Raiden worried he'd gone too far with his darkly possessive comment, but rather than slap the words from his lips, Liria subsided against him in obvious relief.

Wrapping his arms around her all the tighter, Raiden pressed a kiss to her hair. Damned Nurus and his constant meddling; bad enough that he and Taos had dealt with more than two decades of pithy, unwanted advice, let alone starting in on Liria. Or perhaps Raiden was more angry at himself? In his haste to crack Liria open and wrap himself in her essence, he'd forgotten what it would mean to have a relationship with her - beyond being happy, of course.

"I'm sorry," he murmured, tipping her head up with a knuckle beneath her chin. "I should have thought to speak about this with you before we gave in to each other."

"You didn't mean to upset me," she sighed. "I understand that much, at least. And some of the fault is my own; I've never had the opportunity to decide things for myself before. The idea that I could choose you, that you could be, in some way, mine... it was a heady thought."

The phrase 'and now it is too late' hung in the air between

them, and Raiden found it difficult to breathe. "You said before you didn't regret what we've become. Has that changed?"

Violet eyes snapped to his, and though there was a hefty dose of uncertainty in their depths, there was also the steely determination which had attracted him from the first.

"No," Liria growled, fisting her hands in his shawl and dragging him down until they were nose to nose. "I will never regret you." A pause, her brow furrowing where it rested against his. "I... It was just a shock."

"And now?"

"Now, I find it difficult to think because your touch clouds my better judgement." She smiled, the soft quirk of lips soothing the sting left by her words. "I do not know the way forward, but I'm accustomed to fighting. I suppose the battleground is simply different."

"Oh?"

"Do not forget, Prince of Egypt, that I grew up in far more vicious courts than this one. Being thrust into the limelight is not my choice, but neither will it prevent me from doing my job." She sighed, her breath tickling his cheeks. "Our shackles may be different, but you and I have both been slaves to duty the entirety of our lives. Perhaps, together, such duty will be easier to bear?"

A curious sensation curled through Raiden's chest and he realised that it was the echo of Liria's heart, the pace having picked up with her words. He shifted to cradle her head in his hands. "Are you saying you're willing to admit your worth?"

"No." Her gaze flickered away from his. "I'm still just a shadow, and you should never forget that." He opened his mouth, but paused when her gaze swung back to his face. "But I am also the woman who loves you, and I'm willing to stand side by side because that is what you need."

Raiden leant forward to capture her lips in a sweet, soft kiss. Less than five minutes ago she'd been ready to run, terrified by the things Nurus had so gloatingly revealed. Now, she'd gathered those shattered pieces of herself into a weapon and was swinging it on his behalf, even when it was clear she believed that she'd be the one left bleeding in the end. His body shook as he kissed her, trying to pour every ounce of his bottomless respect and devotion into the place their bodies connected.

"Taos and I have long been alone in the world," he whispered, feathering kisses over the swell of her cheekbones. "Now, we have you."

Liria sighed. "Yes."

And neither of them, though it hung in the air like the echo of a dream, mentioned Ione.

The diffusion spell wavered, and a grunt of surprise came from a long way away. Raiden glimpsed a foggy silhouette and squinted to try and make out who it might be. Liria rolled off his lap with a snarl, yanking him up behind her. There was such strength in her pull that Raiden stumbled, wings spread for balance as Liria dropped her diffusion spell and faced the interloper.

"Healer Nurus." Liria's voice was the cool whip she'd employed on Raiden when they first met. "I wasn't aware your status allowed for interrupting the Crown Prince during a private moment. I can only assume there's some sort of emergency." She reached into the shadows created by her body and withdrew a curved dagger, the blade bent back along her forearm. "Is there someone for me to kill?"

The older man took a step back, jolly face blanching and sweat breaking out over his brow. "I merely worried for my Prince's safety."

"Oh?" She tilted her head. "As his personal guard, I think that's *my* concern."

Nurus cleared his throat and stepped back further. "I, er... My Prince?"

"Now that Ione is Queen, Liria has become part of the Pharaoh's guard - and my partner in all things." Raiden crossed both arms over his chest. "Safiyah should have updated you upon your return."

Nurus waved a chubby hand. "She was gone by the time I arrived."

"Is she all right?"

"How should I know? I had things to attend to following the conclusion of my pilgrimage. The affairs of one tardy healer can wait."

Raiden fought the urge to roll his eyes and stepped to Liria's side, draping a possessive wing about her shoulders. Her dagger pricked his side in warning, and he grinned. "Shall we go and see our friend Balai, my Lady?"

"I'll show you a Lady," Liria muttered - but she swept the dagger into the shadow between their bodies and when her hand came back, it was empty. Reaching up, she adjusted his wing like it were a cloak, then nodded. "Very well. I think the poor boy's waited long enough."

They swept past a sputtering Nurus and into the healing temple proper, Raiden trying - and failing - to choke back the laugh in his chest. "Balai's in his twenties. He's not really a boy."

"Young twenties, if anything." Liria snorted. "Trust me, he's still a boy."

"Because you're so much older?"

She lifted a brow, but didn't look at him. "I'm older than you, and Ione, and Taos; you know that already. But no, I meant because you've protected Balai, allowing him time to *be* a boy."

"You're talking about a man with the Touch of the Underworld."

"Are you, an Egyptian, trying to tell me that death is anything other than a doorway?" Liria snorted and shook her head. "Balai has the powers of the great beyond in a world where such a thing is an honour and a blessing. He's about as terrifying as strawberry syrup on a pancake."

Raiden's laughter bubbled out, echoing through the corridor as they walked. Liria steered them past a nurse's station and took two left turns before his mirth had faded enough for him to say,

"How do you know where we're going? Nurus never gave directions."

"No, because he wanted to show how important he was by guiding us himself." Liria's violet eyes turned heavenward for a moment. "I can sense your young embalmer's power. I know where he is."

Fascinated, Raiden drew her to a halt in the hall. "You can sense the Touch of the Underworld?"

"I can sense everyone," she answered, tapping a taloned finger against his sternum. "I can tell who - and what - is around me at all times."

Raiden tried to expand his mind and sense the world around him, and was rewarded with little more than an ache in the back of his head. "I can't do that. Who taught you?"

"The naga, perhaps?" Liria pursed her lips, considering, then shrugged. "Truthfully, I've no idea. My training, if you would term it such, was unconventional at best. I recall being strapped to a table, Coranna's voice, bright light and lots of pain. I just... am, I suppose."

Something cold sucked the breath from his lungs. "How old were you?"

"I don't know, but I was five when I helped Coranna escape the naga grottoes to become Queen of Atlantis, so... perhaps a few years younger?" Liria searched his face, her gaze soft. "Don't look like that, Raiden. I told you, I'm a shadow. A weapon, not a person - and you might disagree, but that is the truth of my upbringing."

Liria pulled gently out of his embrace, spreading her wings in a flash of plum and crimson before resettling them down her back. Raiden watched the motion with a mixture of hunger and awe, marshalling every ounce of his warrior's will to stop from touching without permission.

"The truth of your upbringing enrages me," he said, following her the last few paces down the hall to a closed door.

"And I understand I cannot change it, but, Liria, that is no longer your life."

She shook her head, pushing the door open rather than reply. Raiden followed her inside, where the little healing chamber was lit by soft lanterns and the single bed was taken up by a pale-faced Balai. Clear green eyes opened as they stepped inside, black jackal's ears pricking up. Though his frame appeared leaner than when Raiden had last seen him, the young embalmer was well and truly alert, his hand steady as he waved them to close the door.

"I'm glad to see you well," Raiden murmured, clasping the proffered arm. "I imagine you gave Anubis quite a scare."

"Safiyah exhausted herself healing me, too." Balai sighed, his face pinched with regret. "She passed out and Anubis had to take her home to rest."

Liria blinked, her jaw dropping. "The god of death took a healer home?"

"He said it was the least he could do, and he wanted to reassure her daughter." Balai shrugged. "When I'm well enough, I'll pay a visit to express my gratitude."

"A good idea," Raiden nodded, dropping onto the small but comfortable couch along one wall. "What happened?"

Balai grimaced, running a hand through his tousled black hair while he watched Liria drift about the room. The dark fairy poked and prodded things on trays and shelves, lifting jars of salve to sniff and inspecting the variety of medical tools that sat by in case they were needed. When she reached the bedside table, Liria poured a glass of water and pressed it into Balai's hand, then reached behind him to fluff his pillows.

"I'm not really certain," Balai said at last, allowing himself to be shuffled further back on the bed as Liria rearranged his body to her satisfaction. "I felt fine when you left to look for Liria, and both Safiyah and Anubis agreed I was well enough to move." He stared down at his hands, then shook his head. "When I stood, however, my vision swam and the sucking sensation returned. I...

fainted, I guess. Anubis was here earlier, and he said that there had been a tiny fragment of Thissish's essence buried deep inside, like a seed waiting for the first spring rain to bloom. He believes that the onset should have been more delayed, but my powers forced it to light sooner than intended."

"Hmmm." Liria returned to one of the medical trays, picked up a long metal instrument that looked something like a two-tined fork, and used it to twist her hair into a loose knot at the back of her head. Long, curling strands began escaping almost immediately, tumbling around her face and over her shoulders with a sensual abandon that made Raiden itch to touch. Instead, he laced his fingers in his lap and watched as she propped both fists on her hips. "A delayed infection makes sense, but it attributes her more intelligence than I'm comfortable with."

"The Touch of the Underworld should have kept Balai safe," Raiden replied, brow furrowing. "I'm sure that's what Anubis said."

Liria nodded. "From a direct attack, perhaps. But this more insidious seed? It seems intended to clash with Balai's natural powers and either weaken him, or do the job Thissish could not accomplish in person." She pursed her lips, eyes distant. "Once she'd absorbed Jedda's life force, she had enough fuel to make it out to the gardens, where she was in the process of ingesting the girl's internal organs when I interrupted her. I'd wager that, once restored, she'd have returned to collect Balai for herself."

"Wait." Balai held up a trembling hand. "Did you say that creature was *eating* someone's internal organs?"

"Yes. I believe it enabled her to regrow her own... or somehow transplant them into her own body," Liria answered. "The process infected Jedda, too, for the poor thing awoke in my arms not long afterwards."

"None of that makes any sense." Balai ran a hand over his face. "Are you sure Jedda was dead?"

"Quite." Liria hesitated, then shrugged. "She was torn open from pelvis to throat by the time I found her, most of her organs already gone. After I chased Thissish away, I returned what little there was to Jedda's body and used the skirt of my gown to bind her back together, so that she could be mummified properly."

The room grew silent, and Raiden found himself sitting up straighter. "You tried to honour her?"

"Did I do wrong?"

"No," Balai shook his head, his face soft with wonder. "I just... not many people would have risked their lives for someone already dead. You do us a great service, Lady of Shadows."

Liria blushed. "It didn't matter - I had to walk her into Raiden's lightning before she tried to eat someone, and spread the plague further."

"You kept her safe until the end," Raiden murmured. His own memories of the girl were fractured, his mind a chaos of cascading energy and the driving need to find Liria. "Anubis will surely have been able to take her soul to the Duat."

Balai muttered a prayer under his breath as Liria fiddled with the tool tray, her face etched with frustration. "It doesn't leave us with much to go on, now. Both Thissish and Jedda are dead, their bodies destroyed. Even if we confirm they were made from the demon Apophis, we have no idea why Set sent them to Selekhet, or what he hoped to achieve in directly attacking the Palace on the Pharaoh's wedding day."

"Or why he came to the Palace during breakfast in the first place," Raiden grumbled. "Set may be the Anarchist, but that is unusual, even for him."

Liria lifted a brow. "You don't accept his story about wishing to meet Ione?"

"Not without some other subtext, no."

"Perhaps he has an unholy fascination for pancakes?"

"Ha. Ha." In a move fast enough to surprise even himself, Raiden snagged Liria around the waist and dragged her into his lap. She squeaked in surprise and he felt the cool caress of steel at his throat, a sensation which only made him grin. "Too slow, lover mine."

The chill disappeared and she relaxed into his arms, pillowing her head on the wing he curled beneath her for just such a purpose. "You're lucky I didn't cut your head off, Prince of Storms."

Raiden dropped the head in question to kiss her fast and hard, glorying in the laughter he stole from her lips. He drew back far enough to nip at her jaw, running one hand down the curve of her ribs to her waist for no other reason than that he loved to touch her.

"If I didn't know better," he rumbled, "I'd say someone is looking for trouble under the guise of innocence."

Liria offered a slow, wicked smile that caught him in all the right places. She opened her mouth to respond, then froze. "The guise of innocence."

"What?"

"The guise of innocence," she repeated, rolling off his lap. "Of course."

"Liria, I don't -"

"The healers at the Temple of Bast said Thissish carried the blood of Sobek, right?" Liria turned to Balai. "Did she?"

The embalmer shook his head. "I haven't done those tests yet - the creature attacked me before I had a chance."

"Claiming Sobek's heritage was likely nothing more than a fiction to gain entrance to the Temple," Raiden said.

"What if it wasn't? What if Thissish really was one of Sobek's, but then she was turned? What if she was lured from her home and taken somewhere against her will, on the morning of our arrival in Selekhet?"

"That would give time for the blood of Apophis to take hold, but..." Raiden frowned. "How could Set manage that if he was here, invading our breakfast?"

"He couldn't." Liria grinned triumphantly. "But someone else could - and Set could certainly create enough of a ruckus that we might not find out about the girl's disappearance until it was too late. And we'd never associate

Thissish's absence with the Anarchist, because he was here, with us."

"The guise of innocence," Balai murmured. "Set didn't come to the Palace to retrieve Thissish, or even to ruin Taos' wedding; he was creating both an alibi for himself and a distraction so that someone else could... what?"

Raiden leapt to his feet, his heart stuttering in his chest. "So that someone else could carry out nefarious deeds in his name, and we'd be none the wiser."

"Exactly." Liria drummed her taloned fingers on the end of the bed, her face screwed up in thought. "You cut Thissish in half, thus preventing her from carrying out her true purpose - which, given the toxins in her kiss, we can assume was to subdue you and return you to her master."

"Me?" Raiden spread a hand over his chest. "Why would Set want *me?*"

"I don't know, but if I were Set, I'd be keeping our focus on him as much as possible, while whoever's doing his dirty work tracked down someone else to take Thissish's place."

Balai held up a hand. "Why would Set want to do that? Thissish was discovered. She failed."

"Did she? Because until Raiden cut her in half, she was holding him down with her tongue alone." Liria tilted her head to the side. "Imagine what two such creatures could accomplish. Or more."

Raiden shuddered, recalling all over again the horrid, fake scent of moon lilies and the slimy kiss that had come with it. "I'd rather not."

"Raiden is the Prince of Egypt," Balai said slowly. "Even before Liria stabbed him and forced the gods to donate their blood, he was widely acknowledged as the force behind the Pharaoh's throne. If Set could gain control of Raiden the way he owned Thissish, he would have the means to control the Pharaoh - and through him, not just Selekhet but all of Merged Egypt."

"Why not just go straight for Taos?" Liria asked.

"He's too well protected," Raiden murmured. "Anyone wanting him would have to go through the Pharaoh's guard, and, thereby, me. Also, the gods are in constant mental contact with Taos and are more likely to notice a change in him. Balai is right - if you control me, you control the guard *and* Taos."

"And whilst Thissish was alive, she appeared no different than her peers?" Balai looked between Raiden and Liria for confirmation.

Liria shrugged. "From what the Temple of Bast said, no - but I'd like to return there and search Thissish's rooms, perhaps talk to some of her peers. Even seemingly useless information may help us prevent a recurrence of the situation."

Balai nodded, his eyes wide. "A good idea. As soon as I'm able, I'll test the samples I took from the body, as well."

"The more we know about these creatures, the better chance we have of catching any more Set might have created. It would not do for the Anarchist to become the puppet master behind all of Egypt, with nobody the wiser." Raiden shuddered. "We must protect my brother."

"No, Raiden." Liria stepped in close, fisting her hand in his shawl. "We must protect *you*. If Set gets his hands on an angel with the power of the gods, he could bring the entire world to its knees."

CAVITY SEARCH

THE ROOMS IN THE student section of Bast's Temple were sparsely furnished with a bed, a chair, a desk and a small wardrobe. If Liria were to spread her wings in the space they'd brush the walls on either side, and the narrow window, though providing good natural light, was barely wide enough to squeeze her shoulders through.

"This was Thissish's room?" she asked, drifting further into the space.

The young healer behind her shifted from foot to foot. "Yes, Lady of Shadows."

"Did she frequent anywhere else?"

"The common areas and the healing halls, of course, but Crown Prince Raiden is inspecting those with the High Priestess."

Liria nodded. "Thank you."

Footsteps withdrew, and a moment later the door clicked shut. Liria spread her senses through the room in an attempt to trace Thissish's final movements, but the space had been too well disturbed in the last few days for her to discern anything reliable. A search of the mattress and beneath the bed yielded nothing but soft carpet and a rather indignant spider, who was soothed only when Liria offered him a lift to safer grounds via the back of her hand. She fluttered to the top of the wardrobe, deposited her passenger and then checked for hidden panels; nothing. The same went for both inside the wardrobe and beneath it, though there was a discreet pull-out compartment that, from the smell of it, had once held dried herbs.

The chair was solid wood and bore nothing more sinister than the marks of constant use and the desk, though scarred, was the same. Liria spent the better part of half an hour rifling through the books in the desk drawers, but there were only a compilation of study notes and a journal for daily affirmations. She hissed out a breath, dropping the final book back in the drawer. It was a long shot to assume that Thissish had written down something of her master's plans, but Liria couldn't shake the feeling that there was something in this place for her to find. She smoothed her hands along the carefully rendered walls searching for loose pieces to pull away and discovering only smooth, rendered stone. There were no pressure plates to open a secret vault in the softer plaster skirtings, and nothing hidden under the carpet. Everything was as it should be.

Flopping down on the floor on her back, Liria blew out a frustrated breath and stared at the roof. The decision to search the Temple of Bast for clues had been a logical one, and after leaving a message with Yrini to ensure the Pharaoh and his Queen were well guarded, Raiden and Liria had flown straight over. The High Priestess had welcomed them with quiet concern, abandoning her day's duties to escort the Crown Prince without a second thought while Liria had opted to search Thissish's room instead.

She'd assumed it the most likely place to find information but now, with the early afternoon sun highlighting how very innocent the room was, Liria began to wonder if she should have stayed with Raiden. After all, if one of Set's agents was watching the Palace, he'd have seen them leave - and the Crown Prince was even now wandering Bast's Temple with only a healer for company. Still, for all her desire to protect him, Raiden had insisted he could look after himself - and really, who was she to argue? He'd been doing it well enough for years so far. There was no reason to worry over him simply walking the halls, and even if a creature decided to attack, she was only a shout away from... what was that?

Liria picked herself up from the carpet, eyes trained on the carved light fixture overhead. The wooden edging down one side was frayed, as though someone had stuck a knife inside and levered. Spreading her wings, she fluttered towards the roof. Tiny splinters marked the place, and now that she was closer, she could also see a notch in the ceiling's render. Tugging a small, flat knife from the shadows in her bodice, Liria inserted the tip of the blade into the gap and turned it like a key.

The light fixture detached with a soft, wooden sound, hinging open like a trap door. The newly revealed cavity was no more than Liria's spread fingers, but the smell of decay wafting out was enough to confirm that she'd found something. After a careful sniff to ensure no traps lurked inside, Liria reached into the darkness and withdrew a ragged cloth stained with dark splotches. She lifted it to her nose and drew another, deeper sniff. Old blood, with an unusual, almost bitter edge she'd never encountered before.

Lowering her feet to the floor, Liria laid the bundle on the desk and carefully rolled it out. The roughly woven cloth contained another, finer wrapping inside and this time, she recognised the delicate gauze the Egyptians used in their mummification process. It was so thick with blood that it cracked as she unwrapped it, scattering fine, rusty flakes over the desk's surface. The package had been haphazardly formed, and Liria imagined whoever had done so moving in a desperate rush. After several minutes of careful work, she pried the last few layers open and stared down at the item inside.

A dull piece of bone nestled in the gauze. The surface was

smooth but for a circle of dark iron that had been embedded into the centre, emblazoned with a crest she'd never seen before. The work didn't look Egyptian in style, nor was it Atlantean or even of the naga - but that in itself said nothing other than Liria wasn't particularly well travelled. The sides of the bone were jagged and bloodstained, and as she picked it up with gentle fingers, it fit so easily into her grasp she knew that it had been removed from the body with a great wrench of supernatural strength. The back of the piece was as smooth and flat as the front - so not a rib, with their broad curves. Not an arm or leg, either, given the section was as wide as three of her fingers.

Liria flipped the piece back over to the front and ran a thumb over the iron circle. A coin? Or... she raised her free hand to her chest, and pressed between her breasts. The sternum. Broad, flat, the ideal canvas for such a medallion to be placed. Had it once been a necklace, then? Lifting the bone to her face, Liria tilted it back and forth in an effort to see the edges of the iron circle. It sat flush with the surface of the bone, as though it had grown there rather than been fused to the top. She set the shard back into the gauze and shivered. Iron medallions didn't grow inside sternums, which meant someone had put it there - and for reasons unknown, Thissish had sought it out.

Electric energy tickled the outer edge of Liria's senses and she turned to face the door as it opened, revealing the silhouette of an angel in the hallway beyond.

"Find anything?" Raiden asked as he ducked inside the room. He had to pin his wings close to his back to fit through the doorway and once inside, looked even more cramped than Liria felt.

"How do the angelic healers fare in a place such as this?" she asked.

"There are not so many angels who are drawn to healing, but those that are, cope." Raiden shrugged, settling his wings so close to his spine that it was almost impossible to discern them as a pair rather than a single, fused unit. "This Temple is one of the oldest in Selekhet, and was built before the Merge. These rooms predate the existence of angels."

Such history. Liria took another moment to admire the sparse walls with newfound respect, then motioned Raiden to join her at the desk, explaining how and where she'd found the odd relic as he examined it.

"Sternum," he agreed when she'd finished. There was something in the certainty of his tone that made Liria blink.

"You recognise it?"

"Not the bone, but this design, yes." He rubbed his thumb over the medallion, much in the way Liria had done only minutes earlier. "It's the mark of the Kirrilakh."

Liria flattened a hand over her chest. "Your Kadir did nothing to me whilst I was there - I'd have known."

"No, no." Raiden shook his head, his face softening. "I didn't mean it was for prisoners. Kadir runs the Kirrilakh, and those that work with him have amulets embedded in their sternums to provide a certain resistance to djinn magic. That way, they can move about the prison without being caught in the numerous traps." He frowned, turning the bone over in his hand. "Kadir is selective about who he bestows such an honour upon, so he might know who this once belonged to."

"It's an *honour* to be so mutilated?" Liria demanded, rubbing harder at her breastbone.

Raiden raised a brow. "Kadir is a black jann. He has the power to insert this without it being a torture for the recipient."

"And you know this, how?" Liria stared at Raiden a long moment, then gasped. "No."

He rolled an easy shoulder. "I was a baby; I don't remember it. Besides, mine is different to this one - the royal family have a design all their own. It allows us access to the Kirrilakh, but only minimal resistance to Kadir's magic once we're inside, which is why I had to be careful to follow the sneaky jann's rules when I came to visit you. On top of the royal marking, we also have an individual signifier - so if we die in a way that distorts our features, the medallion can be used to identify our bodies."

Unable to resist the temptation, Liria slid her hands beneath the soft linen of his shawl, stroking her fingers down the length of his sternum. It felt normal enough, but when she applied a little pressure, she found an irregular indentation several inches down from the hollow of his throat, where the pendant of a necklace might rest. She traced the odd bumps and dips with her touch, outlining a perfect circle about the same size as the iron medallion she'd discovered.

"It didn't hurt?" she whispered, examining his face for the truth.

"I told you, I was a baby." His face set into harsh lines all of a sudden. "I forget; that means nothing where you were born, does it? In Egypt, children are sacred, and Kadir is a good guy. He'd never harm an innocent."

Liria nodded slowly, curling her fingers into a fist against the warmth of his skin. He had no chest hair to speak of and the texture was smooth like silk, eliciting an unusual urge to rub her cheek against him, or perhaps to outline the cut of his muscles with her tongue.

Instead, she drew a deep breath and forced herself to take a step back. "So this grisly trophy is not from a relative?"

"No. I'll need to take it to Kadir to learn anything more than that, though."

"Whoever it belonged to was Merged," Liria said, running a finger through the flaked-off blood on the surface of the desk. She touched her fingertip to her tongue and frowned. "The scent and taste are unfamiliar, but there are so many kinds of Merged beings that it's not enough to give us a clue."

If Raiden thought it odd she'd just licked dried blood off her finger, he gave no visual cue. Rather, he frowned and jutted his chin out to the side. "If you came across it again, would you recognise it?"

"Potentially." Liria bent close to the bloodied gauze and

breathed deep. "The blood is old and likely contaminated. I might be able to recognise the species if I caught it again, but as for an individual, I cannot say."

Raiden carefully folded the bone shard back inside the gauze and bundled the outer cloth around it. "It's the best chance we've got right now. Is your ability to track by blood and scent related to your ability to sense species and power type?"

"I assume so." Liria took another moment to run her gaze over the room, while Raiden tucked the cloth bundle into a leather bag he wore on a long strap across his chest. "As I said before, I don't know much about why my magical talents do what they do - I just have them." She straightened and propped both hands on her hips. "I don't think this chamber has anything more to offer. Was your search with the High Priestess fruitful?"

"Perhaps. Thissish was missing for about a week before we ran afoul of her, which matches the timeline of your arrival to Selekhet. Fellow students said she had an ailing mother to care for, so they assumed she'd been called home on an emergency." Raiden ran a hand through his dark chocolate hair, tousling the strands so they tumbled haphazardly across his forehead. "I have the address; I thought we could drop by before we return to the Palace."

"Good idea."

"I also asked the High Priest of Sekhmet to compile a list of any other missing persons in the last few weeks, in case Thissish wasn't Set's first attempt." Raiden clicked his tongue against the roof of his mouth. "Does it bother you that this all seemed to start with Ione's arrival?"

"It does, yes." Liria resettled her wings against her back. "What if the answer is as simple as more sleight of hand? You and Taos - even the gods - were all paying attention to the arrival of the Atlantean delegation, and Set did an excellent job of keeping your attention turned inward when he invaded Ione's welcome breakfast. On top of that, the wedding meant a larger number of people going to and from Selekhet than usual, particularly in the lead up to the actual ceremony. Set could have any number of followers moving about the city undetected, abducting potential victims or doing whatever else they might be here to do." She shot him a look from beneath lowered lashes. "Even the troubles between you and I would've played into the Anarchist's hands. If you're dying, or springing me from the Kirrilakh, then you're not paying attention to your city - and neither are the rest of the Pharaoh's guard, because they're either picking up the slack or worrying about another attack from the god of war and chaos."

"Fuck." Raiden spread his wings, grunting when they slammed into the narrow walls of the bedchamber. "You're right."

Liria reached for the nearest wing and smoothed her hands gently down the leading edge, fixing rumpled feathers as she went. Raiden tucked the other back against his body but left her to explore the wing in her hand, his breathing settling into a gentler rhythm with each caress. When she chanced a glance his way, the Crown Prince of Merged Egypt had his eyes closed, his expression serene. Bending at the waist, Liria pressed a kiss to the long, hard bone that ran down the wing's outer edge, chuckling when he jumped. Raiden didn't retreat, however, so she did it again, trailing soft kisses up the tickling warmth of his feathers until he curved his wing around her hips and swept their bodies together.

"Better?" she asked, reaching up to trace the line of his jaw. The idea that she could give this man comfort... her heart swelled in her chest, and she wondered if he felt the echo of it in his own body.

Raiden nodded, his other wing circling her shoulders. "Thank you."

"Are you ready to go, then?"

"I'm ready to disappear into a bedroom and not come out for several weeks - but that will have to wait." His lips twitched into a roguish grin. "We have a house call to make and a god to thwart first."

"Yes." Warmth curled deep in Liria's belly and she shivered as his feathers shifted against the gossamer surface of her own wings, sending delicious pleasure shooting through her blood. With a deep, steadying breath, she pushed at Raiden's chest and couldn't help but marvel when he immediately released her. Such a simple thing, respecting her choices, and yet... for a shadow who'd never had any, it meant the world. "Do we need to let the High Priestess know we're leaving?"

"It would be polite." Raiden strode to the door and peeked into the hall, beckoning her to follow. "Let me know if you sense anything unusual; Set's agents could be anywhere and you, my Lady of Shadows, are likely the only person in all of Selekhet with half a hope of detecting them."

Liria's heart stuttered at the thought of so much responsibility, but she kept her apprehension to herself. Raiden believed in her, and though the idea was something that still terrified her to the core, she'd die before she compromised that belief. Smoothing her hands down her ribs and squaring her shoulders, Liria Atlannon gathered her courage and followed the Crown Prince of Merged Egypt out the door.

MOTHER MINE

The sun was turning towards late afternoon by the time Raiden swept in to land on a neatly manicured patch of grass on the far outskirts of Selekhet. Getting away from the Temple of Bast had been an exercise in restraint that he wasn't sure he'd have been able to complete if not for the fact that Liria had managed to look both respectful and amused the entire time.

"Is this it?" Liria asked, alighting delicately on the ground beside him.

Raiden nodded, shoving the note the High Priestess had written into his belt. Thissish's mother lived on a dairy farm, the farmhouse old but sturdy and the surrounding gardens tended with obvious care. The flight out over Selekhet had done wonders for his equilibrium, the wind whipping his hair and the endless horizon whispering of the wilds - yet his muscles had burned to push harder, his wings eager to see just how fast he could go now that Horus' blood had finished altering his body. The energy of the storm crackled in his veins, no longer a rabid beast but one that filled him with boundless energy and a thirst for experiencing life to the fullest.

A cool touch on his bicep dragged his spiralling thoughts into sharp focus. He turned his head to find Liria watching him, her violet eyes soft. "Are you all right?"

"Just restless." Raiden curved his wings around them for privacy and ran a finger down the line of her jaw. They'd agreed she should wear her human disguise for this visit, in case Thissish's elderly mother was frightened by the sight of, in Liria's words, a monster on her doorstep. With her cream skin and softer features the shadow looked far more approachable, but it dulled her beauty much the way tumbling a gemstone removed the spectacular fire of the earth's precious treasures. Raiden tipped up her chin with his finger and pressed a kiss to her brow. "I have a lot more energy since Horus made me... whatever I am, and idling away the hours listening to aristocrats drone on has ever been a pain in my side."

Liria's lips curved. "The High Priestess certainly knows how to orate."

"When she sent for the ceremonial tea service, I wished we'd gone out the window," Raiden muttered.

"You'd never have fitted." She smoothed her hands across his shoulders and squeezed. "Too big."

"Too big?" Raiden growled and nipped the shell of one slightly pointed ear. "You like me big."

He'd expected a blush, but to his delight, Liria gave him a slow, seductive once over. "I don't think I've had enough experience to say for sure. You might have to show me again."

Before he could think of something suitably witty to say, she ducked under the arch of his wings and strode for the house. Folding his wings to his back, Raiden trailed after her, admiring the sway of her hips as she mounted the steps to the front porch. Liria raised a hand to knock but as her knuckles collided with the wooden door, it swung open. A noxious odour wafted out and Raiden drew both his khopeshes as Liria tugged her curved dagger from her belt.

"Can you sense anything?" Raiden whispered as he joined her in the doorway.

Liria shook her head. "Only death. Keep your instincts sharp."

They moved slowly into a dimly lit family area and Liria thumped an arm across Raiden's chest, halting his forward progress. Her nose crinkled and her brow creased, the cream pretence of her human skin fading to stormy blue-grey as she brought all her concentration to the task at hand.

A soft, slithering sound caught Raiden's attention and he turned towards an open archway. The shutters were down over the windows but enough light crept around the edges that he saw a shadow flicker than fall still. Bending until his lips touched Liria's pointed ear, he breathed, "Kitchen."

She lifted a hand and held up two fingers, then pointed first towards the kitchen and secondly towards the gloomy interior of the farmhouse. Raiden indicated the kitchen and she nodded, then touched a hand to his sword and made a chopping motion near the side of her throat. With the ghost of a kiss to his cheek, Liria slipped into the hallway and disappeared.

Tightening his grip on his khopeshes, Raiden flattened his back to the wall and inched closer to the kitchen. Had Liria suggested decapitation because that was her way, or because she'd been able to sense something he hadn't? Raiden ground his teeth, fighting back a growl. Since he'd woken with Horus' blood stampeding his system, he'd done nothing but doubt and question every move he made. If he didn't stop, he'd not only be useless to Taos, he'd be dead before the gods could so much as snap their fingers.

Raiden reached the open archway that led through to the kitchen and studied as much of the layout as he could from his vantage point against the wall. His body was partially concealed by a tall, potted plant whose leaves had started to brown at the tips, and beyond, a large island bench bore a subtle covering of desert dust, a chunky wooden chopping board, a kitchen knife and the wilted remains of some partly prepared vegetables. Cupboards lined the walls, with a deep double sink beneath shut-tered windows. The floorboards looked to be of darker wood, well trod and uneven, the lovely knotwork hidden by a series of bloody spatters and smears. The walls and cupboards Raiden could see remained clean, so whoever had left the gruesome trail had entered the kitchen from somewhere else, either on their hands and knees or being dragged.

A soft, squishy sound whispered up from behind the bench and Raiden clenched his teeth in an effort not to gag as the smell of rotten flesh drifted through the air. Slipping around the potted plant, he spread his wings as far as the kitchen's boundaries would allow and jumped, managing a single downward sweep that landed him in a crouch atop the bench. His heavy combat boots thumped on the stone surface, and he dropped a knee over the flat of the kitchen knife in case whoever lurked on the other side made a grab for it. Tightening his grip on his khopeshes, he leant out over clear space and braced for an attack.

The smell of rotten meat was stronger here, billowing up from the figure on the floor. It twitched, the movement creating the soft, squelchy sound that had first drawn his attention, and then it lay still again. Hardened warrior though he was, Raiden pressed the back of one hand against his mouth and blinked through watery eyes. The thing on the floor had once been a person, but it was almost impossible to tell more than that. The torso was mostly intact but had a concave look about it, and the legs were no more than a runny mess, as were the lower arms. The figure lay face down, lank hair matted with blood and skin the slimy, dark shade of a wound that had turned necrotic.

Spreading his right wing, Raiden braced against the cupboards across the way and leant towards to the creature. It didn't seem alive but it clearly wasn't quite dead, either, for the thin eyelids fluttered as though they might open and the putrid tongue poked at equally horrid lips. It seemed oblivious to his presence, in spite of the noise he'd made, but as Raiden lowered himself a little closer, the thing's nostrils twitched and it made an odd, rattling sound.

"Shhhhh," he whispered. "I'm here to help you."

Another rattle came from the ruined throat, but before Raiden could decipher if it was an attempt at communication or not, a bloodcurdling scream rent the air. The thing on the floor jerked upright on rotting bones, crying out in desperate reply. Flesh slid in dripping heaps to the floor as it launched at Raiden, the deathly screech growing in strength even as the body failed. Raiden shoved backwards, striking out with his right khopesh as he vaulted back atop the bench. His blade hit true, decapitating the creature with an awful sucking sound. The head sailed through the air to land with a wet plop in the sink, while the body collapsed in a stinking pile back to the floor from whence it had risen.

"Raiden?" Liria appeared at his side in a flutter of gossamer wings, touching down onto the bench without so much as a sound. "Are you all right?"

He pointed with his bloodied sword at the gooey mess on the floorboards. "I'm better than whoever that was."

"Is that their head in the sink?"

"Yeah." Raiden grimaced. "It sort of stuck to my sword and then flew off at the arc of the swing."

Liria fluttered over to the sink and peered inside. "The woman in the bedroom was in about the same condition."

"Thissish's mother?"

"What was left of her, anyway." Liria frowned at the stains on the floor. "Looks like this person was attacked on the back porch and dragged inside."

Raiden jumped down from the bench and strode through the small laundry to the back door. It was hanging crooked from the hinges, dried blood splattered over the wooden surface and floors. He pushed the door open and stalked outside, where the smashed porch banister and arterial spray on the farmhouse walls told their own story.

"If Thissish's mother was elderly, it stands to reason she had someone on hand to help with the farm," Raiden said. "I'm going to bet the farm hand heard a ruckus at the house and came to check it out."

"Reasonable," Liria agreed, crouching to inspect the shattered banister. "He didn't go down without a fight, either."

"If Thissish's transition was gradual, she may have been weaker here than when we confronted her. That would explain the struggle." Raiden descended the back steps and followed the well-worn path towards an outbuilding, lifting his nose to the late afternoon air as he did. There was no wind, but it was a far sight better than the humid stench of death that had permeated the farmhouse. He paused to wipe his bloody khopesh on the grass and then sheathed both blades, turning his face to the sky to soak in the comforting heat of Egypt's blazing sun.

"Does it help?" Liria asked, the scent of moon lilies and dawn curling around his senses.

"The sun?" Raiden cracked an eye to find her at his side, watching the pathway between farmhouse and outbuilding with a tense expression. "Yes."

She tipped her head back just a fraction, the sun's rays gilding her stormy skin with gold. "The heat in Egypt is near overwhelming, but I have loved it since the moment I arrived. It seems strange to think that though this is the same sun that shines upon Atlantis, there is so much more life in the rays that touch your kingdom."

"You speak of Atlantis as though it is terrible, but we're standing outside a house filled with... whatever those things were."

"Atlantis is not all terrible in the same way Egypt is not all good - but the gentler side of that island is not one I've ever seen." Liria shaded her eyes with one hand as she glanced back at the farmhouse. "As for what we faced in the farmhouse, we already know Thissish's undeath was contagious. I'd say she fed upon her mother and the farm hand before she left here for the Temple of Bast, but because her transformation wasn't complete, the infection was weaker, too."

Raiden shivered. "I wonder if Set knew that would happen."

"You would defend his motives?" Liria asked, falling into step as he began to move toward the outbuilding.

"Set's motives may be shrouded in secrecy, but he's not an evil god," Raiden replied. "My father used to argue that chaos is, in its purest form, one of the basest requirements for life."

Liria paused by the large, sliding wooden door of the outbuilding. "So, what, he's not evil, just misguided? You make him sound like a lost child."

"I'm merely trying to point out that if we shade the Anarchist purely as a maniacal villain, we might miss the real truth of the matter." He laid his hand atop hers and squeezed. "There are two sides to every coin, and in my limited experience, even the most benevolent of gods are multifaceted."

She hummed under her breath, lips pressed into a thin line. "You may be right."

"What are you thinking?"

"That I'd like to talk to those who know Set best," Liria murmured. "I can't shake the feeling that we're missing something."

Neither could Raiden. He shifted his shoulders to alleviate the strange prickling that had settled between them. "I could contact Horus or Anubis, but I think we'd be better to go through Taos for a request like that. We can ask him when we return to the Palace."

"Sure." Liria smiled, and he was struck by how much more at ease she was since Anubis had lifted the extra layers from her soulbinding.

What would she be like if she were truly freed? Was such a thing even possible? Questions clogged his throat but Raiden swallowed them down, knowing they'd only steal his shadow's smile. With a final squeeze of Liria's fingers, he released her to grasp the heavy door and pull it open. There was a little resistance and then a loud, metallic sound. It took Raiden a moment to realise the door had been locked, and he'd broken the mechanism when he hauled it open. A blush tinged his cheeks when Liria paused to inspect the damage.

"It can't have been a very good lock," he muttered.

She raised a brow, prodding at a twisted shard of metal. "More like you still don't know your own strength."

"But I... but you..." he tapped the side of his head with a finger.

"Yes, but that doesn't automatically teach your body to exert different amounts of force when you've spent your entire life doing things a certain way." She stepped into the doorway and lifted her nose to sniff. "The healers at the Temple of Bast said this was a dairy farm, right?"

"Yes."

"Where are the animals, then? This building has row upon row of stalls, but they're all empty."

Raiden ducked inside the building and blinked as his eyes adjusted to the dim light. They stood at one end of a wide aisle, with waist-high stalls lining the walls on either side all the way to an identical rolling door at the far end of the building. Each stall's doors were open, and the shed smelt of clean hay with the faintest overtones of barley. Though he trusted Liria's nose, they walked the aisle and checked each stall, then headed back outside and took to the air, making a circle of the property until Raiden spotted a small herd of cows and goats in the back corner of a field, crowded together under a stand of trees. The grass had begun to brown from the sun but the animals appeared sleek and healthy, their drinking trough filled to the brim with shimmering water.

"Why doesn't the water evaporate?" Liria asked as they turned back towards the farm house.

Raiden landed on the front porch and waited for her to touch down beside him. "All the farms in Selekhet - particularly ones with livestock - have automated water systems. The cattle will be fine until we can arrange someone to take them in, or to take over the farm."

She nodded, and together they examined the front of the farm house with fresh eyes. It looked no different than when Raiden had first arrived, but now that the doors were open, the pervasive stench of death gave the building a melancholy feeling.

"You want to search the house, in case Thissish left any clues?" Liria asked quietly.

"Yes. I know it's a stretch, but any information might help us work out what's going on." Raiden glanced at the timepiece on his wrist. "Taos will be expecting us back in time for dinner, but that still leaves a good hour or so before we have to head for the Palace."

Liria clicked her tongue against the roof of her mouth a few times, her brow furrowed in thought. "All right. Let's go."

They worked with swift ease, scouring each room from top to bottom. With the exception of the grisly remains in the main bedroom and the kitchen, everything seemed normal enough. Raiden thumped a clenched fist against the wall in the guest bedroom and loosed a low growl. "Nothing. What a waste of time."

"Not entirely." Liria straightened from where she'd been checking the side of the mattress for hidden slits. "From what I can tell, Thissish was living here for a while before she lost control. That says to me that whatever was done to her was either deemed a failure and she was released, or that Set deliberately intended it to be a gradual process."

"I don't buy failure, but the gradual process theory has merit." Raiden tapped his foot on the floor. "It would mean Set could hide his agents among the population of Selekhet, then provide himself an alibi for the time frame they turned nasty."

"For all we know, Thissish could have been working for Set for weeks, even months, before he called her to more decisive action. She's certainly linked to that piece of bone we found at the Temple - I could smell the same bitter blood in her room."

"From someone alive, or from the fragment?"

"The fragment. It was an old scent, and faint." Liria screwed up her face. "Before that bone was hidden in the Temple, it was taped to the underside of Thissish's bedside table."

"I wish we knew if she recovered it herself, or if it was passed on by someone else." Raiden rubbed a hand across his brow and sighed. "I feel like we've got more questions than answers right now."

Liria's scent drew closer and a moment later, her arms wrapped around his ribs and her body moulded to the front of his. Raiden startled, then curled his arms across her shoulders, careful not to crush her wings. She laid her cheek against his chest and he bent his head to kiss the top of her hair, tension leaching out of him in a steady wave.

"I think we should take samples from the dead bodies," Liria said, her voice muffled by the linen of his shawl. "Then Balai can test them alongside Thissish's. It'll give him a better idea of how the infection functions and whether it can be stopped or even reversed should we come across any more of Set's creations." She nuzzled against his chest, then drew back far enough to look up at his face. "I know you're frustrated, Raiden, but I feel like we have a whole lot of the puzzle pieces now. All we need to do is work out how to fit them together."

He brushed a stray strand of hair back from her forehead. "I'm not really a puzzle kind of guy."

"Luckily for you, I am. I've spent my life reading between the lines, even when the lines are invisible." Liria turned her face into his hand and pressed a kiss to his palm. "We can do this."

"All right." Raiden brushed his thumb across her cheek. "I saw some preserving jars in the kitchen. We can use those to take samples."

She nipped at his thumb, then released him and made for the door. "Come on then, Prince of Egypt. The sooner we get this done, the sooner we can go home."

COMING HOME

Selekhet's Palace was a truly awe inspiring sight, towering above the city and gilded rose by the setting sun. Liria followed Raiden to a modest balcony not far from the Pharaoh's suite, touching down beside him after he'd landed in a flurry of feathers and muscle. The fading light made the rust-coloured feathers in his wings glow with their own inner light, and when he turned to face her, the rich, strokable tones of his skin were etched in brilliant bronze. He looked strong, raw, and beautiful beyond all measure.

"This is my balcony," he said, sweeping a hand at the smooth sandstone area in which they stood. "Ours, now."

Ours. Liria swallowed, eyeing the folding glass doors with trepidation. When Raiden moved to those very doors and pulled them open, it took everything she had to follow him over the threshold. The sitting area was furnished in earthy browns and beiges that offset the natural colour of the sandstone floors and walls, with pops of white and olive green that gave the room character. As Liria looked around, she spotted signs of Raiden throughout - a whetstone and rag, a half emptied glass of

Egyptian beer, a rumpled linen shawl tossed carelessly over the back of the couch.

"Do you like it?"

"It's lovely," she replied, turning to find him twisting his hands in the dark mustard sash at his waist. "It's so much like you."

He hitched a shoulder. "Anything you don't like, we can change."

Liria's mouth dropped open, but he spun on his heel and strode through the doorway behind him. After a moment's indecision, she followed and found herself in a large, airy bedroom. "Oh."

A cream rug took pride of place in the middle of the floor, and atop it, a four-posted bed carved from honey coloured wood. Dressed in a thick comforter of deep khaki green and accented with rust coloured pillows, it looked soft and inviting. The cream gauze canopy was tied neatly to the bedposts at the head of the bed, and matching wooden tables stood at either side. An open archway in the east wall displayed a bathroom that was a triumph of sandstone, glass and shimmering gold, with a bright green vine climbing the walls to provide a brilliant splash of colour. The west wall held a floor length mirror, and beside it another open archway through which Liria glimpsed shelves and hanging rods filled with clothes.

She took a step forward, then stopped and blushed as Raiden unpinned his shawl and tossed it in a wicker basket just inside the wardrobe. The sight of his bare chest stole her breath and set her mind whirling, and when his golden eyes lifted to catch her gaze, she wondered if she would faint.

"Are you all right?"

"I... I'm sorry. I'll... let you change." Liria stumbled back into the sitting area, a hand pressed to her chest as she struggled for air. Her knees went weak and she sagged, only for a pair of strong arms to sweep her off her feet.

"I can see you thinking," Raiden growled, carrying her back

into the bedroom and sitting on the bed with her cradled in his lap. "What is it? You don't like the bedroom?"

"No, it's beautiful." Liria pressed a hand to his chest, then startled away from his bare skin. "It's just... I..."

Raiden shifted his grip and yanked the medical fork from her hair, tossing it carelessly onto the nearest bedside table. With a start, Liria saw that the two jewelled silver pins she'd brought from Atlantis were already on the same table. Her hair spilled over her shoulders and across Raiden's lap, and he combed his fingers through it for a long moment before gripping her chin and turning her face towards his.

"If you don't want to live here with me, I can get you your own suite," he said quietly.

"No! It's not that. I'm just... a little overwhelmed."

"Tell me."

Part of her wanted to rebel against the command, but it was spoken with such tenderness that Liria dropped her head against Raiden's shoulder while he returned to running his fingers through her hair.

"Nobody's ever fought for me before," she murmured, letting her eyes drift shut so she could enjoy the warm sand and burning sunlight of his scent. "You'll either be my salvation or my ruin."

Raiden chuckled, the whisker-roughened edge of his jaw tickling her skin as he kissed her brow. "It's the Prince thing again, isn't it?"

"I suppose so. The moment I see you as Raiden, something happens to remind me that there's still a yawning divide between us - and I don't know how to cross it."

"It frightens you."

"Yes." Liria shivered. "When I think of leaning over the edge, I hear only a screaming abyss."

His fingers tightened in her hair a moment, then relaxed. Gentle kisses fluttered over her brows and cheeks, Raiden's breath warm against her face. "You're forgetting three very important facts."

"What?" Liria opened her eyes as he leant back, enchanted by the softness in his expression.

"One; you have wings." Raiden ran a gentle hand down the gossamer surface of the wing draped across his knees. "However wide the abyss, you can fly across it." He stroked her wing again, the corner of his lip twitching when she shivered in sensual pleasure. "Two; I also have wings. If you can't fly all the way, I'll come to meet you. Gods of the underworld, I'll carry you if I need to." His hand shifted to her hip, and he drew the curved dagger she'd jammed into the waistband of her borrowed trousers. "Three; we're warriors. There is no battle we cannot fight."

Liria swallowed as he tossed the dagger onto the side table with a loud clatter. "I know how to be a warrior and I know how to be a shadow. I don't know how to be a person. I don't know how to be the sort of woman a Prince needs."

"This Prince only needs you to be yourself." Raiden flopped backwards on the bed, dragging Liria atop his chest. His wings spread wide across the khaki comforter, the soft feathers begging her touch. She gave in, propping her chin on one hand and threading the other through the warm, silky mass of feathers near his ribs.

"I'm not really sure how to do that, either," she said at last, fiddling with a feather that was mottled with an enchanting mix of white and rust.

Raiden shrugged. "You'll learn, and Taos and I will be right beside you."

"You make it sounds simpler than I think it's going to be," Liria grumbled, flexing her talons against his chest.

Raiden returned to his rhythmic combing of her hair. "It's not hard, just daunting – and the best way to learn is by facing the situation head on. Why do you think I promised Taos we'd be back in time for dinner?"

Liria covered her face with a groan. Dinner with the Pharaoh? Really? She drew a deep breath and tried to think past the instinctive rush of panic. Raiden and Taos both professed a desire for less formal gatherings, so it was unlikely a family dinner would be the stilted, cold affair she'd escorted Ione to in the Atlantean court on a monthly basis.

"How long do we have?" she asked finally, lifting her hand to find Raiden watching her with tenderness in his golden eyes. "I'll want to wash and change."

Raiden glanced at the chunky timepiece on his wrist. "About an hour?"

She sighed. It was tempting to lay on Raiden's chest all night, but she needed time to wrap herself in some semblance of her customary armour if she wanted to survive the dinner intact. Pressing a kiss to Raiden's sternum, Liria pushed upright and made her way into the bathroom. The luxuriant tub beckoned but she was in no mood to recline, so instead turned her attention to the shower. It was simple enough, just a larger scale version of what she'd used in Ione's quarters when they first arrived. She reached behind her back for the ties on her borrowed top and gasped when strong, warm hands beat her to it.

"It'll be faster if we shower together," Raiden murmured, unwrapping the top and tossing it aside. His hands slid over her ribs to cup her breasts, then moved down to the ties on her pants. "Unless you'd prefer to shower alone?"

"Can you behave yourself?" Liria whispered, curling her fingers over the tops of his. "I don't want to be late."

When he tugged on the ties at her hips, she let them unravel, wiggling so that her clothes slid to the floor in a soft whoosh of fabric. Raiden pressed his naked front to her back, his erection nestling in the crease of her buttocks. He wrapped one arm under her bust and the other across her abdomen and lifted, kicking her discarded pants and underwear aside before setting her gently back on the floor.

"I don't want to behave myself," he murmured, nibbling and kissing his way down the side of her neck to her shoulder. "But I will."

Liria relaxed into him with a sigh, revelling in the feel of so much masculine warmth around her, the way it tingled through her wings and caused her knees to wobble. When Raiden nudged her towards the shower she went, allowing him to reach around her to swing open the enormous glass door, then prod at the panel which controlled the water temperature and the spray.

The shower was just the right side of scalding and Liria stepped into it with a groan, ignoring Raiden's chuckle as he closed the door behind them. A second later he was pressed against her again, lathering his hands with scented soap from the automatic dispenser and then smoothing it all over her body. Part of Liria protested being so thoroughly pampered but it was a small part, a part easily overruled by the larger part of her that was enjoying the way Raiden's hands felt as they traced her every dip and hollow. He scattered kisses over her skin as he went and though his want for her was obvious, his touch was tender more than sexual, the tone of his voice reverent as he bade her move and stretch so he could reach different parts of her body.

When the soaping was done, Raiden turned her towards his chest. While she rested bonelessly against his heartbeat he massaged shampoo through her hair, rinsed it off, then repeated the process with a conditioner that smelled of lavender and honey. He hummed in the back of his throat the entire time, lulling Liria into a state of relaxation so deep she feared she might drop off to sleep, even as her heart cried out his name. She'd never felt so... cherished, never believed such love was possible for a shadow. What else had she been raised to believe that was actually a lie?

Raiden's hands settled on the base of her spine and his chin came to rest on her head. They stood like that for a long minute while the water cascaded over them, then Liria blinked and lifted her head. "What about you?"

"Me?" He raised an eyebrow.

She blushed. "Can I... can I..."

"Sure." He lowered his arms and took a half step back. "I'm yours to handle as you wish."

Liria cleared her throat, then placed her hand beneath the soap dispenser as he had done. Raiden's skin was slick and hot, the soap adding an extra bubbliness to the sensation of stroking her hands over his body. She washed him with as much care as he'd shown her, struck by the trust he placed in their relationship that he didn't so much as flinch with her taloned fingers so close to his vulnerable areas. He bent so she could do his hair, bracing his arms on the wall either side of her shoulders and nuzzling at her breasts while she managed, through sheer teeth-gritted effort, to stay upright through the process.

Raiden shut the water off and kissed her softly before he opened the shower to snatch up a couple of towels, drying himself vigorously in a way that seemed inescapably male. Liria rubbed her own skin dry, twisted her hair into the towel and hesitated.

"What?" Raiden asked, watching her in the mirror as he applied black kohl to his eyes.

"I just realised I don't have any clothes here." Liria frowned. "I'll have to wear my dirty things back to the other suite."

"No, you won't. The clothes you brought from Atlantis are already in our wardrobe, along with a few new things I arranged on your behalf." He lifted his kohl-blackened pinky. "You want some smudge before you go?"

Liria stared. Opened her mouth to remind him she was just a shadow, and shadows didn't get wardrobes, or wear makeup. Shut it again. Swallowed the heartbeat that seemed to be fluttering in her throat, and stepped in close.

"Close your eyes," Raiden murmured, turning to face her. Liria obeyed, and a moment later the soft brush of his fingertip moved across her eyelid in little circular motions. Once he was done with the top, his finger swept gently along the base of her lower lid, then repeated the process on the other eye. "There you go. Take a look."

Liria lifted her lashes, faced the mirror and gasped. Her violet eyes seemed to leap out of her face, the kohl so well blended it was almost impossible to tell where it ended and her real skin began. "Amazing."

"If you like it, I can teach you how," he offered.

"I..." Liria cleared her throat. "I like it when you do it for me."

"Really?" Raiden's expression turned smoky, and he curled his body down to kiss the hollow beneath her jaw. "Then I shall always do this for you."

Something warm tingled inside her chest. "I have nothing to offer in return."

"Not everything has to be an exchange of service, you know." He nipped at her ear as he straightened. "Love is payment enough."

Love is payment enough. The concept seemed so foreign and yet Raiden's words tolled deep inside her. She'd followed Ione to Egypt because that was her duty, and she'd dared to think she might attain a better life by improving the life of her mistress. Now, if she was brave enough to fight, the reward would be not just freedom, but Raiden himself.

"Yes," Liria said, turning to press a clumsy kiss to his lips. "You're right. Love is payment enough." He looked so stunned that she kissed him again, tilting her head a little to get a better fit between their mouths. "No more fear, Raiden. You're mine and I will fight for us."

Pink tinted his bronze cheeks and he wrapped his arms around her, squeezing tight. "Thank you. I should warn you, though..."

"What?"

"If you don't go and put some clothes on, we're not going to make it to dinner."

Liria laughed and tugged out of Raiden's embrace, giving his erection a playful swat before she retreated into the bedroom. Thunder rumbled in the room behind her and she laughed again, ducking into the wardrobe before he decided to chase her and exact revenge.

It didn't take long to discover a set of drawers with a variety of underthings inside. Liria took a moment to swallow her trepidation as she dug through piles of silk and lace, finally settling on a matching bra and panties in a purple so dark as to be almost black. The panties tied at the hip with a soft ribbon, and the bra was edged with thick lace that appeared to depict moon lilies. Everything fit so perfectly that Liria knew Raiden had commissioned them specifically for her, and she couldn't help but smooth her palms over the swell of her breasts to admire the way the silk clung to her skin. A groan from the door drew her attention, and she looked up to find Raiden watching with his fingers curled so tightly around the stone archway that his knuckles were white.

"How did the tailor know the correct accommodations for my wings?" Liria asked, angling her body so that he could see where the back of the bra sat against her ribs. "This is so much more comfortable than anything I've had before."

"Angels have a similar enough shape that it wasn't difficult to guess," Raiden answered, his gold eyes glinting as he looked her up and down. "Gods, Liria, you're so beautiful."

Blushing furiously, she turned to the part of the wardrobe that was full of elegant gowns and selected one at random. It was a long sheath of pale mauve that belled out around the knees, with a slit in the skirt that reached almost to her hip and allowed enough freedom to fight if she needed to. The bodice fit snugly to the base of her wings, the neckline low enough that the leading edge of the dark purple lace on her bra peeked out. Raiden watched while she adjusted the crystal encrusted straps, then stepped in and handed her a silver hair comb set with pale amethysts.

"How can I -" she began, then cut off when he shook his head. *Love is payment enough.* "Thank you."

Further exploration revealed a set of brushes perfect for her long corkscrew curls, so Liria set about untangling her hair and setting the comb above one ear - and when she looked in the mirror, she could hardly believe the woman who stared back was the same Liria Atlannon who'd been born a slave to the naga.

Raiden sauntered out of the wardrobe wearing his customary loose trousers in soft cream, paired with a sash that was the same mauve as Liria's dress. He belted his swords over the top, then took up a shawl in Selekhet's palm frond green from the end of the bed and looped it over his shoulders, securing it in place with a beaten gold pin in the shape of a falcon.

"Ready?" he asked, running a hand through his dark chocolate hair so that it tumbled becomingly around his face.

"Almost." Liria turned to a shelf of weapons, some her own and some new. She strapped a trio of throwing knives to the thigh revealed by the slit in her dress, then selected a thin silver belt which enabled her to hang her favourite curved dagger at her hip.

Raiden beckoned her out into the bedroom and handed over a coiled silver bracelet which twined around her wrist like a snake and proved to hide a thin, flexible rapier inside it. She was so busy admiring the craftsmanship she was taken completely aback when Raiden cleared his throat and offered her a slimmer version of the timepiece he always wore. The face was made of silver and the time was marked out in Egyptian hieroglyphs, with the blue eye of Horus in the background. The hands on the timepiece, though, weren't Egyptian at all - they were delicate fairy wings.

"Do you like it?" Raiden asked, curling the timepiece around her right wrist.

"Raiden, I..." Liria shook her head, blinking back sudden tears.

"You said you'd never owned jewellery before and didn't know what you liked, so I had to guess," he said, showing her how it fastened in place. "I hope you don't mind."

Liria shook her head, unable to speak past the lump in her throat. When he bent his head to kiss her, she trembled in his arms, pouring every single one of her emotions into the place where they connected.

"It's wonderful," she whispered against his lips. "There's just one thing."

He leant back with a frown. "What?"

"I can't read hieroglyphs."

Raiden threw back his head and laughed, and Liria thought it was the most incredible sound she'd ever heard.

SNAKES AND ANCHORS

R AIDEN STRODE INTO THE Pharaoh's private dining room with his
heart lighter than it had been in years. He nodded at Dyrian and
Gallin, who stood guard by the door in their leathers, and
grinned when their mouths dropped open at the sight of Liria's
fingers curled trustingly over his arm.

Taos rose from the elegant glass and iron dining table with a
shout, crossing the space between them with a solid downward
sweep of his wings. Raiden opened his arms and they locked
together in the fierce embrace of two siblings who'd weathered a
lifetime of storms side by side.

"Brother," Raiden chuckled, releasing his Pharaoh with a
smile. "It hasn't been that long since you saw my face."

"No, but after speaking with young Balai, I was worried
about your face," Taos returned, his deep brown eyes sparkling as
he turned to Liria. "I see now I should never have bothered -
with the beautiful Lady of Shadows at your side, it would be very
difficult to get in trouble."

Liria inclined her head respectfully. "Thank you, my
Pharaoh, but I fear your brother's penchant for mischief will try
even my abilities."

Taos tipped back his head and roared with laughter, the sound light and pure and wrapping Raiden in the familiar warmth of family. Though Liria's face remained bland, her violet eyes glittered with humour. While she murmured a polite response to the Pharaoh's joy, Raiden examined the rest of the room. Queen Ione sat regally at the round table with Yrini by her side, the angel doing her best not to look bored. Zsil loitered behind the chair Taos had vacated, and he winked at Raiden as their eyes met. The table was elegantly set with a glass dinner service in Selekhet's palm frond green, accompanied by gold cutlery and white fabric napkins folded into the shape of angel wings. Cut crystal jugs of Egyptian beer and wine were set in the centre of the table around a tall vase with three midnight blue moon lilies inside.

"Shall we?" Raiden offered his arm to Liria, and together they made their way to the table. He paused by one of the vacant chairs and inclined his head to the Queen, who wore a floor-length gown in a deep, sapphire blue that complemented her midnight eyes and raven hair. The moon lilies had no doubt also been chosen to complement her colouring, but all Raiden could think was that they carried Liria's scent within their delicate petals. "Ione, you look most lovely this evening. I trust Yrini has been guarding you well?"

Queen Ione inclined her head in acknowledgment. "Thank you, Prince Raiden, yes. Yrini has been most attentive to my needs."

"Just Raiden, please," he urged, tugging out a chair and settling Liria before seating himself. "Dinner shouldn't be a formal occasion when surrounded by close family and friends."

"Of course." Ione hesitated, then turned her dark gaze to Liria. "My shadow, you are well?"

Liria bowed her head. "Yes, your grace."

"I..." Ione licked her lips, then drew a deep breath and spoke in a rush. "I owe you an apology for my behaviour yesterday. It was remiss of me to speak such when I had promised to do better. Forgive me, my shadow."

"Of course, your grace."

Raiden fought the urge to clench his fists under the table, reaching out instead to fill Liria's glass, then his own, with Egyptian beer. He watched as she took a delicate sniff of the thick liquid, then a tentative sip. Her eyes widened.

"This is good," she murmured, sipping again. "Like nothing I've ever tasted before."

"Egyptian beer is a far cry from the unpalatable stuff by the same name you get elsewhere," Taos agreed, his grin broad as he dropped back into his seat. "It's both refreshing and good for you, Lady of Shadows."

"And the low alcohol content means that we're all still thinking straight the next day," Raiden chuckled, toasting his brother before taking a large gulp.

Taos glowered. "I'm never going to live that down, am I? How was I supposed to know the Mayans drink fortified liquor like it's water?"

"The Mayans?" Ione blinked slowly. "You're on good terms with the city of Tikal?"

Raiden laughed at the look on his brother's face. "Egypt is on good terms with Maya, Sumeria and Greece - and now Atlantis, of course - but Taos has a special place in his heart for King Gabor."

"A special place in my liver, more like," Taos grumbled, taking a sip of his beer. "I'll never drink like that ever again. I couldn't walk straight for three days afterwards."

Raiden opened his mouth to ask whether that was a remnant of the alcohol or Taos' encounter with King Gabor's younger cousin Sacniete, but shut it upon catching his older brother's pointed look. He was saved from his potential gaffe by the arrival of the soup course, and jumped up from his chair to help Dyrian and Gallin bar the door so they could join the meal.

"I find myself intrigued by your political relations," Ione

murmured as she scooped up her soup with dainty motions. "How do you come to be so well regarded by countries so far away?"

Taos shrugged. "Trade and tourism, mostly. When the airships were first perfected back in my grandmother's time, Egypt formed a treaty with Sumeria and the gods of Mu donated the crystal caps to the pyramids - and for Sumeria's ziggurats - to symbolise our ability to chart a path of light and peace in the darkest of days. The Mayans saw the crystals glowing at night to light the way for the ships and wanted to be included. Shortly thereafter, Greece followed suit. I'm hoping that in my lifetime, and with the help of the gods, I'll be able to form connections with even more far-flung areas of the Earth. That way, as the Merge expands, we can create peace and harmony for all races and peoples, even help them through the transition to Merged life."

"World peace? Equality for all? Connecting Earth's people via airship travel?" Ione's eyes crinkled as she smiled indulgently. "It is a lovely dream, but I fear that is all it can ever be. There is no such thing as true equality."

The Pharaoh set down his spoon with a frown. "How so?"

"You are a Pharaoh - a king, an avatar of the gods, an angel." Ione smoothed a hand down Taos' bicep. "How can you possibly take a mere human from the street and say they are equal to you? Common people need structure, and it is up to us as royalty to provide it for them. If there was nobody around to tell them what to do, they'd languish and fade to nothing."

Taos drummed his fingers on the table. "I disagree. If we're not prepared to put ourselves in the shoes of those we care for, how can we properly care for them?"

"We all eat and we all shit," Raiden added, biting his cheek to keep from laughing when Ione looked scandalised. "We all love, and grieve, and breathe and hope. We're all mothers and fathers and children and siblings - and in the end, we all die, our souls ceding to the Soulcatcher for the journey to the Underworld."

Queen Ione scrunched up her face and pushed her soup bowl aside. "It appears I still have much to learn about your culture. I'm fortunate the goddess Isis agreed to tutor me in the ways of ruling a country such as Egypt."

"Indeed." Raiden let his spoon clunk against the edge of his bowl and wiped his face with a napkin. "We're dining unusually well tonight, brother. Is there a special occasion?"

The Pharaoh shifted uncomfortably in his seat, setting his own empty soup bowl aside. A curious silence fell as the rest of the guard waited for his answer, and when Taos finally looked up, his cheeks were dark with colour. "No special occasion. I merely thought to bring Ione into our world gradually."

Raiden sat back to allow a waiter to remove his bowl, murmuring his thanks when it was replaced by a hearty plate of roasted chicken and vegetables. When the servants had all withdrawn, Ione cleared her throat and laid a hand on her husband's arm.

"I don't want you to alter your lifestyle specifically for me," she purred, lowering her lashes coquettishly. "I came to Egypt to be part of your world. I'd be honoured to see how you really live your life."

Taos looked uncertain for a moment, then nodded. "Very well. Tomorrow night, we dine as normal."

"Thank the gods," Zsil muttered, spearing a piece of chicken and swirling it through his gravy. "Formal dining is worse than being dunked in the ocean."

Laughter rang out through the room, and the subtle tension that had pervaded the atmosphere began to ease. As conversations sprang up around them, Raiden curved his wing across the back of Liria's chair and leant in close.

"Are you all right?" he asked, keeping his voice low.

"Of course." Liria darted him a look from the corner of her eyes. "Why say otherwise?"

Raiden ran a fingertip over the back of her hand, and

watched her fingers twitch in reaction. "You've not said a word since we sat, and you've barely eaten."

"Perhaps I'm not hungry."

"*Liria.*"

"Raiden." She gave him a cool look that set a fire burning deep in his gut, then sighed. "If you must know, I have a... different constitution to the rest of you."

"Like the vampires?" He jerked his chin towards Dyrian and Gallin, who were quietly sipping glasses of blood. "I can ask for blood, if you need it."

Liria shook her head. "I can take sustenance from blood, but it's not my preferred meal. I..."

"What?"

"Nothing," she muttered, pushing the food around on her plate. "I can get by like this. Please."

Raiden stared at her profile for a long moment, then sat back and withdrew his wing. What was it about her diet that was such a bother? He racked his brain for all he knew of fairies, and came up with precious little. They were rare, and tended to keep to Mu for the most part - meaning he could likely ask the gods to find out more, but he wanted Liria to tell him herself. He wanted her to trust him enough to reveal every secret, let him beneath every shield to the woman hidden deep inside. She'd given him her body and her heart; what was so unusual about her eating habits that she felt she couldn't share?

Unless... Raiden snuck a glance across the table at Ione. The Queen was doing her best to monopolise Taos' attention, as though she feared he'd divorce her if he had a spare minute to think for himself. Was it possible she had no idea what Liria truly ate, after living a lifetime with her shadow by her side? He recalled their first shared meal and the scandalised expression on the faces of the Atlantean contingent when he'd suggested Liria eat with them. Gods of the sky, it *was* possible nobody knew - and with the compulsion she'd been under, Liria would have been unable to tell anyone.

His knuckles ached, and Raiden glanced down to see he'd clenched his fork so tightly in his fist he'd bent the handle. He blinked at it for a moment, then Liria's delicate arm reached across to coax his fingers apart.

"I have made you angry." Her shoulders drooped as she retrieved his ruined cutlery. "That was not my intention."

Raiden tossed around several possible replies before settling at last on the truth. "You don't trust me. It hurts."

Liria pressed her pristine fork into his grip and then set about smoothing the mangled one back into shape with careful fingers. She fiddled with the angle of the handle until it was as close as possible to the original, then carefully set it against her plate and pushed the meal aside. From what Raiden could tell, she'd barely eaten a thing, merely moved the food around on the plate to make it look like she had.

"It's not that I don't trust you," she whispered at last, her gaze fixed firmly on her lap. "It's that I don't want you to look at me differently."

"I'd never -"

Liria's chair scraped on the floor as she surged to her feet and for a moment Raiden feared he'd upset her, but then something heavy collided with the dining room doors, followed quickly by the unmistakable pounding of fists.

"Help us!" Someone shouted. "Please, help us!"

"Stop." Liria held up a hand when Gallin and Dyrian made to step forward. She ran her eyes over the room, then settled on Raiden. "Stay with the Pharaoh. He, the Queen and the Crown Prince are your priority."

It was word for word what Raiden drilled into the Pharaoh's Guard every day - except for the part about himself - but hearing the words from Liria's mouth twisted his stomach.

"You can't open that on your own," Ione protested, shoving ineffectually at Yrini as the angel tugged her back from the table. "My shadow!"

"It is my honour to stand between you and danger," Liria

answered, her gaze still locked with Raiden's. "This is my purpose."

Before he could protest, she strode to the door and pressed an ear against it. Dyrian and Gallin rushed to flank the Pharaoh and his Queen, with Yrini making the point of the defensive triangle. Raiden started towards the door and gaped when Zsil stepped in front of him.

"Liria's right," the sand sprite murmured, his expression apologetic. "You're being hunted by the god of war and chaos - and your foremost duty is to protect Taos."

Raiden drew both his khopeshes with a growl, manoeuvring to place himself between his brother and the door. Damn the crown Taos had jammed on his head! If not for the weight of it, he'd be standing beside Liria and nobody in the room would think anything unusual.

Gasps echoed and he looked up to see Liria brace her hands beneath the enormous beam blocking the door and lift it as though it weighed little more than a glass of water. She stepped back and the doors swung inwards, revealing two terrified Egyptian soldiers supporting a third in bloodstained Atlantean blue and silver.

"Help us," one of the Egyptians cried. "Please!"

Liria narrowed her eyes, using the wooden beam to bar their way. "What ails you?"

The man in Atlantean armour raised his head, face bloody and torn and his eyes dull with horror. "We were attacked. There was no stopping them. The General sent me to warn... the Princess..."

"What?" Ione shrieked, pressing her hands to her mouth. "Warn me of what?"

"Snakes. Snakes, everywhere," the man croaked, then promptly fainted.

The Egyptians struggled to maintain their grip on the unconscious man. "We saw it," one said. "We were at the docks, supervising the Atlantean dreadnaught as it prepared to sail in the morning. It was overrun and sunk."

"By *snakes?*" Raiden demanded. He made to step forward again, and smacked at Zsil's hand when the sprite held out a restraining arm. "How can snakes sink a ship?"

"There were hundreds. Thousands, maybe." The soldier shook his head. "And something underneath the ship; something enormous."

"Snakes," Ione wailed. "My shadow, the naga have found us! We're doomed!"

"No, we're not," Liria snapped. She twisted her head to see further down the hall, and abruptly raised one end of the wooden beam to let the soldiers through. "Get inside. Ione, see if you can keep the Atlantean alive; I'll need to question him later. Zsil, with me. The rest of you, protect the royal family."

Zsil rushed to Liria's side. "What do you - god of the desert! Are those crocodiles? How did they get inside the Palace?"

"Wait a minute." Raiden shoved around the wounded soldiers and strode for Liria as she ushered Zsil into the hallway. "I'm going with you."

"No." Liria turned back long enough to heave the enormous wooden beam at Raiden, giving him no choice but to catch it, staggering backwards under the weight. "Guard your brother; I'll deal with this."

She swept out the door after Zsil, and Raiden didn't get so much as a glimpse of the hallway before the enormous doors slammed shut. He dropped the wooden beam with a howl of fury and rushed to follow, but no matter how he strained at the doors, they wouldn't open.

Liria had trapped him inside.

CROCODILES ON THE ROOF

Liria stared down the length of the Palace's stately hallway and wished for a longer blade than her dagger. Crocodiles large enough to swallow an entire person slithered along the marble floors, their bodies pressed so tightly together they moved as a single, undulating unit.

"Raiden would have been a better choice for this, you know," Zsil muttered, jumping up and down on the balls of his feet. "I'm surprised he's not out here already."

"He's being hunted by a god. Would you have me sacrifice him to Set's magical minions?" Behind her, the door to the dining room vibrated as Raiden pitted his brute strength against her sealing spell and lost. His energy reached for hers, blazing a path of heat across her senses and setting her hair crackling with the raw fury of his emotions. Gritting her teeth against the urge to call him to her side, Liria waved a hand at the approaching crocodiles. "Look closer and you'll know why I asked for your help, and nobody else's."

Zsil squinted at the beasts which were now less than ten paces away. "They're... made of sand."

As though hearing his words, the crocodiles stopped their

silent advance. This close, it was possible to glean what Liria's senses had picked up; their incredibly detailed bodies were put together out of millions upon millions of grains of sand.

"Can they hear us?" Zsil whispered, edging closer to Liria.

"I don't know. Best to assume they can," she replied, shifting her grip on her dagger. "Can you do anything with them, sand sprite?"

Zsil's clear green eyes narrowed in concentration. "There's a barrier on the surface, but if we pierce the outer shell, perhaps. I'll need to be touching them, though."

"Stay close to me, then, and we'll attack one by one. With such a neat formation, it should be simple enough to -" Liria cut off as the crocodiles began to move, some of them inching further down the hall while several others dug their claws into the sandstone walls and began to climb.

"God of the desert," Zsil breathed, tilting his head back to watch. "They're on the roof."

Liria blew out softly through her nose. "When I next see Set, I'm going to gouge his pretty eyes out."

The faintest echo of a masculine laugh reverberated through the stones of the Palace, accompanied by the merest suggestion of a desert wind.

"I guess that answers the question of whether or not they can hear us." Zsil shuddered. "On the upside, their magic is definitely similar to mine if they can bond with the sandstone like that."

"Keep to the plan, then." Liria put her lips against Zsil's ear and used magic to blur her words. "We cannot let them break through to the Pharaoh. If they do, Raiden will be their only defence and I'll not have him in any more danger than is necessary."

Zsil's lip twitched, fear fading from his face to be replaced by amusement. "If you expect the Prince to stay put, you don't know him as well as you think. Any minute now, Raiden will calm down enough to realise the dining room has windows."

"Surely he'd not leave his brother undefended?"

"He'll see it as helping rather than desertion - and he's used to being a warrior, not a prisoner." Zsil shrugged. "That, and he cares about you."

"My safety is nothing in comparison to theirs," Liria growled, her insides turning cold at the thought Raiden might put himself in danger after all. "Our best option, then, is to remove this threat before he makes stupid choices."

"Yes." Zsil bared his teeth in a feral grin. "Lead on, Lady of Shadows. Let's pit ourselves against the very god to which I pray."

Liria darted towards the foremost crocodile, keeping her body low and her dagger back against her arm. The creature opened sandy jaws wide enough to swallow her whole, so she tucked her wings tight to her back and shot straight into the gaping mouth. Flattening her free hand against the sandpapery tongue, she slashed out with her dagger as she pushed forward, emerging half way down the crocodile's spine amongst a fountain of sand. The conjured creature began to thrash and hiss, but Zsil thrust his fingers into the spilled grains and a moment later, the crocodile dissolved.

"Are you crazy?" The sprite cried, tossing a handful of the now harmless sand into Liria's face. "What if that didn't work?"

Liria shrugged. "Then I'd have cut the head off."

"From the *inside?*"

A crocodile chose that moment to drop from the roof, twisting in mid-air as though to slam them both flat with the sheer weight of its body. Liria stepped aside, slashing out with her dagger to open a wide gash in the creature's flank. Zsil immediately set his hand to the wound, and once again the crocodile dissolved.

Liria snatched her trio of throwing knives from the sheath on her thigh, and sent them thumping one by one into the other crocs on the roof. The moment they hit the floor, Zsil was there to destroy them, collecting Liria's knives as he went.

"This is too easy," Liria muttered, sidestepping another of the floor crocs and running her dagger down the length of its spine. "What are you planning, Anarchist?"

Another ghostly laugh teased the edges of her senses and Liria growled low in her throat, redoubling her efforts. Less than a minute later, the crocodiles were gone and she and Zsil stood ankle deep in sand in the middle of the corridor.

"Why do I get the feeling he's just messing with us?" The sand sprite asked, kicking at the sparkling granules.

Liria shook her head. "It has to have something to do with the ship sinking."

"Does it? He's the Anarchist."

"And yet you pray to him."

Zsil shrugged. "Set is the god of the desert, too, and it is from those sands that I was born. He may be fickle, like the desert, but that should not make him less deserving of love - even when he does things we morally disagree with."

"Egypt is a complicated place." Liria looked over the soft sand in the hallway and frowned. "Does this look bigger than before?"

Zsil turned in place, hands on his hips as he inspected. "The sand is probably settling. It is loose, and we made quite the pile."

Liria chewed on her lower lip as she watched the grains hiss and roll against one another. "No. It's moving towards the door." She lifted her eyes to the dining room and spread out her senses. "Damn. Raiden's gone. We need to get in there before the sand does."

The moment Liria tried to move, the sand solidified around her ankles, holding fast. Zsil uttered a sharp cry, arms windmilling as his lower legs began to dissolve, his body melting into the pile that moved with sharper purpose towards the dining hall.

"It's taking me apart!" The sprite cried, looking desperately at Liria. "I can't stop it!"

She reached to grab his hand, but Zsil's fingers turned to sand in her grip, his arms going the same way as his legs until he was only a head and shoulders, floating inexorably towards the double doors.

"Zsil!" Liria dragged at her feet but the sand had set like stone.

"Protect the Pharaoh," Zsil croaked, lifting his chin to keep his face above the surface as his head began to dissolve. "I'll try to -"

He was gone.

Liria's breath clogged in her throat. She wanted to scream and rage, but she'd spent too long as a shadow to come so completely undone. Instead, she turned the chill of her fury into resolve, and wrenched a leg free from the sand with a loud snapping of bone. Agony threatened to black out her vision but she clenched her teeth, setting her wings aflutter to avoid placing weight on her broken ankle.

"You will not best me, Anarchist," she hissed, bracing herself to free the other foot. "Nothing can hold me - most especially you."

In silent answer, the sand curled up her leg to mid-thigh and held tight.

Cursing in the spitting language of the naga, Liria used the tip of her dagger to slice a thin line around the exposed skin of her thigh. Sliding the dagger back into its sheath, she dipped a fingertip in the blood and began smearing characters around the top of the cut. Unlike the ugly hate culture King Vasilios had encouraged during his reign, the written language of the naga was a beautiful, sweeping creation of swirls, curling lines and elegant dot work. Liria had been a poor student but she knew enough to get by, enough to chant a spell to elevate the water content in her blood until it slicked down her leg and turned the outer layer of sand to a sodden, sticky mess.

Fluttering her wings harder, Liria twisted and tugged - and her leg slid free of the sand with an awful sucking sound. She wasted no time flying down the corridor, being sure to keep away from the surface of the sand as it began to slip beneath the door of the dining room. Lowering her shoulder, she slammed the doors open with her body weight and dashed inside.

Taos and Yrini had backed up against the open window with Ione sandwiched between them. Gallin was carrying the unconscious Atlantean, while Dyrian and the two Egyptian soldiers stood protectively in front.

"Don't touch the sand!" Liria snatched a jug of wine from the table and sloshed it across the floor, destroying the leading edge of the creeping wave. "Where's Raiden?"

"He flew around to try and reach you from the front," Taos answered, his jaw set in a way that said he'd disagreed with his brother's plan. "Where's Zsil?"

Liria's heart stuttered in her chest and she pointed at the sand. "He was swallowed."

"Damn." The Pharaoh's eyes closed briefly and he heaved a sigh. "We need to get everyone out of here."

"You take Ione. Yrini, take the injured Atlantean." Liria turned to the vamps. "Can you carry the soldiers on your back and climb?"

Dyrian pressed his lips together in a thin line, then nodded. "Probably."

"Go, then." Liria shooed them towards the window. "Get out of here."

"What about you?" Ione cried, clutching at Taos as he swept her into his arms. "You must come with us!"

"It's my job to keep you safe," Liria answered, tossing the second jug of wine at the sand trying to creep up the wall. "Stay with the rest of the guard and you'll be fine."

Ione shook her head, eyes brimming with tears. "What if we're attacked while you're here? What then?"

"Then I'll come for you," Liria answered gently. "You know I will."

"Promise," Ione breathed, her eyes wide and fearful.

"I promise."

The Queen nodded, and Taos inclined his head in thanks

before he ducked out the window, Yrini hard on his heels. The two vampires urged the soldiers onto their backs and a moment later they, too, were gone, leaving Liria alone in the dining hall with the murderous sand.

"All right, Anarchist," she muttered, picking up a jug of Egyptian beer. "Give my friend back."

This time, there was no laughing answer, no teasing gust of desert wind. The sand on the floor began to bubble and swirl, dragging itself together to form a serpent so enormous it barely fit inside the room. Instead of a snake's head, the creature had the face - and teeth - of a crocodile. As it opened giant jaws to hiss at her, the sandy surface melted together until she stared into the maw of a flesh and blood monster.

Liria drew her dagger and flipped it into a reverse grip down her arm, then lifted the beer jug to her lips and took a fortifying swig. She swirled the thick liquid around her mouth, releasing the paralytic toxin in her minor fangs as she did so. When her gums ached from trying to produce such a large amount, she spat it back into the jug and fluttered closer to the monster. It hissed again, revealing a long, forked snake's tongue nestled in the crocodile's mouth.

The monster lunged and Liria twisted aside, raking her dagger across the tip of the leathery snout. It was little more than a scratch but the beast jerked back with a squeal of pain and yellowish ichor blossomed in the wound. The serpent's tail, thicker than Raiden's broad shoulders, swept through the air. Liria launched herself skyward, the top of her head brushing the roof as the giant tail swung by beneath, slamming into the glass and iron dining table and shattering it into pieces. Shards of glass and twisted iron embedded into the snake's tail and it screamed in rage, a high-pitched sound like nothing Liria had ever heard before. While it thrashed and shrieked, she darted forwards and poured the entire jug of contaminated beer down the creature's miserable throat.

It gurgled, choked and swallowed, snapping those crocodile

jaws together with an ominous crunch. Liria felt a tug on her arm and looked down to see half the jug missing, shards of cut crystal covering the monster's face in a sparkling rain. She slashed out with the remains of the jug, opening a second gash across the snake monster's snout. It flinched away with a fresh scream, shaking its crocodile head - and as it twisted, she caught sight of a pair of leather boots in the depths of the snake's gullet.

"Similar magic," Liria whispered, her heart kicking up a notch. "Sand becomes sand, and flesh becomes flesh. I'm coming, Zsil."

"Liria!" Raiden sprinted into the corridor, the walls too narrow for him to fly. He had a khopesh in each hand, his golden eyes wide with shock as he took in the open dining room doors and the giant snake creature.

Beneath Liria, the monster shuddered and started to sag, opening its mouth on a long groan. Raiden started to run again, but there was no time to wait or to explain what she hoped to do. If she were to act, it had to be now.

Tucking her dagger close to her chest, Liria took a deep breath and dove head-first into the monster's mouth.

SPIT THAT OUT

RAIDEN WATCHED THE MONSTER's jaws close over Liria's feet as though it happened in slow motion. A deafening boom echoed through the halls as lightning struck the roof - lightning intended for the creature who had swallowed Liria. The Palace shook from the force of the blow, and it was only the deep seated love for his brother that stopped Raiden calling the lightning over and over, until the Palace of Selekhet lay in ruins and the strange serpent monster was dead.

Horus! He cried, sprinting down the hall as fast as he could. *God of the sky, father of angels, help me!*

The serpent turned its crocodile head towards Raiden and hissed, displaying a long, forked tongue. With a flick of his wings, he cartwheeled over the creature's head, slashing with a khopesh as he went. The creature jerked back and Raiden landed on his feet in the hall, ducking as the giant mouth opened... and the monster burped.

"Faugh!" He covered his nose with the back of one hand, eyes watering as the scent of blood and Egyptian beer swamped him. The snake-monster looked equally horrified, crocodile eyes wide and an odd gurgling noise coming from deep in its belly.

Not gurgling, Raiden realised. Chanting.

Together, he and the serpent craned their heads to see the midpoint of the long, sinuous body, where a large bulge had begun to wriggle. The monster gave a squeal of pain, and another burp, and a groan - and all the while, the voice kept chanting. A dagger thrust up through the snake's body, clutched in a stormy blue-grey fist. The monster began to shriek and writhe as the dagger, curved and marked with dark runes, switched to a reverse grip and sliced a long incision in the creature's back - from the inside.

"By the gods," Raiden whispered. "Liria?"

As though summoned, her head popped out of the hole. Yellowish ichor smeared her skin and her hair was slicked to her face with fluid, but her violet eyes were bright as they settled on him.

"Don't just stand there," she cried. "Kill the damned thing!"

What? He blinked, then turned to see the snake shivering and groaning where it lay prone on the ground. Tightening his grip on his khopeshes, Raiden strode over and cut off its head. By the time he straightened, Liria was half out of the hole she'd carved in the body - and she was dragging someone with her.

"Zsil!" Raiden wrapped his arms around the sand sprite's torso while Liria freed his legs. "God of the Sky, what happened here?"

"What *happened* here?" Liria paused in her extraction to set her fingers against Zsil's throat. "I trusted you, and you ran off!"

"Huh?" Raiden blinked. "What are you talking about?"

"Zsil's alive." Liria's face softened, and she sagged in relief. "Just unconscious. Thank all the gods for small mercies."

"Liria - ouch!" Raiden flinched as she slapped him hard across the face. "What was that for?"

"What happened here? What are you talking about? What was that for?" Liria mimicked, spreading her wings with a snap. Ichor and mucus flung off in all directions, splattering the Palace walls and painting a macabre pattern over what little of Raiden wasn't already filthy. "I told you to guard the Pharaoh. I barricaded the door to protect him - and everyone else - from Set's creatures. I trusted you with Ione's life, *my life,* and you ran off and left them to die!"

Raiden backed up a step, tightening his grip on Zsil as the sand sprite's body lolled to one side. "You locked me in that room like a helpless twit. I had to -"

"I trusted you to work as part of a team!" Liria bellowed, lips peeling back to reveal all twelve of her fangs. "Set has been hunting you, so it didn't make sense for you to be on the front line, but that doesn't make you useless - you and I are the two most powerful beings in this Palace. If I'm fighting the magic fucking crocodiles, it's because I'm trusting you to defend everyone else from the rear. But you decided that you didn't want to be an equal part of the team, did you? You decided I couldn't do my job by myself. You decided I needed rescuing, and you left your Pharaoh and your Queen and your friends to the mercies of a god, while you *acted like a pouting child!*"

Something cold twisted in Raiden's gut. "No, it wasn't like that."

"Wasn't it?" Liria's wings began to whir, and he noticed that one was slightly slower than the other. She lifted into the air, her body at an odd angle as it pulled slowly free of the enormous carcass. "Why did I have to rescue the Pharaoh and the Queen by myself, then? And fight the monster snake? And rescue Zsil after he melted?"

"I... I..."

"You abandoned your post, Raiden," she hissed, ramming her dagger back into its sheath. "You said you wanted to walk by my side, with me by yours, but the first time I trust you to do it, you can't. All that talk about equals, about love and trust and honour - and at the first test, it's proven a lie." Liria shook her head, and he was horrified to see tears shimmering in her eyes. "*You* dragged me into this world. You were the one who told me there was something there, that I was a person who could stand on her own. Ironic that when I finally decide to rely on you, you're not actually there. Congratulations, Raiden, you proved yourself right - I *can* stand all on my own. I had to."

She wrenched Zsil from his grip, tucking the sand sprite's head into the crook of her neck. Her body shuddered in the air, her injured wing struggling to cope with the weight, but when Raiden reached for her, she jerked backwards. Her heart pounded in his chest, setting up an ache that matched that of his own.

"Liria, please," he murmured, taking a step forward. "I didn't mean for it to seem that way. I'm sorry."

She gave him a long, sad look, then turned away. "So am I."

Raiden made to follow as she launched out the large, open window which he'd used to exit the dining hall earlier, but paused when a hand gripped his shoulder.

"Let her go," Horus said gently.

Raiden turned to face the god of the sky with a snarl. "How can I? Did you hear what she said?"

"I heard." Horus inclined his head. "The question is, did you? I think you need to consider her words carefully, my brother, before you confront her again - or you may lose her in truth."

Shame edged through Raiden's heart and he cleared his throat. "You're late."

"Anubis and I went first to Taos. Set had blanketed the area with static, and it was hard to get a lock on your location." Horus shrugged. "The Soulcatcher remained behind to look after the Pharaoh, and I came here to find you."

Raiden threw his khopeshes on the floor and sagged into one of the few chairs that had survived the battle. "What is wrong with me, Skywatcher? Ever since you gave me your blood, my life has become a shambles."

"So it's my fault?" Horus looked amused, his mismatched eyes twinkling. "Shall I apologise for saving your life, Prince of Egypt?"

"No." Raiden groaned, tipping his head against the back of the chair to stare at the roof. "That's not what I meant."

"I know." Horus sighed, feathers rustling as he resettled his wings. "Do you want my honest opinion?"

"Yes."

"You're used to being in control - as a Prince, as a soldier, and as bodyguard to the Pharaoh. You've grown up analysing situations and turning them to your will." The Skywatcher stepped into view, his handsome face gentle and his black hair shimmering in the light from the overhead fixtures. "Since the Atlantean contingent arrived in Selekhet, however, you've been unable to mould the world - though not for lack of trying."

Raiden's heart sank. "Liria was right."

"Oh, yes. She's a rather intriguing creature, your shadow."

He sat up with a snarl. "She's not my shadow - she's a woman, a *person*, and I love her."

"Relax." Horus held up both hands for peace, his smile easy in a way that reminded Raiden of Taos. "I was merely teasing. The thing is, brother of my blood, if you truly want Liria in your life, you need to accept that she is - pardon the expression - going to cause a little chaos."

Raiden dropped his head into his hands, wings drooping until they spread across the floor. Horus gripped his shoulder and squeezed, and it was the first time since his youth that Raiden felt the touch of a father. Before he knew what he'd done, he wrapped his arms around the god of the sky and buried his face in the soft warmth of Horus' fighting leathers.

"I just want to keep them all safe," he mumbled, hot tears slicking his cheeks. "I don't want to lose anyone else."

Horus' fingers smoothed through Raiden's hair. "I know. But you must accept that you cannot keep everyone safe by yourself. You cannot carry the entire Merged world upon your shoulders - not even the gods can do that."

"I let Liria down today. And Taos."

"Yes. The positive is that by realising the truth, you can work to change your choices in the future." Horus' wings draped across Raiden's spine, comforting and warm. "Nobody has died, and even Liria's injuries will heal. This lesson has been hard, but not nearly as expensive as you think."

Raiden stiffened. "What do you mean, even Liria's injuries? I only noted a sprained wing."

"Anubis is reporting a broken ankle, moderate blood loss, some acid burns and a nasty cut on one leg, in addition to the sprained wing." Horus paused, and Raiden felt a fluttering at the edge of his thoughts, as though butterflies were tickling the inside of his ears. "The healers have taken shifts to cure the worst of it, but the injury to her ankle was severe. The Lady of Shadows won't be able to walk for a few days, but she will live, and that is what matters most."

"Gods around us," Raiden groaned. "If I'd stayed where she'd asked me to, I could have helped her."

"Without a doubt."

He sat up, pushing against the Skywatcher's hips. "I should go to her."

"She's asleep; Anubis knocked her out."

"I should still go."

The god of the sky paused, and again that fluttering at the edge of Raiden's senses. "Taos and Ione are with her. I think it best you avoid them, for the moment. They're all rather angry at you."

Taos, because he'd been deserted by his own brother. Ione, because Raiden had almost gotten Liria killed. And Liria, because the man who claimed to love her had betrayed her trust.

"I'm such an idiot."

"We all make mistakes," Horus said, his tone so dry that Raiden wondered what mistakes the Skywatcher had made in his past. "The true test of mettle is how you choose to learn from those mistakes."

Raiden tugged from Horus' grip, and this time the god released him and stepped back. He wiped at his face, then gathered his khopeshes from the floor and jammed them into their scabbards. "If you're expecting me to go and take a nap, then you're going to be disappointed. I have too much energy for sleep."

"I'm not surprised. You're carrying a high concentration of my blood - you won't need as much sleep as you used to."

"I'm going to the Kirrilakh." When that earnt him an odd look, Raiden quickly explained everything he and Liria had discovered during the course of the day. "I need to ask Kadir about that medallion."

Horus pursed his lips, then nodded. "That's probably a good idea. The flight will give you time to clear your thoughts - and we cannot stop investigating the situation, particularly after this latest attack."

Raiden stared at the incision in the dead monster's back, reliving the moment of relief when Liria had cut her way free. Curving his wing in front of himself, Raiden plucked out a feather with a downy white base and a tawny coloured top.

"Would you make sure Liria gets this?" he asked, offering it to Horus. "If she wakes while I'm gone?"

The Skywatcher took the feather as though it were made of glass and bowed over the top of it. "It would be my honour, Prince of the Storm."

"Thank you." Raiden glanced down at himself and grimaced. "Maybe I should shower before I go."

"An excellent idea. If you'll excuse me, I'll convey your information to Anubis." Horus curled his fingers carefully around Raiden's feather, spread his wings, and disappeared.

Raiden stepped out the window and spread his own wings, sweeping around the curve of the Palace to land on the balcony he shared with Liria. He showered quickly, doing his best to ignore memories of the shower they'd shared, the vulnerability she'd entrusted to him. So many soft edges, hidden beneath her sharp tongue and sharper mind. Such courage and heart.

"Dammit," he growled, towelling himself dry with jerky

motions that left his feathers ruffled and his hair sticking out in all directions. He glared at himself in the mirror. "You're a fucking idiot, Raiden Horushood. Now put the mistake behind you and focus instead on fixing what you broke."

He strode into the wardrobe and dug out his fighting leathers, drawing comfort from the familiar way they hugged his body. He wasn't the Crown Prince of Egypt when dressed like this; he was a warrior, and he would fight for what he loved. He strapped his sword belt over the top, settled a khopesh into place at either hip, then ran a hand through his hair and let it fall where it would. When he stepped out onto his balcony in preparation for flight, he glared at the god who awaited him.

"Don't you have better things to do than follow me around?" Raiden snapped, propping both fists on his hips.

Horus shrugged. He still wore his fighting leathers, but a long sword was strapped down the middle of his spine and the gauntlets on each forearm held two throwing knives apiece.

"Set is hunting you, remember?" He handed Raiden a granola bar, then snapped his fingers to produce another one, which he promptly took a large bite out of. "And it's been an age since I visited with Kadir. Taos said he'd deliver your feather for you, as long as you grovel appropriately later."

Raiden grunted, snapped his granola bar in half, and shoved both pieces in his mouth simultaneously. *As long as you can keep up, I suppose you'll do.*

Horus' laughter followed him into the sky, the setting sun having long given way to a star-specked carpet of inky night. With his dark leathers, dark wings and dark hair, the god of the sky was almost invisible as he flew - but there was an indefinable knowledge in the back of Raiden's brain that meant he always knew the Skywatcher's location.

It's because we share blood, Horus said, tucking his wings around his chest and doing a barrel roll. *We can always find each other, if we try hard enough.*

And play peeping angel on one another's thoughts?

Horus snorted, flaring his wings wide and sweeping up to fly alongside. *It isn't my fault if you're thinking overly loud, blood brother.*

I've never been one for stealth.

Lucky your shadow excels at it, then, eh? Horus buffeted Raiden's wing with his own, then laughed as Raiden had to tuck and roll to correct his flight path.

Liria's better company, too, Raiden growled, flipping the god off. *And much prettier.*

Horus howled with laughter and Raiden sped up, pushing his body to the limit as he shot across the night sky. Selekhet glittered below him, a soft mixture of naked flames, flickering shadows and the gentler lights from the solar lamps dotted around the streets and inside homes. Before long the city gave way to the desert, the enormous crystals glowing atop their pyramids to light the way for incoming airships. Raiden banked before he could be highlighted in the glow, turning towards the eternal sandstorm which was no more than a smudge on the horizon. Horus tucked himself in closer as they approached, and the sandstorm had barely begun to part before the two angels were spiralling down through it to land on the partially exposed roof of the Kirrilakh with a satisfying thud.

"Kadir!" Raiden shouted, shaking excess sand from his wings. "Let us in, you old bastard."

The floor beneath their feet rumbled, and several large sandstone blocks recessed to reveal a staircase leading downwards into darkness. Raiden followed Horus down the stairs, pausing as the hole in the roof closed behind them, plunging the entire area into pitch black. A heartbeat later, several large braziers at the base of the stairs flared to life, illuminating the foyer with which Raiden was familiar. Instead of the spartan accommodations of his previous visit, this time the room was laid out with plush cushions, a thick burgundy rug and a low table set with plates of cured meats and cheeses.

"An old bastard, am I?" Kadir strode through the opposite

doorway, knotting his white shendyt at the waist. "And here I was going conjure you a stiff drink."

"Master of the Kirrilakh," Horus bowed low. "It is good to see you again."

"God of the Sky," Kadir laughed, returning the bow before dragging Horus into a hug. "It's been decades since your head was beneath my roof."

Horus winced as Kadir's large hands thumped between his shoulders. "Time flies faster than I do, I'm afraid."

"That is fast indeed, judging by the speed you both came in." Kadir ruffled Horus' hair like one might a child, then turned to clasp arms with Raiden. "Crown Prince of Merged Egypt. You seem frownier than last we met - I didn't think such a thing was possible."

"It's been a long day," Raiden muttered, accepting his own hair tousling. When Kadir snapped his fingers to produce a tumbler of amber liquor, he accepted with a grunt and tossed the entire measure back in one go. It burnt all the way down his throat and set a fire in his gut that he closed his eyes to breathe through. "Gods save us all, but I needed that."

"Come now, little angel. Sit, and tell old Kadir what has you looking so worn - and the Skywatcher escorting you, no less."

Raiden flopped onto his stomach on a pile of cushions, his wings draped carelessly over the soft velvet edges. He propped his chin on the back of his wrists and, as Horus and Kadir also made themselves comfortable, launched into the long tale of everything that had befallen him since he'd seen Kadir last. Grim silence had fallen by the time he finished, and he dug inside his leather armour to pull out the bloodied gauze bundle Liria had found at the Temple of Bast.

"First of all, my thanks for returning this. Second..." Kadir accepted the bundle in one hand, then smacked Raiden across the back of the head with the other. "You're a fucking idiot, Prince of the Storm."

Raiden closed his eyes as the room spun. "I know."

"Do you have any idea how she wept, when your astral form kissed her and then your physical form forgot all about it? Do you?" Kadir glared down at him, obsidian eyes glittering with temper. "Are all angels as careless with their priceless gifts as you are?"

"Hey," Horus protested, then flinched when the djinn cut a look in his direction. "All right, all right, so I'm no poster boy for perfection."

"None of us are - but unlike your god of the sky and this useless old jann, you, Prince of Egypt, may yet get another chance." Kadir leant in so close his breath wafted over Raiden's hair. "Though if you don't want that little shadow, I'll happily keep her for myself."

Raiden launched himself from the floor, hitting Kadir square in the chest and taking them both down to the rug. "Stay away from her!"

"Ah." Rather than look bothered, Kadir tucked one burly arm behind his head and grinned up at Raiden from the floor. "Interesting."

"Raiden," Horus sighed and shook his head. "He's baiting you. Relax."

Struggling to tame the volcano inside him, Raiden leant in close to Kadir. "I'll fix it."

"You had better." Kadir gave a firm shove, and Raiden found himself sprawled inelegantly back in his pile of cushions. "I've a soft spot for that poor creature, and if you hurt her any further, I'll use your bones to pick my teeth."

Horus leant forward to snatch up a hunk of cheese, his eyes narrowing. "It's not like you to develop such an attachment, Kadir."

The jann picked himself up off the floor and dusted his shendyt, golden muscles rippling in the firelight. He clenched the bloodied gauze in his fist a moment, then relaxed and snapped his fingers to conjure a fresh tumbler of liquor.

"The shadow and I have something in common," he said at

last, taking a small sip before setting the glass on the table. "We are both slaves."

Raiden's eyes tracked to the golden cuffs that circled Kadir's wrists and ankles, but he kept his mouth shut. Precious little was known about the powerful jann save that he was bound to the Kirrilakh and could never leave, but he'd dropped enough hints over the years that Raiden knew the service wasn't voluntary.

Horus jerked his chin to the bundle in Kadir's fist. "What do you make of that?"

As subject changes went, it wasn't a subtle one, but Kadir appeared not to notice. He unwrapped the blood-stiffened gauze with the same care Liria had shown, his face tightening as he tipped the medallion-set piece of bone into his opposite palm. "Huh."

"You know it?" Raiden asked, picking himself up and resettling his wings down his back.

Kadir rubbed his thumb across the surface of the medallion. "I know it. What I don't know is how it came to be hidden in the roof of an Egyptian temple, nor what it has to do with Set." The jann gazed off into the distance, his black eyes narrowed to slits of night. "Last I saw this, it was in Sumeria."

"*Sumeria?*" Raiden's jaw dropped. "What was Set doing in Sumeria?"

"Probably the same thing he does everywhere else," Horus said, his voice dry. "Being a dick."

"Hah!" Kadir grinned, then frowned. "This medallion... if Set were to have disturbed its resting place, he would have caused a magical shockwave that even those with the barest of Merged energies would have felt. The body of the person who once bore this... they were protected with a spell not unlike those curses which guard the tombs of your past Pharaohs." The jann shook his head. "Much as I would like to solely blame the god of war and chaos, he had help for this."

Raiden thought back to what he and Liria had found at

Thissish's mother's farm. "Would the blood of Apophis have been able to grant protection enough to get inside?"

"Perhaps, but if you think your Thissish did this, she would have brought down a terrible curse upon herself no matter her power." Kadir frowned. "Also, I've known Apep - or Apophis, as you call him - a long time. He was born in darkness and is far from perfect, but I do not see him willingly creating servants for Set. His blood is caustic and would ultimately lead to their death."

"A gruesome death?" Raiden paced across the room and back again. "A death where the skin blackens and the body melts?"

Kadir's eyes widened. "Yes."

Horus swore under his breath. "That medallion - would Set have gained any use from it?"

"If he'd gotten his hands on it, perhaps." Kadir tightened his fist around the bone fragment. "Now that it's here with me, no. Not even the Anarchist can come here without my permission."

Horus scrubbed both hands over his face, looking suddenly and unaccountably worn. "Are there any more medallions he could get hold of?"

"No. The rest are here with me." Kadir studied the medallion a final time, then tossed it up in the air and snapped his fingers. It disappeared. "We need to find Set before he does something truly foolish, Skywatcher. Can you contact Ra? Those two were ever close - he might know where to look."

"Ra is missing," Horus grumbled, tipping his head back to contemplate the roof. "Nobody's been able to contact him for nigh on a month now. And before you ask, Nephthys is gone too - she hasn't been seen for almost three months."

"*What?*" Raiden shouted. "Set's closest friend and his estranged wife disappear and you don't think that's worth mentioning before now?"

Horus crossed his arms over his chest and huffed out a breath. "What do you think I've been doing for the last six weeks?

Sunbathing? No, I've been hunting them - but Osiris didn't want to alarm anybody, so he ordered me to keep it quiet."

Raiden barked out a sharp laugh. "Set's been attacking the Palace left, right and centre, Liria and I have been tearing our hair out trying to work out what on earth is happening, and two of the gods best suited to finding the perpetrator disappear - but you don't want to alarm us? Have you stopped to consider, for a fraction of a moment, that these events might be *related?*"

"Of course I have," Horus snapped. "Why do you think Anubis has been keeping such a close eye on everyone while I scour Mu from ass to tit? It's not so simple as you seem to think, however; Set is one of the most powerful gods to walk either Earth or Mu, and the people best situated to oppose him are his own brother and sister. Neither Osiris or Isis will lift a hand without hard proof of wrongdoing, for to start a war between the gods could destroy us all."

"What aren't you telling us?" Kadir asked quietly, kneeling beside Horus' cushion. "What is occurring in Mu that could possibly birth a war?"

Horus thumped a clenched fist against the floor. "Are you familiar with the Ennead?"

"The collection of nine powerful gods who are responsible for containing the energy of Mu," Kadir supplied. "Your parents, Isis and Osiris, along with Set and Nephthys. Your grandparents, Geb and Nut. Your great grandparents, Shu and Tef, and your great-great grandfather Atum, Father of All and creator of Mu."

"You remember your history better than I." Raiden grabbed a handful of meat and cheese, and dropped back onto his cushion. "Most of those gods haven't been seen on earth for centuries."

"For good reason." Horus stared down at his hands, his face mournful. "A long time ago, our world was destroyed in a great cosmic accident. Nobody truly knows what happened, but the energy upheaval was catastrophic. My great-great grandfather Atum and his consort created the magical construct of Mu to keep as many people safe as possible - but it was built upon and sustained by their life forces. Though they searched as quickly as possible for a place in which to resettle, the journey was long and the construct of Mu drained Atum's consort until she died. The ensuing shockwave crippled Atum, dragging him into a comatose state from which he has yet to recover. In his final moments of consciousness, he sought the most powerful energies he could find and tethered their life forces to the construct in his consort's place - and so the Ennead was born."

"I'll bet that pissed Set off something shocking," Kadir snorted, clicking his fingers to materialise fresh glasses of liquor for everyone.

Horus shrugged. "Not at first. Apparently - this is before I was born, mind you - Set was as passionate as Osiris about finding a safe haven for the people who depended on him. Together, the Ennead, led by Osiris and Set, discovered Earth. The energies of the young world were compatible with those of Mu, but if the magical construct was forced to merge with such a young planet in one forceful sweep, there was a high chance of destroying the world and everyone upon it."

"Let me guess." Raiden accepted his glass and saluted Kadir with it. "Set wanted to take the gamble, and Osiris didn't. They put it to vote, and Set lost."

"Yes, but he did so gracefully, or so I was told." Horus waved a hand at the room around them. "The decision was made to join the worlds slowly, so both realms and peoples would have time to acclimatise - and so the Merge was born. The problem arose when, over time, the gods of the Ennead realised they were weakening. The construct of Mu, the heart of which is the city Lemuria, is draining them as surely as it drained Atum and his consort. Set argued that they should chance the sudden slamming together of the worlds in order to prevent risking their lives, and this time, he had some support. The vote was closely tied, but went in favour of Osiris when he provided calculations to say that the Ennead could hold the Merge for long enough to complete the process without anyone dying. By that time, however, the gods involved will be so drained they're apt to be as comatose as Atum."

"Now *that* is what will have pissed Set off," Kadir announced, shivering. "Nobody wants to feel helpless."

"Exactly - but there's no way to break free of the Ennead save through death, and then that god's place would just be taken by someone else." Horus wrapped his arms around his chest. "Mother assures me that once the Merge is complete, their powers will recover and they will awaken, but it is only conjecture. There is no proof either way."

Raiden frowned. "Meaning that Set believes that because there's no hard evidence for destruction should the process be hastened, he wants to try it in order to save his own hide."

"Exactly."

"I can see why that would be apt to cause a war between the gods, but what does it have to do with Set's attacks on the Palace of Selekhet?" Kadir asked, his brow furrowed.

"Nothing," Horus growled, "or perhaps everything. Who knows? Like I said, Anubis and I have been searching for proof that Set has overstepped the line, but there appeared no reason to involve - or alarm - the Merged citizens of Earth, because for now, it's purely a Lemurian problem."

"A Lemurian problem that could kill us all," Raiden snapped, but felt the fire go out of him almost as fast. "You're right, however. I cannot see any way possible that the drain upon the Ennead could be linked to Set's actions in Egypt these last weeks."

Neither Kadir nor Horus said anything to disagree, and the three men sat sipping their liquor in silence. When all the glasses were empty, Kadir lifted his eyes to the god of the sky. "In your heart, you believe this is all connected."

"Yes," Horus whispered.

The jann nodded. "So do I. Whatever resources I have, they are yours, Skywatcher."

"Thank you." The god's face relaxed ever so slightly. "That means a lot to me. In the meantime, I'll -"

Raiden lurched to his feet as Horus went deathly pale, his empty glass sliding from his fingers. "What? What is it?"

"We must return to Selekhet," Horus whispered, his eyes unfocussed. "The city is under attack."

I'M STILL MAD AT YOU

LIRIA WOKE TO THE soft rustle of feathers and the warmth of a blanket. She drifted peacefully between sleeping and waking, safe in her cocoon while two men spoke quietly nearby.

"...with your wife," one said, the tone huffy and officious.

"I made a promise, and I will see it kept," the second replied, his voice firm and smooth. It reminded her of Raiden, though it wasn't deep or rumbly enough. Which meant...

Liria's eyes snapped open. "Taos?"

The two men fell silent, and she rolled to face them. They were all in a small, well-appointed room that Liria recognised instantly as a healing chamber in the heart of the Palace, for it was identical to the one where she and Raiden had visited Balai. A faded but comfortable chair and been pulled up beside the bed and Taos lounged sideways in it, one of his wings laid leisurely over the chair's back and the other along the side of Liria's bed. The Pharaoh was dressed in the same billowing trousers Raiden favoured, though these were in Selekhet's palm frond green, his matching shawl a green so dark as to be almost black and edged with gold embroidery. Though the angel's posture and expression were serene, the angle of his body placed him squarely between Liria and the man in the doorway.

"My Lady of Shadows," Taos murmured, his handsome face creasing into a smile. His golden-bronze hair was combed neatly to one side and his deep brown skin, several shades darker than his brother's, glimmered in the light from the solar lamps. "Welcome back."

"Thank you." Liria raised herself onto one elbow and cleared her throat. "And Healer Nurus, no less. Have you come to disapprove of me again?"

The older man in the doorway clasped his hands over his portly stomach. "Merely pointing out facts, my Lady."

"As was I," Taos said, his tone firm. "That will be all, Nurus."

Nurus blinked. "But, my Pharaoh -"

"I said that will be all, Senior Healer," Taos snapped, his shoulders stiffening. "Or do I need to start wearing my crown whenever I visit, as a reminder to whom you speak?"

Nurus pressed his lips together in a thin line, bowed, and left, closing the door behind him.

"You don't need to defend me, you know," Liria said quietly. When Taos raised an eyebrow, she shrugged. "I'm used to attitudes far worse than his."

"And you don't think Raiden would beat me senseless if I sat by and let Nurus lecture me on how unsuited you are for a Prince's affections?" Taos snorted, propping his boots on the opposite arm of the chair. "Don't think my position as Pharaoh protects me from his temper - or him from mine."

Liria flopped back onto the bed with a grunt. Her body ached, but not so much as it should have, and though her ankle was strapped in stiffened bandages, it tingled in the manner of a wound knitting itself closed. "Who healed me?"

"Who's to say it wasn't Nurus?" Taos' teasing tone had Liria rolling her head to look at him, all glittering brown eyes and deep, dimpled smile.

"Nurus might hold the title of Senior Healer, but I'll bet you a stack of home-made pancakes that he's not treated an actual patient in years, and uses the authority of his title to force others to do his work while he takes the credit." She watched the Pharaoh's face turn from amusement to surprise, and added, "I'll up the bet to include berries and syrup and say that if you go digging, Safiyah is the real heart of this place."

Taos blinked. "Who is Safiyah?"

"Ah hah!" Liria grinned. "Take my bet, Pharaoh, and see if I'm right. Or can't you cook?"

The angel's eyes narrowed. "Oh, I can cook. You're on, Lady of Shadows."

"Excellent. I look forward to seeing Nurus get his comeuppance," Liria chuckled. She pulled herself into a sitting position, wincing as her body protested. "How long was I out?"

"A few hours." Taos rolled out of the chair and took up a cup from the nearby side table. "Here. Water."

Liria eyed the cup and then the man holding it. "Just water?"

"Just water," the Pharaoh repeated, the corner of his lip twitching. "I'm not Anubis, to put you to sleep without asking first."

"Could you..." Liria took a deep breath. "Could you add some sugar to it?"

Both Taos' brows shot up but he turned to the small refreshment area and rummaged through the selection of canisters. "Sugar or honey?"

"Um."

"It's floral honey, gathered from the Palace garden." Taos held up the little jar, showing off the dark amber honey inside. "I can even heat your water up so it melts."

"You'd do that?" Liria blushed when he glared, then nodded. "Yes, please. Honey."

Taos popped the cork off the top of the jar, poured a generous amount of honey into the cup, then stuck it in the heating unit and flicked it on. A minute later Liria was sipping hot, sweet honey water, and she let her lashes drift shut as it coated her tongue and throat.

"So, sugar, huh?" Taos laughed when her eyes snapped open. "Don't look so scandalised. I should have thought of it sooner; everyone knows the stories about fairies and their love of sweets."

"Hmmm," Liria managed, sipping her honey water again. "The Atlantean contingent… what was the damage?"

The Pharoah's laughter faded as abruptly as it had appeared. "The dreadnaught is destroyed and all upon it, including General Barin, are dead. The young man who came to warn us is the sole survivor – Barin's son, Corbett Dormisculae."

"Corbett." Liria searched her memory, a frown creasing her brow. "I never had occasion to spend much time with him, but his reputation as a soldier was solid. To lose his father and the entire crew like that…"

"Yes. He's currently under the care of the healers, but soon enough, I'll have to send word to King Theon about what happened here." Taos clicked his tongue against his teeth. "Would it be better coming from Ione, do you think?"

Liria shook her head. "I cannot say, but you could always ask Ione." She hesitated, dropping her gaze to the thick woven blanket. "And what of Raiden?"

"I told Horus we didn't want to see him, so they went to the Kirrilakh to talk to Kadir." The Pharaoh sighed, then reached into a small pouch at his waist and carefully withdrew a feather. "He left this for you, though."

Liria set her water aside, accepting the feather in her cupped palms. It was long enough to stretch from the tip of her fingers to the base of her wrist, and was easily three fingers wide. The bottom was a soft, downy white and the top Raiden's unique tawny rust, with the faintest hint of darker brown at the very outer edges.

"He plucked it fresh," she said, running her finger over the dried blood on the feather's stem. "Will he still be able to fly?"

Taos chuckled. "Oh, yes. With Raiden's will, not even iron shoes could keep him grounded."

"I said some terrible things to him."

"Were they true?"

"Yes." Liria shifted uncomfortably. "They were true, but they would have hurt him."

The Pharaoh tilted his head to the side as Liria described her interaction with the Crown Prince of Merged Egypt. By the time she finished, he was grinning broadly. "Your first argument, huh?"

"I suppose so." Liria considered that, staring down at the feather in her hands. "I've argued plenty before, but it's never been quite so personal as this."

Taos perched carefully on the edge of the bed, his expression gentle. He really was lovely, Liria thought, trim and fit and not at all anything like his rough and tumble younger brother. Yet it was Raiden she craved, in spite of her anger.

"Raiden loves you," the Pharoah said softly, reaching to take Liria's free hand in his own. "Everything you said about him was right, but he's walked a hard road. We lost our parents and our sister so young, and in the years since... all he's done is dedicate himself to me, and to the throne. He's always the first into danger, always the first with a plan, always the first to serve, and he's never asked a single thing for himself in return." Taos sighed. "I'm not in any way excusing his actions, but I want to make sure you understand that they come from a place of love - and likely also confusion."

"I don't know what to do now," Liria admitted, staring down at their joined fingers. "Letting him in was the most difficult thing I've ever done."

"First off, he needs to realise what he's done wrong," Taos said, squeezing her hand. "Then, we make him grovel for forgiveness."

She blinked. "Grovel?"

"Oh, yes." Taos chuckled, reaching into the pouch at his belt to withdraw a strip of leather. He motioned to the feather. "May I?"

Liria handed it over and watched as the Pharaoh deftly tied the leather around the feather, then knotted it into a cord which he slipped over her head. The feather nestled between her breasts, the soft edges tickling her skin as though Raiden was touching her himself. She stared down at the necklace in amazement, then back up at Taos. "Thank you."

"You're welcome."

"Can I ask a question?"

He spread his hands in invitation. "Consider me a brother, Liria Atlannon. Ask anything you wish."

"Why did you agree to marry Ione?" She waved a hand at his face. "You're virile and charming and unfairly handsome. Surely finding a Queen couldn't be really that difficult?"

Taos' wings drooped down to lie across the end of the bed, and he sighed. "The truth is, my initial instinct was to discard the proposal. The King of Atlantis' letter sounded like he was selling his daughter for a flock of sheep." The Pharaoh snorted, toying with the gold embroidery that edged his shawl. "It was also pointed out to me that a King offering the hand of his fifth daughter was more a veiled insult than anything else. I've never struggled to bed a woman should I need one, so why trouble myself with such a blatant grab for an alliance with Merged Egypt?"

"Hmmm." Liria frowned. "What changed?"

"Yrini came to Raiden and I one night, saying we'd received a secondary correspondence - from Princess Ione herself. Yrini knew we intended to reject King Theon's offer, but felt it couldn't be done without all the pertinent information. She put the letter into my hands, and though it was almost a novel, I read it." Taos' face softened. "I don't think King Theon ever intended me to receive that letter, for it was vastly different to the first. I could see immediately that Ione was spoilt and hungry for the crown, but underneath, I felt a kinship to her. Like me, she's bound to her position by an accident of birth. Like me, it made her lonely. And like me, she wanted to be free, and to find love. So I said yes - not to King Theon, but to Ione."

Liria fisted her hands in the blanket. No wonder the King and Queen of Atlantis hadn't attended the wedding - they'd tried to subvert it before it even started, but Ione's interference meant Taos had accepted, and Atlantis could not withdraw unless they wished to offend Egypt and her allies. She shook her head. "Ione has come a long way from that viper's nest. I pray you can find happiness together."

"So do I." Taos' cheeks darkened and he glanced up from beneath his lashes, looking suddenly younger than his years. "She is with child."

"*What?*" Liria did a quick tally of days, then shook her head. "It's been only a fortnight. How is that possible?"

The Pharaoh's cheeks darkened even further. "Apparently one or both of us is very fertile. Isis popped by you while you slept, and she sensed the baby." He cleared his throat, looking apologetic. "It's why Ione wasn't here when you woke; Isis whisked her away to check her over."

Liria's mind reeled and she took a deep, steadying breath that was no help whatsoever. "Great gods above us."

"I believe I said something similar." Taos pressed a hand to his cheek. "I must admit to some cowardice on my part; I used my obligation to deliver Raiden's feather as an excuse not to go with them. I know an heir is important, but I didn't expect it to happen so quickly. I feel quite overwhelmed."

"There's no shame in that," Liria murmured. A child. Wouldn't it have been better for the Pharaoh and his Queen to know each other first? To learn to love each other, before they grew a new life? "Ione is part naiad. There's a chance her innate healing energy makes her more fertile than a normal person."

Taos' wings lifted and his eyes went wide. "I never thought of that. How many children am I going to end up with?"

The look on his face was one of such stark terror that Liria couldn't help but laugh.

"Fear not, mighty Pharaoh - she cannot conceive another whilst already carrying. I'd say you're safe for a while yet." Liria gave him a conciliatory pat on the knee. "Besides, would it really be so bad to have a beautiful daughter with your deep brown eyes and luscious hair? After all, you are quite pretty."

He stared at her for a long moment, then grinned wide and leant forward to give her a playful shove. "I see why Raiden loves you, Liria Atlannon. Your heart is large enough to house us all. Did you tell him he was pretty, too?"

"Of course not." Liria rolled her eyes. "Raiden's ego is large enough as it is."

A knock sounded at the door, and it swung open to admit a tall man carrying a stack of towels so high it was impossible to see his face.

"Not now," Taos said as the servant kicked the door shut behind him. "The Lady of Shadows isn't allowed out of bed yet."

The man sauntered across the room and bent to deposit his bundle on the floor, tousled ruby hair swishing over his shoulders as he moved. Liria's eyes narrowed. There was something about his bearing, something about the smooth, dark gold of his skin that seemed familiar. Then he straightened, his handsome face stretching into a smile that displayed fangs, and waved a be-ringed hand. "Good evening."

"Set," Taos hissed, drawing a short sword from the belt at his waist. "What are you doing here?"

The Anarchist looked at the sword, then the Pharaoh, and clicked his tongue against his teeth. "Everyone was so concerned about our dear, sweet Lady of Shadows that I thought to come and check on her myself. I hope I wasn't interrupting anything... clandestine." Set tipped his head to the side, eyes the colour of old blood twinkling with mischief. "Actually, that's a lie. Not only do I hope this is a tryst, but I'd rather like to join in. Three can make quite the party."

"You are not welcome here, Anarchist," Taos growled, fingers tightening on the hilt of his sword until his knuckles turned white. "Not after what you've pulled the last few weeks."

"My dear Taos, if only you knew how I regret our misunderstandings." Set sighed and shook his head. "You always were the more fun of the two brothers. That Raiden is rugged and virile, but so uptight." The god of war and chaos shifted his attention to Liria and winked. "Though from what I hear, he had no trouble unlocking your treasure chest, little shadow."

Liria reached into the shadows beneath her blanket and drew forth a throwing knife. It thunked into the wall where Set's head had been, but the Anarchist was no longer there.

"Did you pull that from nothing?" Set asked, appearing on the bed. His body was warm as it stretched out beside Liria's, his long legs tangling with hers beneath the blanket. "What an interesting talent."

"Get away from me." Liria pulled a dagger from the shadows behind her back and struck, but Set caught her wrist with a laugh.

"Such romance," he purred, twisting the dagger from her fingers and dropping it to the floor. The Anarchist's free arm twined around Liria's shoulders and dragged her against his chest, where he studied her from only inches away. "You are so beautiful in your natural form." Liria shuddered and tried to shove free, but the god's grip was stronger than iron. With a snap of his fingers, Set had Taos sprawled atop both of them, his sword gone and his eyes wide. "Now, this is much better. If only I had two mouths, I could kiss you both at once. Looks like I need to think creatively."

Taos wrapped an arm around Liria's waist and braced his other against Set's chest, trying to push away. "We've had this discussion before, Anarchist. The answer is still no."

"Oh, come on," Set cajoled, nuzzling the hollow beneath

Taos' jaw. "I'll only bite a little." He glanced at Liria. "I wouldn't, if I were you. When I deflect that spell, it will slide to the Pharaoh, and that would be a terrible shame."

Liria ceased the spell she'd been chanting under her breath and let the magic go. "What do you want, Set?"

"Does a lonely god always require motives?" Set lamented. "Can't he create a distraction in the city to draw his fellow gods' attentions, sneak into the Palace, block the Pharaoh's ability to call telepathically for help and immobilise a shadow's magic just for some TLC?"

"No." Liria twisted closer to Taos, evading Set's attempt to lick a path along her jaw. "I don't believe it for a second - but it doesn't matter, god of war and chaos. You have failed. Raiden's not here."

Set grinned, and an invisible force squashed Liria's cheek against Taos' until the corners of their mouths met. She tried to move, but her entire body was frozen as Set leant in and kissed them both simultaneously.

"My dear shadow," the Anarchist breathed, nipping playfully at her nose. The world began to tilt and fold around them, the healing chamber fading into darkness. "Whatever made you think I was after Raiden?"

IT'S A TRAP

Raiden swept over Selekhet's docks to find them in chaos. Snakes slithered over the piers and up the sides of ships, while crocodiles snapped and snarled in the streets.

What in the world is Set thinking? He demanded, passing over an Egyptian trade vessel in time to see the crew leap screaming into the water. Tucking his wings close to his back, Raiden dove to collect one of the crew, with Horus and several other angels following his example.

I don't know. Horus set the woman he'd rescued on a nearby rooftop and returned to the ocean for another. *Anubis is several blocks over, at his temple. A man with super strength and a sharp sword cut down five priests before he was overcome.*

Raiden shivered, setting his own burden down on the rooftop. *Another like Thissish?*

Anubis thinks so. He's ordered all the bodies burnt, even though that goes against custom. Horus swung in to deposit his latest rescue, followed by the rest of the angels who'd lent their wings to the cause. The god folded his wings to his back and walked to the edge of the roof. "It won't be long before the unusually aggressive wildlife thinks to look up."

"We could set fires," said a bedraggled man with a captain's pin on his tunic.

Raiden raised an eyebrow. "And burn down the docks?"

Sekhmet is with Anubis. Horus winced, putting one hand to his ear as though to block a shout. *She destroyed a similarly strong creature at her own Temple. They're now cutting down the crocodiles.*

Raiden joined Horus at the edge of the roof, staring down at the wave of snakes oozing steadily onto the stone streets at the end of the dock. A peculiar tingling spread from his chest and down his arms, and before he'd thought about what he was doing, he raised his face and his hands to the sky. Clouds gathered overhead, darkening to stormy grey between one moment and the next. Thunder rumbled and when Raiden glanced down at the streets, lighting struck where he looked. The impact chipped stone from the street pavers and sent fried pieces of snake flying, leaving a cleared - if singed - space behind that was approximately three paces across.

Strong fingers twined through his and Horus directed their joined hands at the edge of the dockyard, where the snake concentration was heaviest. *Strike the edge of the wood. I'll ensure the fire is contained.*

Rather than destroy the piers themselves, Raiden called lightning into a stack of crates nearby, then again to a wooden food cart which had been abandoned in the rush to flee, and a third time to a collection of wooden barrels. There was a whoompfing sound as the barrels lit, spitting oil high into the air, but the fire quickly spiralled back into itself, spreading outwards to light the leading edge of the snakes on fire.

The scent of cooking meat filled the area, punctuated by the shrieks of people desperately trying to escape those creatures who'd been missed by the strike. Raiden turned to offer what aid he could when all of a sudden the snakes stopped, rolled over as one, and dissolved into sand. The grains rose into the air, higher and higher, swirling together until an enormous cloud hung over the city.

Horus snarled under his breath and waved a hand. A great gust of wind forced Raiden to his knees, the trees in the streets bending double under the strain. The sand cloud twisted and twirled, fighting to retain shape before the wind overpowered it, sweeping the entire cloud out of Selekhet and into the desert beyond.

Good job, brother, Anubis' voice tolled clear as a bell in Raiden's mind, and he flinched.

Hmmm. Horus used the hand still twined with Raiden's to drag him to his feet. "Are you all right, Prince of Egypt?"

"Yes." Raiden squeezed Horus' hand, then let go. *What was that all about?*

I don't know, Anubis answered. *One moment I was decapitating croc-odiles and the next, they turned to sand and floated away. What of the snakes?*

The same, Horus answered, propping one fist on his hip. *It's the motivation I don't understand. What does Set gain from this constant fussing at the city?*

I don't know. Let me get rid of Sekhmet, and I'll meet you at the Palace.

Head for Liria's room - that's where Taos will be. Horus narrowed his eyes at Raiden. "Can you behave yourself? We don't have time for a romantic dispute right now."

"Liria and I are both warriors with a duty to Egypt and our Pharaoh," Raiden growled, thumping a fist against his chest. "Don't insult us, Skywatcher."

Horus grinned and spread his wings. "Last one there's a wingless wonder."

Raiden watched him launch skyward and shook his head.

"Prince of Egypt?" The ship's captain stepped forward and cleared his throat. "What do we do now?"

"Take an inventory of the damage to both the ships and the port." Raiden winced as he spotted several masts poking out of the water where once whole vessels had been. "Bring the report to the Palace and I'll arrange for salvage and repairs. What's your name?"

The captain's chest puffed out ever so slightly. "Grego, your highness. Captain of the *Everlast*."

"Captain Grego, you are hereby in charge of the clean-up, evacuation and resettling of the area. Have your crew direct the injured to somewhere safe nearby, and set up a defensive perimeter in case the creatures return." Raiden spread his own wings and graced the soggy crew with an encouraging smile. "I'll keep a personal eye on your progress. Selekhet thanks you for your service."

Captain Grego thumped his fist. "Gods go with you, my Prince."

"And you." Raiden launched himself into the air and swung in the direction of the Palace, heading straight for the healing Temple within its sacred heart. He tucked his wings close and shot through the tunnel, landing with a thump by the healers' front desk. "Send word to the Temples of Bast and Sekhmet that they're needed at the docks for medical attention, salvage and repair."

"Yes, my Prince." The wide-eyed nurse bowed his head, adam's apple bobbing as he swallowed. "I shall ask Senior Healer Nurus -"

"No." Raiden waved a hand. "This instruction comes directly from me and has nothing to do with Nurus. Pen it yourself and ensure the message is delivered directly to the hands of the High Priestess of Bast, or her partner, the High Priest of Sekhmet. Can you do that?"

The nurse bowed again. "Yes, my Prince. At once."

Raiden checked the roster to find out which room was Liria's, then eyed the vase of flowers on the desk. Should he take one with him? He owed her an apology, no matter what Horus said about the dire nature of the situation. With a grimace, he turned and strode into the corridor. Second hand flowers from the desk were not the way to prove his love; even a hormonal teen would know that much. He'd have to hope that the feather he'd left would buy him enough favour to have a conversation without the

Lady of Shadows trying to cut out his liver. He rubbed a hand across his chest, the phantom echo of her heartbeat seeming fainter than usual. Did she regret her decision to commit to him? What if she had decided not to give him a chance at redemption? His instincts told him to fight, but he'd die before he stole Liria's free will. Where, then, did that leave him? The door to her room loomed ahead and Raiden sighed. If he couldn't fight, there was really only one course of action.

He'd have to grovel.

He lifted a hand to knock, but the door swung open to reveal Horus on the threshold. The god startled backwards, then just as quickly stepped up to fill the doorway. "Raiden. Um. Hey."

"*Raiden?*" Anubis squawked from inside the room. "Blood of the gods, that's just what we need."

"Maybe you should..." Horus flapped a hand vaguely. "Do something else for a bit."

"Why? You told me to meet you here." Raiden's eyes narrowed to slits. "What's going on, Skywatcher?" He raised his voice. "Soulcatcher?"

There was a silence, during which Horus pasted an odd caricature of a smile to his face and phantom butterflies fluttered their wings inside Raiden's ear canal. He put a finger to his ear as though to ferret out the uncomfortable feeling, then realised with a start that the two gods were having a conversation - and trying to keep him out. Rather than ignore the tickling sensation, Raiden focussed on it.

...find out eventually anyway, Horus said.

Anubis let out a sigh. *Could be worse - it could be Ione. Still, I'd prefer to -*

I can hear you, Raiden growled, drawing an intense amount of satisfaction from the way Horus paled and Anubis yelped from inside the room.

You can? Anubis' voice faded to a barely intelligible whisper that sharpened when Raiden mentally reached for it. *He shouldn't be able to do that, brother.*

Horus winced. *What am I supposed to do about it? It's not like I knew how much blood to give him - I've never done it before.*

*I can **still** hear you,* Raiden said, lacing his mental tone with a healthy dose of temper.

Anubis grumbled to himself for a moment, and Horus sighed. *I'm letting him in.*

The god of the sky stepped aside, waving Raiden into the room. As soon as he was over the threshold, Horus tugged the door closed and flicked the lock.

"What's going on?" Raiden asked, running his eyes over the rumpled bed - over which Anubis was currently bent, sniffing the sheets - and then the rest of the room. "Where's Liria?"

Horus leant against the door and crossed his arms over his chest. "Gone."

"Gone? What do you mean, *gone?*"

"We've only been here a moment. You know as much as we do, Prince of Storms." Anubis' face blurred and elongated until the black-furred head of a jackal rested upon his human shoulders. He planted his canine nose against the bed's bottom sheet and began snuffling at it like a pig, even going so far as to bury his head under the pillow.

"Well?" Horus asked, when the Soulcatcher finally surfaced for air.

Anubis' face returned to his human countenance, his black jackal's ears drooping. "Set was here. From what I can tell, he took both Liria and Taos."

"Dammit!" Horus slammed a fist against the wall. "The attack on the city was a distraction, and we walked right into the trap. Again!"

Something cold and hard connected with Raiden's knees, then his buttocks, and it took a moment to realise his legs had given out and he was now sitting on the floor. "He took them? Where?"

"Mu, most likely; Taos is an angel, he has enough Merged blood to survive there - and Liria's so strong she may as well be purebred." Anubis wrapped a hand around his long, black braid and tugged. "Set's stronger in Mu than he is here. It'll be nigh on impossible to find them."

Horus growled low in his throat. "I've been hunting Set for a while now, so I know where he isn't - I'll head back to Mu and start searching anew. Brother, will you notify Father?"

"I suppose so." Anubis inclined his head. "Perhaps now he'll finally listen to us."

"Wait." Raiden scrambled to his feet and grabbed Horus' arm. "I'm coming with you."

The Skywatcher shook his head. "We need you here, Prince of Egypt. You need to keep Selekhet calm and news of the Pharaoh's disappearance contained."

"Taos is my *brother*," Raiden hissed, clenching Horus' arm so tightly the god winced. "And Liria is my heart. How can you ask me to sit here and do nothing?"

"You won't be doing nothing," Anubis murmured, prying Raiden's fingers free. "Taos would be the first to remind you of your duty to Selekhet - and with both he and Liria gone, it's also your duty to protect Ione." The god of death hesitated, then lowered his voice. "She carries your brother's child within her belly, Raiden. A niece or nephew for you, and heir to the throne of all Merged Egypt. Now, more than ever, they need you to keep them safe."

Raiden's jaw went slack and he stared at Anubis in amazement. "Ione is *pregnant?*"

Horus disappeared, but Raiden barely noticed. The room tilted, and Anubis steadied him with a firm grip on his shoulders.

"Isis verified the pregnancy herself." The Soulcatcher snatched a glass of water from a nearby table and pressed it into Raiden's hands. "Here. It's not much, but it might help."

Raiden took a sip and choked on the sudden influx of sweetness. "Ack! Who in the world drinks water laced so heavily with honey?"

"Honey?" Anubis blinked down at the cup, then took a sip himself. "Huh. This was probably Liria's."

"What makes you say that?"

The Soulcatcher frowned. "She's a dark fairy."

"So?"

"She didn't tell you?" Anubis raised a perfectly shaped brow, and when Raiden only glared, shrugged. "All fairies, both dark and light, require a sugar based diet to survive. Light fairies also consume flowers, pollen and nectar, while dark fairies consume night-blooming flowers, poisonous plants and blood."

Raiden frowned, recalling all the times he'd watched Liria with food. "She ate the pancakes and the fruit and the ice cream, but at dinner tonight, she pushed the meat and veg around on her plate."

"It would have made her ill." Anubis' brow furrowed. "Didn't Ione tell you what Liria needed before they arrived?"

A sharp laugh broke free, and Raiden shook his head. "We didn't even know Liria was coming until she arrived. As a shadow, she's little more than animated luggage. In fact, I'm willing to bet my ability to fly that Ione doesn't even know what Liria needs to eat." He sighed. "I asked her to tell me at dinner, but she seemed embarrassed."

"Given the way she's been treated, I'm not surprised." Anubis crossed his arms over his chest. "I need to have a word with Poseidon about Atlantis. The more I hear about that place, the more I want to sink it into the sea."

Raiden passed a hand over his face. He could care less about Atlantis right now; all he wanted was to find his brother and the woman he loved. When he dropped his hand back to his side, it was to discover Anubis watching him as though he might sprout a second head.

"I suppose I better go to Ione." Raiden drummed his fingers on the hilt of his favourite sword. "And co-ordinate the clean-up effort."

Anubis' gaze unfocussed. "Isis is with Ione; she'll break the news gently and tend her for the time being. Focus on your city and your people. I'll speak with Osiris, and return when I've got news."

"And when will that be?"

"As soon as I have any." The Soulcatcher's face softened and he gave Raiden's shoulders a squeeze. "We won't stop until we find them, Prince of Storms. You have my word."

Raiden nodded. The god of death disappeared, and he stared for a long minute at the cup of honeyed water on the table. So much about Liria that he didn't know, and now he might never get the chance to find out.

No. He wasn't helpless; hadn't been helpless since the day he'd learnt his parents and sister had been crushed to death when Petra collapsed. The gods might think they outranked him - might even think they'd outmanoeuvred him, trying to distract him with duty - but he wasn't the quitting kind. Raiden glanced at the timepiece on his wrist. Midnight had come and gone, meaning the Palace would be quiet, interruption unlikely. The perfect time to make his preparations, then slip out unnoticed.

He'd find Liria and his brother, or he'd die trying.

NOW WHAT?

Cool stone kissed Liria's cheek, and she opened her eyes to the thick gloom of yet another cell. Where the Kirrilakh had been well appointed - for a dungeon - this one was in sore need of attention; the floor stones were cracked and slimy, the air rank with the scent of mildew, and the iron door warped and rusty.

She reached out with her magic and was met by a thick, buzzing interference. Set's ethereal footprint was so strong she could almost taste his essence, dark and rich like a finely aged wine. Though the barrier made no move to harm, neither did it budge when the full weight of Liria's power slammed against it and recoiled, stealing the breath from her lungs and setting her mind awhirl.

With no other option than to explore manually, Liria pushed onto her hands and knees, breaking free of the prickly blanket that had been wrapped clumsily around her body to serve as both mattress and covering. Her stiff muscles protested and though she managed to swallow her groan, it was impossible to mask the popping of joints and the rasp of fabric over stone.

"Who's there?" A male voice whispered.

"Taos?" Liria sat back on her heels and peered around the cell. There was no light source to speak of, but her eyes had no issue with the inky blackness and before long, she spotted the Pharaoh hunched against the far wall, wings wrapped tight to his body. Liria crawled to his side and laid a gentle hand on one exposed leg, shushing softly when he flinched. "It's okay, it's me."

"Liria," Taos' tone cracked with relief and he clutched at her hand before she could draw away. "Can you see anything? Where are we?"

"I can see, yes. We're in a dungeon cell."

"Is there a..." the Pharaoh cleared his throat. "I need to... you know."

"Oh." She took a moment to examine their surroundings and then pushed to her feet, setting her wings aflutter as she tested her injured ankle. It twinged, but between whatever the healers had managed and the stiffened bandage, she was able to place her weight fully on the floor. Folding her wings to her back, she tugged Taos upright. "There's a crude toilet in the corner. I'll guide you."

Liria shifted his grip to her forearm and together they paced out the cell, ending up in the opposite corner to the door. Taking Taos' free hand, she helped him feel out the location of the toilet, then made to step back so he could go about his business.

"Wait!" His grip tightened on her arm. "Don't go."

"I know you said to think of you as a brother, but I really don't need to watch you urinate."

Still he clung to her. "Please, Liria."

"You're as bad as Ione," she grumbled, shoulders slumping. "Fine, I'll close my eyes."

Taos immediately began tugging at his trousers with his other hand, and Liria closed her eyes before they saw more than they ought. A long, tinkling minute later, the Pharaoh cleared his throat. "All done."

"Congratulations."

"Sorry, I just..." He sighed, and his wings drooped to trail on the floor. "I guess I'm not brave like Raiden."

Liria winced. "It is I who should apologise, my Pharaoh. Without the compulsion keeping my thoughts and words forcibly contained, the first thing that pops to mind is tumbling out of my mouth. I did not mean to intimate you were in any way lacking as a person."

They crossed to the other side of the cell in silence, Taos gripping Liria's arm bruisingly tight. She arranged both their prickly blankets into some sort of order on the floor, then bade him sit atop it - and when he tugged her down beside him, she went, pressing close enough that their thighs and shoulders touched.

"It's true, though," Taos said at last, easing his grip on her arm but pressing harder into her side. "I'm not as brave as Raiden."

"Don't confuse bravery with bloody-minded stupidity," Liria muttered, then groaned. "I did it again. How do you live like this all the time?"

Taos chuckled. "You have to either consider your thoughts before you speak them, or be willing to deal with the consequences of having your foot perpetually in your mouth."

"Let me guess: you choose the first option, and your brother the second?"

"How very astute of you, Lady of Shadows." A pause. "So, you don't think I'm a coward?"

Liria set a hand on his knee and squeezed gently. "You rule the entirety of Merged Egypt. How can that possibly be cowardice?"

"Oh, I don't know," he drawled, "maybe because I'm too scared to piss by myself in the dark?"

"We were kidnapped by the god of war and chaos, and unlike me, you cannot see a thing in this ghastly place - am I right?" When he nodded, she patted the Pharaoh's knee again. "Considering how fragile and bizarrely dangly a male's genitalia is, I don't think I'd be all that keen on waving it around in similar circumstances, either."

Taos' mobile face contorted and after a long moment, he snorted and shook his head. "I'm not sure if I should be offended or amused."

"Either will provide you a shield from your nerves," Liria replied. When he dropped his head against her shoulder, she startled, then reached up to pat his hair. "Have you always been afraid of the dark?"

The Pharaoh grunted. "When I was a young boy, perhaps five or six, Raiden and I were paying our respects in the tomb of my grandparents. In the way many children are, I was curious, and I wandered off. I soon became lost, panicked, and tripped, extinguishing my torch."

"How long did you wander alone in the pitch black?"

"Several hours. Raiden eventually found me. Even though he's two years younger, he was always the stronger of us - lit my torch from his own, and led me unerringly back to our parents."

"Protecting you, even then." Liria smiled, imagining a fierce young boy with Raiden's gold eyes and dark chocolate hair. "He's going to be crazy with worry for you."

"And for you; I've never seen him so in over his head as he is with you, Liria Atlannon."

She sighed, slumping back against the rough cell walls. "I'm still angry with him. Yet my heart... it belongs to no other."

"Such is love," Taos murmured, shifting so his right wing spread over them both like a blanket. "My advice is to hold tight and never let go."

Liria ran a hand over the warmth of the Pharaoh's feathers, so similar to Raiden's and yet so very different. "First, we need to get out of here."

"Out? We're in a dungeon. There is no out."

"I'm not so sure. Will you trust me, Taos?"

"With my life." He retracted his wing and allowed her to tug him upright.

Liria guided the Pharaoh across the cell, trying not to feel overwhelmed by the swift surety of his declaration. Ione trusted her, but that seemed a moot point - as long as Ione possessed the soul ring, there was no possible way Liria could betray her. Raiden had said he trusted her but had stumbled at the first hurdle, the wound he'd created one that still smarted. And Taos? He had neither Ione's security nor Raiden's great strength; should she wish it, she could kill him here and now and nobody would ever know. To place his trust in her so fully and readily... her stomach knotted.

The stone wall of the dungeon loomed ahead, and she drew Taos to a halt before he walked into it. Setting her free hand against the rough bricks, Liria began to feel her way across.

"What are you looking for?" Taos whispered, his wing sliding across her shoulders. The touch felt intimate, reminiscent of Raiden - except that this was not Raiden at all, and she was seized with an almost unbearable urge to shove the Pharaoh's wing away and press her knife to his throat.

"I'm not sure. Set has blocked my magic, so I'm relying on my other senses." Liria took a deep, steadying breath as his wing tightened, reminding herself the poor angel was blind and terrified. "Something about this area feels off."

There. Liria curled her fingertips around an odd corrugation in the side of a brick. An alien magic brushed her skin, cool and soothing like a clear, spring night. A spark of power lit in her veins and Liria grabbed hold, banishing the simple illusion to reveal a hollow in the stone very much like a handle.

"What was that?" Taos sniffed the air. "It smells like... like a desert oasis."

"Magic. Not mine, and not Set's, either." She shifted the arm to which he clung, guiding the Pharaoh to a safer position, and tugged on the handle. "Stay behind me."

With a soft grinding noise, part of the wall swung open and flickering torchlight spilled into the cell. Liria blinked and ducked her head but Taos gave a sigh of relief, his fingers tightening on her wrist before he let go. "Thank the gods."

"Wait." Liria peered cautiously through the doorway. The narrow tunnel looked harmless enough, and felt that way to her limited senses, but that didn't mean there were no traps hidden out of sight. Taking advantage of the meagre shield the alien magic provided, she reached into the shadowy gloom behind her back and withdrew her favourite dagger. Flipping it into a reverse grip down her forearm, Liria motioned for Taos to stay put and edged through the oddly shaped hole.

A gentle draft caressed her face, bringing with it an earthy scent and the faintest hint of day-old bread. Torches had been mounted at ten-pace intervals along one wall, their flickering flames casting an orange glow that would have been comforting, except that there was no fuel for the torches and the fire itself gave off no discernible warmth. The floor of the roughly hewn tunnel was cool beneath Liria's bare feet, with a slight coating of sand that stuck to her soles and made her wish for a stream in which to rinse clean. The door she'd opened was set in the side of a gentle cul de sac, giving her just enough cover to peek around the corner and get a view of the journey ahead - a long, straight path with enough of an incline that the far end was out of sight.

"Well?" Taos' face was pale when she turned back, his hands twisted in the dark green shawl draped around his shoulders. His golden-bronze hair was tousled, a sure sign he'd been tugging at it, and there was a shadowy quality to his gentle brown eyes that Liria had never seen before.

"A tunnel, leading upward. I cannot see the top, so we'll have to progress carefully." Liria gently pried the angel's hands free from his shawl. "The tunnel is well lit, my Pharaoh, and I am with you. From the sword you brandished earlier, I assume you know how to fight?"

He nodded slowly. "I'm not as good as Raiden, but he insists I keep my skills up where I can."

"Good." She ran her eyes down his body and back up again, cataloguing his muscle tone, stance and balance. The woman in her, newly awakened and distractingly aware, took it upon herself to point out all the ways Taos was different than Raiden, setting her heart aching for the Prince of Storms. "You need a weapon."

The Pharaoh grimaced, patting his naked waist. "Set disarmed me."

"That's not an issue." Liria stuck her hand into the shadows and manifested a dagger similar to her own. "Will this do?"

"I..." He stared down at the curved edge and swallowed. "How did you do that?"

"Magic."

"Didn't you say Set disabled you?"

"Yes. However..." Liria pushed at the suffocating blanket that had lain over her senses since she awoke. "Whatever strange spark was inlaid in the door seems to have loosened the noose, so I have access to some of my subtler skills. The god of war and chaos is not omnipotent, it seems."

"None of them are," Taos muttered, but his expression was much lighter than it had been moments earlier, and he accepted the dagger with a wry smile. "I'm not entirely sure I can use this properly. That backwards way you hold it... I've never seen that before."

"I'd show you, but it takes practice and we don't have the time. It will work as well as any other blade if you hold it however you're comfortable, or I can materialise you something else."

"A sword?"

"Too big. Unless..." Liria reached into the shadows and closed her eyes, concentrating on a dim, distant memory. "What about these?"

Taos' eyes widened as he focussed on the weapons she offered. They were a matched pair of short swords whose blades were the length of his forearms and as wide as his splayed fingers. He shoved the dagger through the sash at his hips and accepted one in each hand, testing the balance and giving an experimental twirl. His left hand was clumsy but the right worked smoothly. "I'm not much into dual wielding, like Raiden, and these are quite short, but... I think I can make it work."

"I'm afraid that is the biggest I can manage." Liria smiled and spread her hands. "Even a shadow has limits."

The Pharaoh's wings opened and closed, his eyes on his new swords as he tested the leather grips. When he finally met her gaze, his brown eyes were dark and serious, his face set. "I appreciate your trying to arm me. I know I'm not the angel you'd prefer, but I won't let you down."

"Taos." Her heart twinged at the determined set of his shoulders. "You are the Pharaoh of all Merged Egypt and Avatar to the Gods. Don't tell me you look at your younger brother and feel inadequate?"

He raised a perfect brow. "I may be the pretty face on the throne, but Raiden is the substance behind it. Surely, by now, you realise that."

"You sell yourself short." Liria's lip twitched. "Also, don't tell your brother that. He's insufferable enough already."

Taos chuckled, then gave her an incisive look. "You're going to forgive him."

"After he finishes - what did you call it? Grovelling? Perhaps." She shrugged. "Raiden is the first person who ever made an effort to see me for myself, and though it's selfish, I love him. I promised I'd fight for us, and so I will; even if it's him I have to fight with." Liria settled her dagger better against her forearm and stepped into the tunnel. "For now, however, we must focus. Neither of us will have an opportunity to slap that crooked grin off his face if we remain in the dungeon."

With a deep, resigned breath, Taos nodded and slipped into place behind her, positioning himself so that his stronger sword arm faced the vacant space at their rear. Liria eased into the tunnel and crept forward on silent feet, her eye twitching every time the Pharaoh's boots crunched on the gritty floor. It was a shame the tunnel was too narrow for his wings - but then, the booming thump of an angel flapping would be as bad, if not worse, than the sound of his walking.

A smile teased Liria's lips as she recalled Raiden's indignant protest that angels did not flap. Of course they did. Birds flapped, and what were the angels' wings, if not bigger versions of those a bird wore? The notion of *not* flapping was ludicrous. How else did they fly? Willpower? Flatulence? Liria shook her head ever so slightly, reigning in the urge to spread her own wings. She'd long come to terms with the fact that she flittered and fluttered like a delicate butterfly, though in truth the movements were more reminiscent of a hummingbird. Her wings might lack the strength and versatility of the angels, but she was silent in the air, far more nimble than her angelic counterparts, and capable of hovering indefinitely. What the angels lacked, she made up for - and the same was true in reverse, making them an ideal pairing. It was a shame, really, that fairies were so rare.

She glanced back to check on Taos and was pleased to see he hadn't so much as broken out in a sweat. His fighting skills may not be equal to his brother's, but at least he was fit enough to handle the steep incline. Liria could feel the burn in her thighs and calves by the time they reached the top, where a solid iron door awaited.

Steadying herself on the wall, she lifted her weight from her injured ankle and rotated the joint. It ached, but there were no sharp pains, nothing that made her think the bone still carried a weakness. After a moment's grimaced indecision, Liria used her dagger to slice through the stiffened bandage and tossed it aside.

Taos frowned. "Are you sure that's a good idea? The healers said you were to rest for another day or so - and I realise that's impossible in this environment, but the stiffening bandage is supposed to help."

"If we run into anything untoward, having my movement hampered by a medical aid could mean the difference between this world and the next. I'd rather risk revisiting the healer when we return to Selekhet." Liria hovered a hand over the door's surface and tried to prod it with what little magic she'd managed to retain. "Hmmm."

"Problem?"

She shook the frigid chill of the metal from her palms. "Iron's not good for fairies. As a dark fairy I have a certain resistance, but…"

"Not immunity?"

"No fairy is immune to iron." Liria chewed her lower lip, then shrugged. "It's also a barrier to my magic. I can't sense anything beyond."

Taos eyed the door. "So we either stay here, or brave the unknown?"

"Yes."

The Pharaoh paced back and forth, swishing his swords as he went. "What do you recommend?"

"Me?" Liria blinked.

"Don't try that 'you're the Pharaoh' look on me," Taos growled. "You're better equipped than I am for this. Like I said before, consider me your brother. Forget about the damned crown."

Liria took a deep breath. Forget the crown? She'd spent her whole life tethered to one crown or another. To put that notion aside and step into a position of authority herself was…

Freedom.

Taos was offering her freedom.

Exhilaration and terror swept through Liria in waves, and she shivered. Ione was so far away that her bond to the soul ring was a distant, stretched ache in the back of her mind, and whatever Set had done to dampen the bulk of her abilities made the connection fuzzy, the sensations so slight that should Ione call, Liria doubted she'd know about it, much less be forced to respond. She was, in truth, as free as she'd ever been - freer even than those moments she'd been with Raiden, her heart and body focussed solely on him.

"All right." Liria turned to Taos with a smile. "Shall we?"

He tightened his grip on his swords and gave a nod. "I've got your back, Lady of Shadows."

Ignoring the brutal burn of the iron against her skin, Liria grabbed the thick handle and yanked open the door.

IT'S DANGEROUS TO GO ALONE

Tiptoeing through the Palace in the dark made Raiden feel like a teenager sneaking out to kiss girls in the garden. He kept his wings tight and his body hunched, sticking to pools of shadow and making sure to keep out of sight of the windows. The door to the Royal Study opened on silent hinges to reveal a darkened interior and Raiden slipped inside, closing the door quietly behind him and then pressing his shoulders against it.

After ten minutes of insect chatter and the occasional hoot of an owl, he slipped over to Taos' desk and tapped the solar lantern that rested on one corner. Soft light spread across the intricate parquet surface, revealing an empty desk pad and several neat stacks of paperwork arranged in size order from smallest to largest. Raiden eyed the piles as he lowered himself carefully into the Pharaoh's overstuffed leather chair, his heart thumping in the back of his throat.

Taos had always, *always* taken care of the administrative side of things, and Raiden the military. It suited their personalities and interests, and merely contemplating dipping his fingers into his brother's area of expertise felt like... usurping.

No. Raiden forced his racing heart to calm. He wasn't usurping, he was doing what Liria had trusted him to do - what he should have done before - and making sure he upheld all his responsibilities before he raced off blindly into the desert. Wiping sweaty palms on his battle leathers, Raiden reached for the leftmost stack. His brother was organised, and he'd not let Raiden down - the pile was laid out in chronological order, and sectioned into categories according to the order of their importance.

"What are you doing, my Prince?"

Raiden jolted, wrapping a hand around the hilt of one of his khopeshes as a second desk lamp flared to life. A wizened old man blinked muzzily from across the room, his body wrapped in layers of loose brown linen and ink staining his hands and arms up to the elbows.

"Jhariv." He let out a breath and relaxed his grip on his sword. "You startled me."

The Royal Scribe hobbled over to Taos' desk and leant heavily on the edge. "*I* startled *you?* You weren't the one who woke to an intruder in the middle of the night."

Raiden endured the sharp cuff to the back of his head with good grace. Jhariv had been the Royal Scribe for his grandfather, his father, and now for Taos. For all his gruff manner, the old man had been a pillar of strength and support after the death of the previous Pharaoh - and unlike the empty platitudes of Nurus, the Royal Scribe had done an admirable job of supporting two young boys attempting to govern a kingdom before they'd truly learnt to become men.

"Sorry, Jhariv." Raiden's gaze drifted towards the Scribe's desk, which was a haphazard mess of inks, brushes, paints, and parchment piled so high that the stacks teetered and swayed of their own accord. "I didn't think you were supposed to sleep in the study anymore."

The Scribe's hand cuffed the back of his head again. "I didn't think you were supposed to sneak about the Palace unannounced anymore. And yet, here we both are. What's going on, whippersnapper?"

"I..." Raiden raised a hand to rub the place where he'd been struck. Uncertainty rose, and all of a sudden he couldn't think, couldn't breathe, couldn't see.

Jhariv grunted. Taking hold of Raiden's free hand, he pressed something hard into his palm. "Eat."

It was the habit of a lifetime to obey, and a moment later the sweet tang of barley sugar invaded Raiden's mouth.

"Suck, don't chew," Jhariv warned, and Raiden relaxed his jaw to follow the instruction. "Breathe, little Prince. Just breathe."

Raiden sucked on his barley sugar and concentrated on breathing while the Royal Scribe rubbed his back in smooth, soothing motions. Raiden's shoulders slumped and he braced his elbows on the desk, winnowing both hands into his hair.

Breathe. Suck. Breathe.

"Now," Jhariv said - and how he knew the barley sugar was gone, Raiden had never been able to figure out, "talk to me."

With his eyes shut and his fingers clenched in his hair, Raiden spoke. Jhariv continued to rub his back while he talked, relating everything that had happened since he and Taos had greeted the Atlantean ship at the docks, and he'd first laid eyes on Liria.

When he finished, Jhariv braced his palms against the Pharaoh's desk and hopped up to sit atop it with a grace that belied his age. Shuffling sideways until they were both eye height, the Royal Scribe propped one sandalled foot on Raiden's knee and leant forward to grip his jaw in a warm, dry hand.

"Most of this I knew from your brother already, but I'm glad to hear it in your own words. First off, you must stop being so hard on yourself." Jhariv's grip tightened on Raiden's jaw, preventing it from opening. "I mean it, young Prince. You cannot help anyone if you cannot forgive your own mistakes."

Raiden grunted, working his jaw to get out a few mangled words. "Hardly young anymore."

"Bah!" Jhariv gave him a warning prod in the gut with the toe of his sandal. "When you're as old as I, everyone is young. Now, stop your panicking and start listening, whippersnapper."

"Yes, sir."

"Better." Jhariv whipped another sliver of barley sugar from the pouch at his belt and shoved it between Raiden's lips before he could protest. Grey eyes glittered in amusement, the old man's grip tightening to prevent the reflexive action to chew. "Always so impatient. Taos, he learnt how to wait, how to plan. You, no. Always rushing to and fro like the winds in the desert." The Scribe's head tilted, his multitude of shoulder-length white braids swishing. "Taos, though? Sometimes he's too slow to act. Too careful. While you're there to leap right in, sword blazing, and sort things out by force. You each have strengths and weaknesses, and they complement each other. Years of shared experience, trial and error, blood and tears have taught you to work as a team. Yes?"

With his mouth full of candy and his jaw crushed in an iron grip, Raiden could only nod.

"Good. Now, whilst the Lady of Shadows seems, from all accounts, the perfect balm for your ragged edges - and you hers - you've known each other, what? Two weeks?"

Another nod, this one more tentative. Jhariv must have noted the change, because his face softened.

"Don't doubt your love, whippersnapper, nor hers." The Royal Scribe sighed. "Love is a funny thing. It can happen in an instant, or after years of long association. It can strike you down like lightning, or slowly creep over your heart like ivy. However it happens is irrelevant; the strength is the same. It's not love that's the issue here, it's shared experience." Grey eyes bored deep. "You made a mistake not because you're a buffoon - though you are rather thick headed, sometimes - but because you haven't worked with Liria long enough to have the natural understandings and rhythms that you've sculpted with Taos. Now you panic, not because you are wrong or less, but because that confusion, added to the strangeness of your new blood, is blinding you from thinking clearly."

Raiden blinked, and swallowed a mouthful of melted barley sugar.

Jhariv grinned, displaying perfect white teeth. "See? This old man still has some things left to teach you, Prince of Egypt." He leant back, releasing his grip on Raiden's jaw. "Now, how about you let me take care of the things behind this desk, while you go do the rescuing?"

"I..." Raiden shifted his gaze to the stack of paperwork, then back again.

"Do you think I'm too old to do my job, Prince of Egypt?" Jhariv raised wiry white brows. "I've been Scribe to this kingdom since I was a child. I can handle the Pharaoh's administrative duties for a few days without the Palace crumbling around us."

"You should be resting more, not working more," Raiden pointed out, jerking his chin at the sleeping mat unrolled behind Jhariv's desk. "If Taos finds out you're still sleeping in here, he'll lose his mind. We care for you too much to endanger your health."

Jhariv waved a knobbly hand. "Yes, yes, I know. He's been at me to take an apprentice for months."

"And will you?"

"Oh, for -" The Royal Scribe huffed out a breath and crossed his arms. "Tell you what, whippersnapper. You let me do this for you, and once Taos is back safe and sound, I'll consider it."

"Consideration isn't enough."

"Fine! I'll accept an apprentice - but they must live up to my standards," Jhariv growled, eyes flashing. "I won't have just anyone."

"All right." Raiden nodded. "And once we settle on an apprentice, you'll drop these bad habits and sleep in your bed."

Jhariv's eyes narrowed. "Very well."

They shook, and then the Royal Scribe reached out to ruffle Raiden's hair. He smiled, feeling suddenly lighter. "Thank you, Jhariv."

"Where do you go?"

Raiden stood. "Mu. The gods are sure Set took them to Mu."

"You plan to go there via the old road?" The Scribe clicked his tongue against the roof of his mouth. "It would be better to ask one of the gods. Safer."

"Anubis and Horus already refused to take me." Raiden pushed back the Pharaoh's chair and helped Jhariv off the desk. "I have nobody else to ask."

"In that, Prince of Storms, you are mistaken."

Raiden shoved the Royal Scribe behind him as the air in the centre of the study shimmered, and two women appeared in a sparkling rainbow of light. The solar lanterns around the outside of the room sprang to life, illuminating a goddess with golden skin, blunt-cut black hair, a flowing white gown and feathers sprouting from her arms.

"Isis." Raiden bowed deeply. "It is an honour."

"Allmother, you are welcome here," Jhariv added, hobbling out from behind Raiden to add a bow of his own. He bowed again, though not quite as low, to the second woman. "Queen Ione, it is a pleasure."

Ione clung to Isis' arm and gave the Royal Scribe a short nod. She'd dressed in flowing black pants and a long sleeved black blouse with a black leather tunic belted over the top, her raven hair braided in a crown around her head. When she caught Raiden staring at her unusual attire, she squared off her shoulders and lifted her chin.

Raiden looked between the two Queens and shook his head. "No."

"No?" Isis raised a perfect black brow. "No, what, Prince of Storms?"

"No, I'm not taking Ione into Mu with me. Or did you dress her so for fun?"

Jhariv, too short to reach Raiden's head while they were both standing, swatted his bicep instead. "Show some respect to the Allmother."

"This is a matter of life and death," Raiden gritted out, "and

Ione is pregnant. You want me to risk the heir to the throne by dragging her into a dangerous situation?"

"How dare you?" Ione gasped. "I am the *Queen*. I decide for myself where I will and will not go."

"You may be the Queen, but you're not my Queen," Raiden snapped, thumping a fist against his chest. "I answer to no-one but Taos - and he'll gut me the moment he sees I've brought you into danger."

Isis' face softened, and she draped a feathered arm over Ione's shoulders. "You are a man of such heart that it humbles me, Prince of Storms." When Raiden opened his mouth to speak, she gave a minute shake of her head. "In this, I agree with you, but we have little choice. Ione can do what nobody else can - she can find the Pharaoh."

"She can?" Raiden narrowed his eyes at Ione. "How?"

The Queen stepped forward, wiping her hands on her leather tunic and flinching from the texture. "I can track Liria through the soul ring."

"And Liria once told me I could track her through the heart bond." He thumped a fist against his chest, where the faintest echo of a fairy's heartbeat was all that kept him moving forward. "I have no need of you."

"My bond is stronger than yours," Ione hissed, brandishing the soul ring as though she'd punch him with it. "I have a higher claim."

"Enough!" Isis held up a hand, her eyes glowing with an otherworldly light. "Raiden, you are correct. You can track Liria through the heart bond." Seeing his victorious smile, the goddess held up a slender finger. "So long as she lives. If something were to happen - and I pray it does not, but we cannot ignore the possibility - then only the soul ring will do. It has the capacity to find Liria no matter what."

Raiden's breath cut at his lungs like a razor. "She's alive. I know she's alive."

"For now, but the longer we delay, the less the likelihood."

Isis' tone gentled. "I will also add that the heart bond is new. Do you understand it? Do you know how to track through it? Because Ione has a lifetime's worth of experience using the soul ring to trace Liria's whereabouts. Though you find the notion unpalatable, it truly is our best chance of finding her - and, through Liria, Taos."

"Assuming they're together."

"I believe they are," Isis murmured. "I've known Set a long time. He prefers to keep all his treasures in one place."

"Even if they are separated, finding Liria will give us the means to recover Taos," Ione said, lifting her chin. "I shall simply command her to find him."

Raiden's world tilted and he clenched his hands to fists. "If you're so all powerful, why not simply command her to return home, like a good little shadow?"

"I did," Ione snapped, then blanched when he growled. "There's something blocking the connection. I can feel through the ring that she lives, but my instructions bounce back."

"Good." Raiden thumped his fist on Taos' desk, and thunder rumbled low and dark through the room. "*Good.*"

Ione huffed out a breath and turned an indignant look on Isis. "See, Allmother? I told you he wouldn't help, no matter the logic. He hates me."

"He hates slavery," Isis demurred, her smile indulgent as she stroked a hand over Ione's hair. "Particularly when the woman in question is the one he loves."

"Liria isn't a slave," Ione rolled her eyes. "She's my shadow. It is her purpose to love me, and her honour to serve me."

"She's a *person,*" Raiden snarled. A savage wind whipped through the room, earning him another swat from Jhariv as the paperwork on the desks took flight like a flock of birds.

Ione's huge navy eyes blinked, ever so slowly. "Of course she's a person. I can't have a chair as a shadow, can I?"

"You snide little -"

"Raiden." Isis glared him down, her deep green eyes glowing

ever brighter. With a snap of her fingers, the wind died and the papers flew back to the desks, reassembling themselves into the piles from whence they'd come. "Queen Ione is not used to our culture. I'm doing my best to teach her, but we cannot expect her views to alter in the space of an evening. For now, we must focus."

He forced air in and out of his lungs, and managed to speak through clenched teeth. "Horus and Anubis wanted me to stay here."

"And I agreed, until I realised that Ione has the means to turn the tide against Set." Isis sighed, squaring her shoulders as though preparing for a blow. "I want to send you and Ione to Mu in secret. If Set gets wind of your arrival, he could move the Pharaoh, or damage him. For the ruse to work, we cannot allow Anubis or Horus to discover your presence. You and the Queen will need to work together if you wish to succeed."

Raiden ground his teeth, knowing he had no alternative - not if he truly wished to rescue Liria and Taos. He blew out a long, slow breath and locked his emotions away, drawing on the warrior's calm he'd spent a lifetime perfecting. "All right. What will you be doing while we're gone?"

"Ensuring Set doesn't suspect anything's amiss." Isis tilted her head to the side, as though listening to something far away. "I'll return to Osiris and take care of our business there as I had originally intended, then I will come back to the Palace to watch over Egypt in your absence. Set, if he's paying attention, will assume I'm giving Ione the lessons I promised - meanwhile, you'll have a goddess to keep your people safe."

Three pairs of eyes stared at Raiden as he ran a hand through his hair. Isis' plan was sound enough, but there was an uneasiness in his gut that wouldn't subside. When an elbow jabbed his ribs, he turned his glare on Jhariv. "What?"

The man held out a piece of barely sugar. "Do we need to repeat your lesson, whippersnapper?"

"No." Raiden took the candy with gentle fingers, and bowed

low to the man who'd helped guide his moral compass after the death of his parents and sister. "I will not fail you, Jhariv."

The Royal Scribe patted his arm. "I know. Go along, now. And remember - suck, don't chew."

Raiden stuck the barley sugar in his mouth and strode to the Allmother's side. She gave him a knowing smile, slipped her free arm around his waist, and everything went black.

PERSPECTIVE

Soft grass cushioned Liria's bare feet and she turned her face into a gentle breeze. The scent of midnight and dew curled through her, relaxing tense muscles and urging her wings to spread of their own accord.

"Stay behind me," she murmured, one arm extended to prevent Taos' unconscious step forward. "It's likely a trap."

The Pharaoh said nothing, his torso bumping her arm as he looked around in amazement. Moonlight filtered down from a clear sky, burnishing the clearing in silver. Rocky walls cradled a blanket of grass, a collection of dark, green trees and a circular pool of water, the surface mirror-smooth and speckled with reflected stars.

A woman stood by the pool, face upturned to the moon. She had sleek black hair cut straight across the shoulders, covered with an elegant netting of silver that glittered with white diamonds. Her skin was smooth and dark, her delicate profile holding an otherworldly beauty. A simple gown of palest lilac was gathered below the bust by a shimmering silver belt, the skirts pooling on the grass in elegant layers. A multitude of thin silver bangles chimed against one another as she lifted a slender arm, beckoning her guests to join her at the water's edge.

"No." Liria shoved Taos back.

"It's all right," the woman said, her voice a soothing, deep thrum. "I will not hurt you."

The Pharaoh curled his fingers around Liria's wrist. "Fear not, Lady of Shadows. That is Nephthys, goddess of twilight."

"Set's wife," Liria growled. "I've done my research. I know who you are, Nightlily."

"Estranged wife," Nephthys corrected, her face serene and her eyes remaining closed. "I'd ask Osiris to officiate a divorce, were I not imprisoned here." Her hand remained outstretched, her posture relaxed. "Come, Pharaoh. Come, dark fairy. Join me, that we can greet each other properly."

Taos jerked forward and Liria stepped in front to block him, raising her dagger with her free arm. "I am not so easily bewitched by pretty words, goddess of twilight. If you wish our trust, you will have to earn it."

"Are you out of your mind?" Taos hissed. "She's a *goddess.*"

"And I promised to keep you safe, no matter what."

"I know her!"

"You know Set, too." Liria bared her teeth. "Shall I turn you over to his tender mercies?"

Nephthys laughed, the sound carrying the deep, throaty note of an owl. She opened eyes the colour of aquamarines and turned to face them. "This one is smart, Taos. She does you credit."

Taos inclined his head in regal thanks. "Where are we, Nightlily? Why are you here?"

"This is a prison." Nephthys waved her arm, bangles tinkling. "You are here, like I, because Set needs something from us." Pale eyes locked on Liria. "You, specifically."

Liria shook her head. "I have nothing to offer the Anarchist, and your words do little to prove your innocence."

"Innocence?" Nephthys' laughter carried a bitter edge, and

she turned to stare down at the mirrored pool. The surface shimmered, shifting to show Anubis standing in an elaborate garden, his brow furrowed as he spoke rapidly. "I am far from innocent." She curled her fingers as through to stroke the line of Anubis' jaw, but the image rippled and disappeared. Nephthys sighed. "Proof of captivity, however? That, I can provide."

The goddess lifted her long gown. Her body was chained at the hips and thighs to a slim stone pillar, hidden beneath the frothy layers of her skirts. The chains were barbed, cutting deeply into flesh so badly burned and twisted there was no way the goddess would be able to stand on her own should they be removed.

Taos gagged and turned away, short swords thudding to the grass as he heaved into a nearby bush. Anger coiled in Liria's gut as she assessed the goddess' injuries, taking note of the hieroglyphs carved into both the stone pillar and the links of the chain. She couldn't read the language of Merged Egypt, but the menace leaking from the characters was more than clear.

"Blood magic." Liria lifted her gaze to Nephthys'. "A curse."

"To bind and to weaken," the goddess of twilight agreed, inclining her head. She let her skirts fall back into place and offered a sad smile. "I cannot move, cannot scry for help, cannot heal and cannot die." The smile turned tight. "To think... I loved him, once."

"Why?" Taos croaked, returning to Liria's side. He swiped the back of his wrist across his mouth and grimaced. "What is the purpose of all this?"

"Ah. That, I can tell you." Nephthys beckoned them closer again. "Please, be comfortable. I cannot hurt you in this condition."

"Liria?" Taos whispered.

"I believe her, but don't let your guard down. Set does nothing without reason." Liria drifted closer, choosing a patch of grass beyond the Nightlily's reach where a small tumble of artfully placed rocks allowed her to sit without folding entirely to the ground.

Taos collected his swords and moved to her side, settling against the rocks with a small groan. "My body is stiff enough to use as planking."

"There are plenty of herbs and flowers here that would ease your suffering, Pharaoh, but I'm afraid I lack the capacity to brew a tisane for you right now." Nephthys waved to a collection of pale blooms in the distance. "Set likes to remind me of what I could have if I submit."

Liria inspected the flowers and recognised enough that she could have brewed a tisane herself, but remained quiet. "You promised us a story, goddess of twilight."

"Indeed." Nephthys' eyes fluttered closed again, and she tipped her head back to the moonlight. "My sister Isis and I were orphaned in the cataclysm that destroyed our home world. The gods Geb and Nut took us in, and we grew up with two foster brothers - Osiris and Set. As we grew, Isis and I both fell for the noble, handsome Osiris, who would go on to become King of Kings, ruler of gods and protector of both Mu and Earth alike." A self-deprecating smile curled Nephthys' lips. "Why I ever thought I had a chance, to this day, I do not know - for Osiris only ever had eyes for Isis. They were built for each other."

Liria exchanged a glance with Taos, and the Pharaoh gave the barest shake of his head. "You can't rush them," he mouthed, settling into a more comfortable position against the rock.

"After Isis and Osiris joined as one, I fled to lick my wounds," Nephthys continued, her face drawn. "Set found me. He confessed he'd been in love with Isis, and in our shared pain, we found peace. From that moment, we became inseparable. He was loud and charming and funny and before so much as a century had passed, my heart had mended and I laid it at Set's feet. We were married the next day."

"A century?" Taos muttered, the corner of his lip twitching. "That's barely any time at all."

Nephthys opened her eyes and raised a brow. "I suppose for you, it feels long, but for us, not so much."

"Indeed." The Pharaoh of Merged Egypt cleared his throat, and Liria had the feeling he was choking back laughter. "Please, Nightlily. Continue."

"Many centuries later, when Isis caught with child, I was happy for her - but Set also saw my pain. He's infertile, you see, and the knowledge that he couldn't gift me our own child worried at him like a poisonous thorn. Though I assured him time and again that our love was enough, with each passing day the bright, sweet man I'd fallen for twisted a little further inside his heart." Nephthys blew out a long, slow breath. "He arranged things so that Isis was called away, and cast an illusion so that I would see Osiris as Set, and Osiris would see me as Isis. Set hid, and watched as we..."

"Gods above," Taos whispered, his face pale.

Nephthys shivered. "Set miscalculated, however. Shortly after Osiris and I were... finished, Isis returned home and the illusion dispelled in her presence. We saw each other for who we truly were, and Set stepped in to explain what he had done. He wanted me to have the child I craved, and thought that since I had once loved Osiris and that Osiris was his brother, it would be enough. That I would be happy, thinking the father of my child was Set, and Osiris would never know. The betrayal... we were all devastated, and Set was furious that we didn't react the way he'd hoped. He stormed out."

"That is... I don't know what to say," Liria whispered, her heart tight and her stomach sick.

"It gets worse," Nephthys admitted. "Though it was only one occasion, Set had planned well. I was pregnant."

"Anubis," Taos murmured.

The goddess of twilight nodded. "Horus and Anubis are half-brothers, born a few months apart." She blew out a soft breath. "Anubis knows the truth of his parentage, and because the fault of the matter lay with Set, Isis was able to forgive us - but I do not know if Osiris, like myself, was ever truly able to forgive what we had done."

"It wasn't your doing!" Liria cried, caught by the tale in spite of herself.

"No, but the knowing doesn't negate the act, does it? I moved in with Osiris and Isis, and we raised Horus and Anubis together, with two mothers and one father. Set was banned from the premises." Nephthys' mouth turned down. "I suppose I should have divorced him then, but for all his mistakes, I found I pitied what my husband had become. I truly believed, in my naivety, that simply being apart was statement enough." She frowned, then shrugged. "Besides, I had my hands full with two bouncing baby boys who had quickly become my entire world. Life, for me, was happy enough, but as time went on, Set became more and more bitter - he loathes Anubis, to this day."

"And Horus?" Taos wondered. "What of him?"

The goddess of twilight hesitated. "That is between Set and Horus."

"As much as we are honoured by your sharing, Nightlily, I have to wonder how this is all relevant to our current plight." Liria shifted sideways to avoid Taos' warning elbow. "I mean no disrespect, but I fear we are on borrowed time."

"I am coming to the meat of it, never fear." Nephthys frowned, then gave herself a shake. "It was during his time of exile that Set realised the magical energy of Mu was slowly draining the Ennead of their powers - the construct needs more to survive than we can provide. He returned to Osiris, citing that the older gods were too weak to maintain the merge and would die before the process could be completed. The impact of their deaths would be catastrophic, both to the rest of the Ennead and to Mu in general. At best, we, too, might become weak. At worst, we would all be destroyed."

Something twisted inside Liria's gut. "Was he lying?"

"No." Nephthys' lashes lowered, the moonlight shimmering over a tightened jaw. "There are nine gods in the Ennead, but of those, only seven are still conscious. It was impossible to refute Set's claim, so we set aside our differences and began to seek a solution. After a time, we worked out a speed at which the Merge could continue that would be safe for Mu and Earth alike - though by then, the gods of the Ennead would most likely be drained so completely they'd be comatose." She shrugged. "We'd recover, of course, but it would take time."

"Set didn't like the decree to stand down?" Liria asked.

"Can you blame him?" Nephthys wrapped her arms around herself. "The calculations are educated guesses only. Nothing is certain. But, what can we do? Breaking the Ennead means smashing the worlds together at catastrophic speed. It could tear the Earth apart, destroy Mu, and kill everyone in both realms. At least this way, there are only nine lives at risk."

Taos pushed a hand into his hair and tugged at the bronze strands. "As alarming as that revelation is, I do not see what it has to do with the attacks on the Palace, nor our kidnapping."

"Always rushing," Nephthys tsked. "Set lacks the power to shatter the merge alone, but he determined that if he could find a proxy strong enough to endure the Ennead's punishing demands, he could swap places with that being and be free. The surrogate won't last the length of time the gods can, but in Set's mind, the vessels can be refreshed as necessary - and their deaths are a small price to pay for our own survival." She tilted her head to the side. "Set needs my magical skills to create the vessels, Merged beings that he's trying to strengthen with the blood of Apophis. He lured me away from my home by posing as my son, then brought me here by force. I refused to co-operate, and... here we are."

Liria looked around the idyllic prison, no doubt created as another instrument to torture Nephthys. Her mind churned, the events of the last two weeks playing over behind her eyes. "The blood of Apophis isn't working, is it?"

"It can only do so much without my interference. Apophis was birthed directly from the primordial darkness, and his blood is a direct connection to both nothing and everything. An inept explanation, but suffice it to say that drinking the demon serpent's essence aligns the subject with the very energies Set needs to manipulate in order to tamper with the Ennead. However, the process cannot be completed unless the intended surrogate is..." Nephthys waved a vague hand. "Empty."

"Empty?" Taos frowned. "Empty how?"

"What my darling wife is trying to say is that their souls get in the way." The air shimmered, and Set appeared at the edge of the little pool. He was dressed in black battle leathers, ruby hair wild about his face and not-quite jackal's ears cutting an impressive silhouette in the light of the moon. His face was in shadow but his eyes glowed from within, a soft burn the colour of old blood. "Apophis' blood strengthens the body but twists the soul, rendering the vessels inappropriate to take on the burdens of the Ennead. If I didn't know better, I'd say that old serpent was doing it on purpose. Still, no matter." Set's grin was a slash of white in the darkness. "I found the perfect solution."

Liria's body turned stiff and cold one muscle at a time. "No."

"Yes!" Set laughed, the sound full of boyish glee. "You don't have a soul to be poisoned - it's brilliant."

"Wait." Taos grabbed Liria's wrist as she made to stand. "Don't."

Set's shoulders shook as he continued to chuckle. "To think it was just chance one of my underlings was snooping at the Palace the day King Theon's marriage proposal arrived. I was intrigued by the backhanded offer the Pharaoh was clearly intended to decline, so I paid Atlantis a little visit. Once I realised what the Princess Ione had trailing her around everywhere, I... how would you say? Waved my magic wand, and ensured the *real* proposal, the one Ione had penned herself, arrived safely in Taos' hands." The god of war and chaos winked at the Pharaoh. "Your soft heart didn't let me down - you accepted, and Ione and her glorious shadow came to Egypt."

"It was a test," Liria said, her mouth dry. "The invasion at breakfast, the attacks, Thissish - it's all been a test."

Set clicked his fingers and then pointed them at her, grinning so wide she feared his head might split open. "Correct. You don't have a soul, so in theory, you were the perfect candidate - but I had to be sure. Oh, and Liria Atlannon, you far exceeded my expectations. You're powerful now, but with the blood of Apophis? You'll be unstoppable." He clapped his hands, then looked suddenly morose. "It's almost a shame to use you up in the Ennead, but... better you than me." Set tilted his head, running appreciative eyes over her body - and then Taos'. "Although, I'm still hoping we can have a little fun together first. My wife has been sorely neglecting me."

Taos spluttered, his cheeks darkening with a blush. "Leave off, Anarchist. I tire of repeating over and over that I've no interest in sharing your bed."

"A pity." Set leered, then laughed. "Never mind. I can make do with our pretty little shadow."

"How *dare* you." Liria shoved free of Taos' restraining arm, flipping her dagger into place. "First you seek to steal that which doesn't belong to you, and now you suggest I'd betray Raiden by rolling between the sheets with the very man who intends to use me like an object?"

Set inspected his nails, heaving a dramatic sigh. "My dear Liria, you and I both know how soulbinding works. As a shadow, you are the property of whomever owns the soul ring - you're already an object. If it salves your ruffled feelings, however, once I transfer the power of the Ennead to you and am free to go about my business, I have no issues with how you choose to live your life and no reason to be in it. And if the experiment works..." He grinned again, showing pointed canines. "Then I know for a fact my most wonderful wife possesses the necessary skills to make more shadows. The gods will bow to me if they wish to live, and Osiris will get his comeuppance at long last."

"I will *never* make shadows for you," Nephthys hissed, fury contorting her delicate features. "To separate a soul from the body is an abomination I'll have no part in."

"Oh, you'll change your mind." Set gave her a knowing look. "After all, you wouldn't want anything to happen to your precious son, would you?"

Nephthys went pale. "You are not strong enough to kill Anubis."

"Not right now, no. But once I'm free of the Ennead and my full powers have returned? That brat stands no chance."

"He was meant to be *your* child!" Nephthys cried. "Yours! You saw to his creation, Set, not anyone else."

"He was meant to be mine - but you threw my gift back in my face," Set snarled, gripping his wife's chin in taloned fingers. He kissed her, hard and raw and furious, then hissed in her face. "I loved you. I made the ultimate sacrifice to give you what your heart wanted, and you turned on me like I was trash."

Tears spilled down Nephthys' cheeks. "I loved you, too. We could have adopted, but you made a different choice - and in making that choice, you cut your own throat. Don't press the blade into my hands and declare it my fault, because it's not. My son, *my son*, is twice the man you'll ever be."

"Which brings me back to my point," Set purred, nipping none too gently at her nose. "When I have the power to end *your* son's life, you'll do anything I ask to keep him safe." A knowing smile twisted his lips. "Anything and everything."

Nephthys' strangled sob wrenched at Liria's heart. Curling her fingers through Taos', she squeezed his hand and then slowly set it aside.

"Look after the goddess," she murmured, brushing a kiss to the Pharaoh's temple. "When Raiden comes, tell him I would have been honoured to learn from our mistakes, to grow together into the future. Tell him I love him, no matter what."

"No." Taos' dark eyes went wide. "Liria, *no*."

"I'm sorry, Taos, but this is the only way. For what it's worth, I have enjoyed being your sister." Ducking away from his reaching hands, Liria drew a throwing knife from the shadows by her side and sent it whizzing towards Set's head. The Anarchist ducked at the last moment, eyes narrowing as he released his cruel grip on Nephthys' face.

"Be careful what you invite, little one," he purred, curling his top lip to show fang. "You might not like the games I play."

Liria laughed, spreading her wings and raising her dagger. "You want to play, Anarchist? Come and get me."

A KING'S RANSOM

THE SKIES OF MU were similar to those of Earth, and yet, at the same time, unutterably different. Raiden's wings beat through air that shimmered with latent energy, causing just enough drag to make him work and leaving fine trails of white mist streaming from the tips of his wings. The atmosphere was a shade too blue, the scenery passing by underneath similarly saturated in colour. With every breath, a sherbet-like tang coated the back of his throat until he had to either swallow heavily or choke.

Tucked safely against his chest, arms around his neck and eyes squeezed tightly shut, Queen Ione looked even more uncomfortable. The moment Isis had materialised them in Mu, Ione complained that moving her body was akin to swimming in molasses and promptly decreed that Raiden would have to carry her wherever they went. Since the best way to travel was by air in any case, he'd exchanged a long-suffering look with Isis, gathered Ione close and surged skyward.

The Queen had immediately declared the horrors of flight too nauseating for her pregnant body, and in the hours since had kept her eyes closed and her lips compressed, stirring only to alter Raiden's direction if he drifted off course. The silence left him plenty of time to think of Liria, alternating between pure panic, strangling regret and furious determination. He didn't dare think on their bedroom escapades lest Ione catch a hint of the inevitable reaction and assume it was aimed at her, so instead, he began to build an extravagant plan to apologise for his brutish pigheadedness and earn Liria's trust all over again.

Isis had explained that Mu and Earth were merged enough to share times of day, but that weather would change depending on where they were within the magical realm. So it was that as Raiden flew, a too-orange sun rose in the sky, coating the area in balmy warmth. The landscape beneath had been that of a green, idyllic spring, then flowed to dark, craggy mountains and was now a shadowed, misty swamp whose creeping chill rose goose-bumps across his skin and beat back the sun as an unwelcome intruder.

In the early afternoon, Raiden caught the dip of wings on the horizon. Changing angle, he dropped into the chill clouds concealing the swamp and landed on a squelchy hillock, the backdraft of his wings eddying the mist around them.

"What are you doing?" Ione hissed, her eyes popping open as he ducked into the relative shelter of a nearby bush. When Raiden curved his wings around them for further camouflage, the Queen's jaw dropped and she shoved roughly at his feathers. "This is entirely inappropriate."

Raiden clapped a hand over her mouth and jerked his chin at the sky. Ione's midnight eyes glittered with rage, then she froze as the heavy beat of wings broke the silence and a shadow passed by overhead.

"Horus," Raiden mouthed, praying the thick cloud cover and his mottled feathers would be enough to blend them with the gnarled brown branches of the bush. "Quiet."

Ione nodded and he released his grip on her mouth, straining with every sense as Horus circled overhead a few times, then went on his way. When the Queen made to move, he shook his head and held up a finger. After almost half an hour passed with no sign of the Skywatcher, Raiden folded back his wings and let out a soft breath.

"I still don't see why we should hide from him," Ione mumbled, poking a strand of raven hair back into her braided crown. "Surely Horus would help us."

"Yes, but he could as easily draw Set's attention. The element of surprise may be all that stands between those we love and their death."

"Fine." She grimaced. "Can we go now? I'm dreadfully uncomfortable."

Raiden stared down at the Queen, cradled in the protective circle of his arms and thighs as he crouched. "*You're* uncomfortable? I'm carrying you!"

"And?"

He opened his mouth, closed it again and shook his head. "You have absolutely no concept of how spoilt you are."

"Excuse me?" She stiffened in his grip. "I am not spoilt."

"Then you can walk." Setting the Queen on her feet, Raiden stood and shook out cramped muscles.

"I thought we were flying." Ione wrapped her arms around her torso and shifted her weight, squeaking when her boots made a squelching sound on the damp ground. "What was that?"

"Mud," Raiden grunted, cracking his neck. "It's what happens when you mix dirt and water together."

"You condescending asshole." Ione jabbed a furious finger into his chest. "I've received nothing but insults since I arrived in Egypt, but have I complained? No. I committed myself to Selekhet, to your brother, and became Queen." She bared her teeth. "Even if that Queendom is a farce."

"A farce? How is it a farce? You have a crown. Taos coronated you himself."

Ione stuffed her fist in her mouth and screamed, the sound muffled by her skin and the heavy gloom. Her chest heaved unevenly and tears had gathered in the corners of her eyes by the time she tore her fist out and thumped it against his breastbone, saliva and all. "I want to be Queen of *everyone*. I deserve to be!"

"And back we come to the spoilt comment. Someone who cannot handle sharing responsibility for an entire country's welfare with her husband and brother-in-law isn't suited for governance of any kind." Raiden glared at her down the length of his nose. "You walked into a kingdom that Taos and I have bled for, and honestly expected to take it over? Respect must be earnt - and so far, you've not done much to warrant any." He spread his wings. "Now, are you coming with me to rescue Liria and Taos, or am I to leave you here to fend for yourself?"

Ione gaped. "You can't leave me here. I'm pregnant."

"Watch me."

They stared each other down for long minutes, until Ione cleared her throat and lowered her gaze. "I may have spoken in haste. My apologies, Prince of Egypt."

"Accepted." Raiden clenched his fists and searched for the diplomacy Jhariv had tried to instil in him as a boy. "This is difficult for all of us."

"I realise I'm not perfect," Ione continued, sidling closer. "I am endeavouring to change. The goddess Isis has been most gracious in helping me."

It was said through gritted teeth, but Raiden couldn't help admiring the effort. He swept the Queen into his arms and offered a tight smile. "You're family now," he told her. "Even if we disagree, we stick together."

She blinked, and he threw them into the sky, wheeling westward. Ione's arms looped around his neck and she swallowed, but this time her eyes remained determinedly open. With murmured words and the jerk of her chin she directed Raiden onward, and by the time he was squinting into the setting sun, the Queen announced that Liria's soul signature was almost directly beneath them.

"Are you sure?" Raiden stared down at the idyllic tropical archipelago laid out like emerald jewels in a viridian sea. The island Ione indicated was neither the smallest or largest, with wide, sandy beaches and tropical undergrowth wound around clusters of silver-grey boulders barely the height of two men.

"Of course I'm sure," Ione said at last. "The pull of the ring is never wrong."

"I'm not trying to cast doubt, it's just... this doesn't strike me as the sort of place Set would hide."

The Queen's brow furrowed. "He's god of the desert, is he not? There's a lot of sand here."

"And fire?"

She pointed to where thick curls of steam rose from the greenery. "In Atlantis, we had several naturally occurring hot springs. They're caused by volcanic activity - and, if there's volcanic activity, there's a high likelihood of caves or grottoes under the island itself."

Fire. Sand. Raiden looked to the horizon, where the final rays of Mu's setting sun reached for him in blistering glory. Heat, much like the desert.

"You're right," he said. "It's the perfect hiding place, more so because it appears the opposite of what Set would find appealing."

Ione's face slackened, then she blushed. "Thank you."

"How do we get in, do you think?" When she looked even more shocked, Raiden grinned. "You're the one who grew up on an island, not me."

"Hmm." The Queen's expression turned pensive. "Sometimes there are steam vents for the volcanoes in the areas around a hot spring. Sometimes, tunnels that open into the ocean."

"I can't see Set making regular use of a water entrance, but a steam vent - yeah, I'd buy that." Raiden clicked his tongue against his teeth. "Problem is, if it's too hot, we won't be able to use it without having the flesh stripped from our bones."

Ione stared at the enormous sapphire set in the middle of the soul ring. "Neither Liria or Taos are impervious to fire. There must be an entrance that's safe."

"Only one way to find out." Raiden circled lower, landing with a bone-jarring thud on the beach. He fell to his knees and groaned as Ione tumbled unceremoniously into the sand. "Sorry. Long day."

The Queen stared for a moment, then rolled upright and staggered to his side. Her hand clamped down on the exposed flesh of Raiden's bicep and tingling warmth swept through his body, driving away the hours of fatigue he'd accrued while flying.

Raiden exhaled in relief, then noted the way Ione's face paled and tugged free of her grip. "Save your energy."

"I'm perfectly fine," she snapped, shaking her hand as though his sweat were somehow infectious. "I'm also not egotistical enough to believe we'll be safe without you at full strength, so retain your lecture for someone else."

"All right." Raiden cleared his throat and gained his feet. "In that case, thank you."

Ione blinked, then her stony expression softened ever so slightly. "I... you're welcome."

Spying a familiar tree, Raiden strode up to it and gave the trunk a shake. Several pieces of ripe fruit plopped onto the sand and he scooped them up, brushed the sand off and offered one to the Queen. "We haven't eaten all day and you should keep your strength up, too. Lemurian guava?"

"Oh." She accepted the fruit, turned it back and forth in her hands, then shot him a look from beneath black lashes. "Don't think this makes us friends."

"Wouldn't dream of it." Raiden bit into his own fruit to hide his grin.

They wandered off the beach, making short work of several guavas each while arguing over where was the most likely place to find an entrance underground. The soul ring gave no more information than that Liria was 'down,' a directive that gave Raiden hope even as it frustrated him. He'd spent all day checking the echo of Liria's heartbeat inside of his own and though it had steadily strengthened as he followed Ione's directions, he was no closer to tracking her through the sensations than he'd been the night before. He thrust his hands into his hair and tugged, swallowing the growl he wanted so badly to loose. The more they fluffed about looking beneath bushes and poking rocks, the more time Set had with Liria and Taos to do... whatever it is he was trying to do with them.

Ione stumbled upon a hot spring and they washed sticky juice off their hands as the last of the sun's rays burnished the world in shades of rose and plum. The mottled colours reminded Raiden of Liria's wings, and he couldn't help but stare at the heaped collection of rocks and vines at the edge of the spring, drinking in the glorious wall of shifting colour while a lump built in his throat.

Where are you?

When she didn't answer - of course she didn't - he wiped his hands on his leathers and moved to press a damp palm against the warm stone. Tears spangled Raiden's lashes and blurred his vision, twisting the environment into a kaleidoscope of brilliance and shadows. He leant his forehead against the rock, closed his eyes and drew deep, shuddering breaths.

"What are you doing?"

Raiden's eyes shot open at the sound of Ione's voice and he made to step back from the pile of boulders - only to freeze. "Looking at something."

Easing along the rough surface, he pulled the clinging undergrowth aside and slipped his hand into the dark crack he'd spotted. At first glance the crevice was barely large enough to warrant checking but the more Raiden wiggled his fingers, the more of his arm was swallowed - with only empty space beyond.

"There's no way we'll fit through there," Ione groused, peering over his shoulder.

Raiden studied the slab top and bottom. "I think it's a door."

"How will you open it?" Ione scoffed. "You'd need the strength of a god."

The strength of a god? Tossing the Queen a feral grin, Raiden wedged his shoulder against the boulders and took as good a grip as he could get on the lip of the crevice. Muscles strained and bones ached as he heaved, throwing every bit of his supernatural strength into his arms. The stone gave a ponderous groan and slowly began to shift, swinging away as though on a giant hinge. Gasping with effort, he gave a final shove and collapsed, his heart throbbing in his ears and black spots dancing across his vision.

Wiping sweat from his brow with the back of one wrist, Raiden refocused to find Ione's jaw dropped and the stone door open just enough for them to squeeze through. He grimaced. "It's not much, but it'll do."

"How did you - are all angels that strong?"

Raiden tested his teeth with his tongue, debating how much to reveal. For whatever reason, Taos hadn't shared the secret of Horus' gift; it could be as simple as oversight, seeing as Ione had been unconscious during Raiden's transformation... or his brother might not entirely trust the woman he'd married.

"No," Raiden said at last. "I'm different."

"As strong as a *god?*"

"Clearly not, or I wouldn't be risking a hernia just to get the door open a crack." Before she could ask more questions, he used the rocks to drag himself upright. His limbs were a little wobbly but held when tested, so Raiden slipped through the gap he'd made and into the tunnel beyond. He checked the area over then held out a hand to guide Ione through, surprised when she didn't release her grip on his fingers.

"I can't see," she whispered.

"Give it a minute." Raiden counted in his head, watching as the Queen squinted into a darkness through which he could see perfectly fine. "Now?"

Her face twisted into a very un-royal grimace. "I can make out basic shapes, but that's about it."

"All right. Stay close to me, then." Raiden lifted a wing as the Queen sidled into him, then draped it around her shoulder to prevent her getting lost. The action felt stilted in comparison to his friends or even Liria, who fit against him as though they'd been cast from complementing moulds.

The tunnel sloped steadily downwards, the floor rough but not impassable. Ione bumped into both Raiden's body and his feathers as they walked, her grip on his fingers all that saved her from more than one stumble. When she stepped unknowingly into a hollow and Raiden scooped her against his chest to prevent a twisted ankle, they leapt apart as though burnt. Ione dusted frantically at her leather tunic while Raiden shook his wing out and then they resumed their uncomfortable journey, breathing a sigh of relief when flickering firelight seeped far enough into the tunnel that the Queen could walk unassisted.

When Ione made to stroll into the light, Raiden yanked her into a pool of shadow and held her still while he peered around the final lip of rock that separated the tunnel from the cavern beyond. The rough-hewn chamber was lit by iron torches whose cradles burned with a fire that looked natural enough, but gave off no sound and appeared to require no fuel. Three tunnels split from the small antechamber, devoid of any feature that might indicate which way to go.

After several tense minutes Raiden eased into the light, Ione so close behind she was stepping on his heels. He walked up to one of the torches and held his hand out to the flame, unsurprised when it gave off no heat. "Magic."

"Well, this is the home of a god," Ione replied, her voice pitched as low as his. She waved at the three tunnels. "Which way?"

Raiden inspected each of the entrances, seemingly identical to each other. "I don't know."

A soft breeze wafted down the one closest, and he leant into the scent. Some sort of garden? The air was cool, too, not the humid press of the tropics from which they'd come. It reminded him of kicking back on Taos' balcony in the evening, sharing beer. It reminded him of moon lilies, deep kisses, and Liria Atlannon.

He took an instinctive step backward. "That one's a trap."

"How can you tell?" Ione slipped closer to the tunnel and inhaled. "It smells wonderful."

"That's why it's a trap."

The Queen gave him an incredulous look. "How can something so perfect be a trap?"

Raiden simply raised a brow, and she blushed and stepped away with a nod. When he was certain Ione wasn't going to make a break for the fragrant tunnel, he crossed to the centre one, pausing smack in the entrance to breathe deeply. "Nothing. Musty, maybe. Unused."

"No," Ione shook her head, brow furrowed as she stepped to his side. "Ash. Dust. Almost like a tomb."

"Hmm." They moved to the third tunnel in unison, breathing together. Raiden catalogued the scent in his brain, watching Ione do the same. "Water?"

She'd gone stiff. "Deep ocean."

He eased into the tunnel and sure enough, around the first bend, the tunnel ended in a pool of dark water that smelt strongly of salt. Raiden returned to Ione with a nod. "It's flooded."

"So that leaves us with the one that smells like paradise, or the one that smells like death." The Queen blew out a soft breath. "Every instinct I have says we should stay away from the tomb, which means we should probably go that way - but then, it could as easily be the reverse, and the safest route is the pretty one."

Raiden spread his wings and tucked them back in again. He took a few steps into the musty tunnel, following the gentle bend. It led deeper underground, the path smooth and well lit by more of the strange, magical torches. Retreating back to the antechamber, he followed the sweeter scented tunnel an equal distance, noting the way the floor angled downwards and the heady fragrance of flowers grew stronger. His feet begged him to go forward, insistent that Liria lay at the far end, but Raiden forced himself to go back to Ione.

"Not that way," he wheezed, shaking his head to clear the dizziness which had taken hold. "We'll choke on whatever that scent is, and whoever comes through next will find nothing but smiling corpses."

Ione eyed the musty, dry tunnel in the middle. "Forcing us to go this way could be as much a trap as any of the others."

"There's little choice." Raiden coughed, spat blood into his hand and showed it to her. "We either have our lungs dissolved, drown, or take a chance on the middle road."

The Queen stared at his bloody palm, lips pressed into a line. With a muttered curse, she latched her fingers around Raiden's wrist and tingling warmth spread into his chest. The sensation wasn't as strong as the first time and was gone almost an instant later.

"The damage wasn't so bad," Ione murmured, though her face was pinched and pale. "But you're right; we'd be dead quickly if we went that way."

Raiden wiped his bloody hand on his leather pants and then drew both khopeshes, their familiar weight comforting. Ione hooked her fingers into the back of his belt, and together they walked into the tunnel that smelt like a tomb.

THE BLOOD OF APOPHIS

Freezing water sloshed over Liria's face, jerking her awake with a gasp. Coughing and spitting brine, she blinked stinging eyes and snapped her teeth in case whoever was foolish enough to douse her remained close by - but her fangs tasted only empty air. Her senses swirled out, the darkness inside her reaching, reaching, reaching... until she turned her head to the side and retched noisily.

"My apologies, child." Slick like grease and deeper than the ocean, the unfamiliar voice wrapped Liria tighter than any chains, pressing down on her chest and making her ears pop. "I did not mean to ensnare you."

Liria moved to sit and found herself bound wrist and ankle by chains of iron. She hissed as the metal bit into her flesh, tugging and twisting in a desperate attempt to get free.

"Stop," commanded the voice. "You will hurt yourself."

Liria fought harder. A frustrated hiss filled the void between her ears and she clenched her teeth to avoid crying out, yanking against the chains which held her flat on her back on the stone floor, arms and legs akimbo.

"Daughter," the voice intoned. "Stop our guest before she causes an injury even she cannot heal from."

The fuzzy outline of a woman bent over Liria. "If you do not stop your wild thrashing, I will make you."

Unlike the soul-crushing tones of the being who called her daughter, this new voice was so soft it was almost a whisper, hissing over Liria's senses like sand in an hourglass. Straining upwards as far as her bonds would allow, Liria snapped her teeth at her mysterious captor's face. The action earnt her a ringing blow to the head, slamming Liria back to the floor and ending her struggles while she gasped for breath.

"Daughter," the huge voice chided.

"It made her stop, didn't it?"

"Did I raise you to be cruel?" A rumble, as of stones grinding together. "She is as much a prisoner as we are."

Silence, and Liria forced herself to keep panting as though distressed while she listened for the reply.

"No, Father." The silhouette hunkered down close by Liria's side - though not close enough to be struck by her claws. "Forgive me, stranger. I cannot free you but if you promise not to gouge me, I can put fabric beneath your chains so they won't burn."

Liria spat blood on the floor. "All right."

"Promise," the deep-dredging voice rumbled, the word edged with a roughness that may or may not have been a chuckle. "Your word, dark fairy."

"I swear not to harm you while you're rendering me aid," Liria croaked, testing her split lip with the edge of her tongue. Whoever the 'daughter' was, she'd struck true - and carried the strength of a mace in her fist.

This time, there was no mistaking the gravelly grinding as anything but laughter. "Well put. Help her, daughter."

The woman's silhouette disappeared, and when she returned, Liria began to make out the first inklings of form. Long, slender features, wide set, almond shaped eyes with glorious lashes. Dark hair hung in thick dreadlocks to her backside, held back from her face by a dirty length of linen worn like a headband. An equally dirty tunic stretched to mid-thigh, ragged and worn through in several places. Her feet were bare, her body lean and her gait graceful in a way Liria identified as deadly.

She returned to Liria's side and began poking torn rags beneath the chains, bringing blessed relief from the burn of the iron. Once finished, she sat back on her heels and pursed her lips. "It is done, Father."

"And what, my child, comes next?"

The woman grimaced, finally meeting Liria's gaze. "My name is Sylvan."

"Liria."

"Welcome." Sylvan heaved a sigh and looked over her shoulder. "Is this really necessary? They never stay long."

"Excuse my daughter's manners." Something slithered in the darkness, a shape so giant that Liria's brain scrambled to make sense of what her eyes presented. "I am Apep, Great Serpent of the Deep. I have many names, but the one perhaps with which you are most familiar would be Apophis."

Out of the gloom, Apophis coalesced into a creature of flesh and blood. A serpent so enormous Liria and Raiden together would struggle to get their joined arms around his girth, covered in palm-sized grey scales that looked rough, like flint or shale. The cragginess exacerbated around his giant, wedge shaped snake's head, giving him a dark grey collar of rocky protrusions that shimmered faintly in the meagre light. Two enormous silver eyes were bisected down the middle with a snake's slitted pupil, and when he opened his mouth on what she could only hope was a smile, a pair of fangs longer than Liria's arms flicked out. Apophis inched closer, the murky shadows behind him writhing in response and leaving Liria's stomach to knot as she registered coil upon coil upon *coil* of serpent.

"They said you're a demon," she managed, for the first time

missing the way her compulsion had once made it impossible to put her foot in her own mouth.

Apophis lowered his head, easily big enough to swallow Liria whole, down to ground level. When he nudged at her arm, the touch was warm and gentle. "I am. *The* demon, in fact."

"It is not our blood that defines us, but our decisions," Sylvan said, as though reciting from an oft-read text. "Our actions."

"Indeed," Apophis rumbled, the sound so *much* in Liria's ears that she flinched. The serpent blinked, an eerie, sideways motion, and the tip of a forked tongue appeared between his lips. "My voice is hurting you, little one?"

Sylvan leant closer and squinted. "One of her ears is bleeding."

Apophis hissed, jerking his head back. Scales slithered and ground against the floor and then he reappeared, looming over Liria until all she could see were the enormous caverns of his nostrils. His tongue flicked out again, tracing a ticklish path over her cheek until it found the tell-tale trickle at her left ear. With deft motions, the serpent painted two thin stripes along Liria's cheekbones in her own blood, then tipped his chin downward until they were eye to eye - or would have been, if not for the fact that each eye was larger than her head.

"I can taste the darkness in you. Stronger than I anticipated," Apophis announced - and somehow, his voice was modulated, sliding over her rather than into her. "You have my apologies, little one."

Liria looked between the serpent and his 'daughter' and took a leap of faith. "You don't seem to be very evil, for demonic creatures."

Sylvan blinked, but Apophis laughed, a musical hissing sound that filled the space around them.

"As my daughter said before - it is not our blood that defines us, but our decisions." Apophis' mirth died as suddenly as it had come. "I am enslaved to the god Set. Enslaved in a way that you, as a shadow, should understand all too well."

Liria blinked. "And your daughter?"

"Thrown in as a babe for food." Apophis bent to rub his enormous head along Sylvan's cheek. "I adopted her instead."

"Set... tried to feed you a baby?" Liria stared at Sylvan, taking in her features all over again. "What sort of threat do you pose to the god of war and chaos?"

"A threat?" The other woman jerked back in surprise. "I'm no threat."

Liria shook her head. "Then you're either stupid, or he never meant you to die in the first place."

"It's generally unwise for someone chained to the floor to call her cell mates stupid."

"Enough," Apophis rumbled. Though it was hard to truly gauge his expression, his tone sounded thoughtful. "I've never considered it in that light, but... the shadow may have a point."

"Tsk tsk, Liria Atlannon." The darkness by Liria's other side rippled, and Set appeared. No longer clad in battle leathers, his dark gold skin shimmered beneath the flowing black garb of a desert nomad. Deep ruby hair tumbled becomingly about his handsome face, his square-edge, not quite jackal's ears poking out of the mess at an adorable angle. Draped once again in copious amounts of gold jewellery, he looked the sort of man who under-stood pleasure, pain and the various ways in which to give both. When he smiled at Liria, it took every ounce of her willpower not to smile instinctively back. "Giving away all my secrets already?"

Liria sank her fangs into her own lip until she tasted blood and the illusion shattered. "Whatever tricks you hope to pull, Anarchist, think again. Or have you forgotten what happened last time?"

"Oh, I didn't forget." Set raised a hand to the slash mark that traced across his jaw and grinned. "One might even consider it foreplay."

Apophis leant over Liria's body to sniff the wound. "You stripped her powers and she still cut you?"

"Our shadow is an enigma. It seems the soul binding prevents a full stripping," Set replied, patting Apophis affectionately on the nose. "She took me by surprise - but, in the end, I am a god. I prevailed, and here we are."

"Were the chains not a bit much?" The demon serpent retracted his head to look down at Liria. "It's not like she can escape."

"Don't be so sure," Set snorted. "Liria Atlannon can do all manner of things she shouldn't be able to." Apophis' eyes flashed with silver, and the god of war and chaos laughed. "No, no, my pet, don't go getting ideas. As much as I'd love to leave Liria with you a while, I'm afraid circumstances have forced my hand. I have some... political matters to attend to."

Liria growled, ignoring the way Sylvan's face clouded with pity before it went carefully blank. "What have you done with Taos?"

"Taos?" Set tilted his head to the side. "He's safe. I have no wish to harm the Pharaoh."

"He'll be safer with me." Liria strained against the chains, but the iron cut her strength to less than human. "He's my responsibility."

"I'm afraid that won't be the case for much longer." Set's eyes narrowed. "Your rather tenacious lover has arrived."

Raiden? Here? Liria bared her teeth in a feral grin. "He's going to tear you apart."

"On the contrary," Set murmured, crouching to pluck playfully at Liria's nose. "*You're* going to tear *him* apart. Apep?"

"No," Apophis rumbled, pressing back into the shadows. "I won't do it, Setekh."

The Anarchist's face softened. "You don't get to make that choice."

Liria could only watch as Set held out a hand, and Apophis groaned. The floor shook beneath her and magic gathered thick enough in the air that breathing became difficult.

"Stop it! You're hurting him!" Sylvan reached imploringly towards Set. "Let him go!"

The power abruptly cut off, but Set's burgundy eyes glowed with an unholy light as he turned his face towards the younger woman. "You're right. He's been fighting this whole time, and the constructs are weakened as a result. Much better if he acts voluntarily, don't you think?"

Between one moment and the next, Wasceptre materialised in Set's hands. With a flourishing spin, he took a two handed grip and thrust the forked base deep into Sylvan's gut. She choked and gasped, wrapping her hands around the shaft as Set lifted her body into the air. Apophis roared in fury and rushed forward, rocks raining from the ceiling to pepper Liria's vulnerable flesh.

Transferring the sceptre to one arm, Set held up a hand and spoke in a voice that rang with power. "Stop."

Apophis froze, jaws wide, bare inches from the Anarchist's face.

"You want to help her?" Set wiggled Wasceptre and Sylvan cried out, slumping further over the weapon as her blood dripped to the floor. "I'll give her back to you, Apep. I'll return your daughter - when you bleed for me."

Apophis' body trembled with effort, but Set held him without breaking a sweat. Silver eyes flashed down at Liria.

"I'm sorry," the serpent whispered.

"It's all right," Liria replied, though her heart thundered and her bones ached. "I understand."

Set's hand retracted and Apophis sagged, manoeuvring himself into a position that had one of his huge coils poised over Liria's face. The serpent turned hate-filled eyes on his master and hissed. "Do it, Anarchist."

"I'll need your word, Apep - give the shadow everything, or our deal is off and your daughter is mine."

"No!" Sylvan gasped. "No, Father. Don't do it. Let me die."

Apophis closed his eyes. "I swear to give the shadow the full power of my blood. She will be yours to command in every way, her body a vessel for your power like no other has ever been."

"Will it work?" Set took a half step closer. "Is she strong enough to set me free?"

"You know I cannot answer that with any degree of accuracy. I can only make her a monster. *Your* monster. What happens after that will be up to you."

Set clicked his tongue against the roof of his mouth, then materialised a sword and slashed it deep into Apophis' side with no heed for the heavy armour his scales should have provided. Black blood bubbled up, and Apophis angled his body so that it poured over Liria's face, fetid and sticky in a way she'd never seen.

"Drink," Set crooned, his eyes fastened on Liria's face. "Drink it all, little shadow."

Liria held her breath as long as she could, but there was no escaping and at last she gasped, her mouth filling with blood she had no option but to swallow, gagging on the vile taste of demon. She glared her loathing at Set and hoped he felt every ounce of it. "I'm going to suck the marrow from your bones, Anarchist."

Set laughed, and Liria coughed as more blood sloshed down her throat.

"I'm sorry," Apophis said, his head bowed low. "I'm so sorry."

The words turned fuzzy, Liria's body buzzing with a blackness so great it had no end. The magic native to her as a dark fairy rose and was swamped, drowned in a tide of something far more sinister. It slicked her insides with poison, burned her thoughts to ash and dragged a gurgling shout from her mouth. Against her will, her lips parted and she drank eagerly of the blood that poured from Apophis' wound, Set's grin stretching wider with every greedy, gulping sound she made. She was screaming, but the sound came from a distance; first agony and then unbridled ecstasy as the sucking black took her over, pushing her innermost self back and back and back, as though to evict her from her own mind.

From a great distance, she saw Apophis pull away. Set flicked his sceptre and Sylvan's body flung off, landing in a crumpled, moaning heap amongst the copious grey coils that filled the dungeon almost to overflowing.

"You said you'd give her back!" Apophis roared.

Set raised a cultured brow. "And so I have."

"She's *dying!*"

The Anarchist looked confused. "Well, I did stab her in the gut. Those sorts of wounds tend to be fatal."

"You... you..."

"Now, now. I never promised I'd fix her, only return her." Set ran a hand down Liria's cheek and something blossomed inside her, a boiling connection that had her turning her face into his hand and licking the warmth of his palm. "There's only one way to save her life, Apep. Will you take it?"

Apophis roared, his pain so thick that it wrapped around the secret, innermost part of Liria and made it weep. But that tiny piece of her was helpless, drowning. With every second that passed by, it became smaller and smaller until, with a tiny pop, it winked out entirely.

She was nothing.

She was everything.

She was Set's.

"Master," Liria whispered. Set smiled, and the chains at her wrists and ankles fell away. She sat up, colour bleeding from her vision until everything was shades of grey - except for the Anarchist, who burned a deep, dark red. "You're beautiful."

"That I am, little one. Belonging to me isn't so bad, now, is it?"

"No." Liria rose to her feet and spread her wings, infernal energy strengthening every bone, sinew and muscle she possessed. "You are perfection."

"That I am." He held out an arm. "Shall we? I have someone

for you to kill, and then I'll bestow upon you the greatest honour of your life."

The demon serpent was still roaring and thrashing behind her, but the sounds were irrelevant, his grief no more than fuel for the fire of her master's glory.

Liria smiled and placed her hand on Set's arm. "Where you go, I will follow, master. Always."

Heart and Soul

Raiden emerged from the long, winding tunnel into something so unusual it could only be built by magic. Every sense he owned insisted he stood in a large clearing that could have been part of any enchanted forest, except that Raiden knew beyond doubt they were underground. Grass flattened beneath his combat boots and a soft breeze lifted his hair from his brow. Stars winked overhead, the constellations as alien as they were beautiful, framing a fat, low moon that gilded the area in pale blue and silver.

Underground, he reminded himself. *We're underground.*

And yet his wings arched of their own accord, as though to launch him into that woven dark. Would it prove real, or would he slam face first into a craggy roof?

"Oh," Ione whispered, coming up close behind him. "It's beautiful."

"Pretty sure it's a trap," Raiden grunted.

A soft, feminine laugh crossed the grassy expanse. "Not so long ago, your lover said the same, Prince of Egypt."

Raiden narrowed his eyes on the collection of dark trees across the glade. Moonlight refracted off a small, circular pool of water, and beside that pool slumped a woman, her body bent at an odd angle as she strained to reach a misshapen mound at her feet.

"Nephthys?" Even in the shadows, it was impossible to mistake the goddess of twilight - she was almost identical to her twin sister, Isis. Raiden blinked to bring the shape at her feet into better focus. "Taos!"

He was there in a sweep of wings, barely registering Ione's bark of protest. Blood trickled from a wound in Taos' hairline and his normally deep brown skin was pale.

"I cannot reach him," Nephthys said quietly, "but I think he's all right."

"How long has he been like this?" Straightening his older brother out on the ground, Raiden ran shaking hands over his chest and legs, then back up to his head.

Ione arrived in a flurry of panted curses and dropped to her knees by Raiden's side. "Let me see."

"Looks like it's his head," Raiden began, but cut off when Ione shoved him aside, placing her palms flat on Taos' torso. Recognising a dismissal when he saw it, he looked to Nephthys. "Where's Liria?"

The agony on the goddess' face told him all he needed to know, but she gave the words voice anyway. "Set took her."

"You didn't try to stop him?"

The goddess' lips pressed into a thin line, and she lifted the voluminous skirts of her lavender dress. Raiden's jaw dropped at the twisted, bloody mess her lower body had become. "What is *wrong* with the Anarchist?"

"He's afraid," Nephthys replied, and though her hands shook, her tone was hard. "He thinks he's saving us, but he's really just afraid."

Raiden turned that over in his mind, bracing a fist in the grass as he bent to inspect the horrible, barbed chains that bound Nephthys in place. He touched a finger to the metal and hissed as it shocked him, bright and hard.

"Raiden?"

The sound of his brother's voice had Raiden turning like a flash. Deep brown eyes blinked up at him and he dropped into Taos' arms with a sob of relief, tumbling Ione backwards out of the way. "Taos. Thank the gods."

"Set took Liria," Taos croaked, clinging to Raiden even as he was clung to. "She fought - gods, you should have seen it - but she didn't have all her powers and she lost. I tried to step in, but..."

"It's okay." Raiden pulled back enough that Taos could see the conviction in his eyes. "It's okay, brother."

Taos nodded slowly, chewing on his lower lip. "I also tried to call for help. I can't reach anyone from here."

"Oh?" Raiden closed his eyes. *Horus? Anubis?* Nothing, only an oddly ringing silence in his own head. He opened his eyes again. "I can't reach anyone, either."

"Set." Taos sighed, then his eyes flickered to Ione. "You came."

"Of course." Her voice was tight and snippy. "I'm the only one who could find you."

She must have flashed the soul ring, because comprehension dawned on the Pharaoh's face. "Thank you."

Raiden pulled back, helping Taos into a sitting position against a nearby tumble of rocks. Ione folded herself into her husband's side and he left them to their mumbled conversation in favour of investigating Nephthys' chains again.

"You cannot break them," the goddess of twilight murmured.

Raiden shot her a look from beneath his lashes and saw defeat in her expression. "If I could, would you be able to call for help?"

Nephthys blinked. "Pardon?"

"Taos and I can't get through the veil of Set's energy. Would you be able to?"

"Maybe." She wet her lips nervously. "In normal circumstances, yes - but I'm weaker than usual."

"You have a blood link to Anubis, right?"

Her face flickered. "Yes."

"I'm going to get these chains off," Raiden told her. "Then, I want you to call Anubis and tell him to bring anyone he can get hold of, all right?"

Nephthys studied his face for a long minute, then slowly nodded. Raiden poked at her chains again and was shocked for his trouble - but after the last time, he'd registered that the sensation was more a surprise than anything else. So, with warning zaps of energy tickling the veins in his arms, he explored. Silver and sharp, the chains dug cruelly into Nephthys' flesh with barbs both physical and magical. The hieroglyphs tracing each link were tiny, but he was able to make out spells for binding, draining and blocking.

"The enchantments are linked in a pattern similar to the chain itself," Nephthys murmured. "If you can break one, you interrupt the entire flow." When Raiden shot her a look, she flushed. "I made them a long time ago, when Set sought a means to cage Apep."

And now she was bound by them. Raiden shook his head at the irony, searching for a place he could wriggle a finger between the goddess' skin and the metal. Nephthys hissed but made no other protest as he worked, the barbed links biting into his skin until his blood provided enough lubrication for Raiden to get a reasonable grip on the chain. Magical energy zipped through him in a constant cycle, setting his teeth on edge and making his heart race. The echo of Liria's was there, too, fluttering along at a far higher speed - as though wherever she was, she was afraid.

I'm coming, he promised, tightening his grip on the barbed metal in hand. *I promise.* Once Nephthys was free to call the other gods, Raiden would be free to hunt Liria, and he'd find her if it took his last breath.

Fortifying himself with that knowledge, he dug deep inside for the power of the storm. Thunder rumbled in his chest and the air began to thicken, clouds forming overhead to blot out the illusionary sky. His chest rose and fell in great pants as he strug-gled to mould the energy how he wanted it. The hair on the back of his neck stood on end, then his arms, then finally, the hair on his brow began to lift. Still he folded and built, clenching his teeth until the thunder was an echo of his own groaning voice - or perhaps they were the same - and the crackling air was painful to breathe.

Now.

Lightning struck, arcing down from the cloud in a thin but intense stream. It connected with the back of Raiden's hand and flowed down his fingers into the chain, burning away both his own blood and Nephthys' in an explosion of white hot force. There was a loud crack, a woman's scream, and then silence.

Raiden opened his fingers to reveal an empty palm. The intensity of the storm had faded to nothing, and as he watched, the chain binding Nephthys began to dissolve, one link at a time. She fell into Raiden's arms less than a minute later, whimpering and shuddering... but free.

"How?" she whispered, eyes cloudy with pain as they gazed up at him.

Raiden grunted. "I almost died. Horus saved me with his blood. A lot of his blood. So much so, I don't think I'm even remotely human any more."

"You're beautiful," Nephthys whispered, then gave a weak little cough. "I need some time to recover before I can call for my son. The backlash of that broken spell took a toll."

"I understand. I'll -" Agony clenched in Raiden's chest and he cried out, doubling over the goddess in his arms until they were crushed together. His heart wrenched as though it would come out of his chest, his vision swimming to black as a burning pain unlike anything he'd ever known swamped his body.

He must have passed out, because next he knew, Raiden was flat on his back and Taos was leaning over him with a concerned expression. Ione was propped against the tumble of boulders with Nephthys draped in the cradle of her thighs, the goddess breathing shallow and the Queen of Egypt's eyes screwed shut. Healing her, Raiden realised - or at least trying. He doubted Ione had the power to do more than ease Nephthys' pain, but if it helped her reach for assistance sooner, more the better.

"Brother," Raiden croaked, then groaned and clutched at his chest. "What happened?"

Taos shook his head. "I don't know. You just collapsed. The Nightlily said it wasn't quite magical, but something else."

"Liria," Raiden murmured, rubbing at the ache. "I think it was Liria." He turned his attention inward, concentrating on the strained thumping of his own heart - and the echo beyond it. "She's alive, at least."

"We need to find her." Taos cast a worried glance at his pregnant wife and lowered his voice. "You can't protect us all, and I'm no use against a god."

Raiden forced himself onto his elbows, breathing through waves of dizziness. When the world was steady, he levered himself to a proper sit, then a kneel, and finally staggered to his feet. While he stood with hands braced on thighs, Taos related the tale of everything that had befallen himself and Liria since Raiden had last seen them.

"Pawns in a game of gods," Raiden muttered, shaking his head in an attempt to clear the lingering cobwebs.

"Isn't that normal?" Ione's voice was weary. "Where I come from, it's all about one being trying to claim power over another."

"Not in Egypt," Nephthys croaked, her eyes no more than pained slits. "I will admit Osiris has kept the problems of the Ennead from the Pharaoh, but it wasn't intended to cause harm - more that it will take hundreds of thousands of years for the worlds to completely Merge, thus making the issue redundant."

"Until Set came along and tried to kill us all," Raiden growled.

Nephthys inclined her head. "Indeed."

The soft breeze in the clearing picked up, bringing with it the scent of sulphur. Beyond the pool, the grass began to dance in a swirling eddy of energy, the atmosphere rippling. Raiden eased his spine straight and drew both khopeshes, moving in front of his brother.

"Go to the women," he murmured. "I'll buy Nephthys time to call for help."

Taos hesitated, then his hand clamped on Raiden's shoulder for a quick squeeze. "Be well, brother."

"You, too."

Raiden moved to the side of the pool and waited. The rippling darkness condensed, coalescing into two forms, one male and female. When the shadows withdrew, Set stepped forward - with Liria on his arm.

"Well, well." The Anarchist flashed Raiden a toothy grin. "Crown Prince of Merged Egypt. Or perhaps Prince of the Storm is more accurate, in this instance? It is, after all, that glorious flare of power that alerted me to your presence."

"Call it what you will." Raiden shrugged. "This ends now, either way."

Set laughed, the sound so lovely it grated on Raiden's nerves. He took the opportunity of Set's distraction to examine Liria, silent by the Anarchist's side. Dried blood coated a great deal of her body but he'd lay wager that none of it was hers, judging from the easy way she held herself. Her expression was as closed and cold as when he'd first seen it, the perfect mask of indifference, but her eyes -

He froze.

Liria's beautiful violet irises were black, the creature who stared out at him dull and empty.

"Liria?" Raiden lifted a hand to his chest, where the echo of her heartbeat didn't so much as hitch in recognition. "Can you hear me?"

She looked him over as one might something on the bottom of their shoe, then turned to Set.

"Answer," the god of war and chaos murmured, his lips curled into a sadistic grin.

"I can hear you," Liria said. Her voice was hers, and yet not. A slithering quality distorted the cadence of her words, and she spoke without a hint of the icy steel he'd come to associate as uniquely hers. This Liria was... flat. Lifeless.

"Are you all right?"

Another glance at Set. Another nod.

"Of course." Liria's fingers curled over Set's forearm in an unmistakable caress. "My master is perfection."

Raiden stared. Behind him, he heard a gasp that was unmistakably Ione's and a scrabbling sound as she no doubt struggled with Taos.

"My shadow!" Ione screamed. "What have you done to my shadow?"

"*Your* shadow?" Set reached up to chuck Liria's chin. "She belongs to me, now. She will be the vessel that saves me from the Ennead and, eventually, the key to saving all the gods of Mu."

"I'll never let that happen," Raiden growled, spreading his wings.

"Melodramatics already? Very well." The god of war and chaos kissed Liria's cheek, then pointed at Raiden. "Kill the Prince of Merged Egypt, my pet. He's standing in my way."

"No!" Ione cried. "Liria Atlannon, I command you to stand down!"

Something in Liria's expression flickered for the barest moment, but it did nothing to prevent her walking smoothly across the grass towards Raiden. She spread her hands as she went, and two of the long, wickedly curved daggers she favoured appeared.

Raiden moved to meet her, twirling his khopeshes lazily in a display he could only hope kept her attention on him, rather than on the trio behind him. In reply, she flipped both daggers into a reverse grip down her forearms. The movement was simple, but so elegant and deadly that Raiden's gut clenched.

"Liria," he whispered, knowing she could hear. "Don't you know me? Don't you remember?" She paused, and he lifted one hand to his chest, rubbing his clenched fist over his fracturing heart. "I love you."

"I feel nothing." Long lashes drifted to half mast over black eyes, the expression on Liria's face completely devoid of life. "I exist only for the perfection of my master."

"Kill him, my pet," Set called, sounding impatient. "Kill him and bring me his heart."

His heart? Raiden snuck a glance at Set, whose expression was cheerful enough on the surface, but carried an underlying tension. Blood quickened in his veins, and he searched Liria's face for any sign of recognition, anything that would show him she was really there.

"Yes, my master," Liria returned, her pace unhurried as she closed to within striking distance. "I will kill the Prince of Egypt and bring you his heart."

"It's just Raiden," Raiden said softly. "Just Liria. You know that."

She raised her blades and settled her stance, the heartbeat echoing in his chest a dull, monotonous thumping. Nothing. There was nothing. And then her lips twitched in a twisted parody of a smile. "Prince. Of. Egypt."

Raiden barely got his swords up in time to parry the first blow. She moved like a whirling dervish, the strikes of her dagger so fast it took all he had to block her blurring movements. Raiden swallowed past the lump in his throat, working not to give ground as Liria dashed and leapt and spun and struck, her body little more than a smudge in the false night.

"You're in there," Raiden grunted, catching a dagger in the cradle of his blades. "You wouldn't taunt me like that if you weren't. Fight, Liria."

"I am fighting," she returned, ducking his backhanded slash with ease. "And you will die."

Liria attacked with renewed vigour, pushing Raiden back

until his heel splashed in the shallow edge of the circular pool. With a twist of his shoulders and a flare of his wings, he dodged her thrust and shoved her hard in the spine, toppling the dark fairy into the water even as he vaulted back to the centre of the clearing.

After a moment's silence, Liria's head broke the surface. She rose slowly from the pool, flicking water off first one wing, then the other, before they began to whir, lifting her body into the air.

"Why bother with your new pet, Anarchist?" Raiden called, gathering power to him in a wave that made his voice boom with thunder. "Are you too scared to fight me yourself?"

Set laughed, Liria shot forward without so much as the flicker of an eyelash - and Raiden had his answer. He launched into the air in a violent sweep of wings, shooting under Liria's guard and tackling her across the clearing and into the trees far beyond. They hit the ground hard and rolled, blades flashing as she tried to keep up her attack in spite of Raiden's advantage.

"It's another test," he hissed, using his greater weight to pin her body to the grass. "Can't you see? Set wants you to kill me to prove your allegiance. That means he's not sure, Liria. That means there's a chance."

"He is my master."

"No one's your master." Raiden kissed her, hard and fast, begging silently for even the barest flicker of recognition. "You're a real person. Your own person. And I will love you beyond my last breath."

Something fluttered in his chest, the faintest hint of a caged butterfly. Liria shifted underneath him and Raiden twisted his hips to block the blow, but it gave the other opening she'd needed. With an almighty heave made all the more eerie by the complete silence in which it was executed, Liria shoved him up, gathered her legs to her chest and kicked so hard he went flying.

Raiden had barely time to curl his wings around his body before he crashed, sliding on his shoulders for several body lengths. Liria was already overhead, her leap mirroring the arc of his tumble, both daggers at the ready. Even knowing he'd be too late, Raiden began to lift his swords; not for fear of his own life, but for knowledge of how crushed Liria would be if she were the one to end it. He wouldn't do that to her - she was his to protect, even from herself.

The air around Liria shimmered. Horus appeared, swinging a warhammer almost as large as he was tall. It collided with Liria's side and sent the shadow shooting back towards Set, out of Raiden's line of sight.

"No," Raiden gasped, his heart crumbling as the god of the sky landed beside him.

Horus gave him a sharp look. "Fear not, Prince of Storms. She lives."

He shook his head, unable to believe. The hammer was too big, the blow too heavy. Every bone in Liria's body would be pulverised. When Horus gripped his arm and hauled him upright, it was all Raiden could do to stand. He didn't want to look, didn't want to *see*, but his eyes went across the clearing of their own accord - to where Liria was picking herself up gingerly from the ground, a long divot in the grass showing the sign of her passage.

"How?" he rasped, allowing Horus to drag him through the trees to where Taos crouched with Ione and Nephthys. "How is she alive?"

"Set gave her the blood of Apep. It makes her impossibly strong." Nephthys' brilliant aquamarine eyes shimmered with emotion as she looked to Horus. "You came."

Horus knelt by her side, dragging Raiden down with him, and stroked the goddess' cheek. "We both came."

Raiden glanced over his shoulder to see Anubis in the middle of the clearing, his body clad in leather armour as black as his midnight skin. His head was no longer human but that of a jackal, and he twirled his double-ended scythe in one clawed hand. The other he held at chest height, a ball of purple fire crackling in the cradle of his fingers.

"Anarchist," Anubis boomed, his voice that of the deepest tombs. "I never took you for such a coward."

Nephthys winced. "He's angry."

"So am I." Horus gently lifted the hem of Nephthys' dress and glowered at the ruin of her legs underneath. "This needs Isis."

"Where is she?"

"Coming." Horus made a face. "She went to find Osiris first. We'll need them both to best Set."

Set chose that moment to stride into the clearing, his own human face dissolving into that of an animal the likes of which had never been seen on Earth - or perhaps even in Mu. Reminiscent of the jackal, as were his ears, with a longer snout and a face that was all sharp edges over Anubis' sleek lines. He conjured his sceptre with a blood curdling howl, and then Anarchist and Soulcatcher met in a storm of blades and fur and fire.

"We don't have time to wait for Osiris." Nephthys clutched at Horus' arm. "If you work with your brother, you can win."

"We already talked about it, and we're not leaving you undefended," Horus returned equably. "Anubis can handle it until backup arrives." When Nephthys opened her mouth to reply, he caught her jaw in gentle fingers. "Trust him, Nightlily."

Raiden stared at Liria, who was dusting herself off and retrieving her daggers. "I'm going after her."

"She'll kill you." Horus blocked the way with his warhammer. "The blood of Apep binds her to Set. There's nothing left now. I'm sorry, Raiden."

"No." He thumped a fist to his chest. "Liria's in there, somewhere. I felt it."

"It won't be enough," Horus said softly. "We'll have to put her down."

"No!" Raiden and Ione, together.

Nephthys held up a hand for silence. "She's a shadow, yes?"

"Yes." Ione flashed the soul ring. "My shadow."

The goddess of twilight turned her gaze to Raiden. "And the bond I sense in you?"

"She gave me her heart. Some sort of naga spell." He rubbed his chest for what felt like the billionth time. "I can feel her heartbeat."

"Heart and soul," Nephthys murmured. "Heart and soul... it might be enough."

An explosion sounded, and Raiden looked up in time to see Set hit the ground hard, Anubis' scythe swinging for a killing blow. The Anarchist screamed in fury and rolled away, slamming his fist against the earth. The ground rumbled and split open, and the biggest serpent Raiden had ever seen reared out of the hole.

"Apep," Horus cursed, rolling to his feet. "Now I've no choice. Prince of Egypt, guard them well."

Without a backwards glance, he gripped his hammer and launched into the air.

"Listen," Nephthys tugged on Raiden's arm, bringing his attention back around. "Forget guarding us for the moment - there's a chance to save your lover."

"Tell me," Raiden growled.

The goddess of twilight pursed her lips, her gaze sliding to Ione. "What will you give up for her?"

"Anything," he answered. "Everything."

"I was talking to the Queen."

Ione blinked. "Me?"

"Yes. Liria is bound to Set by Apophis' blood, but the bond of a shadow is a claim that runs even deeper. Likewise, the naga's gifting of their heart is a sacred spell with great power. Alone, neither are strong enough, but together... whoever carries both Liria's heart *and* her soul has a chance to save her."

"I'll do it." Ione looked expectantly at Raiden, oblivious to the roaring and smashing going on over his shoulder. "Give me her heart."

He opened his mouth, but Nephthys held up a hand. "He

cannot. Liria gave it freely, and only she can take it back. But you can give Raiden the soul ring."

"No." Ione clutched her beringed hand to her chest. "No, no, no. Liria is mine."

Nephthys' lashes drifted low, as though her meagre energy had run out. "Then she will be put down as soon as the other gods arrive."

"Ione," Taos began.

"No! She's mine! I need her," Ione wailed, shaking her head. "I've given you enough already. Liria belongs to *me!*"

"She's a person," Taos murmured. "She doesn't belong to anyone."

"She does," Ione hissed, tears streaming down her face. "She's mine. My friend. My confidante. My protector. *My every-thing.* If I let her go... how will I know if she loves me?"

"You'd have to trust her." Raiden dredged the depths of his patience and gentled his voice. "If you can't part with the soul ring to save her life, I'll set her free with death."

"She'll kill you." Ione's voice wavered, her dark blue eyes wide.

"No. I'd never let her suffer that way."

"Then how -"

"She told me once that the heart bond tied her life force to mine. My death means she, too, would perish - something Set has overlooked in his arrogance, I'd wager, or he'd never have asked her to carve me to pieces." Raiden squared his shoulders. "If there's truly no other way to save her, then I'll turn my blade upon myself."

Ione's jaw dropped. "You wouldn't."

"I would. I promised Liria we'd stand side by side, and I plan to keep my word. Where we go, we go together; even to the afterlife."

The Queen stared at him, her face slack, then over his shoulder where Liria was no doubt already looking to join the battle against Horus and Anubis - if she hadn't already. Tears silvered Ione's cheeks and her hands shook as she raised them, drawing the soul ring from her finger.

"I relinquish my shadow into your care from this moment forth," she whispered, taking Raiden's right hand and sliding the band onto his ring finger. The enchanted silver stretched and flexed, moulding to fit his larger finger perfectly. Something clicked into place deep inside him, a warmth that spread through his body like an embrace. Raiden's senses expanded and contracted in a sudden sweep, leaving him swaying sideways into Taos. When he straightened, he felt... Liria. Her soul, warm and light, twining around his, filling every crack he'd never known he had.

"Gods above us," he murmured. "She's... everywhere."

Ione wrapped her arms around herself as though cold, and nodded. "Now, Prince of Egypt. Go and get her back."

SPOILT FOR CHOICE

HER MASTER'S PRESENCE FILLED the illusory glade, the flames he conjured in defence of his perfection shimmering tangerine in Liria's grey on grey world. The centre of the Anarchist's focus was a tall, broad-shouldered man with the head of a jackal, his entire body dusted with fur so dark it was true, world consuming black. He swung a double-ended scythe with easy ripples of muscle which Set's lean figure could never, for all its perfection, quite match. Like her master, this enemy wielded fire - but unlike her master, he wore only loose flowing pants and a hefty belt, leaving an impressive torso on full display.

Anubis, said someone, from somewhere. Her master, most likely, since she was so closely tied to his glory she could feel the edge of his emotive state.

Fury. Despair. Hatred. Determination. Fear. And when he clashed with that midnight enemy... pride.

Liria might have thought that odd, if she'd had time for such things. Instead, she stood by Apep, most gloried of her master's servants, and waited for her fractured bones to snap and crackle back into place, mended with fierce agony by the demon blood in her veins.

"Little one, can you hear me?"

Apep's voice, though the serpent's mouth hadn't moved. Not inside her head so much as... an understanding of having already spoken. Liria didn't know how to answer, but Apep was of her master as she was of her master, so she tipped her chin back and looked up to find his shining silver eyes trained on her face.

Odd, that. In a world of black and white and grey - bar the magnificence of the Anarchist - those eyes were definitely silver. Liquid mercury, with a hint of glitter, as of silicate beneath the sun. Carrying hints of colour she couldn't quite grasp, and didn't try to, for in service to her master, it was unnecessary.

Only the perfection of Set mattered.

"Good," said Apep. "You can hear me."

Liria continued to stare. Apep was not the master... but, being that he was of the master, as she was, it seemed they shared a bond of their own.

"Yes," the serpent agreed. "We are prisoners together. I am sorry."

Liria blinked. Her master was perfection. There was no shame in being shackled to the glory of his divinity.

Apep seemed to sigh, though he hadn't actually moved. That, in itself, was another oddity. Set, in his divine understanding of things that were beyond one such as she, had summoned the demon serpent. Why didn't he fight?

"May I ask you a favour?" Apep's voice was soft, carrying something she identified as sadness.

Liria tilted her head. What could she possibly grant that their glorious master couldn't?

"My daughter." Apep's eyes nictitated, and when the clear membrane subsided, he seemed to be peering inside Liria, to a level that should be reserved only for their master. And yet, because Apep was of their master and she was of Apep, Liria didn't mind. She waited for the great serpent to finish. "Save her."

Liria blinked, foggy memories of a woman's silhouette pushing through the many layers of her mind. Sylvan, adopted daughter of Apep, wounded by the master but returned in divine grace to Apep's side.

"Not now," said Apep, as though he knew she'd been about to turn and look. "After. When it's done."

After? She knew not what the great serpent spoke of, but he was of Set, and she was of Set, and they were of Apep, and together, they were perfect.

She nodded.

"Your word, shadow. I cannot resist him much longer; I want your word."

Resist? As though from far away, Liria registered the sound of clanging and shouting and burning, the crack of thunder and the pounding of flesh against flesh. Beneath it all, a calling, a *need* - her master was summoning her, and she was standing with Apep, unmoving.

Odd. Because if Apep was of Set and she was of Apep and they were of each other... Liria paused, brow furrowing. No, she could feel it now - Set was their master, the divine perfection who they gloried in serving, but he was not of them at all. He was something other, something greater than the sum of Liria's parts, and Apep was... keeping them separate. A wall, built from a lifetime's strength forged in forced servitude. A wall that, once it came down, would leave Liria exposed, but which reminded her, in this instant, that for all her master's perfection, she was of Apep, and Apep was of her, and therefore, Apep's daughter was also hers.

She nodded again, and because it seemed necessary for reasons she couldn't fathom, spoke. "You have my word."

Apep seemed to relax, and in the deepest burning depths of her veins, in a pulmonary chamber engorged with his blood, she felt his smile.

"Thank you," he said.

Then the veil lifted, and the full force of her master's screaming demands wrapped around Liria and throttled until she choked for air.

Defend me!

Liria lifted from the ground, her body having finished the last of its agonising repairs. Apep, first and foremost of the master's slaves, gave a great roar of sorrow and flung himself at the Anarchist's shadowed enemies. His sadness permeated Liria even as she darted forward, targeting the god who had once been a handsome-faced man but who now wore the imposing head of a falcon.

Horus. Again, that voice - though now that Liria had heard her master screaming in her head, she knew it was not the voice of his divine perfection, but someone else. *Skywatcher. Friend.*

Friend? Another odd notion. Liria hesitated, turning as though she could pinpoint the origin of the voice that so clearly came from within her own mind. Nothing. Nobody. Sinking into the glory of her master's aura, Liria moved to engage Horus alongside Apep - and was tackled heavily into the trunk of a tree by something large and hot that smelt of warm sand and burning sunlight.

The tree cracked ominously beneath their combined weight, and Liria grunted as the bark tore into her sensitive wings. When she raised her eyes, it was to stare into the face of the Crown Prince of Merged Egypt. Both of his hands were fisted in the bodice of her torn dress as he pinned her to the tree, dark hair that looked black but was really brown hanging over his face. She lifted an arm to stroke it back as if on reflex, then realised what was happening and wrapped her fingers around his wrist instead, digging sharp talons into his skin.

"I'm not letting go." The angel's eyes blazed grey but she knew they were really a deep gold. Blood slicked his skin as she tightened her grip, but he didn't so much as flinch. "Ever."

Liria tilted her head. Unlike Apep, who was of her as she was of him, this one required words. She dug them out and threw them with surgical precision. "Then you will die."

"Seeing you like this is already killing me." The Prince swallowed, his face turning vulnerable as he took her in. "Gods, Liria, you have to remember."

Again with the remembering. "My memory has not been compromised."

"You know who I am?" He looked startled, then pleased. "You know who you are to me."

"I am the chink in your armour, Prince of Egypt." Liria did lift her fingers to his face, then, streaking his own blood across his cheek. In her other hand, she materialised a short, sharp dagger. "You mean nothing to me."

And yet... those words cut at her throat. The odd expression on his face, the agony he tried to hide, it seemed to clench something inside her own chest. His breathing hitched, as though he, too, felt it, and suddenly he bared his teeth in a feral grin.

"You gave me your heart, Liria Atlannon. I'm not giving it back." The Prince of Egypt glared down the length of his nose. "You want it? Carve it from my chest."

Liria lifted the dagger and swung not towards his chest, but his soft throat. If he thought to distract her, it would never work. She would take his life for her master's glory and then -

The dagger stopped.

Quivering with effort, Liria tried to close the final inch between cold steel and hot skin, but her body refused to obey. Her master's command swam deep and dark inside her, but something even deeper kept her still, the two warring forces so intense she emitted a keening cry.

"What... have you... done to me?" Liria gasped. The more she tried to press the blade forward, the more the strangeness inside her pressed back; until she dropped the dagger, watching it wink from existence before it could so much as clip the front of the Prince's leather armour.

"You can't do it, can you?" He gave a bitter laugh and shoved her harder into the tree. "You can't kill me."

Her world tilted, but of this one thing, she was certain. "No."

"Fight, Liria," he urged, leaning in so close they shared breath. "Fight for me. For us. For yourself."

Then he kissed her.

It wasn't like the hard press of lips that he'd bestowed earlier, more punishment than gift. This one was firm but thorough, his mouth moving against hers with heat and purpose until, without her conscious volition, Liria's own lips parted. The Prince's tongue swept inside and she rose to meet it, pushing against him with a desperation that seemed to come from outside herself - or from a place so deeply buried it belonged to someone else entirely. Her heart thundered in her ears, blocking out the sound of the battle, the feel of her master; blocking out everything but this furious, passionate angel who wielded his tongue like a weapon.

"Raiden." Something inside Liria cracked. That wasn't her voice, surely? And yet it happened again, her hands twisting into his dark hair to prevent retreat. "*Raiden.*"

"I'm here," he gasped, nipping at her lips. A movement her body responded to instantly, melting in his arms as though this were not, in fact, a battle, and she wasn't supposed to be killing him to please her master.

Thoughts of Set speared agony into Liria's brain and she groaned, faltering in her desperate attempt to kiss her way inside Raiden's body. A loud voice clamoured that this was her lover, while yet another decried him as her enemy. A third, much more smug voice didn't care who he was, but was insistent that no matter what she tried, she wouldn't be able to kill him - and would, in fact, defend his life against all comers, including the divine perfection of the Anarchist.

Kill him.

Save him.

Hurt him.

Heal him.

Apep's blood glutted her veins, Set's will pounded inside her skull, her body an empty vessel well suited to their purpose because Liria's heart and soul were gone, gone, gone... except there was a steady thumping inside the cage of her ribs, a tingling insistence spreading chills over her skin. The knowledge of *something*, just out of reach, some indefinable fact she couldn't quite grasp. Voices swirled around and through Liria, a cacophony of shrieking commands. A serpent, apologising, begging for aid. A god, demanding service. An angel, insisting she had a choice.

"No," Liria managed, shaking her head. Her bones felt as if they'd begun to melt, her skin ready to peel right off, but this new agony? It was the worst of all. "There are no choices. *I have no choices.*"

"Look at me."

The command swept through Liria with more power than even the Anarchist possessed. She opened eyes she didn't recall shutting and, impossibly, they cleared to focus on his face. Raiden's face. One strong hand gripped her chin, the other laid over her heart, and through the world of swimming monochrome, Liria was shocked to discover his eyes were blazing gold. A knowing settled over her, and in a forgotten, fortified corner of her very innermost self, she began to unfold.

"*You,*" she said, her tone wondering. "I'm yours. I... I am your shadow."

"For now, but not forever." Raiden feathered his thumb along her jaw. "You are your own person, Liria. You make your own choices. All I can do is hope you choose me, because I will never stop choosing you."

He slipped a heavy ring off his finger, one set with an enormous sapphire so dark it appeared black. While Liria stared, he turned her hand over and slid it onto her ring finger, the band adjusting by itself until it fit so snugly it may as well have always been there.

Liria's world fractured in a kaleidoscope of colour, sound and sensation, and with a scream from the very depths of her returning soul, her body gave out and she collapsed into the arms of her angel.

GOT SOUL?

Raiden caught Liria as she fell, eyes rolling back in her head and limbs lax in a way that terrified him to the core. They fell together, he to his knees, her clutched desperately to his chest, gods fighting around them in a spectacle of claws, scales, teeth, fur and magic.

Shudders tore through Raiden's body as Liria's soul streamed out of him. Staring into her eyes earlier, feeling her heart beating in his chest and the heady warmth of her presence in every pore, there'd been a moment when he'd have done anything to keep her. Anything to savour that feeling of completion another few moments. Then he'd seen Ione's face in his mind's eye, heard the obsession in her voice, replayed all the times Liria had suffered, slave to the compulsion that bound her to the ring. He'd understood in a flash why Ione had become so darkly possessive, why she'd fought so bitterly to keep Liria by her side. With the dark fairy's soul inside his body, he'd never felt so warm, so safe, so strong, so... *more.* She was his. Irrevocably, impossibly, endlessly his, a spiritual feast on which he could glut himself forevermore and never be filled.

High on the knowledge that if she had to choose a master,

he'd probably be the one, Raiden had stared into her eyes and seen emptiness. A shell, hollowed out and stolen - first by the naga, then by Atlantis, third by a god, and now, by himself. Stolen, bound and used, never given an opportunity to be whole.

Whoever carries both Liria's heart and her soul has a chance to save her, Nephthys had said. In his arrogance, Raiden assumed that meant himself, but in that shattering instant, he realised he'd been wrong.

Liria could save herself.

Her heart. *Her* soul. *Her* choices.

So he'd dragged the ring from his finger, even though it felt like tearing his hair out by the roots, and slid it onto Liria's.

"You never gave your heart away," he croaked, shoving matted hair back from her face. "You did something even more precious; you shared it. So now you have what you need, Liria - heart and soul. And if that's not enough, take mine. Take whatever you need, but gods above us, please come back to me. *Please.*"

No answer, only limp silence. Raiden lowered his head to her chest, scooping his wings around them for privacy and closing his eyes. Yes, her heart still beat. Barely enough to vibrate in the cradle of her ribs, but there nonetheless.

Fire slammed into the earth beside him, peppering the protective cocoon of Raiden's feathers with embers and dirt. Gods grunted and metal clashed so close they might as well have stood over him, and he was sure he heard Horus shouting, but before he could focus entirely on the words, they went silent.

No, not silent.

Muffled.

Something lurched and fluttered in his gut and Raiden lifted his head. He crouched in a perfect circle of grass, the world beyond blurred as though hidden behind frosted windows. The sounds of battle were muted, so that all he could hear was his own ragged breathing, his heartbeat... and Liria's.

"You really do have a death wish, don't you, Prince of

Egypt?" Her voice was croaky, but warm, and when he met her violet eyes, they glittered with power. With *life*. Raiden let out a sob and buried his face in her throat, squeezing as tight as he could because he knew she could take it. Taloned fingers curled gently into his hair. "Hey, now. Don't I get a little something for my impertinence?"

"Liria," he sobbed, and kissed her. Again, and again, and *again*, covering her lips and her cheeks and her jaw and her throat. "You came back."

"Raiden." She stopped his frantic movements with a knuckle beneath his chin. "Of course I came back. I love you, remember?"

"I love you, too." He crashed his mouth down on hers, shoving his tongue deep and claiming her the only way he knew how. "I love you. Gods, I love you."

His body burned with need, his heart with furious fire. She gentled him again, cupping his face in her palms and wiping tears from his cheeks with the tips of her thumbs. "You gave me my soul, Raiden. I can feel it deep inside, pushing out Set's power, dissolving Apophis' blood. You gave me the strength to fight for myself when I had lost my way." Wonder suffused her features. "It's so warm."

Raiden laughed, then, bubbly and wet. "I know."

"Do you know what the only thing more dangerous than a bound shadow is, Prince of Egypt?" Violet eyes blazed, her lips curling into a smile. "A free one."

He sipped from her lips in joyous reprimand, laughed when she snapped her teeth. They struggled upright, dirty and bleeding but alive and, more importantly, together. Raiden linked his fingers through hers. "Show me."

"With pleasure."

Liria raised her free hand as though to brush away a fly. Raiden felt a tug deep in his gut and instead of dissolving, the privacy shield spiralled out as though in the grips of a strong wind. Anubis and Set, locked together high above, tumbled apart. Horus dove to shield Taos, Ione and Nephthys with his spread wings whilst Apophis took the brunt of the blast, his body slamming to the muddied grass by the edge of the pool. Raiden realised with a start the enormous serpent wasn't fully revealed, the great bulk of his length still hidden below ground in whatever place he'd come from. The sheer size of the demon was almost beyond categorisation, yet Liria strode to run her hand across one enormous ridged nostril as though he were a kitten in front of the hearth.

"I've not forgotten," she told him, pressing a kiss to Apophis' nose. Her wings spread wide as she moved, the tears Raiden had caused when he slammed her into the tree healing before his eyes. Shadow and smoke leaked from her very pores and when she turned to look up at Set, she trailed darkness like an old friend. "Anarchist. We have a score to settle."

Raiden edged to Horus' side, drawing both his swords. The Skywatcher was staring at Liria with something akin to fear in his eyes. "What did you do to her, Prince of Storms?"

"I gave her the soul ring."

"You *what?*"

"You heard me." He have his blood-sire a sidelong look. "You've gone awfully pale."

Horus swallowed heavily. *Anubis! He gave her the ring.*

He what?! Anubis bellowed, flinching back from Set as Liria rose into the air. His sharp eyes locked on Liria's right hand and went wide. *Did our angel lose his fucking mind?*

I can hear you, said Raiden calmly.

Silence crackled between the three of them, then Anubis grumbled, *I keep forgetting. That's going to be really inconvenient from now on.*

What, that you have to be honest for a change?

We haven't been dishonest, Horus snapped, brows beetling. *Just... selective.*

Well then, you've only got yourselves to blame, haven't you? Raiden planted both fists on his hips, grinning when Horus had to jump sideways to avoid a khopesh to the thigh. *Nephthys said Liria only stood a chance to be saved if she had her heart and her soul. It was cryptically worded, but I worked it out. What's wrong with Liria having her own soul back?*

Anubis dropped lower in the sky, his jackal's tail thrashing. As he passed Liria, he gave her a solemn nod, and received one in return. *I've done a lot of research on shadows since Liria Atlannon arrived in Egypt.* The god of death paused, hovering where he could provide support should it be needed. *You must understand - there is no way to free Liria from the soulbinding without killing her. She will always be a shadow.*

But? Raiden encouraged.

But, Anubis grumbled, shooting him a glare, *to be given her own ring means she is her own mistress. The powers which were diverted to bind her at birth are returned, and the feedback loop of the compulsion amplifies her energy threefold. On top of whatever else that means, she cannot be controlled or compelled, because the shadow binding is a compulsion beyond all others. You thought she was dangerous when she defied Set at their first meeting? She's far more dangerous now.*

I didn't think she was dangerous, Raiden breathed, his eyes riveted on where Liria and Set circled one another in the sky, exchanging low words he couldn't catch. *I thought she was beautiful.*

You're an idiot, then, Horus declared. *She's strong enough to kill you, now. To kill us, even.*

Good. He curled his lip at them both. *Unlike the two of you, I'm used to not being invincible. And after recent events, I'd trust Liria over a god any day.* A sudden thought hit him and he smiled. *She really is the Lady of Shadows.*

They fell silent, then, and Raiden could almost taste the emotive current.

He's right, brother. If we'd been more forthcoming, this situation might have been avoided, Horus muttered at last. He scuffed a boot in the dirt. *We owe you an apology, Prince of Storms.*

No, Raiden shook his head. *You owe Liria an apology - and when this is over, I'm going to make sure you give it to her.*

THE COOKIE CRUMBLES

Liria hung in the air opposite the god of war and chaos and watched him move from righteous indignation to trembling fury.

"This doesn't have to go on, Anarchist," Liria murmured, spreading her fingers to show her hands were empty. "You have the power to stop. It's not too late."

Set shook his head, cheekbones sharp against the lines of his face. "Don't you think I've examined all the other options? This was the only way."

"You have the same problem as all the other gods." Liria clicked her tongue against the roof of her mouth. "None of you know how to ask for help."

"How can we? The gods are supposed to care for their people."

Liria encompassed the cavern with a spread arm. "Is this how you care for your people, Anarchist? Murder, poison, mind control?" She pointed at Nephthys. "Torture?"

"I..." Something like shame spread across Set's features before he lifted his chin and stiffened his spine. "What right do you have to question me? You've seen inside my heart and mind. You know how I feel."

She nodded. "It's the only reason I'm not already attempting to cut you down, Anarchist. You care; you've just lost your way."

"You seek to redeem me?" He laughed, the sound beautiful and brittle.

"Should we not be given a chance to atone for our mistakes?" Liria clenched her hands to fists, then forced them to relax. "Surely you know you cannot win now. There is only you, against the rest of us - too great a challenge even for the Anarchist, I think."

"I have Apep."

"The demon serpent fights against his will," Liria said softly. "He's learning to resist you. Help won't come as easily as you believe."

Set's lashes lowered, his face a study in reluctance. When they lifted again, however, his irises glowed blood red with power and he curled his lip to show pointed canines. Power swelled, the god of war and chaos snapped his fingers... and suddenly there was a young woman in his arms.

Though Liria had yet to see her in full light, she recognised Sylvan at once. The young woman's worn tunic was covered in thick, dark blood, and she moaned in pain as Set banded his arms around her middle, her head lolling limp against his shoulder.

Apep, Set called. *Defend me, or your daughter's life is forfeit.*

"You do this thing, Anarchist, and it will be the end of you," Apophis rumbled, his voice echoing both throughout the cavern and inside Liria's head. "You may have dominion over my actions, but if you harm my child, I will find a way to bring about your end."

Set drew a long, taloned finger down the line of Sylvan's jaw, his smile sensual. *You gave her your blood, my pet, and that makes her mine, now, too. The things I could make her do - the things she'd enjoy doing, because I tell her to enjoy them - do you really want to risk it?*

Apophis said nothing, but his silver eyes sought Liria.

I will keep my word, she promised, then offered a cold smile when Set startled. *Oh, yes, Anarchist. I can hear you.*

Set's mobile face worked for a moment, then he laughed, a delighted, tinkling sound. *I wonder if the sweet Sylvan will prove to be as intriguing as you, Liria Atlannon. After this, I rather think I'll find out.*

Apophis charged with a hissing roar, and Horus lifted to intercept the demon serpent, swinging his warhammer as he went. Liria saw the flash of Raiden's swords but was forced to duck away from a brilliant orange fireball that arced close enough to her face to singe her hair. She curled her torso to create a shadow and drew her favourite dagger from within it, blocking Set's scimitar moments before it could cut her in half. The impact jolted her teeth in her skull but she held, twisting to shove his blade aside and landing a solid kick to the Anarchist's exposed shoulder.

"You're faster," Set approved, angling himself so that Sylvan's limp body hung between them like a shield. "Stronger. I see now why your shadow brethren were categorically hunted and destroyed once the making of them was outlawed."

Liria swept beneath the arc of his sword, her wings a whir. She used magic to blur her image and cannoned into Set's exposed side, raking her talons up the straps of his leather breastplate and shredding them. Her dagger came in fast and low but the Anarchist was gone again, and Liria jerked away as fire licked through the place where she'd been hovering.

"He's not even trying," Liria murmured, as Anubis floated to her side.

The god of death inclined his imposing jackal head. "A great deal of his energy is focussed elsewhere. Osiris should be here by now, but Set's scrambling our location."

"You cannot breach it?"

"The Anarchist is the stronger god," Anubis admitted without rancour. "He always has been. Of those here, only Nephthys stands a chance against him alone, and even then, she'd need to be at full strength. What little energy she had, she spent reaching out to me."

Liria watched as Set wriggled out of his shredded leather armour and let it fall to the ground. "Another test, then?"

"Doubtful. He's the god of war, Liria Atlannon; strategy is just as important as brute strength on the battlefield."

"Strategy," Liria murmured. "He'll have a backup plan. Several, perhaps." Her eyes fell on Nephthys, slumped against an equally pale Ione, Taos' arms wrapped protectively around them. She thought of the goddess' story of a love gone wrong, a man who'd gambled and lost, and now resented everyone else because of it. Rubbing a hand over her chest, she recalled the thick, all-consuming zeal Set's possession had incurred but also the finer, more subtle intricacies that had filtered through alongside it - feelings easily overlooked unless you'd spent the entirety of your lifetime living under the oppressive mantle of someone else's desires. She looked up at Anubis. "It's a trap."

"A trap?"

"Not for us - for Osiris."

Anubis glanced around the room and flinched. "Both Osiris' sons are here. His adopted sister. The Pharaoh. The Prince of Storms. Yes, I see it now - our lives, in return for freedom of the Ennead."

"Can it be done?"

The Soulcatcher slowly shook his head. "Not without destroying both our worlds, but Set refuses to believe that. He'll do anything to be free and so long as Apep - Apophis, if you prefer - is under his command, he has the means."

"Is the demon serpent really so strong?" Liria looked to where Apophis battled Horus and Raiden, his head switching back and forth as the two angels dipped and swung and slashed.

"Yes," Anubis answered. "Apophis is born from the primordial darkness beyond life. He can be defeated, but not destroyed. Set, having dominion over snakes, has influence over him like no other."

"Then Apophis is the key." Liria looked to Set, who now cradled Sylvan against his bare chest and watched them with a taunting smile. "If we can rescue Apophis' daughter, he will fight Set's hold."

Anubis blinked. "That woman is his daughter?"

"Adopted."

"It matters not," the Soulcatcher replied with certainty. "Love is love."

By mutual accord, they drifted closer to the god of war and chaos. Storm clouds began to gather and kinetic energy prickled over Liria's skin, calling to the darker side of her nature. She lifted a hand as though to catch falling water, enjoying the thrum and purr as Raiden's energy wrapped around her own, blending and changing until all that he was, all he commanded, was also hers. *This* was why dark fairies were so much rarer than any others. This, here, their natural ability to blend with the magic around them. To borrow strength. Steal it, even. A natural affinity that had seen her ancestors hunted, and her very life force perverted in order to bind Liria's soul to her master's - but now that she was in possession of her own ring, she was free, at long last, to be herself. *All* of herself.

Set raised his sword in Liria's direction. Fire pulsed down the blade, gathered at the tip and then shot out, a steady stream headed straight for her chest. Liria threw up a displacement shield, the same one she'd used to contain Raiden's explosion at his brother's wedding, only this time she directed the force of it outwards. Set's magic thumped into the spell, flowing across the surface in a carnelian wave before a sharp gust of wind puffed the fire out as though it were nothing more than a candle.

Anubis chuckled and twirled his double ended scythe. "I'm not sure if I've said this yet, Liria Atlannon, but I like you."

"Thank you, Soulcatcher."

"Most welcome." He snapped his fingers, and purple fire crackled to life in the palm of his hand. When he laid that palm against the shaft of his weapon, the entire thing became engulfed in cold mauve flames. "Shall I take Set, while you rescue that poor girl?"

"It would be my pleasure." She made to lift the displacement shield, but Anubis held up a finger. "Yes?"

The god of death grinned, showing a mouth full of sharp teeth. "Welcome to Selekhet, Lady of Shadows. Truly, we are lucky to have you."

And then he was gone, a sound curling from his throat that might have been a howl, and might have been laughter, or some blood-curdling mix of the two. Set raised his sword to meet Anubis' attack, mauve fire mixing with orange as they shifted into a speed beyond comprehension. Liria cut in low and fast, using a combination of Raiden's storm winds and her own energy to throw up shields or deflect fire that came too close. Set twisted away as she approached, scoring a fine slice down Anubis' arm and then sending the Soulcatcher flying with a solid kick to the chest. Liria drew a throwing knife from the shadows of her ripped bodice and let it fly, forcing Set to dodge until his back was almost to the cavern wall. His flaming sword shivered through the air near her hip, the bottom edge of her dress catching fire. She put it out with a sharp gust of air, twisting Raiden's magic to send a smattering of rain directly into Set's face.

The Anarchist jerked back with a laugh, shaking his head to clear the water. "Clever, little shadow. You know your lover's magic better than he does."

"Practice," Liria ground out, narrowly avoiding a vicious kick to the knee. "Instinct."

"I hope you're not distracting him, tugging on his energy like a child on their parent's leg," Set mocked, his smile full of mischief. "Such a shame if unknowingly lending you his power left him defenceless."

"If you think I'm foolish enough to fall for such a weak ruse, you deserve to drown in your own arrogance," Liria snorted.

"Oh, you won't fall for that one," Set agreed, his smile growing ever wider. "This one, however, will work just fine."

The Anarchist's sword disappeared and he darted forward, blocking Liria's slashing blade by wrapping long fingers around the underside of her wrist. She anticipated his attempt to wrench her arm and moved through it - only to end up with her back slammed against the cavern wall, Sylvan in her arms, and Set's lips pressed against her own. The kiss was hard and fast, the Anarchist's tongue licking along the seam of her lips as Liria fumbled with Sylvan's dead weight, her wings trapped against the biting rocks in the cavern. A knife flashed in the corner of her eye and she groaned as it sank deep into her ribs, the pain causing her jaw to drop and allowing Set entrance to her mouth.

He took it, his tongue sliding over her teeth even as he twisted the knife he'd buried hilt deep, secure in the knowledge that between holding Sylvan and being crushed to the wall by his body, Liria was helpless.

Except that she was a shadow, a *free* shadow, and she would never be helpless again.

With a growl of fury, she bit down hard on Set's tongue. He yelped and drew back, his own blood leaking from the corner of his mouth.

"Now," Liria panted.

Sylvan opened her eyes, turned her head, and buried unnaturally sharp teeth deep in Set's throat. He hissed in shock, blood-red eyes going wide, focus diverted. Holding tight to Sylvan with one arm, Liria wrapped her fingers over the top of Set's and yanked the knife from her own body. Her talons cut into the Anarchist's wrist and his grip slackened enough for her to turn the blade and ram it deep into his groin. He screamed, the sound so otherworldly her blood threatened to freeze in her veins.

Anubis! Liria cried.

Bloody hellfire, can everyone reach me on this channel? Anubis griped - but Liria saw the flash of purple as a fireball big enough to engulf Set's entire body rocketed their way.

Set's scream ratcheted from pain to fury to sheer terror - and then, with an almighty wrench of both muscle and power, he was gone. Liria was left supporting the entirety of Sylvan's weight, her body slipping from the wall as her wings struggled into action. Blood slicked her side, and she knew Set had caused enough damage that she'd not be quick enough to dodge. Reaching for Raiden down the pathway of his magic, she brushed her mind to his.

Brace, she whispered, and then threw up a displacement shield, tucked her body tight around Sylvan's, and closed her eyes as Anubis' deadly fire slammed into them both.

THE GOD OF DEATH

The concussive boom of magic detonating against magic shook Raiden to the very foundations of his soul. Then, as if that weren't enough, Apophis' giant body slammed into him at the exact same moment as the shockwave from the blast did. Fighting against the two immense forces proved impossible and Raiden went down hard, sandwiched between muddy grass and giant serpent before he'd had much of a chance to recognise what happened. He strained against the enormous weight on top of him, which did little more than put him at risk of self injury, before a voice rumbled, "Keep still, Prince of Egypt, unless you wish to die today."

That was when it registered that the giant demon serpent wasn't trying to kill him at all, but rather had just saved his life.

As though the revelation had been his cue, Apophis' great weight lifted free, leaving Raiden starfished on the grass with Horus' similarly swatted form bare inches away. The god of the sky wore a dazed expression that Raiden supposed matched his own, and they stared at each other in complete confusion for a good ten seconds before Raiden croaked, "What happened?"

"Besides having Apophis sit on us?" Horus levered himself

into a sitting position and Raiden followed suit, his gaze tracking up to the demon serpent who still hovered overhead, the coils of his huge body - most of which were still subsumed in the floor below - blocking the rest of the chamber from view.

"Besides that." Since the snake overhead was very obviously protecting them, Raiden didn't bother reaching for his swords, instead patting himself down to check for injury. "For someone who got sat on, I feel remarkably well."

"Trust me, if he wanted to crush us, he could have," Horus grumbled. Using one of the snakes' enormous coils for support, he staggered to his feet and palmed his warhammer. "Hey, big guy, what gives? You want to let us out?"

"Not unless you want to be caught in a rain of Anubis' soul fire," Apophis replied, his voice taut with strain. "Most of it is gone, but there are still motes."

Horus went white and Raiden was glad he was still sitting down. He'd seen Anubis flinging about the purple fire which stole life with a single touch, but since it had all been heading for Set, he hadn't thought much beyond 'oh, good,' and 'serves you right.' Now, however, he said, "How in the gods' names did it end up exploding all over the place? He could have killed us all!"

Apophis didn't answer.

"How can you possibly be safe?"

Apophis shifted slightly at that. "I am born from the primordial chaos of all creation. The soul fire is not comfortable, but it cannot kill me. Nothing can."

There was a wealth of pain in the serpent's words, and Raiden shivered in spite of himself.

Brother, what the fuck is going on? Horus demanded, his expression strained in a way Raiden had never seen before. *Was it Set? Did you get him?*

Yes and no. Anubis' voice came back hoarse. *Liria had him, so I attacked, but at the last minute Set disappeared and Liria... she... oh, gods, Raiden, I'm so sorry. I couldn't stop it. She threw up a shield but I don't know if it was enough.*

Raiden's hand clapped to his chest and he began to wheeze for air. He tried to think past the panic, to register the fact that there was still an echo to his own heartbeat. *Where is she?*

She fell, Anubis whispered.

"I caught her," Apophis said. "And my daughter. The Soulcatcher can approach and once it is safe, I will release the rest of you."

"Why are you helping us?" Raiden asked, digging his fingers into his leather armour as though to cling tighter to Liria's heartbeat.

The great serpent shivered. "Because Set is gone, and for the moment, my will is my own. And because I owe your Liria a debt of such magnitude that she's earnt my service, such as it is, for eternity."

Horus' brows shot up. "What of Osiris?"

"He's here," Apophis replied. "Set has laid a variety of traps that will need to be navigated before anyone else can safely move in or out. I'm relaying instructions now."

"But we got in," Horus protested, brows drawing close in a frown.

Liria said it was a trap. A pretty, pretty trap for our father, Anubis growled. *This whole time, we've been no more than pawns in the Anarchist's ridiculous game. Apophis, my lord, would you be so kind as to - thank you.*

Raiden shoved upright as Apophis' coiled body shifted and stretched around him, scales that he knew from their battle were as hard as rock sloughing against one another as the great serpent reversed the majority of his body into the hole from whence it had erupted, leaving only enough length to put him at eye height - or thereabouts, for a creature whose head was big enough to swallow several people whole - and revealing what remained of the enchanted cavern.

The small pool was little more than a muddied hole in the ground and a large portion of the trees had been flattened. Grass and flowers were slushy and ruined, and a couple of loose boulders had been tossed or cracked. The small cluster of rocks which had sheltered Taos, Ione and Nephthys seemed relatively untouched, and Raiden could tell from the pattern in the squashed grass that Apophis had protected the Pharaoh with his body even as he fought against the gods.

Anubis arrived, then, and Raiden's vision narrowed to a pinpoint. Cradled in the Soulcatcher's arms was Liria, her skin covered in a thin layer of soot and her arms wrapped tight around another woman, who Raiden assumed must be Apophis' daughter. Blood had turned the entire side of Liria's already ruined dress a dull, muddy colour, and it trailed over Anubis' flexing arms to drip, drip, drip on the ground as he walked. An inarticulate cry gurgled in the back of Raiden's throat and he leapt forward, dragging Liria into his own embrace and crushing her to his chest.

"Liria? Liria," he rasped, pushing matted hair from her dirty face. "Gods, Liria, look at me."

Her heartbeat still worked inside his chest, an echo that fluttered and became more thready with each passing moment. Her lashes remained flush against her cheeks and she didn't stir to his voice, didn't protest the way he squeezed her tight enough to make his own bones creak.

Raiden dropped to his knees and, though it cut at him, laid her out on the ground. He tore at her dress to reveal a brutally deep stab wound, the flesh shredded in such a way that Raiden knew Set had twisted the weapon as he'd buried it to the hilt inside her. He covered the bleeding hole with his palm and pressed down hard, tears blurring his vision. "Can any of you heal? Anyone?"

"I can," said a new voice. A woman with blunt cut black hair and feathers sprouting from her arms knelt at his side. "Let me see, Prince of Egypt."

Raiden didn't want to let go, but when Isis gently touched her fingers to the backs of his hands, he shifted to pull Liria's head into his lap, instinct curving his wings around them as best he could. When his feathers brushed Isis, the goddess didn't so much as blink, her face calm as she laid her hands over the stab wound. Isis' brilliant green eyes unfocussed, and a nimbus of golden light began to leak from her skin.

"The wound is deep," the goddess announced. "I will do what I can, but there are no certainties."

Raiden curled over to press his forehead against Liria's, the hot salt of his tears dripping onto her face. *Don't leave me,* he begged, his soul screaming as it reached for the slowly fading echo of the extra heartbeat in his chest. *Please, Liria. I love you.*

A firm hand gripped Raiden's shoulder, and he didn't need to look to recognise his brother's touch.

"She fought well," the Pharaoh said softly. "She saved all our lives."

"Shut up," Raiden hissed. "She's not dead. She's *not.*"

Taos squeezed tighter, and though Raiden tried to shake him off, he didn't let go. Thunder cracked in Raiden's chest, lightning stuttered in his veins - and with all that power, he couldn't do a single thing but wait, clinging like a madman to the faintest, featherlight rhythm of Liria's heartbeat.

If you leave, he growled, tunnelling every bit of his awareness into the lingering whisper of her presence, *I will follow you.*

Raiden felt, more than heard, the shock and denial of whoever else was listening, but he didn't care. He gathered every ounce of his intractable warrior's will and slid it against the echo of Liria's energy, following instinct over understanding. And then, just like that, there she was; the warmth of her soul blending with his. Not like it had when he'd worn the ring, worn her spirit like a cloak, but a true blending of power and essence and love that kept them separate while making them more. One. Whole.

I can hear you, she whispered, faint amusement in her tone. *You precious, stubborn angel. Don't be so foolish.*

My choices are mine, and I choose you, he snapped back. Where they floated, Raiden couldn't say, but it reminded him of the odd nothing space where they had once merged their thoughts to teach him control of his powers. Bits of him, leaking into her. Bits of her, leaking into him. Learning, even as they changed each other irrevocably.

My choices are mine, now, too, Liria answered, wonder shivering through them both. *So if you choose me, I choose life, for both of us, always. Hold onto me, Raiden.*

He wrapped himself around her as tightly as he could. *I'm never letting go.*

Good. Liria brushed against him in a way that felt like a kiss, then she did... something, and golden light spilled around them, pattering across his senses like rain.

Well now, said Isis, her tone filled with delight. *There you are.*

Yes, said Raiden and Liria together, and in unison, they reached for the Allmother as she reached for them, and her light was everywhere, her magic everywhere, and they rose and rose and rose... and Raiden blinked.

The cavern, wrecked by battle and magic. His brother, still squeezing his shoulder. Anubis and Horus, bickering like old ladies, as much Raiden's brothers now as the one he'd been born to. Osiris, his deep, tolling voice low as he spoke with Nephthys. Isis, moving to join them. The scrape and roll of Apophis' scales, the steady rise and fall of his daughter's breath. And in Raiden's lap, lashes lifting to reveal violet eyes bright with glittering power, Liria Atlannon.

"Raiden," she whispered, lifting the hand with the soul ring to cup his face. Her thumb brushed his cheek, catching the last of his old tears and the first of his new. "My Raiden."

He didn't have words, his tongue too thick in his throat, so he hunched down close enough to kiss her, a trembling, astonishing kiss that carried his whole heart.

"You can't be Liria Atlannon any more," he rasped against her lips, his body shaking as he carefully lifted her closer. "Because if I'm yours, you're mine. Atlantis holds no claim to you."

Too-big eyes widened, and then crinkled at the corners. "That is the worst marriage proposal I have ever heard."

"I don't care about a wedding." Raiden laid his hand over her chest, where her heart thumped reassuringly beneath his palm. "Whatever just happened bound us closer than any vows could ever do. I can feel you inside me."

"Me, too," she whispered, her smile widening. "You're so warm. My soul is so warm. I've never felt so full, so *real*. But if my name bothers you, we can change it." Something cheeky shifted in that glittering gaze. "I suppose, given you're a Prince and I'm but a shadow, that we shouldn't upset Egyptian tradition too much. Liria Horushood sounds fine, don't you think?"

"Yes." More tears, running down her fingers, as he rubbed his face against her hand. "Gods, yes."

"And though you don't care about a wedding, I'm pretty sure your Pharaoh will," she continued, her other hand raising to brush the hair back from his forehead. "So, to your terrible marriage proposal, I say I'd be honoured to be your wife and to have you as my husband." Fangs flashed. "I can't wait to see Nurus' face."

Raiden's shoulders shook, his laughter a hoarse rumble in his throat. "You realise that will make you a Princess, Lady of Shadows?"

"Yes." She huffed out an irritated breath, then shrugged against him. "I'm my own mistress now. I can do that."

Raiden straightened, peering over his shoulder to where Taos watched them with shining eyes. "You hear that, brother? She can do that."

"An adventure for which I cannot wait," the Pharaoh said, his face a picture of relief. He brushed a hand across Liria's matted hair. "Thank you for keeping him here."

"Welcome." Liria nipped at Raiden's jaw. "He's far too good to waste on death."

As though summoned by the word, Anubis came slowly to their side. His jackal head had melted back into a human one, with the exception of his long, black ears, and that human face was a picture of grief. He knelt before Taos and when he opened his curled fingers, a tiny, pale blue flame flickered inside.

"What is this?" The Pharaoh asked, his eyes wide.

Anubis swallowed heavily. "Apophis moved swiftly to protect everyone from the rain of soul fire, but it appears he was not quite swift enough. Ione was brushed by an ember and - and - the Queen lives, but she has lost your child." Tears silvered the Soulcatcher's eyes as he lifted the tiny flame a little higher. "I'm sorry."

Raiden's breath caught in his throat and in his lap, he heard Liria gasp. Taos sagged against him and he wrapped an arm around his brother's hips in silent support as the Pharaoh of Merged Egypt cupped shaking hands around the flickering flame of his deceased child and bent his head in mourning. His lips moved, a soft prayer for peace and deliverance, and when he was done, Anubis closed his fingers tight and the tiny flame was gone forever.

Though his body sagged with exhaustion, Raiden helped Liria to her feet. Together, Taos cradled between them, they walked to where Isis knelt beside both Nephthys and a pale Ione.

"I'm sorry," Nephthys croaked, her face distraught. "I tried to hold the child until Isis arrived, but I wasn't strong enough."

Taos jerked his head in a nod, falling to his knees and gathering Ione into his arms. Her eyes were closed, her face lax.

"The Queen has sustained serious injury," Isis murmured, her body giving off golden light as she moved her hands over Ione's prone form. "The soul fire is a thing that brings death to whatever it touches. I cannot say if she will ever bear another child."

"Ever?" Taos' voice trembled.

Isis shrugged. "She has the healing gift but in such small traces, and it was already expended beyond her natural limit. Her body was completely defenceless." The goddess of life and healing sighed, her green eyes sad. "Her womb is, technically, whole. But the ability to carry life... I cannot sense it. I know this is another blow, so soon after the first, but you should know it now. That way, when she wakes, you can support each other better."

Taos jerked his head in another nod, and Raiden's heart clenched hard in his chest. He'd seen that look before, when they lost their parents and sister. Lost, alone, numb. By mutual accord, he and Liria curled their arms around Taos and pressed their bodies to his sides.

"Brother," Raiden rumbled. "We are here."

The Pharaoh's breathing hitched, and he turned his head into Raiden's neck. With a heavy heart, the Crown Prince of Merged Egypt held his brother as he cried.

RAW EDGES

Under Isis' recommendation, it was decided to leave Ione in her enchanted sleep until the Queen could be returned safely to Selekhet. Once Taos had purged his immediate grief, he curled against the rock with his wife in his arms, rocking her silent form and pressing kisses to her hair.

"Brother..." Raiden began, but Taos only shook his head.

"Later," the Pharaoh croaked. "Isis and Nephthys are here - go and do what you must."

"He's right, Prince of Egypt," Isis murmured, her face pinched as she began to explore the ruined mess of Nephthys' legs. "The immediate danger has passed us by; Set won't return here so swiftly. I will watch your family as I watch my own."

Liria brushed her fingers down the length of Raiden's arm. "Come on."

Though Raiden heaved a heavy sigh, he nodded, and when Liria turned away he followed, his presence a crackling force simmering just beneath the surface of her skin. Their fingers twisted together by mutual, unspoken agreement, and their bodies brushed with every step. When his wing settled over her shoulders Liria relaxed into it, even going so far as to spread her own gossamer and glass wing until it caressed her lover's finely sculpted backside. The sensations that shot through her were an overwhelming mix of pleasure and pain but the look of profound love Raiden shot her way was well and truly worth the effort.

Osiris, Anubis and Horus stood deep in conversation with Apophis, who had emerged from the hole in the floor enough to cradle an unconscious Sylvan in the armoured coils of his body. All four looked up as Liria moved to lay a hand on Sylvan's grimy forehead, examining the younger woman with her senses.

"There is a war inside her," she murmured, looking up at Apophis with a frown. "What has happened?"

The demon serpent lowered his great head to nudge Sylvan's frail shoulder. "You remember that Set stabbed her?"

"Yes."

"After he forced me to taint you with my blood and left, there were very few options." Apophis shifted his coils, the sound like crumbling shale. "Sylvan knew she was to be used as leverage. She told me to let her die, but I... could not. We have experimented some, over the course of her life, and she has a certain tolerance to my blood. I gave her enough to strengthen her body's natural healing processes - but somehow Set's blood is in her system as well, and the two are not at all compatible."

"I know how it got there," Liria admitted. Though the words cut at her throat, she relayed how Set had attacked her, kissed her, stabbed her, and then Sylvan had torn into the god's throat with her teeth so that Liria could try and save them both.

"Set did *what?*" Raiden demanded, his face turning stony.

"Hush." Liria tightened her grip on his fingers. "It was awful, but I am unaffected. The gesture was simply another weapon in his arsenal."

"One you turned against him," Osiris said, nodding in sharp approval. "It seems that Sylvan drank of Set's blood rather than spit it out - a dangerous move that could even now be her end."

"Perhaps that's what she intended." Horus laid a hand on Apophis' enormous scales. "If Sylvan knew she could be used as an avenue to manipulate your surrender, then by removing herself from the equation, she protects you."

The great serpent's head lowered in defeat. "Yes."

Osiris rubbed a hand across his jaw, jewel-bright eyes hard as they looked the young woman over. "There is no telling what Set's blood will do, particularly mixed with yours, Apep."

"Apep. That is what Set calls me," Apophis rumbled. "Apep is a slave to Set's bidding, a monster sent to slaughter in his name. A story used to frighten children into obedience. If it's all the same to you, King of Kings, I'd rather you chose another name to address me by, particularly while I'm in control of my own thoughts and actions."

"My apologies." Osiris offered a short bow, his normally booming voice somehow contained and condensed by the enchanted cavern so it was, though no less intense, quieter than usual. "Would Apophis do?"

"Yes." Apophis cleared his throat in a hissing surge, then said, "I'd beg for my daughter's life, if you'd have it."

The God of Egypt remained silent, and Liria turned on him with a growl. "No. You will not kill this woman."

"She may yet die on her own," he returned gently. "And if she lives, there's no telling what she may become. You have seen the effects of Apophis' blood - adding Set's makes for a volatile mix, Lady of Shadows."

"I have drunk of Apophis' blood," Liria snarled, slapping herself in the chest. "Will you kill me, too, for the privilege?"

Osiris said nothing, his expression frozen, his body as still as though carved from marble.

"You expunged Apophis' influence," Horus said at last. "And Set is... well, he is the embodiment of chaos."

"I don't care if he's the embodiment of dessert carts - Sylvan does not deserve to pay for his crimes. Nor yours," Liria added, poking Osiris hard in the chest. "This whole situation wouldn't have happened if you'd bothered to open your mouth and treat the rulers of Selekhet as the equals you purport them to be.

Instead, you let Set move us around like pieces on a chessboard, swanning in to save the day when you saw fit. The Prince of Egypt almost lost his life and the Pharaoh has lost his heir. Because of *you*. Innocent Egyptians are dead, because of *you*. Now, Set has escaped and we're standing here discussing the potential murder of a woman in front of her own father, because of *you*." With a flick of her fingers, Liria created enough shadow from which to materialise a curved dagger in each hand. "Let me tell you something, King of Kings. I made a promise to protect Sylvan, and I will see it carried out. Nobody will stop me from keeping her safe - *least of all you*."

Osiris stared down at her, his eyes inhumanly blue and his face a cool mask. Raiden fell into place behind Liria, drawing both his khopeshes with a silken sound. After a long moment, Horus moved to join him, Anubis at his side, both with their own weapons in hand.

"Father," Anubis said, his voice wobbling over the word. "Liria is right. We've cocked this up something shocking. Don't make it worse."

The faintest breath of a breeze filtered through the cavern, and Osiris' lashes drifted closed. "It is a common misconception that gods are immune to errors of judgement, that our word is not only law but also right, purely because it is our word. Such pressures can be dangerous and none, least of all myself, are immune to them."

Horus and Anubis perceptibly relaxed but Liria had a lot of experience with the prevarication of politically powerful beings. Drawing herself up and using her most clipped, court-ready voice, she said, "So you admit to your own arrogance? How enlightening. I'm not so deaf that I missed your lack of offer for reparation, King of Kings, nor suggestions on a path to go forward. You call yourself a god of Egypt and yet the duty for protecting the people clearly falls to Raiden and now, by virtue of fate and my own choices, to me. However Sylvan came to be in this place, she was born in Selekhet, and I claim the rights to her protection."

"Liria?" Raiden's voice was low, unfurling in her chest like a precious flower. His lips ghosted against her cheek, his body vibrating with leashed energy as he focussed on the potential threat in front of them. "Gods, I love you."

"And I love you." She curled her darker magic against his, felt the storm tremble in response, and waited.

Osiris' eyes opened. Bluer than was natural, they were simultaneously soft and hard and carried the depthless wisdom of eternity. The stony stillness that had seized Egypt's penultimate god shattered as he smiled, a full, deep smile that showed all his perfect teeth and crinkled the corners of those penetrating eyes.

"Lady of Shadows, it is an honour to be so rightly castigated," he boomed, his voice pushing against Set's lingering influence to shake the walls of the cavern. "The daughter of Apophis has done no wrong, so I will not judge her prematurely." He craned his neck to peer over their collective heads, more than tall enough to manage the feat. "Her body must fight to accommodate the blood of both Set and Apophis, and if she survives - *if* - there is no telling what sort of creature she will be once it's done. We cannot simply release her, nor can we allow her to stay here. No offence, my lord Apophis, but if Set finds you, there will be no way to protect her."

"Understood," Apophis rumbled, his voice sad and deep, so very deep. "She must be kept somewhere secure, both for her safety and the safety of others, until it can be determined what her future holds."

Raiden stirred. "Send her to the Kirrilakh. Kadir is well placed to contain Sylvan if she gets out of hand, and he's certainly strong enough to protect her should Set get any unusual ideas."

"Kadir," Osiris mused, his nose crinkling. "The Kirrilakh is a good solution, but he may not be amenable to speaking with me."

"No, but he'll listen to me on behalf of the Pharaoh," Horus said, lifting his chin. "I'll take her."

Osiris sighed and gave a tense nod. As Horus murmured goodbyes and collected Sylvan in his arms, the King of Kings ran a hand through inky dark hair and cut Liria a wry smile. "As you've likely guessed, this is not the first error in judgement I've ever made."

"What's at the heart of it all?" Liria asked quietly, returning her daggers to the shadows from whence they came.

"Love," Osiris answered. "Love for my brother, for my wife, for my people, for my children. It makes us do foolish things at the best of times - and lately has not been the best of times."

"Nephthys told us of the Ennead, and of the challenges you're all facing." Liria leant into Raiden's strength and sighed when his arms came around her, swords and all. "Co-operation is more important now than ever before - but after what happened today, you're going to have to work hard to regain the Pharaoh's trust."

"And yours?" Osiris asked, a faint twinkle entering his eyes.

Liria bared her teeth. "I wasn't foolish enough trust you in the first place."

At that, the King of Kings boomed out a huge laugh, and they turned their collective minds to the task of evacuating Set's lair. Osiris took Nephthys and disappeared, while Isis transported Taos and Ione back to their quarters in Selekhet, with the promise to stay until the Queen awoke. Anubis, his face drawn with sorrow, remained by Apophis with Raiden and Liria.

"Little one," the demon serpent rumbled, nudging the Soul-catcher with his nose. "You cannot blame yourself for this."

"It was me, though," Anubis sighed, and Liria was surprised to see him lean against the enormous snake as one might a grandparent. "It was my magic. I threw that fire at Set in a desperate rage and now the Pharaoh and his Queen have paid the price."

"It was an accident," Raiden said, moving forward to clap the god of death on the shoulder. "Taos is in pain right now, but he will not blame you. None of us do."

Liria scratched at the dried blood on her wrist. "If you'd like to be technical, Soulcatcher, the fault is mine. I put up the shield that detonated the fireball into those billions of tiny flamelets."

"No." Anubis' eyes blazed with power until they glowed like miniature suns. "You built that shield to protect."

"The blame, if it is to be placed, lies with Set," Apophis rumbled. "He is an adept puppet master and we have all had our strings tugged in a most ruthless fashion." The great serpent shifted as though uncomfortable. "I cannot linger here. Soon, the soul fire I absorbed will dictate the need to sleep. I must hide from Set before oblivion sucks me under." Enormous silver eyes turned to Liria. "I am holding you to your promise, little shadow."

"I will keep it," Liria swore, reaching up as he lowered his huge head. Apophis nudged at her palm like a horse awaiting apples and she smiled. "Your daughter will be safe."

The eternal serpent hesitated. "And if she becomes a thing that cannot be saved?"

"Then I will deliver mercy with my own two hands."

"Thank you." Apophis' tongue flicked out to caress Liria's cheek, then he pulled back. "I should like to say we will never meet again, because that would mean that Set was unable to wield me like a weapon once more, but somehow, I doubt it to be true. Instead, I can promise only to hide to the best of my ability, and to fight his hold once we are reunited."

"Thank you." Raiden offered the demon a bow. "You know, for the face of evil, you're not a bad guy."

Apophis' eyes nictitated, and then he hissed a gravelly laugh. "I shall remind you, perhaps, that appearances can be deceiving."

With that, the enormous serpent retracted into the ground and when Liria peered into the hole, she could see no trace that he had ever actually been there in the first place. She stared for a long, long time, until Raiden turned her into his chest, large hands splayed across her spine. They clung to each other, and after a moment, Anubis' huge arms came around them both.

"Are you ready to go home?" The god of death asked.

Liria smiled and burrowed deeper into Raiden's chest. "Yes."

AT LAST

THEY RE-MATERIALISED IN THE sitting room of Raiden's chambers. Late afternoon sunlight poured in through billowing gauze curtains, the windows open just enough to let in a soft breeze. As Raiden inhaled, he caught the scent of freshly baked bread and knew that out in the city, vendors were setting up for the night market.

Anubis stepped back and looked them both over, his lips pressed into a thin line. It was the first time Raiden had ever seen the god uncertain - and though there was a small, human part of him that was discomfited by it, the larger part of him was pleased the Soulcatcher was comfortable enough to show his inner turmoil.

"He lost, you know," Raiden said softly.

Anubis blinked. "Huh?"

"Set." Raiden bent to press a kiss to Liria's temple. "He might have escaped today, but he lost."

"How do you figure that?"

Reluctantly releasing the woman he loved, Raiden crossed to the sideboard and poured three glasses of thick Egyptian beer.

He passed one to Liria, put the second one in Anubis' hands and took the third for himself.

"The way I see it, Set's plan was to play us against each other. To divide and conquer, not just to get his hands on Liria, but to strengthen his own position with a view to the end game." Raiden clinked his glass against Anubis'. "Instead, he drew us closer together. Now he's in hiding, while I've gained a... a..."

"Fiancé?" Anubis offered. "Lover? Partner?"

Liria cleared her throat softly. "Mate?"

"Mate." Raiden snatched at the word, four letters that somehow encompassed the entirety of what he felt for the fairy whose name was etched into his very bones. "The Anarchist hides, while I've gained a mate, a sister-in-law, and two new blood brothers who I'm also proud to call friends. In my book, that means Set lost."

"Friends," Anubis echoed, staring at Raiden as though he'd never seen an angel before. "But I almost killed us all!"

Liria snorted. "For the god of death, you did a lousy job. We're all still here, Soulcatcher."

"Not all." Anubis' gaze flickered, and he looked down into his beer. "You really don't think the baby's death was my fault?"

"No," Raiden and Liria said in unison.

"Friends." Anubis looked from Raiden to Liria and back again, his expression softening ever so slightly. "I'd like that."

"To friendship, then." Raiden lifted his glass and drank, and after a moment's hesitation, Anubis and Liria did the same. "Now, talk to me, Soulcatcher - because I have a rather intense desire to strip my mate naked and ensure her good health by inspecting every living inch of her bare flesh, and your reticence is getting in the way."

Liria startled, and Anubis burst out laughing.

"Osiris has taken the burden of the Ennead's drain upon himself," the god said, his face sobering. "It is why he was unable to break Set's traps without Apophis' help. Isis is using a great deal of her energy to support her husband, and Nephthys is hobbled while her injuries heal. Ra is, predictably, missing when we need him most." Anubis took a deep breath and ran a hand over his face. "That leaves Horus and I as the strongest remaining gods in the pantheon. There are a few others similar in strength; Sekhmet, Thoth, Bast... but they don't know the particulars of the situation."

"The point being?" Liria asked, her tone cool and professional.

"The point being," Anubis growled, "that Horus and I together are still no match for Set. We're going to have to trust some of the others, and soon, but it's almost impossible to guess who will be sympathetic to the cause."

"You need allies."

"Yes. Because as Osiris has dedicated himself to the Ennead, Set has drawn back from it as much as possible. He's currently the strongest god, not just in Egypt, but possibly amongst all the pantheons of Mu - and he will do anything, *anything*, to be free of the Ennead. Alone, he's a threat. If he were to recruit other gods..."

"Shit," Raiden whispered. "Could he do that?"

"Yes." Liria nodded, her blue-grey skin pale. "Set is as charismatic as he is powerful. He could convince a fish that water wasn't wet."

Raiden scratched at the stubble on his jaw. "What do you need from us?"

Anubis stared at his beer. Took a healthy swallow. Stared some more. His fingers, elegant as a musician's, tapped a rhythm on the frosted glass.

"Do you understand how a dark fairy's true magic works?" The god asked at last.

Raiden frowned. He'd seen Liria use magic many times since they'd met, but Anubis spoke now as though there was something more.

"Yes." Liria set her beer aside and clasped her fingers at her waist, as composed as though she were at court. "I've never had access to it until Raiden gifted my soul to me, but it was used to taunt me on multiple occasions, and once even as evidence for my execution."

"What sort of power could possibly be motivation for your execution?" Raiden demanded, curving a wing around her shoulders. When he tugged, she allowed him to pull her to his side, where he could run a finger down her cheek.

"The same thing that makes dark fairies the perfect shadows." Anubis finished his beer and set the glass aside. "Liria can blend her power with someone else's and steal it."

Shock coursed through Raiden as he stared down at Liria's face. "Steal?"

"Borrow is a more accurate term." Liria lifted one shoulder in a shrug. "Regarding the soul ring, the blending ability makes it far easier to bind a dark fairy into a crystal and make them a shadow. Outside of that, with physical contact I can use someone else's magic in addition to my own. As soon as the contact is broken, the effect is interrupted."

"Is that the case with Raiden?" Anubis asked, his gaze keen.

"Yes and no," Liria said quietly. "I gain full access to his abilities upon physical contact, but due to the bond we initiated in Set's lair, I have low level access all the time." She flicked Raiden a glance that screamed vulnerability. "I do not need his permission, because our souls and hearts are twined together."

"You don't need my permission," Raiden breathed, brushing his lips over hers. "Because I'm yours. If you ever need my power, you *take it.*"

Liria's lashes fluttered and she leant into him, deepening the contact until it was a proper kiss. Raiden trembled, aching for her, but Anubis cleared his throat and he broke away with a sigh.

"So," the Anarchist said, "together, you are both easily as strong as a god. If Horus and I knew you were willing to work with us, not just to protect the Pharaoh and Selekhet but to oppose Set, it would ease our minds exponentially."

"Opposing Set is in everyone's best interests, but we must be equals in this, Soulcatcher." Liria narrowed her eyes at the god of death. "I will be a pawn no longer."

Anubis bowed deep and low. "Equals. My word, both as the patron of lost souls, and as your friend."

"Done." Raiden swept Liria into his arms, ignoring her squeak of surprise. "Now get out."

Anubis' face creased in a smile, and he disappeared between one moment and the next.

"Raiden," Liria chided.

"No," he shook his head, striding through the bedroom and into the bathroom, where he gently lowered her feet to the floor. "I almost lost you. He can go soak his head for all I care."

Liria shivered. "For a moment, in that place, I thought I'd never see you again. Now you're a part of me, as much as I am a part of you. It cannot be undone."

Raiden crowded her against the bathroom sink, a hand on the bench either side of her hips. He kept shoving forward until they were pressed tightly together and snapped his teeth in front of her face, earning a startled hiss.

"Good," he growled, flaring his wings until he was all she could see, all she could feel. "I don't want it to be undone; I want to do it more. Beyond that, I want to bury myself in your body over and over and *over* and gods, Liria, if you don't want that you better say it right now, because I am this close to tearing all your clothes off and fucking you against this cabinet."

Her violet eyes were wide, her sharp features flushing dusky pink at his words. She slid her hands over the pitted leather of his armour and curled her fingers around the back of his neck, talons pricking the skin at the base of his skull. Leaning in close, she whispered, "I'm waiting."

There was a perfect moment of frozen silence, then Raiden shredded the remains of her dress with his bare hands. Liria sliced her talons through the fastenings of his armoured vest and he shrugged out of it as she turned her attention to his leather pants. Lacings split and then she was shoving them down, and he had to corral his raging need long enough to kick off his boots. Liria knelt to drag his pants off his legs, and then Raiden was naked and she was digging her talons into his buttocks while she swallowed his erection in one swift, decisive movement.

Someone was making a noise like a boiling kettle and he suspected it was him, but it was impossible to focus beyond the hot, wet suction of her mouth as she licked and nipped and generally drove him mad.

"I can't," he gasped, fisting a hand in her matted hair and yanking her up. She panted in his grip, expression somewhere between frustrated and triumphant as he curled his fingers into her underwear and ripped the flimsy garment off her body. It left her naked except for the knife sheath strapped to one thigh, her skin flushed with passion and smudged with mud and blood - and if he didn't have her right this second, he was going to die. "I can't wait, Liria."

"Then why are you still talking?" She dug her talons into his shoulders and jumped, locking her legs around his waist.

Raiden walked them into the shower, bracing her back against the tiles while he curled one arm under her ass and slid balls-deep inside her. His body shook in time to his pulse - or was it hers - and before long his hips echoed the movement, in and out and in again in deep, decisive strokes. Her talons dug harder at his skin as she used him for leverage, taking him every bit as much as he was taking her, and it was everything he'd ever needed. More.

He surged forward to claim her mouth and they fought in erotic bliss, kissing and panting and thrusting and clawing while thunder rumbled in every breath Raiden took and lightning crackled through his veins. Liria's power brushed against him, through him, blending with the primal energy of the storm and dappling it with glorious shadows and bright, violet sparks. He felt the internal walls of her body start to clench on him, felt the rolling tide of sensation that built deep inside her, and it locked his own spine, setting off a chain reaction that had them both crying out as their bodies spent themselves on each other.

Raiden sank to his knees, clinging to Liria as she clung to him, their chests a powerful bellows that worked in perfect unison. His wings curved around her, creating a feathered cocoon that blocked out the world until there was nobody and nothing else; just Raiden and Liria.

"I love you." The words beat in his blood, the very reason he drew breath. It should have been frightening in its intensity but Raiden had never felt more whole, more real than he did at that moment.

"And I love you." Liria nuzzled into his neck, her lips moving against his skin. "I feel like we've been hurtling towards each other since the moment I stepped off the ship. I thought you were insane, but now... I'm glad, Raiden. I'm so glad."

"It's not going to get any easier from here, you know." He shifted beneath her, wrapping both arms around her ribs and tugging her closer. "Set might be defeated for now, but I have no doubt he'll be back. Taos and Ione lost a child, and we have a wedding and your coronation to plan. We'll need to keep an eye on the Kirrilakh, in case Kadir needs our help with Sylvan, and put thought into expanding the Pharaoh's guard now that you and I are going to have our attention divided between Selekhet and the gods. That's before we even start thinking about state issues, like the decimated Atlantean contingent and the implications of Set's failed experiments wreaking havoc in the city."

"Not to mention, when Ione realises you gave me my own soul ring, she's going to combust," Liria murmured. There was something in her voice that made Raiden pull back just enough to look down into her face.

"Are you sorry?"

"I... no," she said slowly, brow puckering. "No. I'm glad to be free, but... she's already suffered so much. As happy as I am, I can't help feeling mildly guilty, as though I've abandoned her. I can tell you now, that's exactly how she'll see it."

Raiden was astounded by her deep capacity to care when from his point of view, Ione had done nothing but torment and torture Liria without reprise for decades. He scattered kisses over her upturned cheeks until his equilibrium resettled enough to say, "We'll do what we can to help, but not at the expense of your soul."

"Never again at the expense of my soul," she whispered, the corners of her lips kicking upwards. "It's mine now, and I quite like it where it is - tangled irrevocably with yours."

Tangled irrevocably. Yes, that's exactly how he felt. Still... "It doesn't worry you? The future?"

"Of course it does." Liria's lips pressed against the hard line of his jaw, followed by the gentle scrape of her fangs. "But, Raiden, like it or not, I'm built to face danger. And together? We're a force to be reckoned with, a force that will only become more dangerous as we learn to work in harmony." She poked him in the stomach. "Don't think I've forgotten that trick you pulled in the palace hallway."

He groaned. "I'm sorry."

"Good. You should be."

Eyes narrowed, Raiden reached up to the tap and flicked it on, dousing them both with a shock of cold water. Liria squealed but he held fast, and as the spray began to warm, his cock began to twitch.

"I think you need a good, thorough cleaning," he purred, leaning down to nip the shell of her ear. "And I still haven't inspected you for injury."

Her laughter was low and sultry. "Do your worst, Prince of Egypt. I can take it."

THE HEART OF A SHADOW

A SMALL MEMORIAL WAS HELD FOR THE BABY.

It was hard, and Liria shed as many tears as the Pharaoh and his Queen. Afterwards, Ione became quiet and withdrawn, spending most of her days cloistered with the goddess Isis in the bedchambers she shared with Taos and refusing any and all visitors.

Taos, though he carried shadows in his deep brown eyes and new lines at the corners of his mouth, began emerging from his shell a couple of days later - and Raiden was there every step of the way, cajoling his brother to laugh and on more than one occasion, to brawl with a complete lack of composure that Liria hadn't seen from the Pharaoh before.

Horus and Anubis visited regularly, and Raiden, Liria and Taos spent hours deep in conversation about both Selekhet and Mu, and what the future might hold for all of them.

Sylvan regained consciousness in the Kirrilakh but not coherence, and Kadir sent word that he'd been forced to lock her in a cell for her own safety. Her behaviour ranged from spitting rage to insane rambling to eerie stillness and though Liria visited her at least once a week, there was yet to be any kind of clarity in the other woman's eyes. Liria returned from the visits discouraged, and twice she cried on Raiden's shoulder, but Kadir promised not to execute the young woman unless there was truly no other option. With that in mind, they could only wait.

Of Set, there was no sign.

Days became weeks, and in that time, Liria succumbed to Raiden's pleading and allowed him to plan a wedding far more decadent and showy than she would have liked. She frowned her way through seemingly endless amounts of dress fittings, her decades of training as a shadow the only thing preventing her from hissing every time the sweet, joyful tailor turned up at her door. It was only when Raiden suggested marrying at sunset, his eyes crinkled with affection as he kissed her frowning brow, that the last of Liria's resistance faded.

"Sunset," she repeated, lifting a hand to trace the line of his jaw.

He nipped at her fingers. "Yes. The truest melding of night and day, when brilliant light and deepest shadow mingle into one. What do you think?"

"I think you're a scoundrel, seducing me all over again with pretty words that serve no purpose," Liria whispered - and when he smiled, she forgot the tailor was present, forgot the pins in her dress, forgot the Palace and the gods and the very air she breathed. She leant forward to kiss him, a soft melding of lips that sent a shock of emotion coursing through the soul she'd never understood, and now wore both on her finger and twisted inside her bones. "I love you."

Raiden's hand fisted in Liria's hair and he made to plunder her mouth, only to leap back with a sudden yelp. The tailor brandished a long, sharp pin and a sharp scowl, but her eyes glittered with mirth.

"The wedding is tomorrow, my Prince. If you do not leave off, the Lady will never be ready."

"My deepest apologies." Raiden swept a flourishing bow, the courtly gesture entirely ruined by the way he rubbed at his behind. "If it please you, dearest clothier, I'll take my leave - I believe my pride has been punctured enough for one day."

Liria watched him go, taking, as he always did, some of the warmth of the room with him. She longed to follow, but instead stood patiently while the tailor finished with the dress fitting, clasping the woman's hands between her own storm-grey ones once it was done.

"Thank you, truly," Liria murmured. "I know I've not been the most patient the last weeks, but I do appreciate your efforts."

The tailor smiled, squeezing their combined fingers gently. "Hush. It is a difficult thing to step into a place of prominence when one is used to fading into the background, but your spirit is as pure as your love for our Prince. You are doing admirably, my Lady - the honour is mine. Now, I think you should rest; I'll attend your chambers in the morning, to help you dress."

Liria nodded in thanks, breathing a sigh of relief as she slid back into the soft linen pants that Yrini had procured for her to wear on a daily basis. The top was similar to the one she'd borrowed from the angel's stash, a simple concoction of straps that tugged the material close and supported her more than ample bosom without impeding the use of wings or weapons. Once she'd finished buckling on her sword belt and twisted her hair off her face with a thin knife in a soft leather sheath, Liria made her way through the Palace halls to the Pharaoh's chambers.

Twice so far she'd attempted to visit Ione and been turned away; this time, however, when the guards barred their ceremonial spears across the doorway, Liria lifted both hands to display the soft, dark tendrils of power that curled between her fingers.

"If you so much as think about reaching for those laser pistols at your hip, I shall melt them into your skin forevermore." She glared first at one man and then the other. "I am here to see the Queen. You may let me in, or I shall let myself in at your expense."

"The Queen commanded that she was not to be disturbed by

anyone, not even the gods," one of the guards managed, his throat flexing as he swallowed.

Liria stared at the rapid thump of his pulse until the scent of his fear tickled her nose, then looked into his eyes and smiled. "Just as well I'm not anyone, then, isn't it? Don't worry, I'll ensure no harm comes to you for disobeying the Queen's order. On my honour, and the Prince's, I swear it."

After a moment's hesitation, the two men bowed their heads and stepped back to let her pass. Liria didn't wait, simply set her hand against the door and used her magic to unlock it, drawing gasps from the guards as the handle spun by itself. She slipped through the gap as soon as it was wide enough, sealing the door behind her with a simple warding spell before she turned to regard the Pharaoh's opulent quarters.

A pervasive gloom hung over the brightly appointed room, heavy curtains drawn so tightly together that not so much as a glimmer of the late afternoon sunlight broke through. The silence was as oppressive as the heat, and every breath slicked Liria's throat with a bitter aftertaste. Following both her nose and her instincts, she made her way not to the bedroom but the enormous bathing room, where a deep pool large enough for ten angels cradled a single occupant.

Ione floated on her back in the water, long, dark hair spread around her like the naiads from which she was descended. Though Liria made no sound as she crouched at the pool's gilt edge, the Queen's lashes lifted, her midnight eyes focussing unerringly in the almost darkness.

"You have some nerve to come here," Ione murmured. Her voice cracked, as though she'd spent so much time screaming it no longer functioned as it should. "Did you kill the guards?"

"No."

"I should have known they'd be useless even before I armed them." Ione snorted, the elegant sound rippling the surface of the water. "Why are you here, Lady Liria?"

Liria considered the mocking whip of words, and the pale,

perfect Queen with such venom in her glare. "I came to see how you were faring."

"How I was *faring*?" Like a snake affronted, Ione reared up from the water, lips twisting into a snarl. "Betrayed by all around me, left to rot while you flounce off into your precious, sparkling fairy-tale, and you *dare* come in here and ask me that?"

Water sloshed against the edge of the pool, cresting the edge to lick warm and inviting at Liria's knuckles. She watched the small tide ebb and flow for a long moment before shaking her head. "Nobody has betrayed you."

"How little you know." Ione tossed her head, flicking a trail of water across Liria's face and chest. "Tell me, my no-longer shadow: why did I come to Egypt?"

"To be free."

"To be *Queen*." Ione spread her hands, gesturing at the ornate chamber around them. "I am of naiad blood, my healing gifts so minute as to be worth little mention. I am the youngest daughter in a proud line of royalty that spans generations in any given direction, and the day I was stolen by my grandfather, Vasilios of the naga, I vowed never to become a pawn ever again." Ione's smile was brittle. "Do you know what I learnt, in those weeks with the naga? I was but a child, the breath of a promise, but Vasilios had all manner of magical creatures under his command. Sensitives who declared that whilst my healing abilities were of little consequence, my naiad blood was strong enough that I'd become exceedingly fertile once I grew. I believe Vasilios intended to use me as a brood mare, until you tore me from his accursed grip - and though that nightmare is one I never intend to relive, I never forgot what I'd heard. And I knew, when I petitioned Taos for his hand in marriage, that I had a weapon to ensure my dominion of not only his life, but his throne and this entire pathetic country."

"You planned to conceive from the beginning." Liria blinked, sitting back on her heels. "That's why you went to bed with him so swiftly."

"Indeed. I waited, hoarding my virginity my entire life, until I could get a king into my bed - I wasn't about to waste the opportunity when it presented." Ione's hand spread across her barren belly. "Now I am as empty as the crown upon my head. A Queen who cannot reproduce, a Queen who is second to the Prince - a Prince whose authority will only increase, for he will ever remain Taos' heir now that I cannot produce one. The power, the *glory* that I deserve, has been stolen from me."

"Stolen?" Liria tsked a denial. "Every effort was made to save that child."

"Who cares about the child?" Ione slapped her hands against the water. "I could have made another - I could have made twenty others! But no, the gods pick and choose who they bestow their favours on, and then they steal from you the very thing which would see you into the future. It's all a ploy to keep us bowing by their feet."

"I thought you cared for Taos," Liria returned, her thoughts awhirl. "You seemed so enthusiastic about learning to be the Queen."

"Pah. All that nonsense about becoming a gentler person and learning at Isis' knee? I did what I had to do to secure Taos' attention - even when it came to you." Ione's eyes glittered, though it was impossible to tell if the tears on her lashes were of rage or grief. "As if I would ever truly let you go! I allowed Anubis to loosen the soulbinding to curry favour, because in the end, you were always going to be mine - but it was for nothing."

Liria rubbed at her brow. "Yet you gave Raiden the soul ring to save my life."

"Of course - who better to help me forge an Empire than my very own shadow? You were mine, in a way that nothing or nobody will ever be mine. I needed you. So, yes, my shadow; I gave the ring to Raiden to save your life, but he betrayed me." Ione hissed, a reptilian sound that rattled in her broken throat. "He didn't give the ring back, as he ought. He gave it to you instead - and you *took it.*"

"It's my soul." Liria leant away from the ugliness in Ione's expression. "Raiden made me whole again."

"Whole? You were not made to be whole, you were made to serve. That soul ring was mine. *You were mine.* You had no right to take it, and leave me so cold and alone." Ione spread a hand over her heart. "A betrayal so deep, so cutting, that I will never recover. Unless..." The Queen held out an imperious hand. "It doesn't have to end this way, my shadow. You can be forgiven, if you return the soul ring to me and resume your rightful place at my side."

Liria scuttled backwards on her hands and knees, pushing upright with a flourish of her wings. "No. Even if I wished - and I do not - to return to being your slave, something happened down in Set's lair. My soul may forever be trapped in the ring, but it is also now twined with Raiden's, and I have never been so much myself as I am now."

"Again you choose to betray me, as I knew you would." Ione's expression was one of hateful triumph, her body sinking slowly into the water until only her head was visible. "So be it."

"I came here to see if you were well. Despite the imbalance of power between us, I have cared for you during our time together - but I will not stand idly by while you speak like that." Liria stared down the Queen, who didn't as much as blink beneath her regard. "You need medical aid, lest your mind twist irrevocably. I will speak to Taos and see you have it, but you must hear clearly, in this moment, that I will never be your shadow again. I am my own person, and more than that, I am in love with Raiden - I would never risk him, or his soul, for your petty greed."

"Then best you leave." Ione's voice was so soft, the water barely stirred beneath her lips. "Marry that Prince, but know you do it without my blessing. I hope you choke upon your wedding wine."

Liria left without looking back, sealing the Queen's rooms from the corridor so that Ione could not get out. She went, heart hurting, to the chambers she shared with Raiden - where she tumbled into the warmth of his embrace and sobbed against his chest.

"We will not abandon Ione," he murmured, wiping her tears with his thumbs. "I will talk to Horus and ensure she has the support she needs."

"What about Taos?"

Raiden's lips thinned. "I hate to hurt him, but I think he needs to know."

"Together," Liria whispered. "We'll tell him together."

Relaying the conversation to the Pharaoh and watching the light fade from his soft brown eyes wounded Liria so much that, by the time she fell into bed with Raiden that night, her soul shivered beneath her skin. Instead of distracting her with lovemaking, Raiden curled his body tight to hers and squeezed, cradling her with his huge heart while she shuddered against him until sleep claimed her.

The morning of the wedding saw her emotionally spent, but also refreshed in a way Liria had never before known - as though a deep, insidious poison had been expelled. Ione had turned her away, and though part of Liria mourned that, another part of her knew the relationship had been toxic. She stared at her reflection in the mirror, her stormy skin smooth and her violet eyes lit with magic. Today, Raiden got his wish and would marry her at sunset, in a frothy affair that made her entirely uncomfortable - but his joy, his pride and his love made it worthwhile, and she would not dishonour this new beginning between them by wallowing in distress.

When sunset came, Liria walked onto the dais in Osiris' temple in a dress the colour of spun silver. It highlighted her skin to perfection, complementing the jewels Raiden had draped her in before he left to get dressed himself. Now, he stood opposite her in a formal gold collar and flowing trousers in Selekhet's palm frond green, his crown glittering in the light of the setting sun and his deep golden eyes locked on Liria as she placed her hands into his.

Osiris began to speak, his deep, booming voice a joy to listen to - but the words washed over Liria like a sweeping tide, her world beginning and ending with the angel who was edging closer with every breath. A cheer went up, and Liria supposed they must be married now, for Raiden gathered her close and possessed her mouth the way he possessed her heart. Their souls sung as they twisted together, a peculiar echo that the soul ring amplified until Liria was giddy with love and joy, so much so that she didn't care the entirety of Selekhet were watching as she melted into Raiden's embrace.

Someone was laughing; Taos, the sound rusted but real. There was a thump, and Raiden grunted, but he'd fisted his hands in her hair and was breathing life into her lungs, so Liria didn't bother breaking the kiss to see what it was the Pharaoh wanted. A moment later, something cool touched her forehead and a peculiar weight settled atop her hair.

Liria jerked back with a start as the Pharaoh swept an arm towards the crowd. "Egypt! I present to you the Crown Prince Raiden and his wife Liria, the Princess of Shadows and my newest sister."

"Princess?" Struggling free of her husband, Liria raised her hands to the crown that sat upon her head. "Princess? Are you *mad?*"

Osiris burst out laughing, the sound shaking the temple - and Liria joined him, swiftly followed by everyone else, until Selekhet rang with the sound.

"Does it bother you?" Raiden asked that night, as they lay side by side in the small, pyramid shaped cottage by the hot springs. There was too much to do for them to take a real break, but Taos had been adamant they take at least a night - and the light in the Pharaoh's eyes had flared so brightly in that moment that neither Liria nor Raiden had the heart to turn him down. So they went, leaving Taos to handle the mantle of governance on his own while they stripped each other bare and made love for hours on end.

"The crown, you mean?" Liria lifted one shoulder. "Not really. I know it was mentioned in Set's lair, but I never expected Taos to actually follow through with it." She screwed up her face. "I'm still not sure I'm worthy, but I'll learn to live with it."

"You're more than worthy - Taos and I both agreed." Raiden drew idle hieroglyphs on the skin of her belly, his brows furrowed. "You should know that Isis went to visit Ione before the ceremony, but the Queen refused to speak to her, merely stared into space as though our goddess did not exist. The gods are more concerned for her welfare than before."

"Ione lost a child," Liria murmured, watching the play of muscles in his arm as he caressed her. "Though she says it doesn't distress her, I cannot believe the words to be true. I saw her crying at the memorial - those tears were no lie."

"We will make sure she gets whatever she needs to heal," Raiden promised. "She will not be forgotten."

"I know." Liria sighed. "I have endured many things in my long life, but nothing as painful as that memorial service. The fact Taos is able to get out of bed every morning and not just func-tion, but function well... I'm in awe."

Raiden's mouth flattened. "We've had practice losing people we care about."

The old pain in his eyes caught at her and Liria wiggled closer, until the length of her side was pressed into the front of his body and she stared up into those bright, golden eyes.

"Would you like to have children one day?" she whispered, swallowing past a sudden lump in her throat. Raiden's eyes flared wide and he lifted his hand to stare first at her belly, then her face. "No, I'm not pregnant. Relax. It was a hypothetical."

Disappointment warred with relief in his expression. "I thought you weren't able to?"

"Not before," she agreed. "But I had a conversation with Anubis this morning, before the wedding. He's been doing some research and he thinks that now I'm in possession of my own soul, it might be possible."

Raiden's jaw dropped. "We could... we could have children?"

"Maybe." Liria put hard emphasis on the word, reaching up to caress his cheek. "It'll take decades for my reproductive cycle to begin functioning, if it ever does. And... if it does, it may never function optimally. I just thought you should know that there's a chance for us, however slim, should we want it."

"Oh, I want it," he murmured. "Decades, huh? That's plenty of time for Taos to heal, for us to deal with Set, and for me to love you blind six ways from sunset."

Liria chuckled. "Yes. You're lucky angels are so long lived."

"Ah. I suppose it's my turn to confess now," Raiden sighed. "I spoke with Horus before the wedding. He says that since I've taken his blood and become... other, an angel's standard lifespan may not apply. He thinks I might... linger. Endlessly. Agelessly." The Crown Prince of Egypt cleared his throat. "Like a shadow does."

Forever. They could have forever - if they dared. If they fought for it.

The sheer rightness of Raiden's words settled in her breast-bone and Liria nodded. "I think your Skywatcher speaks true."

"I'm not sure how I feel about it." Raiden's face pinched. "It means, if Horus is right, I'll one day outlive Taos. On the other hand, if he's wrong, I'll die... and in doing so, I'll kill you, too."

"I do not fear death. If that is to be our fate, then I will meet it without regret." She laid a finger across his lips when he would have protested. "No. My life, my choices. We could die tomorrow, or in five hundred years, or five thousand; none of that matters to me, so long as I do it with you. You have no right to deny me that, so don't even try."

Raiden frowned, but eventually nodded. "I don't like it, but I feel the same way. When we go, we go together."

"Right. As for Taos, you'll always carry him in your heart. And besides, we're friends with the god of death, remember?

Should the day ever come when you are parted from your brother, we'll simply go to the underworld to visit him." Liria offered a bright, wide smile nobody but Raiden had ever seen. "Problem solved."

He snorted, but the corners of his lips began to twitch and the heaviness of the mood lifted, replaced by something lighter and fuller. "So, that's settled then, is it? We walk hand in hand into tomorrow?"

Liria linked her fingers through his. "We walk hand in hand into all our tomorrows - that's what it means to claim the heart of a shadow. Can you live with that, Prince of Storms?"

Raiden kissed her hard, his fingers twisting into her hair and his wings a heavy blanket over her stormy, blue-grey skin.

"Yeah," he breathed against her lips, "I can live with that."

~ THE END ~

Thanks for reading!
Can't wait for the next instalment?
Keep up to date with all the latest shenanigans at:
www.sliceofsammy.com

ACKNOWLEDGMENTS

This book would not have been possible without the love and support of those nearest and dearest to me.

First off, to Mum, who reads everything without comment and is entirely responsible for this particular novel being written in the first place. When I woke up one morning with the idea for Raiden and Liria's story burning a hole in the back of my brain, I called her and said, "It's not the right time!" She laughed and replied, "Just write it already." So… I did, and never has a book poured out of me the way this one did.

Special mention to Bron, as always, for listening to me rant about characters and plot and settings and Ancient Egypt, which I love so very much. And huge thanks for beta reading what turned out to be a longer book than expected! You're an absolute star and I would be lost without you in my life.

Thanks to my ARC team – you guys rock! I love being able to send you copies of a new book and getting such positive, excited responses. It means the world to know you enjoyed something I created.

To all the readers (yes, that's you) who picked this up and gave it a go – I hope you loved this tale as much as I do. I hope you laughed, and cried, and got mad and happy and *ahem* in the naughty parts. If this made you smile, then I've done my job!

Also by Samantha Marshall

A sorceress. A warrior.

A space deer.

The sorceress Arcana and her soulmerged deerken companion have spent fifty years traversing the galaxy, following the song that haunts Caelum's dreams in an attempt to solve the mystery of their creation. When they stumble upon an injured knight in a frozen ruin, Caelum insists on rescuing him – for why else would a knight be in such a mysterious place, if he wasn't somehow connected to the singing inside Caelum's mind?

When he wakes, the knight reveals himself as Fenris, stalwart Guardian of the Weaver and her Timeless Kingdom. Recognising Caelum as a deerken, the tall, brooding Guardian offers to unravel the mystery of Arcana and Caelum's past in return for their assistance in returning home, so that he might liberate his queen from the clutches of a madman.

Whilst Caelum throws himself wholeheartedly behind Fenris' seemingly noble cause, Arcana can't shake the feeling that their handsome guest is keeping secrets. Despite her efforts otherwise, her attraction to Fenris continues to grow… along with the suspicion that if she and the Guardian can't find common ground, his secrets might be the end of them all.

Read on for a sneak preview of Chapter One!

CHAPTER ONE

Arcana drew in a lungful of sharp morning air, expanding her chest to capacity and savouring the chill. Long tendrils of curling gold edged a mauve and crimson sky, promising another clear day. She tightened slender fingers around her steaming mug and exhaled in a gust, the bitter essence of the frozen landscape tingling through her veins and out between her lips. The beacon of warmth in her hands abruptly disappeared.

"Ugh." Arcana looked down. The amber liquid had frozen at an odd angle, partially sloshed up the rim of the mug as though in preparation for a sip.

"Did you freeze your tea again?" A great drift of snow shot up into the air as Caelum stood, shaking himself off in a show of fur and slush.

Arcana tipped the mug upside down in demonstration. "Yeah."

"What is that, the third one so far?" Caelum lowered his shaggy head and scratched at one ice-speckled foreleg. Arcana watched in silence, admiring the elegance of his antler rack, each dip and whorl carrying remnants of the snow which had piled up as he slept. Long, sleek fur cascaded like silk from his muscular frame, a silver grey which darkened to black down his spine and mottled across his hindquarters. Caelum turned towards her, his black eyes bottomless and filled with thousands of tiny, swirling stars. "Well, is it?"

"I haven't been counting." Arcana stared into the mug, where her reflection stared back from the mirror-like surface of the tea. White skin - whiter than snow, starker than salt - and midnight hair which tumbled straight and glossy to the base of her spine. She bore the slightly ovular face and button nose of a classic beauty but her eyes, a deep black without iris, pupil or white, ruined the effect. Without the signature features of most normal eyes they seemed too large in her face, emphasised by long black lashes which further unbalanced her cuter, canvas-worthy assets. Slender, not particularly muscular - no sorceress was - with middling to small breasts and a basic hourglass shape, there was nothing much to distract an onlooker from the full impact of her unusual face. Aware that Caelum was watching her self-assessment with an impatient, if not reproachful air, Arcana raised an ebony brow and leant back against the frigid weatherboard of the shack in which she had spent the night. "Did you regret your decision to sleep outside so much that you spent the entire night dreaming of hot beverages?"

Caelum snorted, pawing at the snow. "I already told you, I won't fit inside the wayhut. Doorway's too narrow."

"Yeah, I know." Arcana shivered, and not from the cold. "I would've felt better with you inside. The warg were howling all night."

"I noticed. If it helps, they're not particularly close - it's just the sound carries so easily over the ice." Caelum yawned, his majestic profile thrown into silhouette by the rising sun.

Arcana rolled to her feet, staring over Caelum's broad shoulders to the icy wasteland beyond. "Say what you like, but this trek is taking us steadily closer to their godawful wailing - or are you going to tell me that's a trick of the tundra?"

"No, you're right," he allowed. "If you're worried, we can go back -"

"Don't be silly. I'm just grouchy after trying to sleep on that frozen bed." Arcana tucked her long, ink-black hair into the collar of her jacket and dragged a knit hat into place atop it. "The wayhut is woefully ill-equipped for this icy hellhole - anyone who wasn't me would freeze to death in a couple of hours."

Caelum turned his head south, where barren drifts of unmarked snow were gilt with morning light. A green tinted mountain loomed in the distance and Arcana knew without seeing that his eyes were trained upon it. "Ice princess status notwithstanding, if we don't get a move on the day will be wasted."

"Suits me – the sooner we get started, the sooner we leave this ill-begotten iceberg." Arcana lifted her leather satchel from the porch and shouldered it in one swift movement, clumping down the steps to halt before a bank of waist deep snow. "South?"

"Yes." Caelum pushed through the drifts towards her, leaving a deep furrow in his wake. "I can hear that mountain singing."

Arcana buried her hands in the fur of his shoulder and swung astride, settling the leather satchel comfortably in her lap. Her legs tucked around Caelum's ribs with the familiarity of long practice and his antler rack rose in two enormous, elegant silhouettes on either side of her field of vision. She brushed a finger along one velvety edge, entranced by the whorled pattern which was unique as any fingerprint. The surface began to smooth and change as she watched, velvet receding and curved edges sharpening until Caelum wore an antler rack of glittering, coffee-black blades. Arcana withdrew her hand from the scimitar curves and said; "Getting the weaponry out already?"

"All that howling set me on edge. Also, I visited the dreambank while you slept," Caelum answered, turning south and pushing into the snow.

"The dreambank?" Arcana sat up straight, fingers clenched to fists in his long, silky coat. "But... here? There's an access point here?"

"Yes." Caelum's voice turned dreamy as he left the drifted snow surrounding the wayhut and began to pick his way across the hard-packed ice of the tundra. "It was fragile and fractured, like trying to catch falling water. Either way, the fact I saw anything at all - and the singing coming from that mountain - means we're on the right planet."

"I never doubted your instincts in the first place." Arcana reached out to flick playfully at a black-tipped ear. "Did you see anything useful?"

"Fragments. Enough to point us in the right direction. It's like looking into a kaleidoscope and makes about as much sense." His ears flickered thoughtfully. "You were right, though. We're going towards the warg, rather than away from them."

Arcana shivered. "We never do anything the easy way, do we?"

"Where would the fun be in that? You never know, we could get lucky and find the temple before we find the warg. It might even be in one piece." Caelum turned his head slightly to regard her, the swirling stars in his black eyes a sharp contrast to the silver-grey fur of his face.

"Oh please. Look at this place - if the warg are here, whatever we find will be a ruin. Even if all they're doing is hiding from the weather, they'll have found the temple by now. It's how they work," Arcana muttered, shielding her eyes with one hand and glaring off into the stark white distance. "I just don't see why there'd be a temple on this miserable haemorrhoid of a world in the first place."

Caelum chuckled. "This planet wasn't always covered in ice, you know."

"Don't be ridiculous." Arcana waved a hand upwards, where the sun winked weakly above them. "It's too far from the sun for anything else."

"It used to be closer. And there was a moon... maybe even a different sun," said Caelum. The amusement was gone from his voice, replaced by the sombre, distant tone that often coloured his memories of the dreambank.

"Wait... you're saying this wobbly hunk of rock used to be in a *different place*?" Arcana demanded. Caelum was silent for so long that she yanked on the arm-length fur at the back of his head, earning herself a sharp snort and a threatening shake of his shoulders.

"I told you, the dreambank is fractured." Caelum's ribs expanded beneath her for a moment, then he sighed. "I saw green, and life, and a bigger sun, and a very large planet off the port side. Some sort of ferrying system, like that ridiculous setup that runs between Jupiter's moons. So yes, I think it used to be somewhere else."

Arcana turned her eyes upwards, where the sky remained a strange shade of after-dawn grey and would for the rest of the day. There was certainly no large planet on the horizon and hadn't been since they landed two days ago. "A different location would certainly explain why the wayhut was so badly provisioned, but who... *what* could move a moon? What happened to the planet?"

Caelum's shoulders rolled in an elegant shrug. "If I knew that, I would tell you." Calm words, but the hackles at the base of his neck were stiff with frustration. Arcana stroked her fingers though his fur until it began to relax, glaring out at the landscape. There was nothing to see beyond the flat, solid ice of the tundra, nothing to hear beyond the stinging wind. For want of anything better to do, she began braiding the long hair that grew down the ridge of Caelum's spine, trusting his instincts to take them wherever it was they needed to go. The sun was well overhead when his steady progress abruptly halted, jerking a complicated braid out of her fingers. Arcana looked up through the swirl of his antlers to see that the landscape ahead rose into a short, stubby hill at the foot of the green tinged mountain.

"It's here," Caelum said.

"It… that?" Arcana frowned. "It looks like a half-built sandcastle."

"Illogical construction or not, somewhere up there is the reason we came." He was silent a moment and then sighed, a great rumbling of his chest. "This place… I feel strange. Edgy. As though there's something I should be doing, or something I should know, but I can't do it because I don't know it."

"That's why we're here, isn't it? To unlock the secrets hidden inside you." Arcana jumped down from his back, her booted feet sliding across the ice. Caelum's head snaked out, his teeth fastening over her coat and steadying Arcana when she would have fallen. "Thanks."

"Welcome." Caelum waited while she regained her balance then turned to look at the mountain, his posture cramped with lines of tension. "I feel like we need to hurry."

Arcana glanced around them nervously. "Warg?"

"No. Something else." Caelum tilted his head, starry eyes roving over the almost sheer ascent. "In the interest of haste, I think a staircase would be handy."

"Only you would ask for a staircase up a mountainside," Arcana grinned, crouching to flatten her hands against the snow-flecked ice beneath them. She called her magic, savouring the chill heartbeat of the landscape that flowed in her veins. Caelum moved closer until his legs almost brushed her shoulder, cloven hooves weaving an intricate dance as the ground beneath them began to reform. The ice buckled and cracked, the inch-deep covering of snow sloughing sideways as first one step, then another, rose gracefully from the tundra's frozen surface.

"Halfway up for now," Caelum murmured and Arcana obliged, continuing to shape the shallow ice stairs until they connected with the hillside where he indicated. Caelum regarded her work in silence, his twitching tail the only sign of life. "That never gets old."

"I'll take that as a compliment." Arcana pushed to her feet, shaking the last few snowflakes free of her clothing.

"You should." He tossed a rogue's grin at her but it was short lived, falling into a frown. "The singing is getting more urgent. Let's go."

"All right." Arcana twisted one hand in his fur, dragging herself onto his back. "But for the record, following the directions of a singing mountain might be misconstrued as crazy."

"It's never stopped us before." Caelum flowed over the hardened ground without fear of slipping, picking up speed until he may as well have been flying. Moments later they stood at the top of the stairs, eyeing the wall of snow and ice before them. "Although I'll admit it's never been this strong before. Are you sure you can't hear it?"

"Not a thing." Arcana clutched at Caelum's fur as he stepped fearlessly onto a narrow ledge, navigating footholds that should have been impossible for his size.

"Here," he said at last, motioning to a section of the hillside that looked like any other. Arcana waved a hand and the snow slithered aside, revealing solid ice. Caelum's ears flickered. "We need to go in."

"I figured." Arcana slid carefully off his back and flattened her hands against the mountainside. She called her magic and pushed, walking forwards. The wall gave way beneath her touch, retreating and widening to form a tunnel big enough for even Caelum to follow easily. It should have become darker as they progressed but the ice projected a soft blue light that filled the tunnel.

"How did you do the light?" Caelum asked.

Arcana paused, looking back over one shoulder. "I didn't." She removed her hands from the ice and the light winked out.

"It's not... that's not your magic?" He sounded uncertain for the first time since their arrival.

"No." Arcana touched the wall again and the light returned,

soft and blue and constant. "Should I stop? We can go back if you're worried."

"The blue light is creepy, but…" Caelum frowned, scuffing at the floor of the tunnel with one neat, cloven hoof. "We need to keep going. Just be alert."

"Okay." Arcana pushed further into the mountainside, Caelum so close behind his breath tickled her ear. They walked in silence, save for the rasp of Arcana's lungs and the soft slither of her feet along the icy flooring. All of a sudden her magic cut off, the feeling akin to that of a solid slap. Arcana gasped and stumbled face first into the wall ahead, rebounding into Caelum and plunging the tunnel into darkness.

"Arcana?" Caelum's voice echoed through the inky black.

"I'm fine." Arcana leant against the side wall and the blue glow returned, revealing an imposing stone slab in front of them. "Whatever that is, it rejected my magic."

Caelum leant over her shoulder, his fur tickling one cheek as he squinted at the door. "I guess that means it's not for you to open. Can you increase the light?"

"I don't know." As if hearing her words, the tunnel brightened, throwing the carving on the door into focus. Arcana gasped and took a half step back. "Caelum – is that your face?"

"Not my face, but one like mine. And look; a keyhole." He jerked his chin and Arcana saw at once that the deerlike face on the door had a soft indentation where the nose should be, and two long, narrow slits at the outer edge of the antler rack.

Arcana frowned. "Are you sure about this?"

"Not at all." Caelum slid past her, placing his nose in the indentation and the tips of his antlers into the stone slits. A moment passed, then another, and then the door began to glow, a gentle green light that emanated from the places Caelum touched and spread until the entire carving's face was illuminated. The slab swung aside with a huge groan, leaving Caelum standing alone in the blackened maw of a doorway. He turned to regard Arcana with gently swirling eyes. "Shall we?"

"Wait - there's no light," Arcana protested. "I can't see in the dark."

"Hmmm." Caelum poked his head through the door and swung it from side to side. "Nothing. What about that magic ice?"

Arcana looked at the glowing wall with a degree of uncertainty. In her experience, it was unwise to trust an unknown source of magic, much less meddle with it - but without a fire handy, what choice did they have? Frowning, she bladed her hand and made a scooping motion against the wall, using her magic to carve out a fist-sized ball of ice. The tunnel immediately darkened but the globe in Arcana's palm retained its eerie blue luminescence, shedding a soft glow around her for several feet. She held her breath a long moment - but nothing happened, save for Caelum to stare at her inquiringly.

"Okay. Here we go." Arcana twined her fingers into the fur at Caelum's shoulder and lifted the orb higher, widening the circle of light. The glowing ice was no match for a proper torch but it alleviated the worst of the gloom, revealing a vast rectangular chamber whose far wall had collapsed in a tumble of rubble and snow. A stone dais stood in the centre of the space, the back end partially covered by debris. As they approached, Arcana made out the crumbling remains of a tall, circular structure with a shorn-off stone pedestal to one side.

"Do you see that?" Caelum's steady, hypnotic pace faltered for a moment and then he shot forward with his nose outstretched, jerking free of Arcana's grip. She stumbled on the uneven floor, the light in her hand zagging crazily across the stone walls.

"Great Gods of Sorcen, what are you-"

"Here!" Caelum's voice bore an urgency which had Arcana hurrying forward. He stood at the base of the dais, head lowered to the armoured figure slumped on the floor.

"What in the name of magic?" Arcana dropped to one knee beside the figure, reaching out to carefully tug the dented helmet free. The face inside was male and bloody, his soft teal skin and high cheekbones framed by a tumble of dark curls. "A knight?"

"Is he-?" Caelum broke off.

Arcana laid two fingers against the knight's throat, pressing down, searching. His skin was cold to the touch, sticky with sweat and blood, but beneath it all Arcana felt the unmistakable flutter of a pulse. "Alive, but barely." Arcana moved her hand over his plated chest, where the metal had been slashed diagonally from pectoral to hip. Dark blood flowed readily from the gash, pooling on the floor and coating her fingers. "We need to get him out of here."

"Put him on my back." Caelum dropped to the ground, silver fur spilling across the stone floor and immediately staining dark with the warrior's blood.

"Yeah, sure. Hoist a knight in full plate armour onto your back," Arcana growled, levering her arm behind the warrior. His eyes flew open at the touch and she gasped as jade fire spilled down his cheeks, mingling with the blue glow of the ice orb and casting eerie shadows over the planes of his angular face. Though the knight's eyes appeared featureless, Arcana knew without doubt the moment he focussed on her.

"Run," he grunted.

"Shhhh. I need you to get onto Caelum's back." Arcana grabbed the knight's chin as his head began to list. "Can you do it?"

"No... leave. Run..." The knight groaned, trying to pull away until his gaze fell on Caelum, kneeling patiently on the floor. His jaw dropped open.

"Please listen to her," said Caelum quietly.

"A deerken," he breathed, and just when Arcana feared he wouldn't move, the knight gripped her arm tightly and pushed himself upright. Even doubled over it was impossible to miss the fact that he was almost seven feet tall, his frame wiry but powerful underneath what remained of the armour.

"Of course. Don't move for me, no, but a big hairy goat? No

worries," Arcana drawled. She inserted herself under his arm, doing her best to provide support as the knight slung a leg over Caelum's back.

"My sword…" He gestured to a long, wide blade on the floor, revealed by the absence of his body.

Arcana bent to heft it and staggered under the weight. The giant sword - it had to be at least as tall as she was - barely shifted an inch. "No way am I going to be able to carry that. We'll have to ditch it."

"No!"

"Put it in the bag," Caelum jerked upright, ears swivelling towards the tunnel. "And hurry. I have a bad feeling."

"A bad feeling? Great." Arcana slid her satchel off and crouched on the bloodied stones. The knight's brilliant green eyes widened as she slipped the mouth of the bag over the tip of the blade and tugged, inch by slow inch, until the entire sword had disappeared. Arcana flipped the satchel shut and repositioned it over her shoulder. "Much better."

"Mage," the knight whispered.

"Sorceress," she corrected, stepping beside him and hefting the glowing ice. "And slave to the first rule of adventuring: always have a magic bag. Now, let's get you out of here."

"Warg!" Caelum's shout echoed through the crumbling cavern, his stardust eyes wide in the pale blue light. A shadow hurtled across the room towards them, claws rasping on stone. Arcana dropped to one knee, flattening her hand against the floor and calling her magic. It rose through her veins, dragging the energy of the stone and the earth along with it. The warg leapt, no more than flashing fangs and whirling claws in the half-dark. Arcana raised her arm and great pillars of stone shot out of the ground, huge and ancient teeth more than twice her height. The warg yelped as the stone skewered his body and the room fell silent.

Arcana stood and dusted her hands. "That was close. I thought you said they were further away?"

"Yeah, and you said they'd be here. One of us had to be wrong," Caelum murmured, ears flickering as he listened to the dripping silence. "This place must be connected to their den. Probably a side effect of the cave in."

"Hmm." Arcana stepped over the gritty rubble, the blue light in her hand spilling across the furred face of a creature who was neither human nor animal, but some bizarre blend of both. The warg's tongue lolled out at an angle, eyes wide and lifeless. "He was only young."

"That's why he was so easy to kill." Caelum high-stepped past the body, nose wrinkled in disgust. "The scent of his blood will call the others. We need to move."

Arcana reached inside the neckline of her top, where a tooth hung on a length of leather. She closed a fist around the necklace and prodded it with her magic. "Whatever energy stopped me opening that door is thick through the whole place. I've got a basic trickle of power, but not enough to charge the tooth. We need to get outside to jump."

Caelum grunted, already moving for the tunnel. "I figured as much. Come on."

Warg. Always warg. Arcana waved a hand and watched as the stone spikes returned to the earth. The dead warg now lay at her feet, his chest a gaping hole. Looking much like the classic bipedal werewolf out of a Terran horror story, the warg were a force to be reckoned with. They bred incessantly, fought without mercy and possessed an innate cunning surpassed only by their physical abilities and natural weaponry. But how did they get out here, to this misbegotten lump of ice and snow? Arcana stepped around the corpse and made for the tunnel, placing her feet carefully to minimise the sound of their passing. It was no use; a terrible howl echoed through the vast room and moments later warg began boiling out of a crack in the corner.

"Run!" She shouted, leaping between Caelum and the slavering, racing bodies. He bounded away and Arcana threw her arm skywards, sending their tiny orb of light up and up and up. In her experience, it was always a bad idea to meddle with strange, wild magic - unless, of course, there were worse things chasing you. So Arcana poured her own magic into the globe, feeling for the spark inside, grabbing it, twisting... Until the orb exploded in a blinding ball of brilliance. The warg howled in pain, falling away from the bright light that spun and shimmered in the air above.

Arcana leapt for the tunnel, blinking the radiance from her own vision as she raced along it, dragging her fingers down the wall for balance. A pool of daylight called her on, Caelum's silhouette framed in the entrance. Together they crept along the tiny goat track, back towards the icy staircase. Arcana forced herself to take deep, steadying breaths, absorbing the cold into her lungs, changing the magic from the earthy interior of the temple to the chill of the frigid outdoors.

"They're still coming," Caelum warned.

Arcana looked over her shoulder, where the tunnel had come alive with the sound of snapping teeth. "Be ready. This could go badly." She closed her hand to a fist, collapsing the icy entrance. The mountain groaned, the warg howled and for a long, terrible moment everything was still. She flicked a glance at Caelum, watched his ears swivel until they were trained on the mountain.

"Get on," he commanded. An ominous crack punctuated the words, followed swiftly by sloughing, swishing and rumbling. Arcana hauled herself up behind the knight as a great wall of snow came crashing down the mountain towards them, dotted with boulders and fuelled by crumbling masonry. Caelum leapt down the icy stairs and Arcana leant over his neck, using her body weight to hold the knight's limp body in place.

The ground bucked and heaved but Caelum didn't miss a beat, his cloven hooves cleaving thin air as often as they did the ice. "Did you have to bring down the whole mountain?" He shouted, his voice snatched by the wind and muted by the roar of the earth.

"I didn't mean to!" Arcana cast a glance over her shoulder to see the avalanche rapidly gaining speed, spitting rock and ice and warg into the air behind them.

"We need to jump! I can't outrun it." Caelum reached the bottom of the stairs and threw himself across the ice, a desperate race to buy them time. Arcana reached inside her furred coat and yanked the leather thong from around her neck. Clenching the tooth in her fist, she crushed herself against the knight's plate armour, wrapped her legs tightly around Caelum's ribs and focussed her attention on the tiny talisman in her hand.

At first, nothing. No more than the roar of the icy doom behind them and the undulation of Caelum's body as he raced over the bucking ground. Arcana closed her eyes and held her breath, anything to shut out the world and focus. She probed the tooth with her magic, finding a crack through which she could gain entry. The inside was a tranquil dream that spoke of lazy summer days, softly swaying flowers and gentle breezes. Arcana melded with the energy and dragged the sensation over them like a blanket, forcing it into Caelum's flesh, into his bones, suffusing their combined essences with an otherworldly presence until the ice, the snow, the land around them shimmered as if in a heat haze.

And Caelum jumped.

For moments that lasted lifetimes, they hung between realms and realities, bound together only by physical contact and shared determination. Then with a gut-wrenching lurch the universe realigned itself and they were no longer speeding across an iced landscape but standing in a carpeted room, face to face with a deerken skull.

"Made it," Caelum wheezed, his head between his knees.

"Are you okay?" Arcana slid off his back, dragging the armoured knight with her in an awkward tangle of clattering limbs.

"I will be. That was close." Caelum shook himself thoroughly and turned towards their guest. "How is - wait, is he *green?*"

"I don't think his skin is green so much as teal." Arcana laid her hands against the knight's chilled cheeks and frowned. "And yes, he's still alive. Help me get this armour off, would you? I need to see his wounds."

"Hang on." Caelum set the sharpened edges of his antlers against the edge of the breastplate and heaved. The leather ties shredded and the entire thing rolled off, thumping onto the floor on the knight's opposite side. "There."

"Thanks." Arcana peeled back the remains of the linen shirt underneath to reveal the great, bloody gash that stretched from the knight's right hip and ended just below his left armpit. "Wow."

"He's lucky he wasn't disembowelled."

Arcana narrowed her eyes at the wound, still steadily pumping dark burgundy blood all over the place. "Actually, I think whoever did this was aiming for heart, then guts - you know what? Rescind that. They were trying to cut him in half." She pressed her lips together. "This is more than a first aid kit job. I'll need fire."

"On it." He moved away, and Arcana busied herself soaking up some of the excess blood with a nearby blanket while she waited. Less than a minute later, Caelum dropped an old-fashioned lantern onto the ground beside her. "Here."

"My bedside lamp?" Arcana stared down at the tiny flame, barely taller than that of a lit candle. "Is that really the only fire we've got?"

"On short notice, yeah." He rolled his shoulders in the deerken equivalent of a shrug. "Everything in the kitchen's powered by the engines – no open fire."

"Frigging spaceships." Arcana flipped the lantern's latch and opened the tiny glass door. She placed one hand above the flame, letting it lick across her palm and between her fingers, filling her with heat and light. It wasn't much, but it would have to do. She set her other hand on the warrior's hip, covering the edge of the gash. The smell of burning flesh filled the air and Caelum snorted, prancing away. Arcana ignored him, drawing on the flame and focussing the heat, cauterising the knight's wound one slow inch at a time. Sweat trickled into one eye and she blinked it away, wishing vainly for a blazing furnace rather than the cheery, tickling flamelet of her bedside lamp.

"Almost there," Caelum encouraged.

Arcana grunted, dragging the magic now, forcing it through sluggish arms, determined not to falter. Too fast, and the flame would go out. Too slow, and it wouldn't be enough to melt that teal flesh back together. She leant forward, pressing her palm against the knight's chest to seal the last part of his wound. "He's lucky he's unconscious." Arcana pulled her hand from the lantern and scrubbed at her face, equal parts relieved and exhausted.

"Will he live?" Caelum asked, taking the lantern's handle between his teeth and lifting it out of the way.

"He bloody better," Arcana snapped, resisting the urge to sag forwards onto the carpet. Instead, she fumbled with the fastenings of her coat, now far too warm for the controlled climate of the ship. She dragged it off, dropping it onto the carpet beside her, and allowed a moment to appraise her strange guest.

His skin was indeed a soft shade of teal; not too light, not too dark. Pleasant, Arcana thought, a pleasant complement to the jade eyes she'd seen inside the temple. His dark curls were stuck with sweat and blood to his face but it was possible to see they were a shade of teal also; almost black, not quite. High cheekbones and long lashes lent him an otherworldly elegance, enhanced by a slender, wiry frame sheathed in muscle rather than overburdened by it. Dirty and bleeding, he was one of the most handsome creatures Arcana had ever seen; she had no doubt that clean and animated, he'd be breathtaking.

Caelum appeared with a blanket and together they drew it over the knight's body, now branded with a livid burgundy burn. Arcana folded her coat and slid it underneath his head, then pushed to her feet to find Caelum watching her, the stars in his eyes swirling gently. "He'd be better in a bed," the deerken remarked.

Arcana shook her head. "I'm not game to move him, not when it might reopen that wound." She sucked on her teeth for a moment. "The carpet will do for now and when he wakes – if he wakes – we can move him into one of the beds. Is our orbit stable? Shields up?"

"Of course. You don't want to leave?" Caelum looked surprised.

"I do, but I'd like to talk to Captain Slashy before we go too far."

"He *is* the reason we were called," Caelum said, his tone flat.

Arcana waved a dismissive hand. "I'm not doubting your instincts - but why? How did he get here? Where is he from? Who tried to cut him in half? What in the name of a thousand suns has he got to do with us?"

"I don't know, but he's ours," Caelum insisted, his voice suddenly petulant. "We were sent to him."

"Do you have any idea how crazy that sounds?" Arcana buried her hands in her hair, tugged in frustration. "We've spent fifty years following your instincts across space and this is the first time we've ended up with a third wheel."

"That alone should show you how important he is," Caelum replied.

Arcana rolled her shoulders in a vain attempt to ease their tension. She wasn't going to win the battle - wasn't even sure exactly what the battle *was*. And yet - "Look, I just want to talk to him, okay? I don't know where to take him, what to do with him, until we at least answer some of those questions."

"All right," Caelum agreed. Then, "He's rather beautiful, don't you think?"

"Exquisite." Arcana regarded the knight through narrowed eyes. "But I don't always trust beautiful. Slashy could also be vain, or cruel, or, you know, a bad guy who wants to kill us."

"He's got laugh lines in the corners of his eyes and my

instincts don't lead us to bad guys." Caelum's voice was tart. "You worry too much. Also… Slashy?"

She shrugged. "Gotta call him something."

"Huh. I guess so. Well, whoever he is, he's not going anywhere for now. I'll watch him," Caelum said.

"Thanks." Arcana stood on tiptoe and planted a kiss on the side of his furry nose. "Now, if you'll excuse me, I have warg to wash off."

OTHER TALES BY SAMANTHA MARSHALL

Sorcery and Stardust

A sweeping science fiction series following the adventures of Arcana, Fenris, Caelum and Flare as they work to save time and space from the bestial warg and their vicious leader.

The Kin Chronicles

A paranormal romance series featuring the Kin, a race of people who can shift into animals and live alongside humanity in an alternate contemporary reality.

The Merged Worlds

A fantasy and paranormal romance series that starts in a time before our written history, when gods roamed the Earth, technology was crazily advanced and humanity shared their space with angels, vampires, fairies and a host of other magical creatures.

A Perfectly Paranormal Anthologies

A collection of paranormal romance anthologies in conjunction with several other wonderful authors.

To find out more about any of these, visit my website:

www.sliceofsammy.com

Get your FREE copy here:
https://sliceofsammy.com/contact

WANT TO KEEP IN TOUCH?

I love to hear from, and hang out with, like minded people (yes, that's you!) and expand my tribe. Whilst I'm most active in my newsletter, you can also find me in other places from time to time! If you've already joined my mailing list and are still looking for more, then check out the following:

BLOG - www.sliceofsammy.com/blog

~

FACEBOOK - Samantha Marshall

~

INSTAGRAM - @sliceofsammy

~

TWITTER - @slice_of_sammy

ABOUT THE AUTHOR

Hi, I'm Sam!

I've been writing my whole life, scribbling stories on anything close to hand – from the shopping list to napkins to post-it notes (don't mention post-its to hubby haha).

I grew up reading fantasy of the likes of Anne McCaffrey, Terry Pratchett, and their peers. I'm also a lifelong vampire fan, along with all things spooky. In my late teens I was introduced to paranormal romance and discovered a whole new layer of story-telling with a bit of a spicy edge! Taking what I learnt from all of the above, I devoted myself to creating full-bodied characters, meaty plots, epic adventure, and a little bit of naughty sauce on the side.

I completed a Diploma of Professional Writing and Editing after high school and spent the next several years in my writing cave, working on a novel that is now in a drawer somewhere, followed by a couple of others who shared the same fate. (What can I say? I'm a recovering perfectionist.)

I came close to debuting my novel career in 2009, then ended up pregnant and took some time off to have kids. I debuted for real in 2019 with *Sorcery and Stardust* and won ARRA's Favourite Debut Romance Author for 2019, which was extremely cool!

I write speculative fiction that is a fusion of multiple sub-genres and therefore doesn't fit particularly well into any of them, but after many years and a lot of angst, I'm okay with that. I love

~

Or send me an email at - samwrites@sliceofsammy.com - I love hearing from readers and authors alike!

See you there ^_^

Love,

Sammy
XOX

all my characters and their stories for different reasons, but have a soft spot for an excellent villain and a tortured protagonist.

I currently live in south east Melbourne, Victoria, with my hubby, two kids, a Golden Retriever and a turtle. I volunteer with the Romance Writers of Australia, and I'm passionate about great writing, interesting characters, chai tea and happily ever afters.

facebook.com/sliceofsammy

twitter.com/slice_of_sammy

instagram.com/sliceofsammy